SAFE HAVEN

Jenny made her way to the edge of the garden, hedged with smooth, round rocks piled on top of one another. Reaching out, she touched the tip of a hydrangea bush, its leaves lush and green, its flowers boasting the palest pink. She closed her eyes and breathed in the scents around her.

Heaven. That's where she was right now. And she could stay here for a good long time, enjoying the sights and smells of beauty. Elliot Drake had created this sanctuary. She could almost see his strong, tanned hands shoveling the dirt into mounds, sowing seeds, easing new flowers from their plastic pots. Yes, she could almost visualize the whole process, but analyze it? No, that she couldn't do.

What kind of a man would create such a place? A beautiful safe haven that welcomed and nurtured, sustained and healed . . .

Also by Mary Campisi

SIMPLE RICHES

PARADISE FOUND

THE BUTTERFLY GARDEN

Mary Campisi

ZEBRA BOOKS
KENSINGTON PUBLISHING CORP.

http://www.kensingtonbooks.com

To my sister, Ann—because you know that sometimes we all order strawberry shortcake without the strawberries . . .

And to my best friend, Charlene Richeson—because you are like a sister to me and neither miles nor years will ever change that . . .

To the Reader

I am the third child in a family of four: two brothers, older than I, and a younger sister, all of us born within five years. Our family wasn't wealthy; as a matter of fact, we were anything but wealthy, though we never knew it. We just thought sharing a bed was normal, *and* a bathroom, *and* a closet, *and* clothes ... as for entertainment, well, there was only one mother in the neighborhood who had a car, and it wasn't for carting kids around to play dates. So, we rounded up all the kids on the street, with my oldest brother Bill as organizer and leader, to play kickball, kick the can, and my two favorites, touch football and soccer. At age ten, I was the only person who could run as fast as my brother Mark. That meant I was the only one who could tag him when he was running for a touchdown! I won't get into the time he actually *tackled* me, put me flat out, and knocked the wind out of me—all so I wouldn't score. He's still very competitive! And soccer was fun except for the time Mark got into trouble for kicking the ball too hard and knocking out my sister Ann's front tooth when she was playing goalie. It was only a baby tooth and I guess it had to come out sooner or later, but still ... there was a lot of blood. We spent our early childhood years together because that's what kids did; we played together, worked together, and, of course, as siblings do, complained that Bill got favored because he was the oldest and Ann got spoiled because she was the youngest and Mark and I, well, we just got all the work. Even today, we both believe there's a grain of truth in that; okay, more than a grain, though our mother says we were all treated the same. Any middle child will tell you that's just not true!

And so, *The Butterfly Garden* is especially important to me because it delves into sibling relationships and family hierarchy as children and as adults. It also deals with metamorphosis on various levels and an eventual letting-go . . . of old beliefs, habits, rituals. Just as the butterfly sheds its cocoon to emerge in dazzling splendor, so too, if given proper nurturing and guidance, do we.

To my readers: I hope you enjoy Grace and Jenny's journey as they discover each other and themselves and learn that love comes at unexpected times in unexpected packages.

And, as always, I am so grateful for my brothers, Bill and Mark, and my sister, Ann. Through the years we have leaned on one another, never more than a phone call away, listened with great empathy, advised with caution, and, above all, loved one another. Thank you, Billy, Mark, and Annie. I love you.

Chapter 1

Inhale, hold. Exhale, *whoosh*. Inhale, hold. Exhale, *whoosh*.

Jenny Romano kept her eyes closed, inhaled again, reached for the handle on the middle desk drawer, yanked it open. Exhale, *whoosh*. She fingered her way over the Snickers bar, the packet of M&Ms, the half-empty package of Chips Ahoy cookies, skimmed past the chopsticks, a half-dozen matchbooks, and a tube of toothpaste. Where was it? Where? Inhale, hold.

Damn it, where was it?

Exhale, *whoosh*. She opened her eyes, plunged both hands into the drawer, and started rummaging. Stefan promised her it would work—*he promised*—said he'd gotten it from a reliable source. *Just a sniff, just one, and it'll make every bone in your body loose, your mind relaxed, mellow,* he'd said. Well, she needed to feel loose now, needed mellow. Now. She scooped up a handful of the drawer's contents, tossed them in another drawer. *Come on, come on, where is it?* There, in the bottom corner of the drawer, hidden under a *CopyPlus* coffee mug was a small, dark brown, glass bottle.

Just a sniff, girl, that's all, just a sniff and it'll take you away. Stefan's words floated in her head as she snatched it up and unscrewed the stopper. Inhale . . . inhale . . . inhale . . . hold. Ahhhhh. She closed her eyes. Inhale . . . inhale . . . inhale . . . hold.

"What are you doing?"

Jenny's eyes flew open, landed on the tall, lanky figure standing in the doorway. "Didn't you ever hear of knocking, Gino?" She took another whiff from the contents of the bottle.

Gino ignored her question, took three long strides, and folded himself into a leather side chair. He was wearing his usual preppy-grunge attire: wrinkled khakis, button-down cotton shirt—Eddie Bauer, no doubt—and scuffed, brown loafers, no socks. "What's in there? Is that another one of your concoctions? You get that from Fredo on the corner?"

"Stefan gave it to me. It's aromatherapy, lavender and chamomile."

"Ah, aromatherapy." She didn't miss the sarcasm in his voice. "So what did your gay neighbor tell you this . . . aromatherapy . . . would do?" He laughed, rubbed his stubbled jaw, "Win you a shoot for the cover of *Time?*"

Jenny closed the bottle, set it aside. "Gino, everything isn't about getting that damn cover for *Time.*"

"It's not?" Gino Strandelli's thick brows pulled together. "And here I thought we were in for a little friendly competition."

"And don't talk about Stefan that way. He's my friend."

Gino held up both hands, "Hey, I have nothing against the guy, but you have to admit, he comes up with some very . . . queer ideas. No pun intended."

Jenny took a deep breath. *Inhale, inhale.* Gino Strandelli was not going to drive her crazy today with his fifty zillion questions. Underneath the Vinnie Barbarino "Who, What, Where" persona was a decent guy—nosy, but decent. Jenny told him she thought he missed his calling—he should've been a reporter instead of a photographer—but the truth was, he was a damn good photographer, too. When you looked at Gino Strandelli's photographs, you weren't just looking at random shots of faces with famous names attached; you were inside people's heads, peering into their thoughts, touching their souls, all with the help of a camera lens.

"So, Jenny, I'm curious. If you're not trying to work some potion to score big with *Time*, what the hell were you doing with that stuff in the bottle?"

She straightened a stack of papers on her desk, avoiding his gaze. When she spoke, it came out more mumble than word. "Relaxing."

"What?" He leaned forward, resting his long arms on his knees. "What did you say?"

Jenny cleared her throat. "Relaxing," she repeated, a decibel higher.

"Relaxing." He said the word as though it had a foreign element to it. "Relaxing. You. Jenny Romano, the original Energizer Bunny?"

She looked at him, cracked her knuckles, frowned. "Well, I was trying not to think about the Italy assignment. It's so big—the Pope and all those cardinals, and the Vatican. And Rome. God, that would be so incredible." She rubbed her neck, trying to massage the knot on the right side. "Joe's supposed to decide who's doing the shoot later today, and since you'll be in Greece, I figure I've got a good chance of landing it."

"You'll get it," Gino said. *"Relax."*

"That's what I was trying to do, Gino—I was *trying* to relax, until you barged in on me."

"I think I liked it better when you smoked."

"Me, too." Jenny rolled her eyes. "Don't let anybody ever tell you that once you're over the hump, you forget about it. That's just not true. Five months and I'm still leaning next to people in the elevator, trying to catch a whiff of cigarette smell on their clothes."

Gino laughed and shook his head. "Well, just think of how many alveoli you're expanding in your lungs and how much healthier you are."

"That's not why I haven't picked it back up," she said, thinking of the two packs of Doral in the bottom of her drawer. "It's because of Stefan and Gerald. They bought me a stack of 'kick the habit' audiotapes, fixed me all these herbal remedies—home-grown concoctions that Gerald created and swears by—and then, if that wasn't enough," she opened her top drawer, pulled out two eight-packs of Strawberry Bubble Yum, "they bought me two cases of Bubble Yum. How can I start smoking again? They'd be crushed."

Gino said nothing, just cocked his head to the side and nodded.

"Do you realize," Jenny went on, thinking about the little glass bottle of lavender and chamomile beside her on the desk, "that everything we do revolves around our breathing?"

"Really?" He shook his head. "Now *there's* a revelation. Everything we do revolves around breathing," he repeated the sentence, rolled the words around on his tongue. "Jenny, tell me the truth—what's really in that bottle?"

"I told you. Lavender and chamomile."

"Then either it's relaxed your brain as well as your nerves or you need a vacation, bad."

"I'm fine. And my brain's fine, too. I just . . . I just needed a few minutes to . . . quiet myself."

"Oh, God," he groaned, "don't tell me you're taking that yoga class again."

"I'm not."

"Thank God."

"I'm taking tai chi."

"Can't you just," Gino started, stopped, "can't you just sit still on your own? You know, just close your eyes and . . . drift—no smells, no instructions, no music . . . no props . . . just you?"

Jenny looked at him as though he were speaking Portuguese and said, "You mean, like meditation? I've tried that, but it didn't work."

"Because you can't meditate listening to Led Zeppelin."

"It was the symphonic version," she said, "no words, and I had headphones on . . . quietly. That wasn't the problem—I just couldn't do it."

"Please tell me there isn't another one of you out there somewhere," Gino said, pulling his hands through his jet black hair. Today he wore it long but he usually tied it back in a ponytail with a shoestring, another grunge concession.

"I'm it. My parents stopped after me."

"Surprise, surprise," he said, but there was a smile on his face.

"Of course, I do have an older sister. Grace. You'd like her—she's nothing like me."

"Ah, she's normal."

"Yeah, she's normal—husband, kids, car pool, minivan."

"Stifling."

"She doesn't seem to mind. Grace is used to taking care of everybody, me included." Jenny shrugged, ripped open a packet of M&Ms, poured a handful in her hand, popped them in her mouth. "It's just what she does," she said, chewing. "It's just Grace."

Grace folded another pair of Blue's Clues underwear and looked out the kitchen window. Spring in Ohio was usually soggy and gray mixed with brown sludge, but today the sun was bright, the sky was clear—the palest robin's egg blue—and the earth was dry and dark, sprigs of life sprouting from the trees, poking out of the ground. A patch of crocuses by the swing set burst alive in shades of purple, yellow, and white.

This time of year reminded Grace of birth, and newness . . . and starting over. She looked away, her chest tight, and grabbed another pair of Natalie's underwear. Cinderella in her ball gown.

It was wrong of parents to let their little girls believe in princes and happily-ever-after. Happily ever after—what? Grace knew there was no such thing, had known it for a while now—three years and two months, to be exact. Most of the time, lives were just made up of the "after" part; after the argument, after the pain, after the nothingness, after the heartache. The heartache . . . she'd buried it deep, so deep that no one would ever know . . . especially not Grant.

Breathe, she told herself, *just breathe.*

The phone rang but Grace didn't pick up, not until the answering machine kicked in and she heard Jenny's voice, loud and demanding, on the other line. "Hey, Gracie, where are you? Hey?"

Grace lifted the receiver, flicking off the answering machine button. "Jenny. Hi."

"What do you know about lavender and chamomile?" And before Grace could answer, she went right on. "Do you think they really make you relax or is that other stuff, patchouli, better?"

"Jenny, you're not taking those herbal supplements again, are you?"

"No, of course not. This is just something Stefan gave me—said it would put me in a mellow mood."

"He gave you the herbal supplements, too."

"Those were to quit smoking, remember? This is different."

"If you want to mellow out, stop drinking five cups of Starbucks a day and cut out the M&Ms."

Silence.

"And the Snickers . . . and—"

"Okay, okay," Jenny said, "I get the picture."

"You still planning to come for Natalie's birthday?"

"Uh . . . sure, sure I am."

"You forgot, didn't you?" Of course she forgot. Grace knew her well enough to pick up the half-second hesitation in her voice, the awkward sway of vowels as she tried to force them together into words that sounded natural, confident . . . like the truth. It didn't matter that Jenny was only three years younger than Grace; their lives were worlds apart, their responsibilities to themselves and others wider than the 2400 miles that separated them. It had always been that way, even in elementary school: Grace sitting at the kitchen table, practicing her alphabet in cursive, writing each vowel with such care, such precision. *Dog, cat, run, stop,* making a round motion with her hand, circle, circle, until the sharp tip of the #2 pencil formed the word. And then Jenny, three years later, pulling out a torn piece of paper and a few stubby pencils, the eraser tips worn down, scribbling the letters with speed and deliberateness. They were the same words, *dog, cat, run, stop,* but their formation was cramped, smudged with attempted eraser marks, a rip where she'd pressed too hard.

That was Jenny, moving through life fast, faster yet, trying to get to one place, then the next, not always a goal, just an experience, making an occasional correction, but always moving. Grace was a planner; she plotted, thought about it, considered, took polls, adjusted her opinion, thought about it again . . . and yet again . . . so that when she finally moved off her mark, the goal had become indistinct, nebulous, less intense. Often, it had become someone else's goal . . .

"Okay, so, I have it marked down here . . . the thirty-first of July, right?"

"The thirtieth is Natalie's birthday," Grace said, shaking her head.

"Oh, right . . . what I mean is, the thirty-first is the day the girls and I will have our own party so you and Grant can do something together." The words came out fast. "I knew that."

"What day is your flight coming in?"

"Well . . . I haven't booked it yet. I've been . . . preoccupied lately, waiting to see if I get this really huge assignment in Italy. That's why I was using the lavender and chamomile, to make me relax so I won't think about it. Joe's making his choice later today and I really want it."

"Good. Great." Jenny wouldn't be here for Natalie's birthday, she knew that. Oh, she'd mean well, even promise the girls they'd do fun things, but in the end, she'd call, last minute, say the plane was delayed, the assignment got extended, the taxi driver drove around in circles for an hour jacking up the meter, and she missed her flight. "I see." And she did. Grace loved Jenny but she also knew her, knew she couldn't depend on her.

"I'll be there. Hey, come on, Grace. Have a little faith, okay? Just as soon as I find out about this assignment, I'll book the flight. Okay? Trust me. I'll be there."

Chapter 2

Grace adjusted her skirt one last time, undid the second button on her shirt. *Too low? Not low enough?* She undid another button, moved slowly from side to side, gaze stuck on the reflection of herself in the mirror, the area of exposed flesh peeking out of the yellow cotton. Too low. She fastened the button, grabbed the overnight bag on the bed, and hurried out of the room.

Could she really go through with this? A surprise anniversary present that included lunch at Victor's and dessert at the Marriott—she being the dessert? Laura had made it sound so romantic, so captivating, so *easy* . . .

"I'm your best friend," she'd said, "would I steer you wrong? Guys love this sort of thing, trust me. When I did this for Hank last year, he made coffee for me every morning for a month. Of course, he doesn't do it anymore, but, well, nothing lasts forever, does it? *So, do it,* Grace. It's your anniversary. After twelve years together, you need a little pick-me-up every once in a while. Have the lunch, get the

room, I'll take the kids . . . and don't forget to stop by
Victoria's Secret.''

"I'll feel so foolish,'' Grace had said, "and what would
I buy? If you haven't noticed, I don't exactly look like a
Victoria's Secret model.''

"So? Do I? I'll bet half the women who go in there
haven't been a size four in their entire lives.'' And then,
she'd leaned in close, lowering her voice. "Last year, I
bought one of those black lace teddies, see-through. You
know what Hank said? Well, actually, we didn't do a whole
lot of talking that night, but the next morning, he asked if
I'd wear it around the house sometime, you know, under
my sweats.''

"But Grant—''

". . . is a guy,'' Laura had said. "You're his wife, the
mother of his children, the woman he's chosen to spend the
rest of his life with, and you've got a lot less jiggle than I
do. But it's not about that, Grace, it's about adding a little
zip—fantasy, call it—where you're the star. Trust me, Grant
will love whatever you buy and he won't say it makes your
butt look big. And after, when you get home, I'll bet he'll
find a way to stop working all those late nights, pouring
over those boring briefs . . . you just watch, he'll prefer a
wife in silk and garters any day.''

Grace thought of the pink teddy folded between layers of
pink and white tissue paper. Would Grant think she was a
fool, an impostor? Would he say, *Where's my wife? The
one who wears brushed cotton to bed? Where'd she go?*

She sucked in a deep breath. *Relax. Relax.* Maybe she
needed some of Jenny's lavender and chamomile concoction.
Jenny wouldn't have this problem; she wouldn't have the
first qualm about marching into Victoria's Secret and asking
the salesclerk to help her find her size in the black garter
belt and stockings. *Size 6,* she'd say, *but sometimes I'm a
4*—no need to lower her voice and pull the clerk aside,

like Grace did. And she'd pick black-and-red, maybe bright blue—no pink, like Grace.

Well, Jenny was different. She'd never had any kids, she didn't have to worry about the extra flab around the middle or the pockets of flesh under her thighs or the back of her butt.

No, if Grace were honest, really honest, she'd just admit the truth. It wasn't about Jenny's size or the fact that she was extremely attractive, exotic even, because she didn't seem to notice or care much about that. In fact, Jenny didn't really care what other people thought about her at all. She did what she wanted, when she wanted, how she wanted, and to hell with everything and everyone else.

Grace wished, deep down, that once, just once, she could be more like Jenny.

The drive to Grant's office took less than twenty minutes. Clarke, Heath & Jackson was located two towns over in the upscale suburban area of Montcrest. Grant was a senior partner and one of the most well respected real estate attorneys in the area. This was the life he'd always planned: a partnership in a prestigious law firm, a house in suburbia, a wife, two children, a retirement plan, a hefty stock portfolio . . . so many grand plans, all of them almost lost, three years and two months ago . . .

Grace pushed the thought from her head, tried to bury it in the past, where it belonged. The present, that's what they needed to focus on; thinking about today . . . tonight.

She pulled the van into the parking lot, then circled around, looking for Grant's green Land Rover. His reserved parking spot was empty.

No. Grace let out a long sigh. *All this planning and worry and now he's not even here?* She considered her options. Louise would know—she knew everything; Grant called her his second mother. Grace pulled into his parking spot and went to find his secretary.

Louise Brumbacker was a thin, wiry woman with gray-black hair and a two-hundred-card Rolodex. Grant said she knew all of his clients' names—spouses, too, even some of the children—knew where they lived, what they did, how much money they made. He said Louise belonged on a game show, *Corporate Secretary's Challenge.*

"Hi, Louise," Grace said, spotting the top of the woman's gray-black head behind a filing cabinet.

"Grace!" Louise popped out from the back of the cabinet. "Hello." She had a habit of rolling her words. "And what brings you here?"

"Well, I was looking for Grant," she gestured a hand toward the parking lot, "but his car's gone."

"You just missed him," she tapped a finger against her chin. "Ten minutes at most."

"Do you know where he went?"

"Sure do. Chantel's. Business meeting with Foster Realty . . . foreclosure," she added.

Business, important business. Maybe she should just wait here for him—not exactly what she had in mind, but at least she could carry out part of the plan.

"Was he expecting you?" Louise asked. "He didn't say you'd be stopping by."

"No," Grace shook her head. "I wanted to surprise him. Tomorrow is our anniversary. Twelve years."

Louise nodded, a knowing look on her face. "Yes, I remember. It's only the closing details on a foreclosure—you should go. I'm sure Grant will be thrilled to see you."

"But, what about his client?"

"If it's old man Foster, he'll look forward to seeing a young, pretty face." She smiled. "Might even speed things along for Grant."

"You really don't think they'll mind?" Grace spent most of her life surrounded by people under the age of ten: mornings as a teacher in Keystone Elementary School's kindergarten program and afternoons with her own two, Danielle and Natalie. The corporate world tended to intimidate her—too many serious faces, no room for laughter or compromise.

Louise shook her head. "Of course not. Go. Surprise them both."

"Okay," Grace said, her confidence building. "Okay."

Chantel's was on the opposite side of town, nestled among a small copse of trees, evergreens and maples, with tailored shrubs lining a brick drive. Tiny white lights decorated the trees, casting a fairy-tale look about it in the evening. The structure itself resembled a ski lodge, its wood stained to a deep brown-black with double gold-encrusted front doors. Grace thought it quaint, cozy, romantic. She and Grant had only been here twice since its opening three years ago. The first time had been two years ago, for his thirty-seventh birthday, and then last summer to celebrate his promotion to senior partner.

Grace pulled onto the brick driveway, spotted Grant's Land Rover on the far end, partially hidden by a flowing oak tree. She parked the van and checked her lipstick in the rearview mirror.

Breathe, she told herself, *just breathe.*

Laura's words came back to her, boosting her confidence. *He'll love it, you just wait and see. You'll be the one getting coffee in bed for the next month. Trust me, okay?*

Okay. She could do this, *Grant would love it.*

Grace walked across the parking lot, her high heels *click, clicking* on the brick, imagining Grant's face when he saw her and later, imagining his face when he saw her standing before him in nothing but a pale pink, semi-sheer teddy.

When she entered Chantel's, the maitre d' gave her a brief smile, bowed from the waist, and inquired in a mix of French American, "May I help you, madame?"

She returned his smile, briefer still. "Yes, my husband is here. Grant Clarke. I'd like to join him."

The maitre d' nodded, checked his reservation list, and said, "If you will follow me, please."

The restaurant was crowded—business people mostly, lunching and making deals. Grace followed the maitre d' past several tables, scanning ahead for Grant. It wouldn't be too difficult to spot him; his tall frame and good looks stuck out in any crowd. Ahead, off to the right, she saw the back of a man's head, the same brownish-gold curls as Grant's. Was that him? The maitre d' slowed his pace before she could get a better look. He stopped, turned, his face flushed a dull red.

"Madame, I am sorry, but it appears Monsieur Clarke is not here."

"Not here? But . . . of course he's here."

He shrugged his shoulders, motioned toward the entrance. "I must have been mistaken. Monsieur Clarke is not here."

"But that man over there," she sidestepped around him, pointing in the direction of the man with the golden brown hair. "He looks like my . . ." The words evaporated, sucked dry by the sight in front of her. The man had turned and was in profile, his lips full, his cheekbones high, jaw strong. It was Grant, and he was as handsome as he'd been the first time she saw him in the laundromat at Ohio University, trying to decide how much detergent to put in the washing machine. He'd smiled at her then, a slow, bewitching smile that brought her under his spell, made her believe in happily-ever-after.

But now, he wasn't smiling at her; he wasn't even looking at *her*. There was a woman leaning partway across the table, her hands clasping Grant's close to her bosom, her lips working their way over his fingers, trailing tiny kisses along the back of his knuckles. Grace felt weak, dizzy; she thought she might pass out, wished she would just disappear . . .

"Madame," the maitre d's voice reached her, uncomfort-

able, perhaps even a bit sympathetic, "let me help you."
He tried to take her arm, but Grace twisted away.

"No." Then louder, "No! I want to see him, I want to
see my husband." A few people looked up, quickly looking
away when she stared back. Others were more furtive about
it, sneakier, like vultures waiting to peck out scraps. Grace
tried to move her feet, tried to get closer, but she was frozen—in time, in place, in reality.

This could not be happening . . . *this could not be happening* . . . and yet it was.

She watched, transfixed in a surreal kind of way, as the
woman with the long, black hair smiled at Grant, laughed,
flicked her tongue over his fingers. She was tall, graceful,
sexual—familiar, in an oddly bizarre sort of way, as though
Grace should know her. Or perhaps it was the dance itself,
the mating ritual of women who prey on other women's
men; perhaps it was that which was familiar.

"Please, madame, please, let me help you—"

Grace swung around, facing the maitre' d. His forehead
was beaded with sweat, his eyes darting from Grace to
Grant's table. It was obvious this man's main concern was
getting her out of here without a scene. He cared nothing
about what was happening six tables away, probably witnessed it every afternoon and evening. And as long as everyone practiced discretion and the tip was sizeable, no one
need be the wiser, certainly not the wife at home with the
children. They were casualties; unfortunate, yes, but inconse-
quential.

"It seems you were mistaken," Grace said, raising her
voice above Beethoven's *Moonlight Sonata* and the quiet
clatter of silverware on china. "My husband *is* here," she
let out a strained laugh, her pitch getting higher, pointed at
Grant. "He's there, see, *right there,* the one with the woman
falling all over him."

Grant happened to turn then, noticed everyone looking at

him, and gently eased away from the woman. He didn't see
Grace at first; she was partly hidden by the maitre d'. Then
she stepped forward in full view. Grant stared at her, stunned,
his forehead creasing as he pulled away from the table.
The woman pouted, reached for his hand, frowned when he
brushed her away. It wasn't until the woman turned and met
Grace's gaze straight on that Grace realized why she felt
such familiarity with the woman. Her eyes were light, maybe
hazel, almond-shaped, her face oval, neck, long and slender.
My God, she looked like Jenny.

Grace turned and ran, stumbling as she tried to find her
way out of the restaurant, past the onlookers, most still trying
to determine what part of life's pathetic little drama they'd
just witnessed. When she was outside, she made it as far as
a row of holly bushes before she leaned over and threw up.

"Grace! Grace!"

Oh, God. Grace wiped her mouth with the sleeve of her
cotton shirt, looked up. He was coming toward her, his long
legs moving in quick strides.

She turned and ran again.

"Grace! Stop! Stop!"

She made it to the van and scrambled inside, but he
was opening the passenger door before she could press the
"lock" button.

"Get away!" she screamed. "Get away!"

"Grace . . . I can explain." He climbed into the van,
closed the door. "I can . . . really. It's not what it looked
like."

The tears were coming, she couldn't stop them, hot, scalding her cheeks, burning the memory of Grant and the other
woman who looked like Jenny in her brain. "What, Grant?
What do you think it looked like?" She plowed on, not
giving him time to answer. "Do you think it looked like a
man having a cozy lunch with *another woman,* one who
wasn't his wife?" Her voice turned shrill, "One who looked

almost exactly like his wife's *sister?* Is that what you think it looked like?''

It was this last that got him, the part about Jenny; she could tell by the way the muscle in the right side of his jaw twitched, once, twice, three times, like it did when he was hiding the truth. ''Grace, you're upset, you don't know what you're saying.''

''Stop it! Just . . . stop it.'' She sniffed, wiped her hands across her face. ''I hate it when you patronize me, do you hear me? I hate it!''

''Okay.'' He held up his hands, nodded. ''Okay. I'm sorry. I . . . I just want a chance to explain.''

Her chest tightened when she looked at him, ached with a pain so deep she thought if she unbuttoned her shirt she'd see blood. How could love be so one-sided, so cruel, so *unsympathetic?* Maybe it wasn't love at all that was thrashing against her, threatening to beat her into the ground, stomp her, bury her alive. Maybe it was the betrayal, maybe that was it.

The betrayal of a man who'd promised to be faithful . . . and was unfaithful . . . again. Three years and two months ago it had been the same . . . no name . . . no face . . . just a letter in a shirt pocket and a Discover Card receipt from the Ritz.

''I,'' Grant was speaking again, his tone low, soothing, ''I had a luncheon appointment with a realtor. We were handling the foreclosure.'' He blew out a long breath. ''I knew as soon as I got here that she was going to be a problem, the way she kept touching my hand when she talked, and the sly smiles. I tried to be professional, tried to just ignore it, but it was just damn embarrassing.''

Grace listened, her grief suspended for a moment, replaced by amazement and disbelief. ''You're saying she *forced* herself on you?''

He shrugged and had the good grace to turn a dull shade

of red. "It's pretty pathetic, isn't it? I should've just left, excused myself, and gotten out of there, but Foster Realty's a big client. I thought I'd just tolerate it."

"Tolerate it?" she echoed, envisioning the woman's lips moving over Grant's knuckles. *"Tolerate it?"* she repeated.

"Right." He reached out to touch her hand, but she pulled away. "I . . . wouldn't do that to you . . . to us . . ."

"Again."

"What?"

"You meant, you wouldn't do that to me or us, again."

"Oh."

"Exactly."

"I love you, Grace. I know I screwed up before, but I love you." He leaned forward, closing the space between them. "I've always loved you."

"Don't, Grant." The tears were starting again. Grace shrank back against the car door. "Don't." It was little more than a whisper. "I know," she said, wondering how she could still be breathing when her heart was ripped in half. *"I know."*

Chapter 3

He stared at her a minute, as if trying to interpret what she'd said. Then, slowly, his shoulders slumped forward and he ran his hands over his face. "Oh, God. Grace, listen, you've got to listen to me. It . . . it didn't mean anything. Honest. She doesn't mean anything to me." His hands were open, begging her to believe his words. "It just sort of . . . happened."

"And she just sort of happened to look almost exactly like Jenny." Grace felt her resolve crumble like a rose left in the sun too long without water. "If I'd seen her from across the room, I'd have thought it *was* Jenny."

"No," he said, "no, that's not true. She doesn't look like her at all."

But Grace wasn't listening. "And the other one, Grant, the one three years ago, did she have long, black hair, too? Did she look like Jenny?"

"Grace, you don't know what you're saying. You're upset—"

"How long, Grant? How long have you been lusting after my sister?"

He shook his head. "I love you, Grace. You, nobody else."

"But you want Jenny." The words hung between them, sharp, painful. To have her husband fantasizing about sleeping with her sister . . . this was almost too much to comprehend.

"Grace—"

"Do you know why I came here today? Do you have any idea?" She didn't wait for him to answer. "I thought I'd surprise you, take you to lunch." She let out a laugh that sounded more like a croak. "And then I was going to really surprise you, maybe even shock you a little, with a hotel room at the Marriott." She leaned forward, unzipped the overnight case, and pulled out the pink teddy. "Here." She threw it at him. "Happy Anniversary."

He caught the swatch of material, held it up, fingered the satin edges. "It's beautiful, Grace. Beautiful. Just like you."

Her shoulders started shaking, tiny convulsions running through her with each word he spoke. *I love you, Grace . . . You, nobody else . . . Beautiful . . . Just like you . . .* They were only words without meaning, syllables strung together that formed sound, that was all. The conviction, the promise, *the pledge* was missing. Maybe it had never been there, maybe she had only imagined it, wished it, dreamed it; maybe he had never really loved her. What of that? Or, and this was perhaps the most plausible, maybe he just hadn't loved her *enough.*

Grace swiped at her eyes and straightened in her seat, avoiding Grant's steady gaze. He would be desperate now, promising his heart, his love, his soul to eternity and beyond; she remembered this from before. There would be flowers and little love notes pasted around the house, in her purse, on her dashboard, in the fridge. Grant Clarke in pursuit was a powerful, all-consuming force, not so different from the Grant Clarke in the boardroom of Clarke, Heath & Jackson. She could expect jewelry—last time it had been a gold bracelet with rubies and diamonds. Perhaps this time she'd earned a matching necklace. And the lovemaking, well that would be superb, selfless . . . dizzying.

Familiar. All of it was familiar, too familiar.

He didn't love her enough. She knew this, just as she'd known from the moment she laid eyes on him in Chantel's that he was having an affair with a woman who by design bore a striking resemblance to Jenny. This last part made her sick, as though it was almost worse than the affair itself, and maybe it was. Jenny was her sister, for God's sake, *her sister*.

"I . . . I was going to give this to you tonight." Grant was talking again, his voice low, almost desperate as he pulled a small, silver box from his suit jacket. "But I want you to have it now."

She stared at the box in his hand. It was small, wrapped in heavy silver paper with a fancy bow, the kind jewelry stores used. Did he really think he could buy his way out of this, just give her a gift and she'd forget he'd slept with a woman who looked like her sister?

Did he?

Bile rose to the back of her throat. She had to get away, now. Grace put the key in the ignition, started the engine.

"Grace? Where are you going? We need to finish this."

She backed out of the space, lurched forward, gaining speed as she headed for the exit.

Out. Out . . . Got to get out of here. Now! Her foot pressed the accelerator, hard, harder. She couldn't get his words out of her head—loud, louder, they taunted her, tormented her. *It . . . it didn't mean anything. Honest. She doesn't mean anything to me . . .*

"Hey! Grace! Slow down! Slow down!"

*I love you, Grace . . . You, nobody else . . . Beautiful . . .
Just like you . . .*

Her brain screamed back at him. *No! No, you don't! You
don't love me, Grant, not enough!* The tears were coming
down now, blurring her vision. *Out! Got to get out!* She
pressed the pedal to the floor.

"Grace! Watch out! The pole!" Grant lunged for the
steering wheel, his big body smashing her against the cush-
ion. He jerked the wheel hard left. The van swerved, spun
around and crashed right into the base of the telephone pole.

Then everything went black.

"I think you should go with the red silk—the fabric
drapes your body, falls to the floor in an elegant display of
allure and temptation."

"Stefan, I'm not trying to allure or tempt anybody,"
Jenny said, throwing the red silk dress on the couch. "Maybe
I should wear the red pantsuit."

"Red leather?" Stefan tapped his finger against his chin.
"That outfit says, 'I'll skip dinner and go right for the sex.' "

"It does?" She stared at the red leather pantsuit with the
mid-belly zipper. "You talked me into buying it—you said
it looked good on me."

He smiled. "It does, sweetheart, it does."

"Oh, for Pete's sake, Stefan, now what am I going to
wear?" She threw the pantsuit on the couch beside the dress.
"Remind me not to take you shopping with me, ever again."

Stefan shook his head, picked a piece of lint from the red
dress. "Jenny, have you been using the aromatherapy I gave
you?"

She eyed him. "Why?"

"Tense, that's all. I sense an extreme tenseness in your
words, around your mouth, even in the way you carry yourself."

"I have been using it," she mumbled. "It just isn't working very well."

"So what are you going to do when you go to Italy and meet the Pope, eh? What then?"

Just the mention of Italy made her pulse race. She'd done it! She'd gotten the assignment that would elevate her world to a new level.

"Tell me, Jenny," Stefan said again, "what are you going to do?"

For heaven's sake, he could be such a nagger, almost as bad as her mother. Almost. "I'll be fine." She threw him a look. "As long as he doesn't make me go to confession."

That made Stefan laugh.

"Touché." He held up the leather pantsuit, examined it, then picked up the dress. "Who is this person you're going to the Photo Finish Awards with, Jenny?"

"Jon Palmer. Acoustic guitar for *Flip Side.*"

"And does this Jon Palmer practice good general hygiene?"

"Of course he does and I know where this is going, Stefan." He was referring to her escort two weeks ago. "Anton wore dreadlocks. His hair was not dirty." But he had shown up to take her to the premiere of *A Beautiful Mind* dressed in ripped jeans, a Hawaiian shirt unbuttoned to the navel, and orange flip-flops. Stefan had not been impressed.

"I wasn't talking about his hair," he said. "I was talking about his familiarity with a bar of soap."

"Don't you have somewhere to go? How much longer until Gerald gets home?"

Stefan glanced at his watch, a black Movado. "Half hour, give or take. Are you hungry? I can have him whip something up for you. How about an omelet, mushrooms, Swiss, red pepper?"

Jenny laughed, nodded. "What would I do without you, Stefan? You're like the mother I wish I'd had."

"You need ten mothers." He said it as though he were annoyed but she knew he was secretly pleased, partly because, beneath the casual jesting, was the truth. Stefan Gunderhaven showed more affection and concern to her than her own mother. How sad that she could find more comfort, more maternal instincts in her gay friend than in Virginia Romano.

The lack of love had always been there, reserved instead for Grace. Jenny was just too different, too confusing, her mother had once said. Maybe what she'd really meant was *Jenny was too unlovable*. It didn't matter anymore, hadn't mattered in a very long time. Really. For the last several years, she'd paid her mother the perfunctory respect that her position required: cards on her birthday and Mother's Day, a phone call once every two months, and an annual visit. Three days tested Jenny's tolerance.

Her mother seemed content with the arrangement, telling all her friends that Jenny was the "Gypsy" daughter who traveled the world taking pictures of people instead of settling down with some nice man and having his babies. The one and only time Jenny had ever shown her work to her mother—a photo of Chief Kenotka, which appeared in *Time* magazine—she'd glanced over it, frowned and asked why, with such a fancy camera, Jenny hadn't touched up the river of wrinkles covering the chieftain's face? Then she'd pulled out a Kmart Christmas spread of Danielle and Natalie and proceeded to inform her daughter that those photographers really knew their stuff.

Jenny would never forget inching the photo of Chief Kenotka back toward herself, slowly, the hurt spreading like the river of wrinkles on the old chieftain's face. She'd slipped it inside her portfolio, and never showed her mother another piece of her work. That was four years ago, yet still, whenever she looked at the old warrior's picture hanging on the wall in her office, she remembered that day, remembered her mother's cruel words.

"So, are you hungry or what? You know Gerald's food is better than anything you'll be sampling tonight. I suggest you eat something," he paused, "just in case the caveman, uh, I mean your date, doesn't find the after party to his liking."

The phone rang before Jenny could think of a comeback. It was probably Jon, telling her what time he'd be by to pick her up. "Hello?" Pause. "Yes, this is Jenny Romano. Who? St. Joseph's Memorial Hospital? In Clairmont?" The room started spinning, fast, faster, the words on the other end of the line fading. "Oh, my God." She gulped in air, sank to the couch. "Oh, my God."

"Is my sister going to die?" Jenny had traveled over twenty-four-hundred miles to ask that question and now, when she was two seconds away from the answer, she almost didn't want to know. Not knowing had its own insignificant rewards, if only temporary. It harbored hope.

Jenny stared at the thin, wiry man sitting on the caramel-colored sofa in front of her. He was dressed in surgeon's green and thick, black glasses. Her gaze flew to his hands. Surgeon's hands. Scrubbed clean, slightly chapped, with blunt nails. A few hours ago they'd been fishing instruments inside Grace's head, trying to remove the clot that was threatening her life.

Jenny's heart pounded in her chest with the force of a boxer delivering his final blows. Hard. Brutal. Crushing. She bit the inside of her cheek.

Dr. Shaffer's next words paralyzed every thought running through her brain. "Your sister's in a coma."

She tried to suck in air, but came up dry. "But you

removed the clot," she insisted. "The pressure inside her skull's gone. Isn't it?"

"Yes, it is," he agreed, rubbing the back of his neck. "But brain injuries are as individualized as the patient." He shook his head. "It's much too soon to predict the outcome."

All she wanted was a *little* reassurance, a gesture, a word, something that would indicate Grace's recovery was attainable. Bile rose in the back of her throat. When was the last time she'd eaten anything? It was almost noon, East Coast time. Other than a cup of black coffee and two packs of strawberry Bubble Yum, she couldn't remember.

"Miss Romano, your sister *is* in a coma. But she's young and otherwise healthy. We're hopeful."

Hopeful. Ironic, that with today's modern medicine and multi-billion-dollar research labs, they still couldn't get past the "hopeful" part. Jenny knew what he meant. He'd done all he could, this man with sixteen letters of the alphabet trailing after his name. Now, it was in God's hands, as Virginia Romano always said. That answer brought no comfort. Jenny needed something more concrete than a nebulous "hopeful" floating around her sister like some mystical aura.

She leaned back in her chair and closed her eyes. She couldn't believe this was really happening. Grace in a coma—a coma, for God's sake. People died in comas, their brains went dead, and they became vegetables, useless bodies that couldn't even breathe on their own. Dead, that's what happened to them. *Dead.* Had Grant told the children? she wondered. Where was he anyway, why hadn't *he* called her, why did she have to hear the news from some clinical voice in the ICU of St. Joseph's Memorial Hospital? Was he with the girls, trying to find a way to tell them why Mommy wasn't coming home for a while, that she might never come home?

"I want to see her," Jenny said.

Dr. Shaffer nodded as he stood. "You'll see a lot of tubes and monitors." There was a brief pause. "And, of course, she's on the respirator."

Of course. She shifted her bag over her shoulder and stood. "I'm ready."

But it was a lie. She wasn't ready, would never be ready to see her older sister hooked up to a machine, fighting for her life.

Her feet moved like a robot's, one mechanical step after the other, as she and Dr. Shaffer headed down a wide corridor. Jenny hated hospitals. The smell of disinfectant mingled with trays of food under plastic covers turned her stomach. Lighting was either too stark or too dim and everything was beige or faded orange. There was too much noise, too. Buzzes, rings, beeps.

She avoided hospitals, hadn't been in one since the day her father died on the operating table two years ago. Too little, too late.

Dr. Shaffer turned right and she followed him, straight to the nurses' station ten feet away. He smiled at the young woman behind the desk and said, "Sally, Miss Romano is here to see her sister, Mrs. Grace Clarke."

The woman named Sally smiled at Jenny. How could this *girl* possibly know how to take care of Grace? She was so young, with her blond braid and pink cheeks.

"She's right in here," the doctor said, moving toward one of several glass-enclosed areas. Jenny followed him, keeping her eyes straight ahead. She didn't want to see anyone else's pain grabbing at her from the other cubicles, trying to suck her in.

Grace. Her eyes blurred, focused, and blurred again. Grace. She stared at her sister. The tears started coming then, running down Jenny's face, trickling over her chin. Grace's head was wrapped with gauze, snug to her skull. Dr. Shaffer had warned Jenny about all the tubes and the respirator with its methodical whooshing sound, but he hadn't said a word about cutting Grace's beautiful brown hair, or shaving her head and wrapping it in white gauze. And that's what tore at Jenny's soul. Her sister, her friend, was lying in that bed, shorn and helpless, with tubes poking out everywhere, looking centuries older than her scant thirty-six years. God. She inched closer, needing to touch her. She reached down and grasped her right hand, squeezing her limp fingers.

"Oh, Grace, what happened?" Jenny whispered. What happened? *What happened?* But the only answer she received was the whoosh of the respirator and the tiny beeps from the machines surrounding her bedside.

Jenny didn't know how long she stood there, holding her sister's hand, tears washing over her grief, blanketing both of them in her sorrow. She and Grace were so different, worlds apart, and yet, they had always understood each other; even now, they understood each other. Even now . . .

Shuffling sounds and scraping wheels yanked Jenny from her thoughts. She swiped at her eyes and turned around to see a flurry of white-and-green rushing into the cubicle next to Grace.

A sharp, piercing noise stabbed the air through the next partition. Jenny held her breath, her gaze flying to Grace's monitor. She didn't know how to read it, but she did know that jagged peaks made the monitor beep, and that meant her heart was pumping, which meant she was alive. Jenny let out a long breath.

"One, two, three, clear." It was Dr. Shaffer's voice. "Let's hit him again. One, two, three, clear." There was a pause. "Let's try a bolus of epinephrine." His voice faded under the piercing sound behind the curtain. Jenny kept her eyes glued to Grace's monitor, concentrating so hard that her vision blurred.

"Miss Romano?"

She pulled her gaze from the squiggly lines. "Yes?"

Dr. Shaffer stood there; his green scrubs were ringed under the arms with perspiration marks. Small beads of sweat clung to his forehead. He rubbed the back of his neck. "I'd like to have a word with you."

Jenny squeezed Grace's hand. "I'll be back," she whispered and followed him out of the room. She'd heard that unconscious people could sometimes still hear talking and if that were true, she wanted Grace to know she'd be back.

Dr. Shaffer led her to the waiting room, and she took a seat in the same caramel-colored chair she'd sat in earlier. He removed his black glasses, rubbed his hands over his face, then put them back on. "I have some bad news."

Bad, as in worse than my sister being in a coma?

He continued, "I wish there were an easier way to tell you this, but there isn't."

He paused. Jenny clenched her jaw.

"Your sister's husband, Grant, was in the car at the time of the accident."

She sucked in a breath. "Where is he? Is he hurt?" *Oh, my God.* She'd just assumed Grace was alone.

Dr. Shaffer shook his head. "We couldn't control the bleeding. It was all internal." Another pause. "I'm sorry."

I'm sorry. That registered through the thick haze fogging her brain. *Sorry?* "He's . . . dead?" The words crept out as though someone else had spoken them.

He nodded. "He was in the cubicle next to your sister."

Grant was the one they'd been trying to resuscitate. Big, strong Grant. Dead. The room started spinning. Jenny tried to breathe, but it felt like a big foot was squashing her chest, choking the air from her lungs. Grant. Dead. The only man Grace had ever loved. She gasped for breath. If the accident didn't kill her, a broken heart would. And Jenny would have to be the one to tell her. And what about Danielle and Natalie?

Who would tell them that their mother was in a coma and their father was dead? Who? *Who would tell them?*

It was more than she could bear. When the dark side of consciousness sank its claws into her, she welcomed it, tumbling headfirst into a black sleep.

Chapter 4

Some god-awful smell jolted Jenny awake. Dr. Shaffer stood over her, peering down through his thick, black glasses. His eyes were brown and small, and he reminded her of a scientist examining some mutant germ under a microscope, she being the germ.

"Miss Romano? Are you all right?"

Jenny rubbed her eyes, squinted. "What happened?" Her head was pounding, her stomach felt queasy.

"You fainted."

"Fainted? I've never fainted in my life." Then she remembered. Grant was dead. Grace was in a coma. Fainting had been a welcome respite.

"Is there someone I can call for you?" His voice was kind. "Someone who can be here for you? A husband? Boyfriend? Mother?"

She shook her head to all three. No husband. Thank God. No boyfriends, not the kind she'd want to see her stripped and raw, hurting like a wounded animal, too open, too exposed, too personal. Her boyfriends, and she used the term loosely, were just for fun, entertainment, a way to pass time, fill in a gap. She tried to picture Anton with his dreadlocks, holding her hand, in his unbuttoned Hawaiian shirt and orange flip-flops. The picture didn't work.

No to the mother question, too. Where was she, anyway? Why wasn't she here, beside Grace? And then Jenny remembered the hip replacement surgery, two weeks ago.

"The girls," she murmured. "She has two little girls." She tried to sit up, but a wave of nausea rolled over her, forced her back down. She ran her hands over her face. "Where are they? Oh, my God, *where are they?*" She felt near hysteria—first Grace, then Grant, and now the girls? Jenny squeezed her eyes shut, took a deep breath.

"Just try to relax," Dr. Shaffer said, taking her hand and speaking in a voice that sounded like the man on her meditation tapes. "That's it. Breathe. Breathe. Relax."

Relax. Relax. An almost hysterical bubble threatened to explode inside her as she pictured Stefan and Dr. Shaffer standing side by side, chanting and dabbing her with lavender and chamomile.

Her breathing slowed and she started to drift off. "I'm tired . . . so tired. California . . . time difference."

"Sleep, Miss Romano."

"Jenny," she mumbled as sleep claimed her. "My name's Jenny."

Something was shining in her face, a bright nuisance, stripping the shades of sleep from Jenny, one layer at a time. Los Angeles sure beat Pittsburgh, but sometimes there was just a little too much sun. She'd forgotten to close the blinds. Again. She turned her head from the light and inched her eyes open. They felt gritty and it took her a few seconds to adjust her vision. She was staring straight into a caramel-covered nubby fabric. This wasn't her bed. But it looked oddly familiar. She blinked and turned her head. White walls. Television in the corner. Scattered chairs of the same fabric. A table covered with magazines. A coffeepot with Styrofoam cups stacked on top of each other.

And then she remembered, remembered about Grace and Grant, and Danielle and Natalie, fatherless, and at the moment, practically motherless. Jenny flung her hair back, pushed herself into a sitting position. The girls. She had to do something. They weren't much more than babies, seven and five years old. Who was going to help them, take care of them?

Who?

There was no one but her. She'd have to protect them, keep them safe . . . just as soon as she found out where they were.

She pulled out her black bag and rummaged through it— pens, notepads, matches, a lighter, Bubble Yum, lipstick, a Snickers bar—until she located her address book. What was the name of that woman who watched Natalie while Grace taught morning kindergarten? Lana? Linda? Laura? She flipped through the pages, went to B for babysitter. There it was: Laura Montgomery.

"Aunt Jenny! Aunt Jenny!"

Two little screaming bundles of wildfire leapt at her, almost knocking her down with their exuberance. Jenny leaned down, pulled them into her arms, buried her face in their hair. They smelled like raspberries and peanut butter. Her chest tightened, her throat clogged.

How was she ever going to tell them?

Natalie pulled away first. "Did you bring me any gum, Aunt Jenny?" She had her father's green eyes, and his dimples—two big ones on both sides of her cheeks. Her hair was just like Jenny's, a jumble of jet black curls falling halfway down her back. When people saw them together, they thought Natalie was Jenny's daughter.

"Was somebody drinking Kool-Aid?" Jenny said, pointing to the faint orange line above Natalie's lip. Anything, *anything* to avoid the inevitable.

"Uh-uh." Natalie shook her head. "Orange pop. Mrs. M says that's for special." She snaked her little hand toward Jenny's black bag. "Gum?"

"Natalie!" This from Danielle. "That is not nice. Wait until Aunt Jenny offers."

Danielle was Grace in miniature with her chestnut hair and big brown eyes. Acted like her, too, always playing the mother, taking care of her little sister, keeping things in order and on schedule. Danielle and Natalie were Grace and Jenny all over again.

"It's okay, Danielle," Jenny said, reaching into her purse. "As a matter of fact, I have two packs of sugarless strawberry Bubble Yum." *And another half a case at home, thanks to Stefan,* she thought. She pulled out the gum and held one out for each girl. "Now, who's been practicing blowing bubbles?"

"Me! Me!" Natalie yelled.

Jenny smiled. "Okay. Show me." She ripped open a third pack and stuffed two wads of strawberry Bubble Yum in her mouth. It wasn't nicotine but at least it kept her mouth busy. There was a pack of Dorals—unopened, of course—stuffed in the bottom of her suitcase, a security blanket of sorts . . . just in case. After five months of not smoking, Jenny wasn't anticipating lighting up but she'd never had a sister in a bad car accident either—in a coma, no less—and whiffs of lavender and chamomile from a dark glass bottle might not be enough.

"Good, good," Jenny said. "Now, let me see you, Danielle. Natalie, try again.'' She watched the girls puff their cheeks out as pale pink bubbles emerged between their lips.

Oh, God, oh, God, oh, God, she had to tell them . . . How? How was she going to do it? She glanced at the woman standing in the kitchen, leaning against the doorway, one bare foot crossed over the other. Laura Montgomery was tall, sturdy, with kind blue eyes and full lips. Her skin was fair, her hair the color of wheat. She wore it pulled back in a fat braid and with her plaid smock jumper and bare feet, she reminded Jenny of Mother Earth.

''Okay, girls, why don't you give me a few minutes with Mrs. M and then we'll go home.''

''Are you gonna stay with us until Mommy and Daddy get home?'' Natalie asked, her green eyes wide and curious.

Jenny choked back a cough. Danielle was watching her. ''I'll be staying for a while,'' she said, avoiding the question. ''Now shoo.''

Both girls scampered off toward the stairs, Natalie yelling that she'd made a half bubble. When they were out of sight, Jenny stood up and walked over to Laura Montgomery.

''Hi, Laura. I'm Jenny,'' she said, extending a hand.

Laura took her hand. ''I've heard a lot about you, Jenny.''

''Most people have.''

She smiled and squeezed Jenny's hand. ''Grace thinks the world of you.''

''Grace thinks the world of everybody.'' This was true. ''Me, you, the local grocer, the mailman.''

''How is she?''

The soft bantering disintegrated into silence. Jenny met the other woman's steady gaze and shrugged. ''She's in a coma, with tubes coming out of every part of her body.'' She shook her head. ''And the respirator . . . She looks so . . . insignificant.'' Tears stung the backs of her eyes. ''Not like the Grace we know.''

''I'm praying for her.''

"Thank you." It was a mumble, half-formed, low. She blinked, but the tears came anyway, spilling down her cheeks, pouring out her pain.

"Oh, Jenny," Laura said, putting her strong arms around her, "it's just so hard to believe."

Jenny sniffed. "She doesn't deserve this. Not Grace."

"God doesn't discriminate when he's doling out pain," Laura murmured. "But I'm . . . having a hard time understanding His plan." She pulled back, looked at her. "You knew tomorrow was their anniversary."

It was a statement, not a question. Did she know that? No, she'd forgotten; actually, she'd thought it was on the thirtieth of this month. But she just nodded, said, "Yes." What kind of person didn't know her own sister's wedding anniversary?

"Grace had planned a surprise for Grant. Lunch at a fancy restaurant," Laura paused, said in a soft voice, "a room at the Marriott afterward."

"Grace?" That was a surprise. The only time Grace had ever talked about "intimacy," as she called it, she'd been advising Jenny on the necessity of safe sex. It was about ten years ago; Jenny had been out of college a year and apparently was dating more than Grace thought appropriate. So, she'd cut out articles from *Good Housekeeping, Redbook,* and *McCalls* and mailed them to her.

"Did you get the articles I sent you?" she'd called to ask about a week later.

"Oh," Jenny had said, "You mean the one entitled, 'Branded for Life: STDs'? Or was it 'Safe Sex Saves Lives'? Wait, there's another one here. 'Sex, Sex, Sex, Just Say No.' Is that the one you meant?"

"You sound upset."

"Why would I be upset? What do you think I'm doing out here, jumping into bed with every guy I meet? Shake his hand and shake down his pants?" She had been upset—

yes, she had been. No one ever gave her credit for having any common sense.

"That's not what I meant. I didn't mean to say I didn't trust your judgment." She'd paused. "It's just that, well, you might not have seen the articles. I know you don't read *Good Housekeeping,* and I thought they'd be good points of reference."

"Did our mother put you up to this? Is she behind this 'safe sex' crusade?"

"No! Why would you say that? She's got nothing to do with it." And then, "Forget it, okay. I didn't mean anything by it."

But she had—Grace always meant something. "Look, Grace, I appreciate your concern, but I'm twenty-three, I have a college degree and a full-time job. I contribute to my 401K plan, and I pay my own car insurance—on time, even—and I take the trash to the dumpster every Tuesday and Thursday without having to be reminded. I'm not the lamebrained screw-up everybody thinks I am."

"I don't think you're . . . I don't think you are." Pause. "It's just that after Reed—"

"Can we forget about Reed? Please? He dumped me fourteen months ago, remember? Said I wasn't 'corporate' enough for his law ambitions, said he wanted someone more . . . like you."

"Jenny, he was a fool."

"I know that, so I'm better off without him, right?" But it had still hurt, still eaten away at her, deep down, the thought that maybe she really wasn't good enough, would never be good enough.

"Right. You're better off."

Jenny had laughed then, tried to change the mood. "Everybody can't be lucky like you and find their Prince Charming the first time around."

"I'm . . . I'm very fortunate, I know."

"So, thanks for the big sister talk, but I don't need it, really. Besides, I keep a twelve-pack of Trojans in my purse, just in case."

Silence.

She really had laughed then. "Just kidding. Really. Just kidding."

That was the extent of "sex" talk between them. And now, Laura was telling her that Grace had booked a hotel?

"She bought this gorgeous teddy from Victoria's Secret," Laura said.

Jenny raised a brow. *"My* sister?"

"Pale pink, kind of see-through."

"My sister?"

"Well, she needed a little convincing."

"Oh, God, how sad."

"And you should've seen what Grant bought her. I'll bet she hasn't even seen it." She looked at Jenny, her eyes bright. "It was a gold necklace with rubies and diamonds, a match to the bracelet he bought her three years ago."

"I don't understand it," Jenny said, a slow rage building inside. "Why did this have to happen? Why? They were perfect together, so much in love, so . . . right for each other. And now this. How is Grace going to go on without Grant? He was her rock, he was everything to her. So, now what?"

A little while later, Jenny gathered up the girls and headed home. They lived three doors away in a two-story house that mirrored Laura's. White siding, small porch, black lamp-post in the front. The only exception was the color of the shutters—Grace's were green, Laura's blue. Oh, and their choice of spring flowers. Laura's flowerbed sported daffodils and hyacinth while Grace had opted for tulips. White and pink. Other than those minor deviations, the houses looked the same.

Jenny glanced down the street. The houses, they were so . . . identical. Did Grace really like this sameness? Didn't she ever feel stifled, like her own ideas had been sucked out, replaced with someone else's? Didn't she ever want to give in to her creative side, just once, say *screw it,* or in Grace's case, *to heck with it,* and do something totally off the wall, like maybe put a totem pole in her yard? Okay, so maybe that was more Jenny's style, but Grace could choose something more discreet, say, a fountain, perhaps, done in a muted stone gray. *Anything* would be better than this.

Pink tulips. White tulips. Pink tulips. They formed a perfect border around the oak tree in the front of Grace's yard. Jenny stared at a pink tulip, the same color as the prom dress Grace wore senior year. Ted Beebleson had asked her to go. He was tall and skinny, with wire-rimmed glasses and a deep dimple on his right cheek. They said he once found an error in his calculus textbook and wrote to the publisher so it could be corrected. He'd asked Grace as she was leaving the library one Monday night and she told him yes, which sent her into an immediate tailspin over the "proper attire necessary to accompany the smartest boy in the school." That Saturday afternoon, their mother had dragged Grace and Jenny out for a frenzy of fabric fitting— too short, too long, too tight, too loose. Too white, too black, too velvet, too polyester. Until, finally, Jenny had spotted a gown, stuffed between a pink organza and a sky-blue taffeta. It was red, silky, with double-wide shoulder straps and a small slit up the back. It was perfect.

"Here, Gracie," she'd said. "Look what I found."

Grace had turned and looked at the gown in Jenny's hands. Her forehead had wrinkled up and she'd just stared for a minute, in her white cotton Playtex bra and panties, saying nothing.

"Do you like it?" Jenny had whispered, not sure why she wasn't using her normal voice.

Grace had nodded. "Yes," she'd whispered back, fingering one of the straps. "I like it."

"Then try it on."

"Okay." She'd smiled at Jenny and her whole face lit up. Jenny had helped her get the gown over her head, settled it around her hips. Then she'd zipped it up for Grace and stood back to take a look.

"Wow." It was the only word Jenny had been able to think of, the only word that seemed to fit. The red gown made Grace look beautiful, or maybe it was Grace's excitement shining through that made her look beautiful; it didn't matter, either way, *she looked beautiful.*

Grace had smiled, a wide open smile that showed teeth and something else . . . Joy? She'd lifted her arms a little and twirled around, stopping to watch the fabric swish around her ankles.

"You're beautiful," Jenny had said in a soft, almost reverent tone.

Grace had twirled around again and then again, laughter bubbling up and over, spilling out of her like champagne.

"Get it, Gracie," Jenny had said. "Get it."

And then, their mother's voice had come crashing through the dressing room walls. "What are you two doing in there?" She'd yanked the door open. Her mouth had fallen open, her jaw went slack. *"What* is that?"

Grace had shrugged, lowering her eyes. "I thought it was kind of pretty."

"Pretty? *Pretty?* It's pretty if you plan to sit on a barstool all day." She'd shaken her head, then held out the pale pink organza gown. "Now this," she'd said, "is perfect for you. Just perfect." She'd handed it to Grace and said, "If it doesn't fit, I'll get you another size." With that, she'd turned and closed the door behind her. "We still need to get you shoes, so don't take all day. Help her, Jenny."

Grace and Jenny had looked at each other but neither said a word.

"Will you unzip me?" Grace had asked, turning away.

"But this gown—"

"Isn't right for me," she'd cut her off. "Pink would be better." Her voice faded. "I'm more of a pink person, anyway."

Jenny had said nothing, just reached up and pulled the zipper tab down. The fabric fell in a blood-red heap at Grace's feet. When she stepped into the pink gown, her eyes didn't shine and there was only a faint smile hovering on her lips. And she didn't laugh, not even one tiny giggle.

All these years later, and Jenny could still remember that day, remember Grace's laughter, remember, too, her quietness, suffocating in its sadness.

As Jenny started up the driveway, her gaze landed on the front door. A wreath hung partway down, decorated with tulips and other spring greenery. She'd seen a similar one hanging on Laura's door, but it was covered with daffodils and hyacinth. Were the people like this, too, all the same, all reconstructed to act alike, decorate alike, *be* alike? Had *The Stepford Wives* come to Clairmont, Ohio?

She thought of her condo in LA, thought of Stefan, who'd painted a galaxy of stars on the midnight blue ceiling in her bedroom. The effect was mesmerizing. Jenny loved to lie in the dark, gazing up at the glittery points as they winked and glowed in the night. But it hadn't stopped there. Stefan had dug into his creative well, exploring bold, abstract interpretations of art that excited and intrigued her as he and Gerald covered her walls with things like sunshine yellow stucco and braided burlap. When Gerald insisted she have her own little garden ... he'd painted one on the kitchen wall ... rosemary, basil, tarragon, and sage.

Jenny loved that "garden" almost as much as she loved the two men who had filled her home with the beauty of their touch and creative genius.

But the people of Clairmont, Ohio, would never understand. Stefan and Gerald would be considered outcasts, freaks, deviants, their work a schizophrenic fantasia.

What would Grace think? Would she agree? *Would she?*

It was hard to tell. Grace was funny that way. She never veered too far to the right or left, but she admired, even encouraged those who did. It was almost as if she wanted to get out of that middle of the road she always chose, that center line where nothing was dangerous, or unfamiliar, or challenging. Or exciting. But it *was* safe. And if there was one thing Grace wanted more than anything in the world, it was "safe." Be safe, play it safe, stay safe, keep safe. It was her mantra.

And it had failed her.

Chapter 5

"Come here, girls. I want to talk to you," Jenny said, patting Natalie's bed. She took a deep breath, blew it out through her mouth. Her old yoga instructor said that was supposed to cleanse and refresh, help center breathing, diminish conflict.

It worked for about a half-second until Natalie bounced on the bed and asked, "Are you gonna stay with us 'til Mommy and Daddy get back?"

Jenny coughed, sputtered. She'd rehearsed the words enough times that she should have been able to say them without strangling on her own incompetence. But then there hadn't been two pairs of eyes staring back at her, one open and curious, the other hesitant and wary. So like their parents. Grant had always dove into every situation, headfirst, no matter how deep the water. Grace wouldn't dip a toe in until she'd strapped her life jacket on and consulted her compass. Even then, when every unforeseeable event had been taken into account, she hesitated. It drove Jenny crazy and she knew it frustrated Grant. He'd never said anything—he hadn't needed to; the way his jaw twitched and his nostrils flared when she acted that way was enough to give away the truth.

But Grace couldn't help it. Not really. She'd been taking care of people and situations for so long that Jenny doubted she knew *how* to be spontaneous. She left that up to everyone else. Grace felt more relaxed standing in the shadows, holding the net, while the rest of the world did flips and somersaults through that crazy maze called life.

"Aunt Jenny?" Natalie tugged on her ponytail. "How long are you gonna stay?"

Her persistence dragged Jenny back to reality. "I'll stay as long as I can." What a horrible response. That revealed less than nothing. God, but she'd always hated the way adults avoided issues, sidestepping them with clever phrases and never answering the question at all. And yet, she'd done just that.

It reminded her of what her mother used to say when she didn't really want to answer a question. Like the time Jenny asked her how Aunt Frannie could have a baby when she wasn't married. She'd been about eight, the same age as Danielle, and everybody she knew who had a baby also had a husband. Except Aunt Frannie. When Jenny asked her mother how that could be, she'd pursed her lips like she'd just sucked a whole lemon, and told her she was too young to ask those questions. That was her answer. Only it wasn't an answer.

Later, when Jenny asked Grace the same question, her sister had pulled her aside, and with her eleven-year-old sophistication, informed Jenny that if Aunt Frannie were going to have a baby, then she *had* to be married. And if nobody was talking about her husband, then maybe they didn't like him or wished she'd married somebody else. But, she assured Jenny, there was a husband. There had to be.

Grace had always answered Jenny's questions the best way she knew how. Now, Jenny owed it to her sister to answer her children's questions in the best way *she* knew how.

"I'm here because your mom and dad were in an accident. A car accident." She bit her lower lip. "A bad one. Your mom's in a deep sleep and we don't know when she'll wake up."

"If you tickle her toes, she'll wake up," Natalie whispered, her green eyes wide and serious.

Jenny reached out, tousled her curly hair. "No, sweetheart. It's not that kind of sleep."

"What about Dad?" Danielle asked.

Jenny looked at her oldest niece, saw the fear and apprehension on her pale face, and wished there was some way she could protect them from the truth. Children shouldn't have to deal with this, shouldn't have to confront the maniacal face of death, or feel its sharp claws digging into their reality, scratching away at their peaceful, safe existences.

"Your dad's in heaven now," Jenny whispered. Her eyes burned with tears.

"Well, he can only stay until Tuesday," Natalie said with the matter-of-fact innocence of a five-year-old. "He promised he'd take me to Toys R Us on Wednesday to get my new bike." She leaned forward and smiled at Jenny. "Pink and purple with a white basket and sparkly streamers."

"Oh, Natalie," Jenny said, wrapping her arms around her niece's small body. "Daddy can't take you, honey."

"But he promised."

Jenny glanced at Danielle. She sat on the edge of the bed, hands folded in her lap, back straight, staring at the floor. "Come here, Danielle."

Danielle looked up and there were tears shimmering in her big brown eyes. Jenny reached for her hand, but she bolted off the bed. "No!" she yelled. "No! No! No!" She ran from the room, slamming the door behind her.

"Danielle! Come back!"

Natalie buried her face against Jenny's shirt. "I'm scared, Aunt Jenny," she said, her small body shaking.

Jenny drew her closer, stroked her silky head. "I know," she murmured. "I know." Of course she knew, because right now fear had a stranglehold around her neck and it was threatening to drag her under. She wasn't just scared, she was petrified. These girls were counting on her to make their world okay. How could she do that when she could barely make a toasted cheese sandwich?

She took a deep breath. *Relax. Relax. You can do this,* she told herself. *Think lavender. You can do this. Think chamomile. You can be the big sister for once. The dependable one. The shoulder that people lean on.*

You can do this.

Can't you?

"What do you mean, Grace has been in an accident?" Virginia Romano's voice pierced the line, sharp and half-accusing, as though she doubted her daughter's words.

Jenny should have waited to call her; she knew this as soon as her mother answered the phone. One more glass of chardonnay might have prepared her better. Or maybe two. Or, perhaps, a whole bottle would have made the confrontation with her mother more palatable.

Jenny took a deep breath and said, "Grace has been in an accident, Mom. It was pretty bad." She hesitated, then pushed on. "She's in a coma."

"Dear God," her mother sobbed. *"Dear God.* My Gracie. Poor Gracie."

"I know."

Silence. "I'm coming. She needs me. Those babies need me."

Jenny closed her eyes, pinched the bridge of her nose. "You just had a hip replacement, Mom. The doctor is not going to let you come."

"These doctors don't know anything. I'm fine." Her voice dropped to a painful whisper. "I have to see her, I have to see Gracie."

"There's nothing anyone can do right now except wait. And you need your therapy."

"Therapy? How can I think about therapy when my daughter is lying in a coma? I have to get to her."

"How do you expect to do that, Mom? You can't even walk right now."

She sniffed, cleared her throat. "How can I expect you to understand? You've never been a mother, never stayed up all night with a sick child. You couldn't possibly know the pain I feel right now."

How many times had Jenny heard that story? Twenty-five? Twenty-five *hundred?* After one, it all sounded the same, blending together into one gigantic heap of nothingness. Jenny had never given birth, therefore she was incapable of real emotion. *Invalidated*—that was the word.

"I'll call you every day and report her progress," Jenny said.

"You?" her mother choked out. "Why would *you* do that? Where's Grant?"

Jenny opened her mouth to speak, but the words wouldn't come out. *Dead. Grant's dead.*

"Jenny?"

"He's dead," she breathed. "He was with Grace."

"Oh, my God," her mother cried, her voice trailing off in agony. *"Oh, my God."*

Jenny blinked the tears from her eyes. "I haven't made any funeral arrangements yet. I guess I'll do that tomorrow."

She got queasy just thinking about it, but there were no other choices. They were the only family Grant had.

"He was like a son to me," her mother said in a ragged voice. "Poor Grant. Poor Gracie. Oh, those poor babies." She repeated the litany over and over for what seemed like a full five minutes, interrupted only by an occasional sob or gasp for breath.

Jenny said nothing. She just closed her eyes and listened, her heart growing heavier as the seconds ticked by. After what seemed like two eternities, she heard her mother sniff one last time and blow her nose. "Jenny," she said, her words clipped, businesslike, "call Laura Montgomery and make arrangements with her to care for the girls until I can get there. Whatever it costs, I'll pay her."

"Mom," Jenny said, twirling the phone cord around her index finger, "I told you, I'm staying. I'll take care of the girls."

"You?" Her mother let out a harsh little sound that fell short of a laugh. "What do *you* know about caring for children?"

Jenny twisted the cord tighter around her finger, watched as it turned red with white marks where the cord bit into flesh. "I know Danielle and Natalie," she said, wondering what her mother would say if she knew Danielle hadn't spoken a word to her all evening and had buried her head under a pillow when Jenny came into her room to say good night.

"You know nothing about children." There it was again, another jab. "You've never even changed a diaper."

"They're not in diapers anymore. I can take care of them." She paused. "And Laura has offered to help."

"You don't even know how to cook."

Jenny could just see her, sitting in her favorite green tweed chair, shaking her head with equal parts dismay and disgust.

"I have expanded my cooking knowledge since the last

time we were together.'' If Gerald's scrambled eggs with Tabasco sauce and Monterey Jack cheese counted, which they probably didn't. She also knew how to make Double Dipped Devil's Chocolate Strawberries, thanks again to Gerald.

''Oh? Now you know how to boil water in one-quart *and* two-quart saucepans?''

Jenny pulled on the phone cord so hard, she thought it was going to amputate her finger. ''I'm not going to get into this now, Mom. I'm staying. And if you're worried the girls will shrivel and waste away, don't. Laura has already offered to help and anyway, I'm not a complete incompetent in the kitchen.'' No need to mention they were going to McDonald's tomorrow night. She didn't need to know that, not unless Jenny wanted to hear the complete, unabridged lecture on the link between childhood obesity and fast food restaurants, which she didn't.

''What about your job?'' Her mother was not going to give up. ''Weren't you supposed to go to India soon?''

Jenny bit the inside of her cheek. ''Italy, Mom. It was Italy.''

''Oh. Well, whatever. Italy, then. Weren't you supposed to go there in a month or so?''

''Right. I already talked to my boss.'' She *had* talked to him ... kind of. Joe knew she was coming to Ohio to be with Grace, and then she'd be flying to Italy from Cleveland.

Her mother was tsk-tsking over the phone. ''Next you'll be losing your job. Again.''

That was one thing about Virginia Romano—she knew just where to sink the knife, twist it in the flesh, force the blood to spurt out. She still didn't believe that last job wasn't Jenny's fault. Not even when Jenny finally told her the truth, that underneath his distinguished air and Rembrandt smile, her old boss, Wesley Edmund Nasrogeron, was a wolf, more interested in the play of light and lens on her *body* than on her *work*. She hadn't had the time or the extra cash to file a sexual harassment suit; she needed a job and she needed money. Fast.

Enter Joe Feltzer. She could see him now, flipping through her latest work, his sausage-size fingers moving with surprising agility. He was a gruff, hard-nosed, transplanted New Yorker with an affinity for Chinese takeout and salami on rye. He didn't talk a lot, not with words, anyway.

But then he didn't need to. In the three short months Jenny had been there, she'd learned that Joe had his own special brand of communication that required neither translation nor interpretation. One look, a raised bushy brow, a creased forehead, a frown on his fleshy face, said more than a library of books ever could. And then there were his hands. They were the size of baseball gloves, rough and meaty, with stubby fingers and blunt nails. When he slashed them in the air, you could feel the breeze brushing by your face.

Joe Feltzer was tough and demanding, but underneath that heavy coat of irascibility and an extra twenty-five pounds was a decent guy and the reason *Fade to Black* was one of the best magazines on the West Coast.

". . . You'll be homeless, left out on the streets. You'll have to move back home," her mother droned on.

That last statement jolted Jenny back to reality.

"What did you say?" Did she really think that moving back home was even a remote possibility?

No answer. Silence stretched through the phone line. Slowly, Jenny released the tangled cord around her finger and watched the skin turn pink again. And waited.

Finally, her mother spoke. "I'll check with my doctor and see when I can travel." The words were brisk, distant, and there was no further mention of doomed employment.

"Fine," Jenny said, anxious to be done with this conversation. Her head ached, pounded with every syllable her mother spoke.

"Fine."

Damn. Now her mother sounded like a wounded animal. What should Jenny have done, let her call the shots, tell her what she was going to do, when, how, why? No, Virginia Romano worked people, made rude, hurtful comments, and then tried to explain them away saying that her age gave her the right to say exactly what she thought. But her passage into the "golden years" had nothing to do with it. Not really. She'd been pushing people around for years. Especially Grace.

"I'll call you every day," Jenny said, anxious to get off the phone.

"Yes." Her mother's voice deflated with the speed of a balloon that's been pin-pricked twenty times. "Poor Gracie. Why? Why her?"

Those were the last words she spoke before the receiver clicked off. *Poor Gracie. Why? Why her?* Who did she think she was kidding? They both knew what she was really thinking, though even someone as bold as Virginia Romano wouldn't speak the words out loud. What she really meant was, *Why did it have to be Gracie? Why couldn't it have been you?* Of course, she'd deny such a horrible thought, deny it to her grave. And maybe she wasn't even aware that it existed. Maybe it only breathed in her subconscious, but Jenny knew it existed.

She knew . . . because she'd been wondering the same thing herself. Why did it have to be Gracie? *Why couldn't it have been me?*

Jenny stared at the plastic tube in Grace's mouth. She'd been sitting here for over an hour, perched on the edge of a "hospital orange" vinyl chair, watching. Sixty seconds had taken on new significance. It had become a basis from which Grace's existence was measured, analyzed, and charted.

Jenny had been counting everything: the drops that fell from the IV, the beeps on the monitor, the whooshes of the respirator compressing and decompressing. Her teeth clicked in rapid staccato as she synchronized her gum chewing to Grace's life-support systems. After two minutes, she stuck the wad of strawberry to the roof of her mouth to give her jaw a break.

When her watch swept another sixtieth second, she let out a quick breath and started all over again. First, she counted the IV drops, then the monitor beeps, and finally the respirator whooshes. After thirteen minutes her vision blurred and her head started pounding. She blinked hard, yanking her shirtsleeve down over her wrist.

Oh, God, help her. Please let her wake up. Jenny let out a long sigh, stood up, and edged her way past the jumble of tubes and cords to stand beside Grace. She touched her hand; it was cool, lifeless. Her gaze shot to her sister's arms. Bruises covered the pale flesh in a kaleidoscope of purples, blues, and yellows. Most probably from blood draws, just one more way to measure and analyze Grace's condition. Stick a needle in and suck the life out of an already-compromised body. *Ah, Grace,* she thought, *you don't deserve this. You, of all people, do not deserve this.* Tears stung her eyes and she blinked them back. *Be strong,* she told herself. *You have to be strong. She needs you now.*

"I'm here for you, Gracie," Jenny whispered, giving her sister's hand a gentle squeeze. "I'm right here for you." She bit her lower lip, swallowed hard.

Jenny forced her gaze past the tube sticking out of Grace's mouth, looked at her eyes. They were closed. There were no lines of fatigue or distress around them, no signs of pain. If she could only block out everything else and focus on Grace's closed eyes, then she could say her sister looked almost peaceful. Even serene. But the second her gaze jumped to her bandaged head, reality pushed its way back.

Grace was in a coma and she was not having a peaceful or serene experience. *She was fighting for her life.*

"Fight, Gracie. Fight," Jenny whispered. "We need you." She swiped at her face with the back of her hand. "I need you."

How weak and pitiful she was, standing here pleading with her unconscious sister to pull through . . . for her. To meet *her* needs. No wonder her mother called her selfish. Maybe she was, maybe she'd just been disguising it under something fashionable like independence or self-direction. But underneath the drive, the single-minded desire for accomplishment, was a woman who saw to her own needs first, always, despite the situations or individuals surrounding her.

She *was* selfish.

But Grace had always let her, had actually made it so easy to take . . . and take . . . *and take . . .*

She'd never seemed to mind rearranging her schedule to meet Jenny's, even though *she* was the one with the husband and two children. Last year, she'd even postponed Natalie's birthday celebration so Jenny could take in a Phil Collins concert before she came to Ohio. Jenny should have at least asked Grace about it *before* she bought the tickets since she'd promised Natalie she'd be there for her birthday . . . *for* her birthday, not three days *after* her birthday. And it wasn't as though she hadn't seen Phil Collins three times before.

But, as always, Jenny had just assumed Grace would make everything work, and she did. They'd had a great visit, done some power shopping without the girls and even chose the same blouse, a gorgeous magenta silk, in some fancy little boutique Grace found. Jenny had drooled over it, fingered the soft fabric, and said she'd just die if she couldn't have it. Grace had looked at her, hesitated, looked at the blouse in her hand, and hung it back on the rack.

Jenny had worn that damn blouse less than five times in the year since she'd bought it. She hadn't needed it; she would have survived if she hadn't bought it. *But she had wanted it.* And now she wondered what made her wanting any more urgent than Grace's? What gave her the right to push Grace's desires aside and jump in line ahead of her, like a high school kid cutting in the cafeteria line? Jenny knew they couldn't both buy the damned blouse; they'd made that pact in their teens. And she'd also known Grace would back down and let *her* buy it.

She stared at her sister, eyes closed, body still. *How many other times have you turned your back on something you wanted? How many times, Gracie? I promise you, I'll buy you five magenta blouses and I'll let you have first pick next time. Only, please, please, please, wake up.*

Chapter 6

Darkness covered her, blanketing her like a cocoon, holding her still, filling her lungs, her throat, her eyes. She couldn't move, could only hear the faintest of sounds, moving over her, around her, through her. A woman's voice, gentle sobbing ... silence.

Where was she? What was happening? She tried to think, tried to form a memory, but the cocoon wrapped itself tighter around Grace's brain, smothered her thoughts.

And blackness took over ...

"So what'll it be tonight?" Jenny hollered from the top of the stairs. "McDonalds or Burger King?"

"McDonald's!" Natalie shouted. "Can I get a Happy Meal?"

"Sure," Jenny called, jogging down the steps.

"With McNuggets?"

"Yes, silly, with McNuggets." Both girls were sitting on

the floor in front of the television, watching *Arthur the Aardvark*. Natalie ran up to Jenny, grabbed her hand, and dragged her back to the couch. Jenny plopped down and pulled Natalie onto her lap.

"Danielle, what about you?"

Nothing.

"Danielle?"

"We're not supposed to eat that stuff more than once a week," she said. "This is the sixth night in a row. And you know it, too, Natalie."

Well, at least she'd spoken—a complete sentence, too. Jenny guessed it was an improvement over the one-word responses she'd been getting the last five days. No matter how many ways she tried to approach her, Danielle didn't want to discuss her father—or her mother, for that matter. Natalie was the one who asked about Grace every day. Was she still sleeping? Did she open even one eye? Did she snore? Not Danielle—she just stared straight ahead, mouth clamped shut.

"I want a Happy Meal," Natalie said, twirling a piece of Jenny's hair around her finger.

"You're gonna get in trouble," Danielle said.

"Am not. Aunt Jenny said it was okay."

"Wait a minute," Jenny said, wondering why it had taken Danielle six days to tell her they weren't supposed to be eating junk food. "Tell me about your mother's rule."

Natalie shrugged.

This time, Danielle spoke in a half-disgusted tone, as though Jenny should have known. "We're not allowed to eat at McDonald's or Burger King or places like that except for once a week."

"Oh."

"Mommy says too many French fries gives you a fat heart," Natalie said with quiet authority.

"A fat heart?"

"Yup." She nodded, her eyes wide, serious. "The fat sticks to your heart and it's bad."

"Oh." Hardening of the arteries? Grace sure was teaching them young. "Well, then, we don't want to break Mommy's rules, so how about eating something here?" Now for the real challenge, but Kraft was quite creative. "I've got four different kinds of macaroni and cheese. Regular, spaceships, musical instruments, and dragons."

"Dragons," Natalie chirped.

"Mom only lets us have the stuff from a box in an emergency," Danielle said.

Jenny smiled at the back of her niece's head. "Good. Then she won't mind if we have dragons tonight," she said, nudging Natalie off her lap and standing up. "Because this *is* an emergency."

She headed for the kitchen, Natalie trailing two steps behind.

Six days ago, she'd been eating Gerald's bouillabaisse, sipping white wine, and munching on homemade baguettes. Tonight, it was Kraft's macaroni and cheese dragons on white Corelle dishes.

Her dietary habits were not the only things that had undergone monumental shifts. In the span of a few short days, she'd transitioned from ambitious, unattached photographer, traveling the world on assignment, to surrogate mother of two, responsible for food, sustenance, and transportation. Thank God, at least the transportation felt normal; the Sebring convertible she'd rented from the airport wasn't the Jag she was used to, but it wasn't part of the minivan brigade this neighborhood belonged to, either.

She was trying, she really was. She'd taken care of Grant's funeral arrangements, attended the service, accepted condolences from his friends and coworkers, thanked them for asking about Grace, and then came home and hauled the kids to Pizza Hut for dinner.

Thank God for Laura Montgomery—she just kind of knew how to work this "mother" thing. The girls got on the bus at 8:10 A.M., off at 3:15 P.M. They ate Rice Krispie treats with milk for a snack or chocolate chip cookies—two, not the four Natalie tried to sneak—and then they did homework, played outside, ate dinner, bathed, and went to bed at 8:45. Laura handled the after-school detail while Jenny went to the hospital. The Montgomerys just kind of rolled the girls into their lives, like cookie dough, blending them together. Even Laura's husband, Hank, a big, burly man with dark hair and a beard, seemed unperturbed by the addition of two more little girls to his household. And their children, Abby and Alexis—well, they subscribed to "the more the merrier" routine.

How could someone be as calm and reassuring as Laura Montgomery, especially when she was surrounded by a bunch of under-ten-year-olds? Maybe she was using an herbal treatment—lavender? Chamomile? St. John's wort?

Laura gave Jenny a list the second day that she called: "An Adult's Survival Guide in a Kid's World."

Lesson one: Peanut butter and jelly sandwiches taste better cut in triangles.

Lesson two: Straws make milk disappear faster.

Lesson three: Milk mustaches are cool. Even for grown-ups.

Lesson four: There *is* a difference between regular Oreo cookies and Double Stuffed Oreo cookies.

Lesson five: Fireflies are magic.

Lesson six: Don't ask a child who she's talking to if she's the only one in the room.

Lesson seven: Check your child's toothbrush at night to see if it's wet.

Lesson eight: Buy lots of bubbles and chalk.

Lesson nine: Let your child "read" to you even if the words are made up.

Lesson ten: Leave the night-light on.

The sixth night ended after a box of macaroni and cheese dragons, a bubble bath, and a story. Natalie chose *Rapunzel,* her favorite. Danielle picked up *Thumbelina* and curled under the covers, facing the wall. By the time Jenny turned off the light, closed the door, reopened the door to make sure she'd left the night-light on, her head was pounding.

She needed a cigarette.

There was a pack in the bottom of her suitcase. Emergency supply. A few puffs, just two or three, that's all she wanted. Who would know? Stefan and Gerald were twenty-four hundred miles away; they'd never find out she'd swapped a pack of strawberry Bubble Yum for a pack of Dorals. *Just this once.* She ran to her room, unzipped the suitcase, and pulled out a pack of Dorals, her palms sweaty with anticipation. And then the doorbell rang. *Damn!* She thought of not answering it, thought of just ripping the pack open and lighting up. But what if it was someone important? What if it was the police returning Grant's car?

What if . . .

Oh, damn. She threw the cigarettes back in the suitcase, shoved it in the closet, and ran downstairs. When she opened the door, Laura was standing there with a glass dish covered in tinfoil.

"Care for a piece of blueberry cobbler?"

The fragrant, sweet aroma of blueberries and cinnamon filled Jenny's nostrils. She eyed the pan and smiled. So she'd eat instead of smoke.

"My savior," she murmured, knowing there was more truth to those words than Laura could possibly know.

"Sugar resuscitation," Laura said, laughing. "Works every time."

"Come on in while I make some coffee." Jenny headed for the kitchen, dug out the Maxwell House. Decaf, no less. No wonder she'd been getting a headache every day; a person couldn't go from five cups of Starbucks Colombian a day to zilch.

"I just bought some triple vanilla ice cream the other day," Jenny said. "Want some with your cobbler?"

"No, thanks. Not everyone's graced with your body. I'll have to run five miles tomorrow to burn up this cobbler."

"Oh, yeah. Exercise." Jenny made a face.

Laura laughed. "Grace told me all about you. How you eat half a pizza in one sitting and then have a hot fudge sundae for dessert." She waved her fork at Jenny. "And don't gain an ounce."

Jenny handed Laura a coffee mug, then sat down and plopped a big spoonful of blueberries in her mouth. "Did she also tell you that she's convinced one day, it will all catch up with me and I'll balloon into a four-hundred-pound ball of fat?"

"Then justice will be served," Laura said, her laughter spreading throughout the room.

"I'm glad you stopped by. I'm really getting worried about Danielle."

"Still not talking to you, huh?"

"Not really. Oh, she did break the no-talking fast for about ten minutes to tell me how she and Natalie aren't supposed to be eating fast food more than once a week. Of course, that's all we've been eating."

"I should've thought—"

"No, it's not your responsibility, it's mine. But, heck, I don't know what kids are supposed to eat. *I like junk food.* I love McDonald's French fries. I thought it was a treat, I mean, when you see all those commercials with kids eating

McNuggets and Big Macs, they're always rushing to the register, laughing, jumping up and down." Jenny shrugged. "You never see them get that excited when they're sitting in front of a plate of green beans."

"Well, you've got a point there."

"So I thought I'd make macaroni and cheese. That didn't go either, not according to Danielle." She leaned over, lowered her voice. "Do you think that's junk food? Why isn't it considered homemade? After all, you cook it at home and it goes on the stove, not in the microwave, right?"

Laura took a sip of coffee, thought a moment. "That's true, but it does have quite a bit of sodium and the cheese is all processed."

Jenny shook her head. "I should've brought Gerald with me—he's a chef. He could've worried about balancing their meals and making sure they got their folic acid or whatever it is kids are supposed to have."

Laura laid a hand on Jenny's. "You're doing fine, just fine."

"What? Oh." No, she wasn't doing fine—she was botching things up, making a huge mess. She couldn't even tell the difference between junk food and real food.

"Are you okay?"

Jenny shrugged, felt her strength start to crumble under Laura's watchful gaze, like a sand castle meeting high tide. She looked away.

"It's all right, Jenny. Cry if you want." Laura touched her hand. "You've been going nonstop since your plane landed. You don't have to be Superwoman."

Jenny sniffed, pressed her fingertips to her temples. "I'm fine. I . . . really." She blinked, hard.

"Oh, Jenny," Laura said, "let it out. Just let it out."

This was where Grace always came in, talking, reassuring; even twenty-four-hundred miles away, she knew what to say, how to say it, to make Jenny feel better, gain perspective.

And now, Grace wasn't here for her, now she was in a hospital bed, and she couldn't talk, couldn't even move. Now it was all up to Jenny . . .

"This is crazy," Jenny said, as a tear slid down her cheek. "I don't know what's wrong with me. Maybe there's something in that cobbler." It was a halfhearted attempt at a joke that hit the ground like a lead balloon.

"Talk to me," Laura said. There was a quiet authority in her voice that demanded a response.

"I thought I was okay. Then, I don't know, I just started to fall apart."

"Welcome to the human race," Laura said.

"Grace would never act like this," Jenny said, swiping at her cheeks.

"Well, we can't count Grace. She's the fourth part of the Catholic trilogy."

"What do you mean?"

"There's the Father, the Son, the Holy Spirit, and then there's Grace."

"That about sums it up."

Laura leaned over the table and lowered her voice. "But you don't want to be within a mile of my house when I come undone," she said. "It's worse than a hurricane."

"You? Lose your cool? No way."

She laughed. "Thanks, but please don't tell poor Hank that. He's witnessed the fallout too many times in our twelve years of marriage." She took a sip of coffee. "It's natural. I'd say even healthy."

"I guess. It's just that I've been practicing all these techniques to relax, de-stress myself—herbal remedies, lavender, chamomile, hot massages, oatmeal baths . . . but they're not working."

"One breath at a time," Laura said. "That's it. You've got a lot on your plate right now."

"I miss Grace."

"Me, too. She could calm me down, get me grounded better than anyone I've ever met before."

"And I really am getting worried about Danielle. Ten sentences in six days isn't good. I feel like in some way she blames me for Grant's death—you know, kill the messenger and all that."

"Maybe, in some subconscious way, she does."

Jenny rubbed the back of her neck, let out a slow breath. *Relax. Relax. Think Hawaii. Think cool water.*

"You know, Danielle's okay with me, a little quieter than usual, but when you've got four girls yapping at once, sometimes it's a welcome relief to have one take a break."

"Well, she's been taking a lot of breaks around here."

"Hmmm."

"What?"

"It might not hurt to have the girls talk to somebody," she said, her clear blue gaze meeting Jenny's.

"Like who?"

"I know someone who helped Hank's niece when her parents got divorced last year," she said. "Actually, his secretary is Hank's aunt."

"A shrink?"

She threw Jenny a look and said, "He's a psychologist, actually."

"Oh. A mini-shrink."

"His name's Elliot Drake, and I think you should consider having the girls talk with him," she said.

"Elliot Drake." Jenny tried the name on her tongue. "Sounds like the name of a ship. Like the *Edmund Fitzgerald.*"

"I met him," she said, ignoring her comments. "He's very nice."

"Did he analyze every word you said?" Jenny asked. "Watch you with hawk-like intensity from over small, black glasses perched on the tip of his pointy nose?"

Laura laughed and shook her head. "You, Jenny Romano, watch way too much television. Elliot does not have black glasses." She gave her a sly smile. "I think they're brown."

Jenny raised a brow and opened her mouth to speak but Laura rushed in. "And his nose isn't the least bit pointy."

"Elliot? Why not *Dr.* Elliot what's-his-name?"

"Drake," she said.

"Drake, Dracula, whatever."

Laura tapped a finger against her chin and tilted her head a little. Her pale-blond braid swayed behind her. "I guess I think of him as Elliot because he's got a very unassuming manner. Relaxed. Casual. You'd never know he was a doctor. And," she grinned, "he introduced himself as Elliot."

"I see—probably some ploy to get you to relax so he can dissect what you're saying."

"He's very nice," she repeated.

"You said that already."

"Well, I guess I did." She hesitated a second, adding, "You've been under so much pressure since the accident . . . you might even want to consider seeing him yourself."

Jenny met her gaze. "No, thanks."

Laura didn't try to correct her this time. "Talking to someone might make things a little easier for you," she said.

"I have someone," Jenny said, forcing a smile. "You."

She shook her head. "I'm not qualified to listen and give you advice—"

"You're a friend," Jenny said, cutting her off. "That makes you more than qualified." She felt her pulse racing and sucked in a deep breath. "I'm sorry. I appreciate what you're trying to do, really. It's just that every person I know who's ever been to see a shrink has gotten more screwed up than when she started out. And besides, I really don't need to see a shrink, or a psychologist, or any other head guy with a bunch of letters after his name. I'm fine." She reached for two pieces of Bubble Yum. "Really." Opening the wrappers, she popped both in her mouth.

"Okay," Laura said, her voice hesitant, as though she wanted to dispute that comment, but decided against it. "Will you at least *consider* taking the girls? Especially Danielle? A few sessions, that's all."

Jenny was working the gum so fast she thought her jaw would pop out of its socket. Strawberry spurted in her mouth in little, uneven gushes. She met Laura's steady gaze and said, around a double wad of Bubble Yum, "I'll think about it."

Chapter 7

Jenny waffled back and forth for the next two days—*take them to see a shrink, don't take them to see a shrink, take them, don't.* But in the end, it was the girls who decided for her.

It was a Saturday afternoon; the sun had spread its rays like a spring jacket, warming everything it touched. Jenny and Natalie were sitting on a blanket in the backyard, blowing bubbles and eating cheese curls. After blowing one incredibly huge bubble, especially for a five-year-old, Natalie leaned over and grabbed a handful of cheese curls. She knocked the bottle of bubbles with her elbow and it spilled on the blanket and the front of Jenny's shorts.

"I'm sorry, I'm sorry." Natalie jumped up, looking at Jenny with something close to fear. "I'm sorry. I didn't mean it, Aunt Jenny. Honest."

Jenny stood up and brushed the soapy liquid off her jean shorts. "I know you didn't mean it, Natalie. It's okay."

The crying started then, huge tears falling down her

cheeks. "I didn't mean it. I didn't mean it. Don't go, Aunt Jenny, don't go." She threw her arms around Jenny's waist, holding tight.

Jenny ran a hand over Natalie's curls. "I'm not going anywhere, sweetheart."

But Natalie went on as though she hadn't spoken. "Please, don't go," she said again, her voice wobbling, " 'cause Mommy can't run and do the kind of stuff you do. I'm trying to be good and quiet, so she can get better. Really, I am."

Jenny hugged her little body close. "I know you are, honey."

"I want Mommy back the way she used to be," she whimpered.

"I know." *So do I.*

"Danielle says I have to behave or I'm going to make Mommy sicker and she might die and then we wouldn't have any parents." Her body started to shake.

"No, Natalie, that's not true."

She sniffed again and this time the tears grew hotter, more insistent. "Danielle says . . ." she stuttered, "that we have to be vv . . . verrry gg . . . goood." Her small body shuddered. "Bb . . . bbetter than with Da . . . aaddy."

"What happened to Mommy and Daddy is not your fault. It wasn't anybody's fault. It was an accident."

"Bb . . . but Danielle says, we have to be vv . . . very good so God doesn't ttt . . . take Mommy, too." More tears, more shudders.

Did Danielle really believe that she and Natalie were responsible for what happened to their parents? *That they could control it?*

Laura was right; they needed help, someone who could talk to them, make them understand the accident wasn't their fault. Laura had given her the name of a doctor. What was

his name? Alec? Alex? Eldridge? Elliot? That was it. Elliot.
Elliot Drake.

Dr. Elliot Drake lived twenty minutes away in the next
town. When Jenny pulled her silver Sebring into a parking
space on Glendale Road, she had to check the address on
her notepad twice. The house in front of her had the same
number as the one on the notepad, but it wasn't what she
was expecting. Actually, she wasn't expecting a house at all.
In California, doctors had offices in sleek, chrome buildings,
several stories high with elevators and walls of windows.

Dr. Drake's secretary—that would be Hank's aunt, she
guessed—had indicated that the doctor's office was in his
house, but somehow, she hadn't expected anything so . . .
warm or welcoming. She'd always thought a psychologist
would counsel patients in an atmosphere that was conserva-
tive, a bit sterile, perhaps even austere.

This house was anything but that. With its long wrap-
around porch and high-pitched roofs, it was an elegant blend
of colonial and Victorian architecture. The color scheme
was perfect; a warm honey-wheat trimmed in Wedgwood
blue and burgundy. The porch led to a small side entry
that had to be the doctor's office. And there were plants
everywhere. Six hanging ferns and several potted begonias
and impatiens. Red, white, yellow, fuschia, orange, all spilling from the porch in an explosion of vibrant color.

Dr. Drake's wife certainly loved flowers, she thought,
climbing the wide steps to his house. Jenny thought of the
blood-red roses and white trellis Stefan had painted on her
dining room wall. They were the only flowers she hadn't
managed to kill.

She followed the trail of potted plants to the side entrance
and stopped before a door with the name "Elliot S. Drake"
on it. For a second, she wondered what the "S" stood for,
and then raised a finger to the doorbell. When she pressed the
button, the first few chords of Beethoven's Fifth Symphony

chimed around her. Interesting. She pressed it again, her curiosity toward the good doctor mounting.

The oak door opened just as she was contemplating another ring. A pleasant-looking, fifty-something woman with huge dimples smiled up at her from her barely five-foot frame. "Hello," she said. "Come in. Come in. You must be Miss Romano, Laura's friend."

Jenny smiled at the woman and stepped past her into the house. "Yes, I am. I have a three o'clock appointment with Dr. Drake."

"Elliot," the woman said, waving a plump hand in the air. "Everyone calls him Elliot." She waddled a few steps and turned around. "I'm Eleanor. Did Laura tell you Hank was my nephew?" she asked. "Yes, of course she must have. Hank's a good boy and Laura's a dear." She lowered her voice. "I'm so sorry to hear about your sister and her husband."

"Oh, well, thank you." Maybe Hank had been paying more attention to her situation than she thought.

"Would you like something to drink? Iced tea or lemonade, maybe?"

"Lemonade, please," Jenny said, wondering if all psychologists' offices were this hospitable. She didn't think so.

"I'll be back in a jiff," the older woman called over her shoulder as she opened a side door and left the room.

Jenny seriously doubted the poor woman could do anything "in a jiff," not with such short legs and so much extra padding around the middle, but she sure did have a kind heart. She reminded her of Aunt Bea on *Mayberry RFD* with her big, floppy gray bun sitting on top of her head and those warm, brown eyes that looked like simmering molasses. And when she smiled, two big dimples carved both sides of her mouth, giving her a girlish appearance.

If Dr. Drake—correction, Elliot—was half as warm and welcoming as this woman, then Danielle might just open up enough to talk to him and Natalie would stop blaming herself for her parents' accident. Jenny glanced around the room, trying to get a feel for the doctor. She'd always been a big believer in observation of surroundings, kind of like taking a snapshot without a camera. It told a lot about the person. Herself, for example. If someone walked into her condo, the first thing they would notice would be a wall of black-and-white photos. Not just any black-and-whites, but photos of people: head shots, full body shots, young, old, in groups or alone. If they were to travel from room to room, they would see more photographs, some colored, others gray-toned, but always with a face or body as the subject. By the time they were finished wandering through the place, they'd know Jenny's passion and her profession, without one peek into the darkroom or one glimpse of a single camera.

She glanced around the waiting room, trying to detect something about Dr. Elliot Drake. Her guess would be that he preferred comfort to style. There was an overstuffed burgundy-and-cream plaid sofa tucked against the far wall with two hand-crocheted cream pillows. A dark blue afghan rested on the back of the couch, compliments of Mrs. Drake, no doubt. Two straight-backed chairs sat across from each other, one done in blue plaid, the other in burgundy. The fabric on both chairs was faded and a little frayed along the edges. Probably something he'd had forever—maybe a purchase made as a newlywed and now, years later, neither he nor Mrs. Drake could part with it.

Her mind wandered off in that direction as she took in the rest of the room. There were two pictures of mountain landscapes and one of a beach. Hmmm. Laura had given no indication of Dr. Drake's age, so she had no idea what to expect. But she'd bet her entire darkroom that he was a white-haired gentleman, pushing sixty, with a kind face, bushy eyebrows, and wire-rimmed glasses. There was

another picture in the far corner—a photograph, actually—
that she had to move closer to see. Jenny squinted hard to
bring it into view. *A motorcycle?* Sure enough, it was a
black-and-white shot of a very large motorcycle. She recog-
nized the style even before she saw "Harley-Davidson"
scrawled on the side of it.

What the heck?

"Here we are, dear," a voice called from behind. It was
"Aunt Bea" holding out a tall glass of lemonade.

"Fresh squeezed this morning," she said, smiling.

"Thank you," Jenny said, accepting the drink.

The older woman's smile deepened, showing her dimples.
"Call me Eleanor. Everyone else does."

"Thank you, Eleanor." Eleanor and Elliot. Mrs. Elliot
Drake. Jenny took a sip of lemonade and puckered her lips
at the sour-sweetness. "I noticed the beautiful flowers on
the porch. Did you plant those?"

Eleanor let out a full-bellied laugh that rolled around the
room, pulling a chuckle from Jenny. "Heavens, no. I have
nothing to do with anything green." She shook her gray
head and her bun flopped back and forth. "That's Elliot's
doing. All of it."

"Well, they're beautiful. I guess I just thought they had
a woman's touch."

Eleanor chuckled. "I'm the only woman around here, and
Eleanor Flatt doesn't do plants."

Eleanor Flatt? Then she wasn't Dr. Drake's wife? "What
about his wife?" The question was out before Jenny could
pull it back and think of a more polite way to ask it.

The smile faded from the older woman's face. "Elliot
doesn't have a wife."

Elliot doesn't have a wife. He must be a widower. She
could tell by the way Eleanor shut down, there was grief
buried in those words. Maybe his wife had died of cancer.
Or some horrible accident. They'd probably been very much

in love and she'd been plucked away in the twilight of their lives, leaving him alone and heartbroken.

"I'm sorry," Jenny murmured, wishing she could yank the last two minutes of conversation back into her big mouth.

Before Eleanor could respond, the door behind Jenny opened and she heard a deep voice say, "Ms. Romano?"

Dr. Drake? Jenny swung around, wondering how a near-senior citizen could have such a young-sounding voice. That's when she came eye-to-eye with the tall, lean man standing in the doorway. *Dr. Drake?* No. It couldn't be. She wiped a sweaty palm on her jeans skirt and held out her hand. "Jenny Romano," she said.

He gave her a wide smile and took her hand. His touch was warm, confident. "Elliot Drake," he said. "Sorry for the wait. I see you've been sampling Eleanor's special blend." He nodded toward the glass in Jenny's hand. "Lemonade and iced tea with a twist of lime." He cast a look at the older woman standing behind her. "Thanks, Eleanor," he said, his deep voice warm with affection.

"You're welcome," she said. "I'll just lock up and go fetch Sydney."

"Fine. I'll see you at six." He turned to Jenny and said, "Right this way."

As Jenny stepped past him into his office, she found herself wondering who Sydney was and what was happening at six. She took a seat in one of two camel-colored leather chairs and looked around. The same decorator who'd placed his mark in the waiting room had added his touch here as well. She'd thought it was Mrs. Drake, but Eleanor had squashed that idea flatter than fly guts on a windshield. The soft leather and polished brass were an extension of the waiting room with their faded yet honest invitation to sit down and relax. It almost made her want to kick off her sandals and cross her legs, Indian style. Almost.

Jenny looked across the desk to find Elliot Drake watching

her with undisguised interest. She returned the stare, lifting her chin a notch. Why did he have to be so young? So . . . virile? Why couldn't he have a paunch and stooped shoulders instead of a lean, wiry body? Why did he have to have coal black hair, dusted with gray at the temples? Why did he have to have hair at all? And those eyes . . . they should be small and beady beneath his horn-rimmed glasses, not large and brown. She closed her own eyes, pinching the bridge of her nose with her thumb and forefinger. It didn't help. She could still see that damn smile.

"Ms. Romano? Jenny? Are you all right?"

Her eyes flew open. Jenny. Something in the way he'd said her name made her stomach jump. He had sounded so casual, so . . . familiar. She crossed her right leg over her left, shifted in the chair, folded her hands in her lap, locked her fingers together. He was watching her a little too closely—analyzing, no doubt. What did he see? Now she knew what an insect felt like when it was pinned to a piece of Styrofoam and shoved under a magnifying glass.

He pulled out a notebook and pen. "You're here to discuss your nieces?"

"Yes," she said, pushing past her discomfort with the man to get to the doctor. "Ten days ago, my sister and her husband were involved in a car accident. My brother-in-law was killed and my sister, Grace, was left in a coma. The doctors don't know what to expect at this point. She may recover, or," she drew in a deep breath, "she may . . . not." She couldn't say the word *die*.

"I see. And you've been taking care of the children?"

"Uh, yes, sort of." She wondered if she should tell him that before the accident, the most care she'd given them was limited to an occasional peanut butter and jelly sandwich or spreading sun block on their arms and legs.

He looked at her over the top of his glasses.

Her ineptitude must have spread across her face like a

summer's rash. "Actually," she said, setting the glass of lemonade down on a cork coaster at the edge of his desk, "one of my sister's friends, Laura Montgomery—I think you know her—has been helping me. More than helping me," she confessed, her words picking up speed, sounding like one long, run-on sentence. "She's been a lifesaver . . . I don't know what I would've done without her . . . You see," she said, fishing around in her purse for a piece of Bubble Yum, "I don't have any children of my own, don't really know much about them." She unwrapped two pieces of gum, popped one in her mouth. "I only see the girls twice a year . . . I live in California and I travel a lot, international kind of stuff, I'm a photographer . . . I'm going to Italy next month . . . Anyway," she chewed hard, went on, "this is all very new to me, all of it . . . Even the cars— they're all minivans, everywhere you look . . . Thank God, the airport had a Sebring . . . I'm trying, though, really, but I'm usually the one getting help, not giving it, younger sister and all that . . . Grace has always been there for me—she was like a mother before she ever became a mother, if that makes any sense." She waved a hand in the air. "And me, well, I'm still trying to figure out the whole food issue, like why is an occasional piece of cake for breakfast such a crime? It's got all the ingredients of a nutritious breakfast— eggs, flour, milk. I think it's fine."

"I agree," he said, with a little half-smile.

"You do?"

His smile deepened. "Yes, I do. Deviating from the tried and true once in a while isn't going to cause permanent damage."

"Oh." Jenny eyed him, wary of his words. *Nobody* ever agreed with her on that subject. Grace had a conniption fit every time she mentioned the word *doughnut* as a breakfast substitute. And her mother, well, she still believed in the five-course breakfast of eggs, bacon, toast, juice, and oatmeal. So why was this man, who was supposed to be able to get inside people's heads and figure them out, agreeing with her? Was it some kind of trick, a setup maybe, to make her see the ridiculousness of her statement?

She looked at him a little closer. He seemed sincere enough. Jenny pried the wad of gum from the roof of her mouth and chomped down hard, trying to get another burst. "Why are you agreeing with me?" she asked. "Nobody ever agrees with me."

He shrugged. "It makes sense. If kids are allowed to eat complete junk food once in a while, then they settle back into good nutrition without much fuss, because they know that on the third Friday of every month, they can pig out."

"That's right," she said, nodding. Of course, she wouldn't admit that her nutrition ideas had nothing to do with the psychology of delayed gratification or whatever theory he was trying to prove. She was simply attempting to break up the boredom of Cheerios seven days a week.

He jotted down some notes on his legal pad. "Why do you think the girls need help?"

She popped the second piece of gum in her mouth and chewed until she got the strawberry gush. "It's really my oldest niece, Danielle, who's having the most difficulty. She's eight and since the day I told her that her father died, she's barely spoken a word to me. She avoids me most of the time, just sits in her room by herself. And the other day, my younger niece, Natalie, who's five, started crying and said that Danielle's been telling her if she doesn't behave their mother will get sicker and maybe even die." Jenny leaned forward, gripping the edge of his desk. "They're scared and I think they really *believe* that their behavior controls whether their mother lives . . . or not."

She could feel the blood rushing to her brain, pounding in and out, searching for a release. *The damn gum wasn't working.* Two wads wasn't enough. She reached inside her purse, pulled out another piece.

"What are you doing?" Elliot Drake asked.

His eyes were on the hand with the gum. "What? Oh. This?" she said with a little half-laugh. "I'm having a piece of gum. Would you like some?"

He lifted a dark brow and shook his head. "No. Thanks."

"It's strawberry. Great stuff." She pulled out another piece.

"You've already got two in your mouth," he said. "Exactly how many do you plan on chewing at one time?" There was a hint of curiosity in his voice.

"Three should do it." She stuffed the wad in her cheek. "I've been known to chew five at one time," she said.

"I'm surprised you have a jaw left," he said, shaking his head.

She shrugged, feeling the strawberry rush on the tip of her tongue. "Better than nicotine, I guess. I quit smoking five months ago." Jenny planted the gum on the roof of her mouth. "Now I chew."

He raised a brow.

"Gum, I mean. I chew gum—it helps calm me down." *Idiot. I'm an idiot.*

"Ah. And . . . do you find it an effective technique?"

She blew a huge bubble, smacked it back in her mouth. "Actually . . . no. I keep thinking I need more gum to enhance the chewing action, but maybe that's not it at all." She rubbed her chin. "My friend in California, Stefan, he gave me this little glass bottle, dark brown, with lavender and chamomile oils. He said if you sniff it, it's a great relaxer. Some people even use it as a perfume, just a dab here and there."

Elliot Drake settled back in his chair and tapped his pen

against his notepad. "And has that worked for you, Jenny? A dab here and there?"

She shook her head. *Shut up! Just shut up!* she told herself. "No . . . not really."

"Maybe you just need a few more dabs."

Was he making fun of her? Hard to say—he was looking at her with those serious eyes and he wasn't smiling. *Nice mouth,* she thought. *Full lips.* She shook her head, looked away.

They talked for several minutes after that, about the girls, their reactions to their parents' accident, Grace, Grant, and finally Jenny.

"I have to go to Italy next month," she said.

"Oh?"

She nodded. "Yes, it's a really big assignment. I'll be shooting the Pope."

"What?" He looked at her as though she were crazy.

"I'll be shooting the—" and then it struck her. "Oh, I mean, I'll be *photographing* the Pope."

"And you've already made arrangements?"

"Yes. I mean, no, not exactly. I have made arrangements with work to fly out of Ohio, but I haven't figured out about the girls yet." She ran both hands through her thick hair. "When I came, I had no idea what to expect. I didn't even know Grace was in a coma and I certainly didn't know that Grant was . . . was dead. I just figured I'd be stopping by to play with the girls a little, provide a diversion, maybe help Grace, run a few errands. I never dreamed it would be this bad and that I'd actually be *responsible* for the girls."

"And now that you are, how does that make you feel?"

Jenny stared at him. *How did it make her feel?* Typcial psychology lingo. "Well . . . I don't know how it makes me feel. I want to help, really I do, and I am, but all these decisions, I'm just used to having to worry about myself and even with that I don't do a very good job. That's why

Grace is so great. She keeps me focused—she makes me see things from a logical point of view without getting all worked up and doing something radical. And when I do, she's always there to bail me out."

"But not now."

"No. Now I'm the one who has to be there for her. And I want to, but I just don't know if I'll be able to." She rubbed her temples, chewed her triple wad of Bubble Yum. "I just don't know."

"Why don't we just take one thing at a time for right now, okay? Maybe we can talk through it and you'll find your answers. But for now, I'd like to see the girls as soon as possible."

"Sure. When are you available?" Jenny sat up straight and smoothed her jeans skirt.

He pulled out a black book and flipped through a few pages. "What about next Thursday afternoon, say three o'clock?"

"Fine."

"Let me just give you a reminder." Their fingers touched as he handed her a card. Jenny was suddenly aware of just how much she'd talked these past forty minutes—blabbered, actually—on and on to this man—a stranger, actually. He walked around his desk to stand beside her, all six-feet-plus of him. There weren't many men who made her feel short, but this man was one of them. "I enjoyed meeting you, Jenny," he said, extending his hand.

"Same here." She placed her hand in his, felt his skin, warm against hers. Jenny pulled away first. Had something just passed between them, a spark, a current, or had it been her imagination? Did Elliot Drake, being a psychologist, have the power to make people think they had a connection with him? Is that how he got his clients to open up? Is that what had happened?

Well, she didn't know, but whatever it was, she didn't like it. Not one bit.

Jenny gave him a quick, hurried smile and a mumbled good-bye. Then she headed out the door and down the flower-lined steps as though the devil himself was after her.

Chapter 8

"So, what did you think of Jenny Romano?"

Elliot looked up from his notes, and nodded at Eleanor Flatt. "We had a very interesting meeting."

"Good." Eleanor half-waddled into his office, plopping herself down on the same chair Jenny Romano had vacated fifteen minutes ago. "But I asked you what you thought of *her,* not the meeting."

He looked up again, and said, "She was a very nice lady."

"Hah!" She slapped her knee. "A *very nice lady?* Do you think I'm blind? That was no Roberta Dunlop in here."

"I didn't say she was Roberta."

"And I'm glad she isn't. What you'd find interesting in a biochemist who totes around a briefcase full of books wherever she goes, I'm sure I don't know. The woman never laughed, never even smiled, what with her tape recorder, her cell phone, her computer—good gracious, she was more boring than watching a stopped clock."

Eleanor was right there; Roberta Dunlop had been boring, extremely boring.

"But this new one, this Jenny Romano, she's not the least bit boring, I can tell."

"Well, you're right there," Elliot said, picturing her stuffing wads of bubble gum in her mouth. "But, Eleanor, she's not a *new one,* she's the aunt of two new clients."

She shook her head and made a *tsk, tsk* sound. "Oh, those two little girls—Hank's neighbors. I heard all about them from Laura, poor things." She leaned over, lowering her voice, "I also heard she isn't married."

"You heard?"

"All right . . . I inquired."

"Eleanor, don't."

"What?" She gave him an innocent look. "What did I do?"

"You know." He looked at her over his glasses. "I warned you the last time."

"Madeline Archer was a very nice woman. If you'd just given her a chance."

He blew out a disgusted breath. "She was looking for a sperm donor."

"Well, once she got to know you she would've wanted more than just your," her cheeks turned a bright rose, "your—you know."

"I appreciate your efforts, Eleanor, but I prefer to choose my own women, if you don't mind."

"Fine. That's fine." She sat there, hands folded over her ample middle, watching him.

He tried to ignore her and went back to his notes, but every ten seconds she sighed or cleared her throat or tapped her foot. Elliot threw down his pen after thirty seconds. "What, Eleanor?"

"Just answer me this and then I won't bring it up again."

She cleared her throat in earnest this time. "Didn't you find Jenny Romano at least a *little* attractive?"

He supposed there was no harm in admitting the truth. "Yes."

"Fine. And didn't you find her quite different from the usual women you associate with, like Roberta Dunlop, for example?"

"Sure," he leaned back in his chair. "Roberta wasn't addicted to Bubble Yum."

Eleanor stared at him. "What?"

"Nothing. Yes, I found Jenny Romano different." Not necessarily in a good way, either, though he wouldn't admit that to Eleanor. Jenny Romano made Speedy Gonzalez look like he was on Valium.

"She's quite attractive, isn't she?"

Elliot picked up his notepad, flipped a page. "In a Bohemian sort of way."

"What does that mean, Bohemian?"

The woman did not give up. He might as well give her some answers so she'd stop. "Well, for one thing, did you notice that gold coin belt that jingled every time she moved . . . and the hoop earrings . . . in her ears and the one on her left cartilage . . . and the bangles on her wrists, five of them . . . and the way she moved, actually kind of swayed, all soft and fluid . . . wild . . . ? And those eyes, don't tell me you didn't notice those eyes, hazel and wide, tilted at the corners, not quite Oriental, maybe almond-shaped . . . and her lips, they were pink and full . . . and all that hair . . ."

Eleanor Flatt stood up, cleared her throat, and smoothed the front of her navy blue skirt. "My, my, Elliot," she said with a sly smile, "for someone who's not interested in the woman, you certainly did notice quite a lot about her, didn't you?"

* * *

"So, Jenny, what did you think of Elliot?" Laura asked two seconds after Jenny walked in the door to pick up Danielle and Natalie.

How to answer that? "Well . . . he seemed very interested in the girls." *And why didn't anybody tell me he was so damn good-looking?*

"Isn't he a wonderful person?" Laura said, obviously trying to draw her into a discussion. Or maybe, the better word was *dissection,* a dissection of her meeting with Elliot Drake. Or maybe not, maybe she was just being concerned, and maybe Jenny was just being paranoid because for some indefinable reason, she did not want to talk about Elliot Drake.

"He seemed very nice," Jenny said, *but I don't like the way he parked himself inside my head and knew what I was thinking even before I thought it.*

"Well, I'm glad you liked him," she said. "I think it's a good thing for the girls to talk to someone right now. He did wonders for Hank's niece." She folded her arms across her chest, shook her head. "Sometimes I wonder how he can be so positive, so giving, after what he went through."

"What?" Jenny asked, before she could stop herself. "What did he go through?"

Laura lowered her voice and took a step closer. "His wife left him," she said. "Four years ago. Nobody knows why and he never talks about it."

"Wow, that's tough." Elliot Drake didn't look like the kind of man a woman would leave . . .

"Worse." Laura shook her head again and her pale blond braid swayed back and forth. "She left their little girl, too. Sydney. She's eight."

"How horrible." No wonder Eleanor Flatt reacted the way she did when Jenny mentioned the word *wife*.

"You've got to give him credit, though," Laura said. "He takes care of Sydney all by himself, with the help of Eleanor. Never complains. Never rails against God for the unfairness of it all. Just does what he needs to do. And really seems to enjoy it."

"And what about the daughter . . . Sydney?"

Laura's half-smile faded. "I guess she's as well as can be expected given the situation." She shrugged, adding, "But she loves her daddy. I don't think she'll like it much if he ever finds himself another wife."

"Maybe he doesn't want one." Not everyone needed to be part of a couple to feel complete. Jenny was a firsthand example of "happy and single."

"Hard to tell, but you've seen him, talked to him—who wouldn't want *him?*"

When the doorbell rang that evening, Jenny was scrunched down on the couch, remote in hand, flicking between *Larry King Live* and *Frasier*. She rolled off the couch, still carrying the remote, and headed for the door. It was probably just Laura, come to deliver another homemade meal. She'd been sending dishes over since Jenny confessed to leaving all of the margarine out of the box of macaroni and cheese the other day because she wanted to make it healthier and ended up with a dry orange paste that stuck in the girls' throats and made them gag. Jenny wondered what Laura was sending tonight; she hoped it was more of that chicken-and-broccoli casserole they had three days ago.

She opened the door but the woman standing on the landing wasn't Laura, didn't resemble her in any way, shape, and definitely not form. This woman was tall and slender, except for her breasts, which were stuffed into a bright blue jersey dress that boasted three inches of cleavage. Silicone-enhanced, no doubt, Jenny thought, working her way up the woman's dress to her breasts. She was a brunette—black, curly hair sweeping her shoulders, running down her back. Her eyes were the color of crystal with a smoky haze.

What was she doing here, on Woodruff Lane, in front of Grace and Grant's house? The answer was obvious; she had a wrong address—definitely a wrong address.

The woman tilted her head to the right and eyed Jenny with a predatory keenness. She pursed her lips, flicking a lock of hair over her shoulder.

"Can I help you?" Jenny asked, running a hand through her own hair. Her fingers got stuck in a gnarl of tangles partway through. She eased them out, ran a hand over her T-shirt and cutoffs.

"I'm looking for Grant," the woman said.

Jenny blinked and coughed. "Grant?" she choked, trying to get his name out. What did *she* want with Grant?

"I need to see him," she said, crossing her arms over her chest in a way that puffed out her breasts so much that Jenny thought she might fall over.

Who was this woman and what did she want with Grant? Whoever she was, one thing was quite obvious. She didn't know he was dead. And Jenny didn't think she'd tell her just yet, not until she found out why this woman was looking for her dead brother-in-law.

"I'm sorry," Jenny said, shaking her head and offering a fake half-smile. "I'm afraid he's not available."

The woman's hazel eyes narrowed to tiny slits. "I'm through with that line. If I hadn't been out of town the past ten days, I would've stormed into his office and grabbed that cold bitch secretary of his by her phone cord and strangled the truth out of her. *Unavailable.* What the hell does that mean, huh? He's not *unavailable* to me, I'll tell you that."

"He *isn't* available," Jenny repeated, her voice firm.

She sniffed. "Who are *you*?"

Jenny raised a brow. "I'm Grant's sister-in-law."

"Oh." She looked at Jenny with renewed interest. "The photographer."

"Who are *you*?" Jenny threw the woman's own question back at her. How and why would she know anything about her? And what else did she know?

"I'm Heather. Heather Eastman." She paused. "Grant's *friend*."

There was something about the way she said *friend* . . . it didn't feel right . . . it felt wrong . . . very wrong.

"Friend?" Jenny said, stepping forward to shut the front door behind her. She wasn't going to chance the girls waking up and seeing Heather Eastman standing at the front door, demanding to see their father.

The woman let out a low laugh, deep in her throat, a practiced sultry sound that floated through the air. "Grant and I *are* friends," she repeated. "*Very* good friends."

"Really? *How* good?" Jenny's heart pounded in her chest like a kettledrum. This woman was talking about Grant. Jenny's brother-in-law. Grace's husband. Danielle and Natalie's father.

"Lovers," she said, pulling her red lips into a smile.

"Liar."

Her hazel-gray eyes narrowed. "The only thing that's a lie is that sham of a marriage he has to your sister. *That's* a lie."

"I don't believe you," Jenny said, taking a step closer. "Grant loves Grace. They're very happy." She meant to say, *Grant loved Grace. They were very happy.*

"If they're so happy, then why is he sleeping with me?" Heather Eastman jerked her head back, flinging her black hair behind her shoulder. "I don't care who knows about us. I told him I was tired of hiding, that I wouldn't sneak around anymore.''

Jenny stared at her, wondering why she would make up such a horrible lie. Why? What purpose could it possibly serve her? She didn't know; she only knew she didn't believe her. *She couldn't.* Because if what she said was true, then what did that say about Grant? And what did it say about Grant and Grace's marriage? Their life together?

"I want you to leave," Jenny said, her voice coming out in a high squeak, sounding strange to her own ears.

"Not until I see Grant," Heather Eastman said, planting her high-heeled feet on top of Natalie's chalk drawing.

"He isn't here." *And won't be . . . ever again.*

"I'll wait."

Jenny let out a frustrated sigh. "Why are you doing this? Grant and Grace have a wonderful marriage. He would never cheat on her."

Heather Eastman raised a dark, sleek brow. "He already did."

She was so insistent, so sure of herself. Tiny hairs pricked the back of Jenny's neck. . . . *As though she were telling the truth. No. No!*

And then the beautiful woman with the tanned skin and bright red nails opened her palm and shattered the illusion of Grant and Grace and "happily ever after." Jenny stared at the plain gold wedding band edged in white gold. A single diamond rested in the center. It was a man's ring. She sucked in a breath of air. There wasn't any need to read the inscription on the inside of the ring to know what it would say. *Grace and Grant Forever.*

"Here," the woman said, handing the ring to Jenny. "Read the inscription."

Jenny hesitated, not wanting to confirm what her heart already knew. Maybe, maybe she was wrong, maybe it wasn't Grant's, maybe this was all a big mistake. If she just refused to read it, then there'd still be a tiny speck of doubt, a crumb of hope that Heather Eastman was lying.

Then again, maybe the woman was telling the truth.

Jenny grabbed the ring and brought it close to her eyes, squinting in the fading light. *Grace and Grant Forever* stared back at her, stabbing her senses, shredding her illusions, ripping her soul in two.

"I told you I wasn't lying." Heather Eastman's voice floated around her in a haze of gloating superiority.

Jenny's hands closed around the ring. "Where did you get this?" She kept her voice steady, void of emotion.

Laughter trickled out of those red lips. "It was our little game. When he was with me, I took the ring off his finger, usually with my teeth and tongue, and tucked it in my purse." She patted the slim leather rectangle at her side. "I kept it until he had to leave."

"How clever of you."

"Yes, it was," she agreed. "It always added to the, uh, shall we say, *allure* of the moment."

"I'm sure it did." If Grant weren't already dead, Jenny would have killed the bastard herself.

"It really turns him on." She laughed again. "But then, tongues and teeth do that to him."

And after she'd killed him, she would've chopped his dick off and cut it up into tiny pieces.

"But it'll be a long time before he gets anything like that again," she said, flipping her hair behind her again. "I'm really pissed and it's going to take more than a necklace to pacify me this time."

Jenny's gaze shot to her neck and the gold serpentine chain hanging around it. A gift from Grant, no doubt. What else had her brother-in-law given this woman? Was she the first? Or had there been others? If so, how many? And then a sickening thought spilled over her, snuffed out her breath.

Did Grace know?

"How long am I going to have to wait for him?"

"What?" Jenny stared at the woman in front of her. Tanned. Beautiful. Heather Eastman. Grant's mistress. Standing there, tall and proud, high-heeled feet smearing the edges of Natalie's blue-and-white chalk house, not one tiny bit ashamed or remorseful that she'd been sleeping with a married man.

"When was the last time you saw him?" Jenny asked, ignoring her question.

"Twelve days ago. At Chantel's." Her tiny nostrils flared. "He went to talk to the maitre d', and never came back."

The accident happened twelve days ago. Blood rushed to Jenny's head. Had Grace discovered her husband and this woman together? Maybe confronted him? Is that why he'd left his lover in the restaurant? Why the woman still had his wedding band? Why he'd been in Grace's van at the time of the accident?

Why she had the accident? Thoughts spilled out from the corners of her mind. *Had* it been an accident? *Or . . . not? Could it have been the hysterical reaction of a woman who'd just learned her whole life was a lie? Could that have been it?*

"How long am I going to have to wait for him?" Heather Eastman repeated. "I don't have all night." She glanced at her watch. "I'll give him two minutes. If he doesn't show by then, you can just tell him to go straight to hell."

Jenny smiled then. It was an evil smile, one she reserved for people she truly disliked. And then she told her that he was already there.

Heather Eastman flicked her long, black hair over her shoulder one last time, gave Jenny a disgusted look, and said, "You just tell him I was here." She turned on her high heels and left, her long legs making their way to the white Mazda Miata parked along the curb. It wasn't until she was halfway down the sidewalk that Jenny noticed some-

thing vaguely familiar about her . . . the hair, the long legs
. . . the way her hips swayed when she walked . . . bits and
pieces flowing together, reminding her of something . . . but
what?

Chapter 9

It was the shrill pitch in Jenny's ear that jolted her awake, with the speed and force of one of her karate instructor's kicks. She grabbed the slim, white phone that had served as a pillow for the last few hours and pressed the "on" button.

"Hullo." Her voice was raw and scratchy. Interrupted sleep and two shots of Jack Daniel's will do that to you.

"Jennifer! I should have known you'd forget to call." Disapproval stretched through the phone line in the tone of Virginia Romano's voice.

"Hello, Mom," Jenny said, rubbing the back of her neck. "What time is it?"

"It's two minutes past midnight. I've been waiting all night to hear from you. Was it too much to ask that once, just once, you behave in a responsible manner and do what you say you're going to do?"

"I fell asleep."

"Harrumph. That's no excuse."

Silence.

"So, how is she? How's Gracie?"

"Grace is the same. And me, I'm fine, Mom—thanks for asking."

Her mother either chose to ignore the sarcasm or perhaps she missed it altogether. Either way, she didn't respond.

There was a deep sigh on the other end of the line. "Pray, Jennifer. You must pray for your sister's recovery."

"I will," she mumbled, knowing that her form of prayer and her mother's were not the same. Virginia Romano recited Hail Marys and Our Fathers, clicking rosary beads like a typist on a keyboard. Fast. Efficient. Error-free. Jenny carried on conversations, disjointed, half-formed, soulful mutterings that left her drained.

"That's the problem with this world. No one prays anymore."

Jenny decided not to comment. The only thing she'd pray for right now, other than Grace's recovery, was Grant's demise. And God, in His infinite wisdom, had already answered that prayer.

"How are the girls?"

"Fine." She wasn't going to tell her about her visit with Elliot Drake. "They're counting the days until summer vacation."

"Thank God for Laura Montgomery," her mother breathed, as though Jenny had nothing to do with the girls. "Those children need her now. She'll give them the security that's so important during this trying time."

Jenny bit the inside of her cheek but said nothing. What would be the point? Her mother wouldn't hear her, anyway.

"And how are you managing, Jenny?" she asked. "Are you wishing you were off on one of your exotic excursions, thousands of miles away from children and responsibilities?"

There was a certain smugness to her voice that grated on

Jenny like sandpaper against skin. "No," she answered, staring at the top of the television. There were two school pictures, 5 X 7's, one of Danielle and the other of Natalie. Danielle's smile was small, hesitant, as though she wasn't quite certain of the camera or herself. Natalie's bold-faced grin boasted two missing front teeth and several haphazard curls poking from a thick fringe of smashed-down bangs. There was nothing shy or reticent about the child or the picture.

"No," Jenny repeated again. "I don't wish I was anywhere but here." Oddly enough, despite the grief and uncertainty of the moment, and Danielle's cold shoulder, it was true. "As for the other, even if I were working, I'd still be responsible for the whole shoot."

"Of course," her mother said, "but we both know that you handle deadlines much better than people."

"Of course," Jenny repeated in a thin voice. "I'm incapable of appropriate social interaction. I'm amazed anyone permits me to be around other human beings."

"That's not what I meant." There was a sharpness in her voice. "And there's no reason to be sarcastic with me, young lady. I was only saying that we both know you tend to avoid situations *and* people that make you uncomfortable."

"Well, I can't worry about that right now, can I?" God, she wished she hadn't answered the phone. "Grace is the one who needs help and that's why I'm here, to help her."

"You shouldn't have to worry about it much longer. Ten more days. Dr. Weiser said ten more days and I can come and take care of my Gracie."

"Your daughter does not play fair," Jenny said, smiling at Grace's still form. "We were having a balloon fight and Natalie attacked me from behind. Guess who got drenched?" She laughed. "I had to peel off my clothes. But not before

I dumped a bucket of water on her head." What about Danielle? What could she say about her? "I think Danielle was the smartest one of all," she said. "She decided to stay in the house and read a book." That part was true.

Jenny's gaze traveled the length of the hospital-white blanket covering Grace's body. Her face looked pale. Gaunt. Maybe thinner? Her whole body was so still. So . . . lifeless. Except for the machines and tubes that pumped life into her frail existence. It had been almost two weeks since the accident. Dr. Shaffer was still "hopeful." His favorite word. It said nothing.

"Do you remember the water fights we used to have when we were little kids?" she asked. "The empty dish-detergent bottles and that old metal tub of water? And then, when we were all done, Mom would bring out Popsicles. Cherry for you and grape for me." Jenny leaned over and stroked her sister's hand. "I loved those days, Gracie. I really did."

The respirator whooshed in her ears. Some days, hours after she was home, Jenny could still hear the steady, rhythmic droning in her head. She hated it and yet she clung to it. For now, that sound meant life. *Grace's life.*

"Wasn't everything so much simpler when we were kids, Gracie?" Jenny covered her sister's hand with both of her own. "I mean, we knew the rules and we obeyed them." A small laugh escaped her lips. "Okay, let me rephrase that. We knew the rules and *you* obeyed them. I was a little less consistent, but I just had a lot of questions. Mom used to get so mad at me." She shook her head. "Dad didn't, though. He was the softie." Tears burned the back of her eyes. "God, but I miss him."

"Anyway, you remember, don't you? Rules were rules. Plain and simple. And words . . . well, they were words. When you said something as a kid, you meant it. There were no hidden meanings, no double entendres. It was all out there in the open. We might not have known the best way to say it, but our meanings were honest and direct.'' She gnawed on her lower lip. "Black-and-white, like one of my snapshots. No gray. And a lie was a lie."

A lie was a lie. Like when the time comes for me to tell you that Grant is dead and I say how sorry I am. That will be a lie. And when I whisper that he loved you so much, more than life itself, that will be a lie, too. And when I tell you what a wonderful man he was, and that we should all be so fortunate to have someone like him, well, that will only be another lie.

Because the truth will be more than you can bear. It would kill you just as surely as pulling the plug on that respirator would do. And I can't do that to you, Gracie, I can't. So, I'll lie.

She'd made that decision before Heather Eastman pulled away in her white Miata. She wouldn't be back. Grant was dead. She'd dry her eyes and find another thirty or forty-something married man with children to be her playmate. They were out there. A lot of them. Jenny had just never dreamed Grant was one of them. *Son of a bitch.*

But Jenny would burn in hell and beyond before she told Grace about her philandering husband. She'd say nothing to make her sister believe that her marriage was marred, her husband unfaithful. Grace deserved better, the best, if only in her illusions.

And Jenny prayed she still had those illusions. A tiny part of her wondered if Grace had discovered Grant's unfaithfulness, tracked him to Chantel's, maybe accused him.

But Grace was too good, too honest, too . . . gullible to discover Grant's treachery. She took people at face value, believed their words, and honored them. Her worst fault had always been believing that everyone possessed the same integrity she did.

Jenny looked at Grace's face, pale against the white pillow. She did not deserve this. She'd never hurt anyone in her whole life. Why her? She blinked back tears. Why Gracie?

Her eyes blurred until she couldn't make out Grace's face anymore. She sniffed, ran the back of her hand over her cheek. It was then, caught halfway between a glance and a stare, that she saw Grace twitch her eyes. Just a small movement, barely discernible, but Jenny saw it.

"Gracie?" she whispered, afraid to take her eyes from her sister's face. "Gracie?"

Grace's eyes twitched again, her forehead creased into tiny lines. Was she trying to tell her something? Jenny squeezed her hand. "Oh, yes! Please, come back to us. Please." The last words fell out as a plea.

Another twitch, followed by three more. Then Grace moved her head from side to side as though she was in pain. What was she trying to tell her? "I'll be right back," Jenny said. "Let me get the nurse. She'll understand what you want." She patted her sister's hand once and practically ran out of the cubicle, half tripping over a chair leg, in search of someone who could interpret Grace's actions. Sally, the much-too-young nurse with the blond braid, was sitting behind her desk, writing in a chart.

"Sally," Jenny said, her breath coming in quick, uneven gulps, "it's Grace. I think she's waking up."

The young nurse's blue eyes grew wide. "I'll be right there," she said, setting the chart aside and hurrying around the Formica station. Jenny rushed back to Grace's cubicle with Sally right behind her.

"She twitched her eyes," Jenny said. "Several times. And she's trying to move her head. And look," she pointed at Grace's forehead. "Her forehead's all creased. Is she in pain?"

Jenny looked at Sally, waiting for some kind of confirmation or explanation. She got neither for several long minutes as the young nurse studied Grace, her cornflower-blue eyes and capable hands taking in every inch of her, assessing, evaluating, palpating. When Jenny couldn't take the silence any longer, Sally's pink lips pulled into a big smile and she said, "This is a good sign, Jenny. A very good sign. Dr. Shaffer will be pleased."

Jenny blew out a long breath and clasped Grace's fingers. "Thank God," she murmured and realized that she really meant it. Thank God for bringing her back to us. Thank God for this gift. *Thank God.*

"We'll be watching for signs that she's ready to come off the respirator. Over the next several hours, I expect she'll start fighting it and that's usually an indicator that we can start to wean her from it."

"You mean she'll be able to breathe on her own?"

Sally nodded. "It takes a little time, but yes, she should be able to."

Jenny dared a smile. "And once she's breathing on her own . . . ?" The question dangled between the three of them.

"She'll be moved to a step-down unit for further evaluation. Depending on her progress, she'll remain there until she can transfer to a rehab unit where they'll work on things like gross motor movement, using a walker, if necessary, speech, occupational therapy and other activities that will assist her with daily living."

Jenny was stuck on the walker part. "Walker? She'll need a walker? Is she going to be a cripple?"

Sally hesitated. "Each head injury is unique, Jenny. We just can't say." She gave her a sympathetic look. "I wish I could tell you that Grace will recover one hundred percent from the accident, that she'll walk without a limp, won't slur her words and will remember everything. But the truth is, we just don't know."

* * *

Two days later, Grace came off the respirator. It was a Wednesday. The next day, she moved her index finger. The day after that, Friday, they transferred her to a step-down unit. At three o'clock that afternoon, she opened her eyes.

Jenny was sitting in her usual faded orange vinyl chair, casually flipping through the latest copy of *New Woman* and sipping a Diet Coke.

"Here's an article for you, Gracie," she said, as she read the headline on the top of the next page. " '10 Foolproof Ways to Look and Feel 18 Again.' " She chuckled. This was her way of communicating with Grace. Jenny talked, suggested, questioned, and stated her opinion. Then, she imagined Grace's answers. Her response to this one would probably be something like *Foolish instead of Foolproof,* or *Is that Dr. Foolproof?*

Jenny chuckled again and glanced at her sister. Grace's eyes were open and she was staring straight ahead.

"Grace!" Jenny threw the magazine aside and sprang from her chair. "Grace!" She rushed to the side of the bed and clasped her sister's hand. Cold. So cold. She wrapped both hands around Grace's fingers, rubbing them gently, trying to work life into them, trying to bring back the old feel of her touch, warm, reassuring. "I've missed you!"

Grace turned her head, just a fraction, enough for her brown eyes to settle on Jenny. Jenny held her breath as she watched Grace watch her. Grace's forehead creased in several tiny rows of confusion. Did Grace recognize her? Her eyes narrowed, just a little. Jenny waited, caught between the delicate balance of hope and despair.

A hundred questions ran through Jenny's brain. Horrible, depressing questions, that made her want to curl up in a ball, weep her fear and frustration. She tried to calm down, tried to remember, *breathe, breathe,* but it came out in quick little panicked puffs.

What if she doesn't even recognize me, her own sister?

And then, Jenny thought she saw her eyes widen. The change was so minute she wasn't certain if it was real or just one last scrap of distorted hope taking form. She stared at those brown eyes so hard that she almost saw double. Jenny blinked and squeezed Grace's hand.

"It's me. Jenny," she whispered, forcing the words past the boulder in her throat.

"JJJJJJJJJ . . ." Grace moaned.

Tears spilled down Jenny's cheeks. "That's it," she said. "Jenny."

"JJJeeennny."

Jenny saw the dim light of recognition in Grace's eyes and sniffed back more tears. "Welcome back, Gracie," she murmured. "Welcome back."

Chapter 10

"How's Grace doing today?"

"Pretty well." Jenny picked up another plate, wiped the soapy cloth over its front. "Dr. Shaffer says she's getting stronger. Maybe another week or two of physical and occupational therapy, then he might discharge her."

Laura let out a long breath. "It will be wonderful to have her back."

"She's ready. Every day, she tells me she wants to come home. She wants to be with her girls."

"Any mention of Grant?"

"Nothing," Jenny said, frowning. "That's what's so strange. I've spent the past several days quizzing her about stuff we did as kids, asking questions and trying to see if there are any gaps in her memory. But she remembers everything, sometimes more than I do." She shrugged her shoulders. "It's weird. I've asked her questions about her job, the neighborhood, the girls. You. But she hasn't mentioned a word about Grant. Nothing. It's as though he never existed.''

''What does Dr. Shaffer say?''

''That the accident may have blocked that part of her memory, wiped it out.''

''What are you supposed to do?''

''Tell her. He wanted to tell her a few days ago, but I asked him to wait.'' Because Grace had just started to smile two days ago, and yesterday she'd laughed. A real laugh, full and rich and deep. Like before. The old Grace was close, hovering, ready to emerge like a butterfly from its cocoon. Just a little while longer. If Jenny told her about Grant, she might sink back into that black hole inside herself and never come out again.

''You can't keep it from her much longer,'' Laura said.

Jenny stared at the suds in the sink.

''Jenny?''

''I know, Laura. *I know.*'' Of course she knew. She knew what she had to do. It was her responsibility. Her *duty.* But the knowing didn't make the job any easier.

''Tell her soon,'' Laura said in a soft voice. ''The longer you wait, the harder it will be for her.''

''I know.'' Jenny sighed, her shoulders slumped forward.

''Tomorrow,'' she persisted. ''Tell her tomorrow.''

Jenny swallowed hard. ''What if she . . . has a relapse?''

''What if she doesn't?'' she shot back.

Silence filled the kitchen, stretching over the cupboards, crawling along the floor, gliding over the ceiling, encompassing them both in a vacuum of stillness.

Laura was right, of course. It was time to tell Grace her husband was dead. ''I'll tell her tomorrow,'' Jenny said, her voice little more than a whisper.

Laura set down her dish towel, laid a hand on Jenny's shoulder. Her eyes were bluer than usual and there were two spots of color on her cheeks. ''I don't mean to be tough on you, but she needs to know the truth. No matter how painful, she needs to know.''

Oh, no, she doesn't. At least not the whole truth. Jenny nodded. ''I'll tell her about him tomorrow.'' His death, not his infidelity.

''Good. You're doing the right thing, Jenny.''

''But right isn't always easy,'' Jenny said. ''In fact, it's hardly ever easy.''

''But it's always necessary.''

''Yeah, I know.''

''Now remember, girls,'' Jenny said as she whisked Danielle and Natalie into the elevator, ''soft voices. Quiet talk. There are a lot of very sick people here.'' She was really only talking to Natalie because Danielle hardly spoke at all anymore and when she did it was just a little grunt or one-word response.

''Mommy's not very sick,'' Natalie whispered, shaking her mop of dark curls back and forth. The bright pink and yellow balloons in her left hand jiggled. ''She's getting all better. Isn't she, Aunt Jenny?''

Jenny hesitated an extra second before answering. In the seven days since she'd opened her eyes, Grace had improved. She could now speak in very slow, disjointed sentences with only minor gaps between words. The initial awkward maneuvering of arms and legs seemed to be disappearing more each day, leaving her with semi-fluid mobility. And yesterday, with Sally's help, she'd actually sat in a chair. So, yes, Grace was definitely improving.

But getting *all* better? Even Jenny, in her most desperate stroke of optimism, could not say that. There was no sparkle in her eyes, no smile on her lips. Not even a glimmer of one. She stared back with blank eyes that could only be described as empty and soulless, transforming her into a stranger. Where was the Grace they all knew, the one who kissed scraped knees, fed stray dogs, and sang silly little lullabies off-key? *Where was she?* Had her spirit died in the accident, leaving behind a hollow shell?

"Aunt Jenny?" Natalie's persistence jogged Jenny from her thoughts. "Mommy's getting all better, isn't she?"

Jenny forced a smile and pushed the words out. "She's better," she said. It was what Natalie wanted to hear and Jenny couldn't disappoint her. Not now. Not when they were steps away from Grace's room. Jenny caught Danielle giving her a sideways glance as though to say, *Liar!* Jenny looked away. But she *had* spoken the truth. Grace was better. Yet, somehow, Jenny did feel like a liar, a teller of half-truths, filling a child with hope that had as much substance as a wad of cotton candy. One lick and it dissolved before your very eyes.

Maybe Jenny felt the sharp edges of deceit pricking at her, because she knew that what Natalie was really asking her, with the trusting naiveté of a five-year-old, was if her mother was going to be just like she was before the accident. And just as surely, Jenny knew she couldn't give her an answer. *Because I don't have one.*

The elevator dinged and the door slid open. They stepped out and Jenny pointed toward the left, down a long, white corridor. "It's this way," she said, eyeing the familiar signs. Natalie laced her fingers with Jenny's and inched closer. Danielle stayed several steps behind.

"Now, remember what I told you. Mommy might sound different when she talks, kind of funny, almost like she's learning to speak for the first time. And her legs and arms will be a little jerky because she has to get used to moving them around." Jenny took a deep breath, swallowed hard. "When the doctor operated, he had to shave her head."

"*She's bald?*" Natalie squeaked, freezing in her tracks, her green eyes filling with equal parts horror and intrigue.

Jenny turned to her and shrugged, pretending it was no
big deal. "Uh-huh. She's got a big white bandage wrapped
around it, kind of like a large headband."

"I want to see what she looks like buzzed," Natalie
whispered, her lips curving into a big grin. "I never saw a
lady with a buzz cut before."

"Shut up," Danielle hissed. Jenny turned and caught her
shooting an *I could strangle you* warning at her little sister.

Natalie stuck her tongue out. "You're not allowed to say
'shut up.' "

"And you're not supposed to stick your tongue out, you
little brat."

"Girls," Jenny said, giving them both her sternest look.
"That's enough. We're here to see your mother, now act
like the young ladies I know you are." She started walking
again, taking longer-than-normal strides to keep them both
busy trying to match her step. They rounded the last corner
and Jenny saw the sign for the step-down unit.

"One more thing," she said, stopping and turning to face
them. She leaned over, just enough so they were eye level,
and lowered her voice. "Remember, Mommy doesn't know
about Daddy. And we can't tell her until she's all better."
She squeezed Natalie's hand, and met Danielle's hard stare.
"Okay?"

Natalie raised her hands and pretended to zip her mouth
shut. Danielle dipped her chin. Not great, but at least it was
an acknowledgement.

"Okay." Jenny straightened and cleared her throat. "I'm
counting on both of you." *Inhale, hold. Exhale, whoosh.*
Grace would have to find out about Grant soon enough, just
not today. Hearing he was dead would crush her, maybe
destroy her resolve to recover. And she couldn't afford that
right now, not in her weakened state. Neither could Jenny.
It would be hard enough to watch her mourn the philandering
bastard when she was well, but it would be impossible now.

The nurse's station was directly in front of them. Julie was working today. Next to Sally, she was Jenny's favorite. Nice, plain, young, with a sweet smile and a soft voice.

"Hi, Julie," Jenny said. "This is Danielle and this is Natalie."

"Hi, girls." A smile spread over the nurse's face, making her appear almost pretty. "Your mother will be so thrilled to see you."

She will? Grace hadn't seemed anywhere near being thrilled about anything since she'd come out of the coma.

"Can we see her now?" Natalie asked in a whisper.

"Of course," Julie replied, her words feather-soft. She met Jenny's gaze and said, "You know the way, Jenny."

"Thanks." Jenny nodded and started the trek to the fourth door on the left. Grace's room. She heard the faint hum of piano music drifting down the hall. That would be Grace's room. Beethoven's *Moonlight Sonata.*

"I hear her music," Natalie said, pointing to a room two doors away. Her voice dropped. "I think she's in there." She jerked her hand away and ran down the hall toward Grace's room.

"Natalie, wait!" Jenny hurried after her, but it was too late. By the time she reached Grace's room, Natalie was already inside, frozen to her spot, the pink and yellow balloons fluttering along the ceiling.

"Mommy?" The word came out, half-whisper, half-cry. "Mommy?" she repeated again, her voice taking on the shrill quality of one nearing hysteria.

Jenny rushed to Natalie, pulled her into her arms. "It's okay, honey. It's okay." She ran a hand over Natalie's curls, letting her bury her face in Jenny's shoulder.

"Mommy?" she whimpered. "Where's my mommy?"

Jenny glanced at the pale figure of the woman seated in the orange vinyl chair. She was wearing a white hospital gown and sky blue booties. Her head was wrapped in white and she was staring straight at Jenny. No wonder Natalie refused to believe this woman was her mother. The mother she knew laughed and smiled, built sand castles and Popsicle stick bowls. The mother she knew wrapped her children in blankets of love and safety. This woman was dead and reheated, a ghost of someone, incapable of feeling, touching, loving.

Oh, Grace, where are you? How can I make you come back?

Jenny cleared her throat and forced a smile. "Hi, Gracie. Look who I brought to see you." She tried to force lightness in her voice, but it fell flat, like a tire with a gaping hole.

Grace moved her gaze to Natalie. Jenny watched as her forehead furrowed into a zillion tiny wrinkles. Her eyes narrowed and she leaned her head forward as though to get a closer look. Natalie stiffened, her small body pushing into Jenny's. Grace's pale lips twitched and contorted, opening at last to mouth one word. "Na . . . talie."

Natalie peeked out over Jenny's arm. "Mommy?" Her words were mixed with confusion and tiny shreds of hope.

"Na . . . talie," Grace repeated, her voice soft and filled with something that sounded an awful lot like pain.

"Mommy!" Natalie wriggled out of Jenny's embrace and took a few timid steps toward her mother.

Grace lifted a hand, and her youngest daughter scrambled forward, throwing her arms around her mother's middle. "I miss you, Mommy," she sobbed. "I miss you." Her tiny shoulders shook as she spilled out her grief.

"Mom?"

Jenny turned and saw Danielle standing by the window, clutching the stuffed yellow-and-white teddy bear she'd brought for her mother. Her knuckles were white and a tiny half-smile wobbled somewhere between hope and fear.

"Dan . . . ielle," Grace breathed her name in a two-syllable sigh.

Danielle's lips trembled, flattened, and she rushed to her mother, throwing her arms around Grace's shoulders. "Oh, Mom," her voice cracked.

Jenny swiped a hand over her cheeks and sniffed. This was what they needed right now, to be a family again. They needed it. *She* needed it. Things were different now. Grace was a widow, a single mother with two small children, recovering from a serious accident. Danielle and Natalie were fatherless, with a mother who, through some miracle, had beaten the odds and survived a car crash and a coma. The wounds were still open, some lightly scabbed, others fresh and oozing, and only time could predict the size or depth of the scars. And there would be scars. For all of them.

"Is Mommy gonna be able to do stuff again?" Natalie asked, scooting out from under her sheet to sit closer to Jenny.

Jenny looked up from the book she'd been reading her and wondered if Natalie had heard anything in the last ten minutes. But then, could she blame her if she hadn't? How could the adventures of a spunky cat and her worrisome sidekick replace the picture of her mother in a hospital with her head bandaged and her words stilted and clumsy?

"Is she, Aunt Jenny? Is she gonna be able to do stuff again?"

"What do you mean?" Jenny hedged. Of course, she knew exactly what Natalie meant, but she chose the adult path and pretended ignorance. Ignorance was useful in measured doses. It bought time and sometimes even made the asker rethink the question. Jenny usually didn't succumb to such ploys, but then again, she wasn't accustomed to being confronted with this kind of brutal, frank inquisitiveness, especially from a five-year-old.

"You know," Natalie said, playing with the pale pink

fringe on her pillow. It was the same shade as the bedspread, "strawberry cream swirl." She lifted her head and her green gaze met Jenny's. "Ride bikes. Play on Mrs. M's monkey bars." Her lower lip trembled. "Go to McDonald's for French fries and chocolate milkshakes."

"Oh, honey," Jenny said, pulling her into her arms, "I hope so." She rested her cheek on top of Natalie's curly head. "More than anything in the world, I hope so."

"Me, too," Natalie whispered. Jenny heard a sniff and then a long silence with nothing but the hum of the air conditioning. Just when she began to wonder if Natalie had drifted off to sleep in her arms, she spoke. "I said a prayer for her tonight, just like Grandma said to do."

Jenny tightened her hold around Natalie's tiny waist. "What did you ask Him?"

"To make Mommy's arms not so wobbly so she can come home."

"That's good."

"And fix it when she talks."

"That's a good thing to pray for, too."

"And one more thing."

"What's that?"

Pause. "To make all her hair grow back."

Two days later, Jenny loaded Danielle and Natalie into the silver Sebring and headed off to see Elliot Drake.

"I don't want to talk to the man," Natalie said, in her new little whiney imitation voice. She'd been using it ever since Jenny told the girls she was taking them to a special doctor to talk about the accident.

Jenny looked at her in the rearview mirror and frowned. "His name is Dr. Drake and he wants to talk to you."

" 'Bout what?" she asked, crossing her arms over her tiny chest.

Jenny sighed. She knew—they'd been over this at least ten times. "About how you wake up in the middle of the night crying. About how you miss Daddy."

Natalie's lower lip puckered, then flattened into a thin line. "He lied to me."

"Natalie—"

"He lied," she repeated. "He said he'd take me to Toys R Us and buy me a pink-and-purple bike with a white basket—"

"Stop it," Danielle hissed.

Natalie ignored her sister. "—and sparkly streamers," she said, her voice wobbling on the last word.

"Natalie, he wanted to," Jenny said, trying to focus on her niece and the road at the same time. "But God took him away before he could."

Jenny heard the sniff behind her and tried to ignore it. Oh, God, she hoped Elliot would be able to help the girls. *Elliot.* Her stomach jumped. She would see him soon, would be standing next to him, talking to him, looking into those warm, brown eyes the color of Hershey kisses . . . and he'd be looking at her, the way he had that first day, deep, deeper, as though he could see inside to the person she kept hidden away from the world, sometimes even from herself.

"Are we almost there?" Natalie asked with another half-whine, pulling Jenny back to the present.

"I think it's just another few minutes," Jenny said, flicking her right turn signal. "Two more blocks and we'll be there."

"I'm tired of being in this car," Natalie said. "I liked Mommy's van better."

"Will you just be quiet and sit still?" This from Danielle.

"There it is, right over there," Jenny said, spotting the house with its bonanza of bright flowers and green foliage. She pulled up to the curb and parked the car.

"Where'd he get all the flowers?" Natalie asked, peeking out the window.

"I guess where everybody else gets them," Jenny said. "A greenhouse or nursery."

Natalie gave her an odd look. "Nursery? The baby place?"

"Not the baby kind, silly, the tree-and-plant kind. A nursery can also be a place where you grow things like plants and trees and flowers."

"Oh." She seemed to be thinking about that. "I like this kind of nursery. We should get some stuff from there."

"It is pretty, isn't it?" Jenny said, fixing her sights on a bright red burst of impatiens as she got out of the car.

"Yeah, especially the green things hanging over there." Natalie pointed to the ferns.

"Maybe we can get your mom one of those. What do you think?" Jenny asked, heading up the steps.

"Yeah."

"Okay. Well, here we are."

"Aunt Jenny?"

It was Danielle.

"Yes?" Jenny tried to keep her voice even. This was the first time Danielle had actually addressed her since the accident.

"Can I have a piece of gum?" Her voice sounded small and hollow, and very far away.

"Sure," Jenny said, digging into the side pocket of her purse. She pulled out a half-open pack of Bubble Yum. "One strawberry, coming right up."

"Me, too?" Natalie asked.

Jenny took out four pieces. "I think we could all use a little strawberry boost right now. One for each of you," she said, plopping a fat piece of gum into their outstretched hands. "And two for me." She jammed both pieces in her mouth and chewed. "Okay, let's go."

Chapter 11

Twenty minutes later, Jenny drained the last of her lemonade and flipped through another page of *Parents* magazine.
Elliot really needed to rethink his magazine selection. Where
was *Vogue? Mademoiselle? Elle?* All he had were old issues
of *Time, Newsweek, Parents,* and *Better Homes and Gar-
dens.* Not even one *People* around. How was a person supposed to learn about the latest Hollywood squabbles,
connections, separations, and all the other important details
of a superstar's life?

Jenny closed the magazine when she saw, "Diaper Rash
Gets Personal." She'd seen enough. Checking her watch
for the fourth time in ten minutes, she wondered how the
girls were doing. They'd been polite but a little reserved
when Elliot first greeted them, but then Natalie had asked
him where he got such a weird doorbell because she wanted
one just like it. He'd laughed and told her only weird people
could get them. She'd giggled at that. Danielle had worked
up a half-smile, too, but it was an effort.

"Would you like more lemonade?" Eleanor asked from her small desk in the corner of the room.

Jenny shook her head and stood up, stifling a yawn. "No, thank you, Eleanor. Not right now." Her gaze shot to the front porch and the kaleidoscope of color out there. "Would you mind if I took a little walk around outside? I want to look at all the flowers."

Eleanor waved her hand a few times and the extra flesh on her forearm jiggled back and forth. "Of course not, child. Go." Her face broke out in a wide grin, showing off her dimples. "If you want to see real beauty, follow the stone path to the backyard." Her brown eyes lit up. "It's glorious," she whispered. "Simply glorious."

"Thanks," Jenny said. "I will." She slung her purse over her shoulder and flashed Eleanor a quick smile. "Be back in a little while."

"Enjoy." Eleanor's sweet voice floated after Jenny as she went out the door and skipped down the steps.

She decided to take in the backyard first, explore the flowers and maybe get a little deeper insight into the doctor. After all, if he was going to be shaping and reshaping the tragic events that would affect them for the rest of their lives, then she wanted to get a handle on him, maybe uncover some quirky behavior patterns or something. If his backyard was clipped, coiffed and weed-free, then she might be able to surmise that he was very thorough and precise, which would be a good thing. If, on the other hand, along with that fastidious care there were hedges and other greenery cut and shorn to the exact same measurement, lending a military appearance, then she might think him too rigid, and that would be a bad thing. She didn't really know what she was looking for, only that when she saw it, she would recognize it.

Grace would think her insane for not just marching into his office and reading the diplomas on the wall. She would do that. Besides, she'd already read a few. University of Pennsylvania. Georgetown. But what did that really tell you? The more schools you went to, the more letters you got after your name? Heck, she didn't even know what half of them meant. Most people didn't but they wouldn't admit it. Grace would know, though, and if she didn't, then she'd find out. So, that would be her job. And Jenny's would be to just dig around in the man's backyard and see what she uncovered.

The front porch boasted free-flowing ferns and mounds of potted impatiens and begonias. The lawn was green and well manicured with two holly bushes on either side of the steps, adjacent to several sculpted evergreens, small and compact. There was a crabapple tree on the corner of the house and four azalea bushes scattered about. Neat, trimmed, welcoming. She'd give the good doctor an A+ for curbside appeal.

But . . . she followed the stone path to a white gate that separated front and back . . . everyone was expected to have a nice front yard. Keep up appearances for appearance sake. Isn't that what they said? Now, a tastefully done backyard, that would tell a whole different story. She lifted the metal latch and entered Elliot Drake's own private little world.

Her breath caught in her throat. There was color everywhere, a bold, beautiful display of depth and warmth, assaulting from all sides. The heady, seductive scent of rose, honeysuckle, and lavender hit her, practically bowling her over with their fragrance. Red, yellow, pink, gold, purple, blue, white, and all of the shades in between scattered in clumps and clusters around the lawn, some tall and heaven stretched, others low and creeping. Shasta daisies opened yellow faces to the sun in brilliant contrast to their neighbor, black-eyed Susan, who presented a soulful, dark visage amid orange-yellow petals.

Jenny made her way to the edge of the garden, hedged with smooth, round rocks piled on top of one another. Reaching out, she touched the tip of a hydrangea bush, its leaves lush and green, its flowers boasting the palest pink. She closed her eyes and breathed in the scents around her.

Heaven. That's where she was right now. And she could stay here for a good long time, enjoying the sights and smells of beauty. Elliot Drake had created this sanctuary. She could almost see his strong, tanned hands shoveling the dirt into mounds, sowing seeds, easing new flowers from their plastic pots. Yes, she could almost visualize the whole process, but analyze it? No, that she couldn't do.

What kind of man would create such a place? A beautiful safe haven that welcomed and nurtured, sustained and healed? What kind of man . . .

"Who are you?"

Jenny's eyes flew open and she whirled around to find a child, a girl, staring at her. Wide, brown eyes pierced Jenny with intensity, scouring over her like a Brillo pad trying to unearth grit and leftover grime from the bottom of an old pot. And Jenny was the old pot.

"Who are you?" the girl repeated, her voice rising with a self-assurance that made Jenny wonder if she were about to converse with a midget instead of a child.

Jenny offered a smile and took a few steps forward, extending her hand. "Hi. I'm Jenny."

The girl looked at her outstretched hand, her big, brown eyes narrowing over it, trying to find a defect, a problem. An ulterior motive. Jenny must have checked out okay, because the girl inched her small hand out and brushed it against Jenny's. Contact lasted no longer than two seconds.

"What are you doing here?"

Jenny dropped her hand to her side and stared at the adult-child in front of her. This must be Sydney. Laura had said she was around seven or eight, but she seemed older. Her skin was pale, almost transparent, as though she spent much of her time indoors, away from the sun. She wore her golden hair in two long braids tied with a blue ribbon at the end that matched the same blue in the striped shorts and tank top hanging on her thin frame.

But it was her eyes that held Jenny, pulled her in. They were familiar eyes. They were Elliot Drake's eyes.

"Are you Sydney?" Jenny asked.

"How do you know my name?" The girl lifted her chin a notch.

"Eleanor—I mean, Mrs. Flatt, told me Dr. Drake had a daughter named Sydney." Jenny let out a little laugh. "And unless you're a wood nymph who lives out here with the flowers, I'd guess you were Sydney."

The girl didn't return the laugh. Not even a hint of a smile. "I am Sydney," she said. "And this is my house."

Jenny nodded. "It's a very nice house."

"And this is my garden," she continued. "My dad made it just for me."

"It's beautiful."

"And you're trespassing."

"Excuse me?"

"I said," she repeated in a very clear voice, "you're trespassing."

Jenny hadn't even known little kids knew what trespassing meant, let alone how to use it in a proper sentence. But this child had it pegged down just right. Except that she wasn't really trespassing—she'd had an invitation from Eleanor Flatt to explore the backyard. And that's exactly what she'd done. Nothing more than take her up on her offer while the girls had their session with Elliot.

"I'm not trespassing," Jenny said, wondering if Sydney used the same bold manner with every adult, including her father. "I was invited to take a look at the backyard. Mrs.

Flatt told me it was beautiful.'' She paused and looked around at the flowering landscape. ''And she was right.''

''Aunt Eleanor told you to come back here?''

Jenny nodded. ''She's your aunt?'

Sydney relaxed a little, her shoulders slumping forward. ''No, not really. But she's like an aunt.''

''I see,'' Jenny said, wondering if Sydney had a grandmother, or cousins. She already knew she had a mother. Somewhere.

Sydney moved to a wooden swing wrapped with purple clematis and sat down, bringing her legs up to her chin. ''So, what are you doing here? Did you come to see my dad?''

''Kind of,'' Jenny said, moving toward her. ''Actually, I brought my nieces here to talk to him.''

''How come?''

She was starting to act more like a curious child and less like the Grand Inquisitor with a ten-dollar vocabulary. Her features had softened; the tightness around her mouth and eyes was smoothing out, the tiny rows of wrinkles on her forehead disappearing.

Jenny moved over to the swing. ''Mind if I sit?'' When Sydney nodded, Jenny sat down and started rocking the swing back and forth, pushing off with her right foot. ''They lost their father in a car accident and they're very sad right now.''

''Oh.'' One small word, speaking volumes.

The old swing creaked back and forth, filling the silence.

''Do they have a mom?'' Sydney was looking straight ahead, hugging her knees under her chin, her voice small and thin.

''Yes, they do,'' Jenny said, watching her. ''But she was hurt in the accident and was very sick for a while. She's still in the hospital.''

''Is she going to be okay?''

"The doctor said she'll be fine. But it was very scary for a while. For all of us."

"Did you cry?"

It was a simple question, yet it was layered with a thousand other questions, all heaped onto one another, spreading out to touch every aspect of Jenny's life, like a cancerous growth with feelers, wrapping itself around the heart, lungs, stomach. Nothing went untouched.

"I cried," Jenny said. "A lot. My sister is one of the most important people in my life. She's always been there for me." She ran a hand through her hair and thought of Grace's shaved head. "She's my older sister, we're three years apart. I don't know what I would've done if something had happened to her."

"I don't have any sisters. It's just me and my dad." Sydney paused a minute and added, "And Ruby Red."

"Ruby Red?" Jenny asked, thinking of pink grapefruit and sunshine.

An almost smile touched her lips as she turned her head to meet Jenny's gaze. "My dog."

"Can I see him?" Jenny asked, not missing the thread of excitement running through the girl's words when she spoke of her dog.

Sydney eyed her up and down, as though she were making a monumental decision that would impact not only herself, but something much larger. The nation, perhaps, or maybe even the world, hung at bay, waiting for Sydney Drake to make her decision. Thumbs up? Or down?

"I guess it would be okay," she finally said, shrugging her shoulders.

"Great."

"Wait a minute." She hopped off the swing and ran toward the back door like a child on a mission.

Something was going on inside Sydney Drake's head. Something big and dark and painful. Something that made her voice sharp and her words cruel, and her face pinched. Didn't her father see it? And if he did, couldn't he do something to stop it?

Jenny watched her run, golden braids flying behind her, and wondered about Elliot Drake's daughter. *Who was Sydney Drake?* Was she really the quick-tongued little tyrant who'd tried to bully Jenny away with words and accusations? Or was there someone else behind those bold, brash words, that defiant scowl, someone who was afraid, hurting, alone? Maybe, right now, she was a little of both.

Jenny heard the dog before she saw him. Her eyes were closed, face tilted to the sun, soaking in the warm afternoon rays, when a heaving, panting sound closed in on her. She opened her eyes just as a big, black ball of fur leapt onto her lap and licked her face.

"Down, boy. Down!" Jenny said, trying to push the dog away. He was huge. And stronger than ten oxen. "Sydney!" she yelled. "Help!"

"Down, Ruby!"

One order from her small mouth and the dog jumped off and settled all fours on the grass at her feet.

"This," Jenny said, wiping dog slobber from her cheek, "must be Ruby Red."

Sydney sat on the ground and threw her arms around the dog's neck. "This is Ruby."

"He's a monster."

"He's a Labrador retriever," she corrected Jenny. "And, he's a she."

"Oh," Jenny said, hazarding a quick glance toward the dog's underside. Ruby Red was lying partway on his/her side and yes, she was indeed a girl.

"She's only two years old," Sydney said, patting the dog's head. "See this bump, right here on top of her head?" She pointed to a slight protrusion on the top of the dog's head. "It's called a smart bump and that means she's really smart."

"Do you have any smart bumps on your head?" Jenny asked, grinning.

That question made Sydney's lips twitch. "People don't have smart bumps. Only dogs."

"I see," Jenny said, determined to pull a smile from the child's lips. She reached down and ran a hand along the dog's back. "Tell me, Sydney, how did Ruby Red get her name?"

"She stole my juice the first day we got her," Sydney replied, matter-of-factly.

Jenny laughed. "Let me guess. It was Ruby Red grapefruit juice."

"Uh-huh."

"I never knew a dog or any animal to like grapefruit juice, Ruby Red or any other kind."

"Except Ruby."

They sat in silence petting the big animal, Jenny covering the dog's back and hindquarters, Sydney, her neck and head. Ruby Red must have thought she was in heaven or at least in the hands of two great masseuses.

"Do you have any kids?" Sydney asked.

Jenny bit the inside of her cheek, missing her bubble gum. "No," she said, maybe a little too forcefully.

"Why?"

Sydney was watching Jenny with those too-wise brown eyes, waiting for an answer.

Before Jenny could think of a response a child would understand, Sydney's gaze narrowed and she said, "Don't you like kids?"

Jenny shook her head. "No, it's not that. I love kids," she said, resting her hand on Ruby's back. "But there's a lot more to it than just loving kids."

Sydney seemed to be considering that response, weighing

it against whatever preconceived notions she had on the subject.

"Do you have a husband?"

Jenny cleared her throat. Twice. This child made Gino Strandelli look meek. "No," she said, watching her fingers sift through Ruby's hair. "I don't have a husband."

"Why?"

Jenny's head shot up. *Why?* What to say to that? *Because the only time I ever let myself care about a man, I mean really care, he dumped me two weeks after I met his parents, told me I wasn't "corporate" enough to fit into his plans?* Or, *Because every man I've ever met wants to change me, reshape who I am so I won't even recognize myself?* Or maybe, *Because all any man really wants is a mother?* And last, but certainly not least, *Because marriage equals commitment and I don't get that whole equation?*

No, she couldn't tell her any of those reasons, so she settled with, "Because, I just never wanted to."

"Never wanted to *what*, Aunt Jenny?" Natalie called from behind Jenny.

Jenny swung around to see Natalie, Danielle, and Elliot coming through the gate.

Elliot's gaze shot from Jenny to his daughter and back. He raised a dark brow but said nothing.

"Never wanted to *what*, Aunt Jenny?" Natalie repeated.

"Nothing," Jenny mumbled, rubbing the back of her neck. She was roasting all of a sudden, cooking like a steak under a broiler.

"Never wanted to get married," Sydney said, sliding Jenny a look from the corner of her eye.

If the world had opened up that instant and sucked her under, Jenny would have considered it a godsend. Heat burned up her face and it had nothing to do with the weather conditions. She was experiencing the ultimate form of humiliation at the hands of an eight-year-old.

"That's not exactly what I meant," Jenny said, trying to salvage a scrap of dignity.

"Daddy used to say some man needed to cut your tail," Natalie said, leaning over and petting Ruby.

"That's not what he said." Danielle shot her a look of disgust. And then, as though she were reciting a nursery rhyme, she corrected her little sister. "He said, some man needed to *clip her wings.*"

Chapter 12

"When the hell are you coming back here where you belong, Romano?"

"Hi, Joe," Jenny said, "nice to hear from you." She looked out the kitchen window—Danielle and Natalie were climbing the monkey bars. If only she could be a kid again. Then Joe Feltzer wouldn't be on the other end of the line.

"We need you here, Romano. The Italy project is less than two weeks away."

She rubbed the back of her neck. "Well, I was thinking I'd just leave from here."

"Jesus, Jenny, I don't like it. You've got all the setup crew, the rest of your equipment—who the hell's gonna be responsible for that?"

"Gino said he'd tag it all for me."

"Yeah, well, Gino's got his ass in a sling, right now. Car accident three days ago, broke his leg."

"Oh, no."

"I'm dying here, kid. I can't stop the magazine until you

decide to come back. And what happens if you change your mind, and you bail out on shooting the Pope? Then I got nobody but second-rate.'' His voice boomed in Jenny's ear. ''What the hell am I going to do then?''

''I'm going to Italy, Joe. I've still got two and a half weeks.''

''You've been there almost four already and I hear from you what, three times?''

''I'm sorry, Joe. Things have been pretty rough here.''

''How's your sister?'' His voice smoothed out, calmed down a little; now he only sounded like half a madman.

''She's coming along. The doctor thinks she can come home in a few days.''

He was silent a minute. ''That's tough, kid.''

That was Joe's way of expressing his condolences. ''Yeah.''

''Okay, well, you call me, you hear? None of these three phone calls in four weeks, that's bullshit. I want you to check in a couple times a week, let me know what's going on. You got that?''

''Thanks, Joe.''

''Take care, kid. Give your sister my regards.''

That was the end of the phone call but it had been just the beginning of a sleepless night for Jenny. She'd known from the beginning that she was leaving for the Italy assignment; she needed this piece, it would boost her career, mark a turning point for her. But, my God, Grace wasn't even home yet . . . and the girls were just starting therapy . . . and Jenny was just learning how to make Laura's chicken-and-broccoli casserole . . . and her mother was counting down the days until she could be with Grace and the girls, a surefire disaster . . . and . . . and . . . Jenny's head throbbed.

Joe wanted her back as soon as possible. If she couldn't carry her load, he'd find somebody else. Two and a half weeks . . .

* * *

"I want to go home."

Grace sat in the dayroom of the Sunset Rehabilitation Center, toying with her empty coffee mug. In her baggy navy sweats and white T-shirt, she could almost pass for a visitor to the facility instead of a resident. Almost. Dark circles smudged the area under her eyes, and her face was pale and drawn. *But then again,* Jenny thought, *so is mine.* She'd slept less than three hours last night, Joe Feltzer's gruff voice rolling over and over in her head. *We need you here, Romano. The Italy project is less than two weeks away . . . I'm dying here, kid. I can't stop the magazine until you decide to come back. And what happens if you change your mind, and you bail out on shooting the Pope?* His words were more potent than three cappuccinos at midnight. They stole sleep, a second at a time, and before she knew it, dawn pushed through night and it was morning.

And there was another, more insidious thief, stealing sleep, destroying the night's restfulness.

Today was the day Jenny was going to tell Grace about Grant. She couldn't put it off any longer. Today, she'd do it today. Actually, *now.* Jenny lifted her wrist, inhaled. Lavender filled her nostrils, poured over her senses . . . calmed her. She'd started dabbing two drops of lavender essential oil on her wrists two days ago, right after she got back from the girls' visit with Elliot, right after Sydney asked her why she wasn't married and Danielle told Elliot that her father said Jenny needed her wings clipped. That had been enough to send her to her room in search of her little brown bottle.

"Jenny," Grace said, jerking her from her thoughts, "I want to go home."

You can't go home. Yet. Not until I tell you about Grant. And then you may not want to go home. "I know you do,"

Jenny said, reaching for her purse. She needed a fix, a jolt to help the lavender. Quick. Jenny reached into the zippered compartment and started rooting around.

"Stop that."

Her head shot up. Grace was staring at her, brown eyes narrowed and . . . angry?

"Listen to me. *I want to go home.* Today."

Jenny edged a finger along the leather lining, feeling for a small, soft square of strawberry. Nothing. *Damn.* She cleared her throat, swallowed. "There's something I need to tell you, Grace."

Grace looked at her, determined. "They can't keep me here against my will, Jenny," she said. "I've passed every ridiculous test they've given me." She held up both hands, wiggling her fingers. "Look. I can move my fingers." Then she lifted her legs, one at a time, bending them at the knee. "See," she said, "my legs work, too."

"It's not that, Grace."

"No? What is it, then? My speech?" Before Jenny could answer, she plowed forward. "It's perfect. So is my memory. I was born on October 13, 1964. My mother's name is Virginia. My father's name was Joe."

Jenny shook her head.

"I have a scar on top of my head somewhere from the time you tried to play gardener and sank a hoe in my skull." She gave her a dry half-smile. "I'm sure with my new hairstyle you'll be able to see it."

"Grace—" Jenny said, but she cut her off.

"I have two children. Danielle and Natalie."

"It's about Grant," Jenny blurted out.

That stopped her cold. "Grant?" There was a hollowness to her voice, a flat, emptiness that washed over both of them.

"I should have told you sooner," Jenny said, grasping her sister's hand. "But I just didn't know how." Her voice cracked. "I just wanted you to get better." She squeezed her fingers. "I didn't want anything to interfere with that, Grace. I wouldn't *let* anything interfere with that."

She felt six years old again, coming to her big sister for help and protection. Grace had always taken care of her, made everything right.

"Where is he?" Grace said, her voice flat, emotionless. "Tell me, Jenny."

Tears burned the back of Jenny's eyes, but she pushed them back, determined to get the words out. "He's dead."

Grace's whole body stiffened with the blow. "Dead." The word slipped through her lips. "Dead," she repeated. And then she sat there, staring straight ahead for so long that Jenny started to fear she hadn't comprehended the words. Jenny held her hand, brushing her thumb over Grace's cold skin in a clumsy effort to comfort her.

"Dead . . ." her voice drifted off.

"Oh, Grace," Jenny said, "I'm so sorry." She took a deep breath. "I know how much you loved him."

Grace squeezed her eyes shut. "Grant," she said on a ragged sigh, one word, spoken with faith and conviction, spanning a lifetime of hopes and dreams.

"I'm so sorry," Jenny said again, feeling stupid, inept. What did she know about the intricacies of a married relationship? Of any relationship involving a man and woman? Nothing. She couldn't possibly pretend to understand it, especially where a cheating husband was involved. Damn him. Grace was falling apart, one breath at a time.

God, but Jenny hated him right now. She wanted to yell and scream to Grace that he wasn't worth it. Not any of it. Her eyes stung with tears, hot and burning. Why was it that the good, honest people were always the ones who got screwed?

Grace sat in the faded orange chair, back ramrod straight, knuckles white, clutching the yellow-and-white teddy bear Danielle had given her. Tears slipped out from behind her closed lids, steady streams of grief trailing down her pale cheeks and onto her sweatshirt.

"I'm here for you, Gracie," Jenny whispered. "Whatever you need, I'll help you."

Grace moved her mouth, just a little, a faint twist of lips that reminded Jenny of the time when they were kids and Grace had the flu. It was the day before her twelfth birthday and their mother had said they'd have to cancel Grace's party if she wasn't better by bedtime. Jenny knew she had to do something to help her, so she sneaked into Grace's room and gave her Stuffy, Jenny's pink rabbit. He'd make her all better, she'd said. Stuffy could make anything better. Jenny still remembered Grace looking at her, her face all pale and sweaty, and working her lips into that same small almost-smile.

She gave Jenny that smile now, the one that meant she needed a lot more than what Jenny was offering, but she loved her for the gesture. Stuffy hadn't been able to help her that day. She'd thrown up most of the night and again in the morning, and the party had been canceled. And now, all these years later, Grace probably thought Jenny wouldn't be able to help her with this, either.

Grace sniffed and wiped her eyes. "Remember when we were kids, and I used to try to beat the light to bed?"

"Sure," Jenny said, wondering what that could possibly have to do with her current situation. "I used to count and you'd turn out the light and try to make it to the bed, before the room went black."

"I really used to think I could beat it."

"I know."

Grace met Jenny's gaze and there was desperateness in her brown eyes. "That's how I feel now. Like I'm trying to beat the light, but I can't. No matter what I do, or where I turn, I can't get away from the darkness. It's all around me, closing in on me."

"No, Gracie," Jenny said, squeezing her hands. "No. It's not going to get you this time. I won't let it."

Grace's lower lip quivered. "Help me," she whispered, leaning forward to throw her arms around Jenny. She held on like a frightened child. "Help me, Jenny." And then the tears came, grief and anguish rolling down her face.

Jenny hugged her sister close, her own pain scalding her cheeks. "I'll help you, Gracie," she vowed. "I'll help you."

Jenny lifted another magenta-colored impatiens from the gray plastic container and brushed the dirt from its roots. Grace had always loved deep, vibrant colors, said they were like a heartbeat, pulsing with feeling, with life.

Grace.

Jenny had gone to the garden center at eight A.M., Danielle and Natalie in tow. Danielle still wasn't talking much, but at least the one-word sentences were getting more frequent, and a few times she'd almost smiled. Almost. Jenny looked at the trays of impatiens sitting on the sidewalk. There were four of them. They'd each chosen a color. Jenny's was magenta, Danielle's fuchsia, and Natalie's salmon. They'd thrown in a little white, too, just because. The girls had helped pull the old impatiens out and each planted a single four-pack of their color before deciding they'd had enough and begged to go to Laura's. Jenny had let them; she needed this time alone, digging in the soil, planting flowers that made her feel closer to the Grace she knew, the one she could call at eight o'clock California time and ask if she thought Jenny should buy the Armani silk pants or the Cerutti sweater. The Grace in the hospital was a shell, a benign, lifeless version of the sister Jenny had known. She wanted the old one back, wanted to see her full smile, hear her voice, soft and encouraging, and dammit, she'd do anything to get her back, starting with a flowerbed of magenta, fuschia, and salmon impatiens.

She placed the base of another flower in its hole and smoothed dirt over the roots, careful not to get any on the petals. A pile of uprooted impatiens lay in a discarded pink-and-white heap in the wheelbarrow next to her. Pale pink, very pale pink, almost medium pink. And white. There were no deeper colors, no traces of red or purple, not even a yellow.

Why? Why hadn't she chosen the colors she loved most? Jenny scanned the street and took in the other neighbors' landscaping. Carpets of muted pink and white wrapped themselves around entrances and beds, up driveways and under mailboxes. There was an occasional salmon or yellow, but nothing as outspoken as magenta or, gasp, red.

Was that the reason Grace had such an anemic display of beauty sitting in her front yard? Was it because of the *neighbors?* Was it because of Grant? She itched her forehead with the back of her hand, the feel of the garden glove's rough cotton scratching her skin. They were only flowers, for God's sake. So, why hadn't she chosen the colors she loved?

Jenny was so involved in her own world, thinking about Grace and her gardening choices, that she didn't notice someone standing beside her until a shadow fell over her arm. Squinting, she looked up and saw an attractive thirty-something woman smiling down at her.

"Hello," the woman said in a strong, well-modulated voice that sounded like the opening greeting for an Infomercial. "I'm Samantha, Samantha Steward. You must be Grace's sister, Jenny."

"Yes, I am," Jenny said, setting her spade down and leaning back on the heels of her old sneakers.

The woman shook her head, her sleek, black hair swaying back and forth under her chin. "We were all devastated to

hear about the accident. Just devastated. And poor Grant,''
she tsk-tsked. ''What a shame. He was such a wonderful
husband and father.''

''Yes,'' Jenny murmured. *If she only knew.*

''To think that less than a month ago, they were just like
the rest of us. A husband, a wife, children. And then in the
space of a few seconds, everything changed. Gone. Just like
that.'' She snapped her fingers and Jenny's eyes settled on
her coral nails. Filed and shaped to perfection, too perfect
perhaps, like the rest of the woman; her skin a bit too tan,
her eyes a little too blue, her ultra-lean shape perhaps the
result of one too many Slim Fasts. Something about the
woman bothered Jenny, though she couldn't say exactly
what it was. Maybe it was nothing more than her voice, a
mixture of one part whine, two parts phoniness.

Or maybe it was because Jenny thought people like this
woman might be responsible for Grace's pink-and-white
impatiens. Jenny pretended to smile and chewed a little
harder on her gum.

''Now, who knows how the children will be affected,''
Samantha Steward droned on. ''No father, no role model.''
She folded her arms over her flat stomach. ''What a shame.''

''Grace will still be their role model,'' Jenny said, not
trying to keep the sharpness from her voice. ''She's a great
mother. She'll handle things once she's back on her feet
again.''

Samantha Steward offered a smile that looked an awful
lot like pity. ''Yes, of course,'' she said. ''But things will
never be the same.''

Jenny bit down on her gum again, hard. ''No, they won't,''
she agreed. *Grace won't have a husband in the house who's
screwing another woman.*

''There are just so many single-parent households today,''
the woman continued, shaking her head. The sun fell on her

black hair and Jenny wondered if it was natural or a salon sample.

"Only one in our neighborhood, though," she said. "Except for Grace. That will make two."

Jenny wanted to ask her if she'd tallied the number of husbands in her neighborhood who were cheating on their wives. She'd bet the count was higher than two. "People do die," Jenny said. "And others get divorced."

"Well, yes," she agreed. "Death is such a tragedy. Divorce, however, is altogether different."

"Why?"

"It's just not an option in my family."

"Why not?"

"Because I'm Catholic," she said matter-of factly.

Ah. So, the Catholic Church was behind her remarks. "So? I am, too. Or at least I was. And I know that Catholics have been allowed to get divorced for years."

"Larry and I are from the old school," she said, shrugging an angular shoulder. "We honor our vows."

"But do you really think God wants a person who gets slammed against the wall by her spouse every night to stay married? And what about the adulterer? The man who sleeps with every new employee, just because he's the boss? Should his wife cling to those marital vows, too?"

Jenny watched the other woman's coral lips flatten into a straight line. "There are always circumstances . . ." she fumbled along. "Of course, it's not right, but . . . we all do the best we can." She looked away, refusing to meet Jenny's gaze. Did she perhaps fit into one of these categories? Which one? Wife abuser or adulterer?

"It's never okay to hit someone or cheat on someone, no matter how much we think they deserve it," Jenny said, amazed that this woman might actually condone such behavior. "And I don't think God would want anyone to live like that."

Samantha Steward cleared her throat twice and hazarded a quick glance in Jenny's direction. "Of course not," she murmured. "Religion isn't the only factor. There are other," she paused, "considerations."

Jenny raised a brow. "Such as?"

"Well," she said, waving a hand in the air, "such as . . . economics and livelihood."

"Oh." *Money.*

"It would be terribly naïve and quite foolish to ignore the ramifications of divorce. Especially for a woman."

Aha! Yup, it was money all right; the Catholic Church was just a convenient scapegoat.

"Just imagine, if a woman in this neighborhood were going through a divorce," Jenny said, casting a glance at the rock on Samantha Steward's finger, "she'd probably have to move out of here and into a smaller house. Maybe even an apartment." She saw her cringe. "And get a job. A real job, not just volunteer work." Jenny's lips pulled into a wide, innocent smile as she watched the woman clasp and unclasp her hands. "No more charge cards. No more extras." She went in for the kill. "I'll bet she'd even have to sell off the tennis bracelet and diamond studs."

Samantha Steward let out a shaky laugh. "She might as well kill herself and be done with it."

"You think so?" Jenny asked, standing up and brushing dirt from her knees.

She nodded. "Absolutely. A life without MasterCard isn't worth living."

Samantha Steward's words stayed in Jenny's head long after the woman herself had disappeared down the street, her black bob bouncing with each step. Is that what middle class suburbia really thought? Did most women just stay in their marriages for the silverware? Maybe that sounded ridiculous, but it all boiled down to *things,* didn't it? Cars, houses, jewels, vacations. Lawn care. Garage door openers.

Things. Objects. Representations of something greater.

Security. The charge card with the fifty-thousand-dollar limit. The bank accounts and financial statements. Stock options. Mutual funds.

Things. Just things.

And what about Grace? Had she discovered Grant's duplicity and stayed anyway? Had she thought there was no way out? Had the accident *not* been an accident, but a subconscious moment of retribution?

Grace was too rational, too even-keeled, *too nice* to even think such a thing. But if her world were threatened, on the brink of splitting wide open like a pus-filled sore, could she have turned the steering wheel, with just one quick, half-second jerk, into a telephone pole? It would have been over before she really had time to consider her actions. *Could she have done it?*

A month ago, Jenny couldn't even have considered such a notion. Absolutely not. But then again, a month ago she didn't know Grant was screwing a leggy brunette.

Chapter 13

"I like the flowers," Grace said, staring out the front window. "They're beautiful." Her voice dropped to a whisper. "So beautiful."

They'd been home less than ten minutes. Jenny had picked Grace up from the hospital in a rented minivan, a navy Plymouth Voyager. The Sebring had to go because it might prove too difficult for Grace to maneuver in and out of on a regular basis. God, she'd actually chosen a minivan over a convertible! She must have been in Clairmont too long.

"You and the girls did a great job," Grace said.

"That's not what Samantha Steward said." Jenny smiled, just thinking about their second meeting. Or rather, confrontation. "She paid me another visit and gave me the address of the garden center where the whole neighborhood buys their impatiens."

"I see you didn't follow her subtle advice," Grace said with a dry smile.

"Hell, no. When have you ever known me to follow

anyone's advice? Especially when it's being shoved down my throat, no matter how sweetly?''

''I'll bet she didn't like that one bit.''

Jenny shrugged. ''She stomped away so fast the little balls on her golf socks almost fell off.''

''Good for you,'' Grace murmured. ''Good for you.''

Jenny studied her sister out of the corner of her eye for a full minute before asking, ''Did you pick the pink and white impatiens that were outside?''

Grace shrugged and said, ''Grant thought we should try to blend in with everyone else.''

So, Grant, dead, two-timing husband that he was, had chosen the color. ''To blend in,'' as Grace said. In other words, originality was not welcomed. Was he just ''blending in'' with the rest of the husbands on the street when he started his affair? Or hadn't he considered what his little extracurricular activities would do to his family and his role as husband and father? She'd bet the second, and she'd bet the only head doing the thinking was the one tucked inside his underwear.

''Would the pinks and whites have been your choice?'' Jenny asked.

Grace didn't say anything for a long time. ''No. I'd have planted the colors you chose.'' Then, a wisp of a smile spread over her lips. ''But I would've wanted poppies,'' she said.

''Poppies?''

''Big ones. All over. Even in the backyard.''

''Poppies,'' Jenny repeated.

''Bright orange-red ones,'' she said with actual enthusiasm in her voice.

''Fine. I'll go to the garden center tomorrow and get some.''

''No!'' She jerked around to look at Jenny as though she'd just suggested streaking through the neighborhood.

"Why not? I'll just pull the other stuff out. I don't mind. Really."

"It's not that," Grace said, with a hesitancy that put Jenny on alert. She gnawed her lower lip. "It just wouldn't look right." A little laugh escaped her lips. "After all, they're poppies."

"Yeah, they are. And I think it's a wonderful idea. Poppies are beautiful."

"But they're *poppies,*" she repeated.

"So?" Was she missing something here?

Grace shook her head and patted her pink-and-white bandana. "So, poppies are used to make opium. That's a *drug.*" Her eyes grew wide when she said the word "drug." "I can't have opium growing on my front lawn."

"Oh, for heaven's sake," Jenny muttered. "Do you mean to tell me you would keep from planting poppies because somewhere, somebody might be harvesting twenty zillion to make opium?"

Grace looked away and shrugged. "It's the principle. It's just not a good thing."

"Says who?" Jenny asked, wondering if this neighborhood were more dangerous than walking along a deserted highway at midnight. At least there, a person knew the harm, and could protect himself against it. But here, among the seemingly quiet, welcoming stretch of houses, one could be blindsided, sucked in by an insipid, all-consuming force that choked, maimed, and killed thoughts and ideas that were different or unique. Here, in this sleepy little development, individuality was cursed, not encouraged.

"Says who?" Jenny repeated when Grace didn't answer.

"Nobody *says.* It's just the way it is, Jenny."

"Oh, baloney. I'm getting you those damn flowers tomorrow." *This was ridiculous.*

"No. You can't." She turned to Jenny and there were tears in her eyes. "I don't want them."

Jenny opened her mouth to speak, but clamped it shut before she said something she'd regret. After all, Grace hadn't been home twenty minutes and Jenny wasn't going to get her upset already. There'd be time for poppies later, and talking about things like rights and choices and being your own person.

What did Grace fear more, not being accepted or being different?

They stood in silence, staring at the splashes of magenta and fuschia blanketing the flowerbeds.

"Thanks for the balloons and the banner," Grace said in a quiet tone, signaling the end of the conversation on the poppies.

"You're welcome," Jenny replied, turning her attention to the three Mylar "Welcome Home" balloons fluttering from the mailbox. A bright red "Welcome Home, Mom" sign hung from the porch, out of view. "The kids picked them out." She glanced at her watch. "They should be here any minute. Or maybe not," she said, shaking her head. "Natalie takes forever to eat three measly Chicken McNuggets."

"I know," Grace said, her voice soft, tender.

"And I think she tortures me on purpose with those French fries. Whoever heard of dipping them in ketchup after every single bite? Do you have any idea how long that takes?"

"Oh, yes. It used to drive Grant—" Grace stopped mid-sentence, her face turning white.

Jenny put her arms around her sister, pulled her forward. "It's okay, Grace. I understand."

Grace sniffed and shook her head. "Who would have ever thought this would happen? *To me?*" Her whole body shook. "Who would have ever thought?"

"I know," Jenny whispered. "I know."

They shared their grief in the quiet of the early afternoon sun, a blue, cloudless sky outside, embracing one another, each mourning their own loss, too painful to put into words. But the feeling was there, pulsing just below the surface, a living, breathing loss.

For Grace, it was more than just the death of a husband. It was the end of a dream. Gone. Forever. In the blink of an eye, the flick of a finger on a zipper, the half-second jerk of a steering wheel. Gone. Jenny mourned her own loss, surrendering all belief that her older sister could make things right, protect herself, her family, *and* Jenny from all harm.

Damn Grant to hell.

The phone rang, interrupting Jenny's curses. She straightened and pulled away from Grace. "Let me grab that. It might be Laura and the girls."

Grace sniffed and swiped at her eyes. "Sure," she mumbled turning back toward the window.

Jenny ran to the coffee table and snatched the phone. "Hello?"

"Jenny? Jenny?"

"Hello, Mom." She tried to keep the tension from her voice but she was in no mood to play twenty questions with her mother today.

"Jenny!" There was a breathless anticipation in her voice. "Is Grace there? Is she home yet?"

"We just got in about twenty minutes ago," Jenny said, eyeing her sister. "Hold on." She walked up to Grace and handed her the phone.

Grace hesitated a minute, as though the last thing she wanted to do was talk to her mother right now. Then she cleared her throat and took the receiver. "Hi, Mom." Her voice sounded weak, tired.

Jenny plopped down on the nearest couch and closed her eyes, listening to the one-sided conversation.

"Yes. I'm fine."

Pause.

"No."

Long pause.

"No. I understand. She's doing a fine job. Really."

Very long pause.

"Okay. Next Thursday. See you then."

Short pause.

"I love you. 'Bye."

Jenny opened one eye and stared at her sister. "Let me guess," she said, letting the sarcasm roll off her tongue. "The cavalry is coming next Thursday to protect the fort. Mom's worried the kids have been taken hostage or, worse," she raised a brow, "have missed a meal."

Grace actually smiled, a half-smile that lit up her pale face. "Don't be so mean. She's just concerned about everyone."

"Can't she be concerned from her own home?" Jenny asked, stuffing a pillow under her head. "God, once she comes through that door, the whole house will be in chaos." She rolled her eyes. "We'll have to eat three squares a day, sit up straight, pick up our wet towels, and be in bed by ten."

"Sounds fine to me."

"It would," Jenny said, making a face.

"She needs to come, Jenny," Grace said, her voice soft and serious. "She's a mother."

"I guess," Jenny muttered. "I just thought that hip surgery would keep her grounded a little longer, say another two months or so."

"How long do you plan to stay?" Grace asked, easing into the recliner beside Jenny. It was a light mauve velveteen. Soft and welcoming, with rounded edges. Just like Grace.

Jenny shrugged. "Well . . . I'm supposed to go to Italy in about nine days to do a photo shoot of the Pope. A really big deal—the Vatican, bishops, cardinals, you know, the higher-ups."

Nine days?" The words fell to nothingness from Grace's lips.

"I know it's not exactly the best time ... but I thought once I finished up, maybe I could come back for a week or two. What do you think?"

If that's," Grace paused, looked away, "if that's good for you."

It was the nine days that had Grace bothered—Jenny could see it from the expression on her face.

"Grace? Are you okay?"

"I'm fine. Fine. It's just that I really like having you here, Jenny." Her lips curved into a faint smile. "There was such peace waking up in the hospital and seeing your face. And even before I really woke up, I *sensed* you were there. Sometimes I heard your voice. And I can't begin to describe how good that made me feel ... how safe."

Jenny pushed back the boulder in her throat and said, "I want to be here for you." *I've just got to figure out how long I can stay here and still keep my job.*

Grace sighed and rested her head against the back of the chair. Her eyes drifted shut. "I'm so tired. Talk to me, Jenny. Talk to me about when we were kids and our biggest worry was finding an old coffee can to keep our bugs in." A little laugh escaped her. "Grasshoppers, beetles, worms." She sighed again. "Remember those days?"

"Of course I do. We used to go in the woods and make 'camps.' Cut those big ferns, the really green ones with the curly ends, and make them into beds."

"They were so soft," Grace murmured.

"And we'd bring cups, white-and-blue plastic ones, and get water from that little creek," Jenny said. She hadn't thought about the camp for years, but now it all came rushing back to her in lush, green detail.

"I loved the blackberries."

"They were the best," Jenny said, remembering the taste of the plump berries. "Big, juicy, ripe ones. We'd pretend they were dinner."

"And we'd lie on our fern beds and look at the sky through the trees."

Jenny closed her eyes and fell back in time. "We were in our own little world. Nobody could touch us."

"And nothing could hurt us," Grace said, her voice slipping away, "nothing in the world."

"So what's up with you and this Elliot Drake?" Grace asked the next day with the casual nonchalance that had sucked more secrets from Jenny than a Hoover ever could.

"Nothing."

"Uh-huh."

"Uh-huh, yourself. He's the kids' doctor." Then, just for extra measure, she added, "He's not even my type."

"Oh?" Grace had a way of saying that one tiny word as though she already knew the answers and was trying to see if Jenny knew them as well.

"No, he's not my type," Jenny repeated, a little louder. She grabbed at the first thing that flew into her mind. "His hair's too short."

"Of course. How wise of you to determine the success of a relationship based on hair length."

"You know," Jenny said, "I can find my own men. If I want to, that is."

"I know." Grace threw Jenny a sly look and her eyes lit up. Tonight, she seemed almost like the old Grace, teasing, bantering, watching out for her little sister.

A slow smile spread over Jenny's face. "Not that I've been extremely successful with any of my choices," she added.

"You just aren't picking the right kind of men," Grace said, easing onto the couch. Jenny plopped down beside her and picked up a nubby, beige pillow. Almost the same color

as the one in Elliot Drake's waiting room. She tossed it
aside and rested her arm on the back of the couch.

"I don't have a specific formula for selecting men," Jenny
said. "I like them to be fun, spontaneous, and . . . extremely
romantic." She tapped her chin with two fingers. "Athletic
is always good, too. Devoted doesn't hurt. Trustworthy.
Dependable."

"Trustworthy? Dependable?" Grace scrunched up her
nose. "Sounds like you're choosing a dog."

"Oh, no," Jenny said, shaking her head. "I'd have much
more specific criteria for a dog. After all, when the man
leaves the dog's still there." She laughed at her own joke,
but it fell flat between them.

"That's it, isn't it, Jenny?" Grace asked, her voice soft
and tentative. "You never choose a man who you might
actually *want* to stay, who you'd want more from than a
little fun and spontaneity?"

Jenny opened her mouth to deny the words, but nothing
came out. Was that what she'd been doing all these years?
Choosing relationships that were doomed to fail with men
who were nothing more than short-term parking?

"Jenny?"

"I don't know," she said. "Maybe."

Grace looked down at her hands, clasped in her lap.
"There's a loving that's beyond sexual. It can't be described
or explained, not in the logical, scientific manner most people
want. It consumes you whole, yet makes you strong, breathing life and hope into every cell in your body." Her eyes
filled with tears. "It's the most wonderful and yet the most
awful feeling in the world."

Jenny reached out to cover Grace's hands with her own.
"I'm sorry, Grace."

Tears spilled down Grace's cheeks. "That kind of love
will tear you up inside," she sniffed. "Rip you apart and

let the birds peck the last shreds of hope from your dead carcass.''

Is that how she felt about losing Grant? Had his death ripped her apart?

"And then the hope dies, one shining ray at a time, leaving you empty and hollowed out." Her voice cracked and her shoulders slumped forward.

"It's okay, Gracie," Jenny said, drawing her close. "It's okay."

Just when Grace seemed to be gaining a little strength, seeming more like her old self, she'd gotten a kick in the gut that doubled her over. And that dead bastard husband of hers was behind it.

"How do *you* think it went today?" Grace asked, the minute the screen door banged behind Danielle and Natalie. Natalie had given her mother a thirty-second version of their meeting with Dr. Drake, starting with "The lady there makes the best lemonade," and ending with "We played with Ruby Red." Danielle's response was more subdued—things like, "Fine. We talked. He was nice."

"I don't know," Jenny said. "They seemed okay when they came out of the appointment." She sighed. "At least, they 'talked.' I think next time will really tell, when Elliot gets them alone." She plumped down on the couch, picked up a nubby pillow, remembered Elliot had one like that in his waiting room, and tossed it aside. Business, she told herself, that's all it was with Elliot Drake, and just because she picked up a stupid pillow that reminded her of the one in his office, it didn't mean a thing.

Grace rested her hands on the end of the recliner and said, "I'd like to go to the next session and meet him."

"Good idea."

She nodded. "I have a lot of questions about the girls,

and,'' she paused, ''how we should handle everything. Should we try to encourage them to talk? Respect their need for privacy?'' She sighed. ''And what about Danielle and the silent treatment she's been giving you, as though you're responsible for everything because you were the one who had to tell them? I don't know, I just don't know. I never thought I'd be in this situation.'' Her voice cracked just a little. ''This is really hard.''

Jenny leaned over and squeezed her hand. ''Yeah, it is, Gracie,'' she said. ''And I'm here to help you any way I can.'' She gave her sister's hand another squeeze.

''I know this is hard on you, too, dealing with me, the kids, Mom. But I appreciate it. I really do.'' Grace forced a smile. ''I might just have to figure out a way to keep you here.''

Jenny laughed. ''You'd kick me out in a week.''

''No, I wouldn't.''

Jenny lifted an eyebrow. ''Remember me, Jenny Romano, your sister, the one who used to hide socks under our bed?''

''And underwear,'' Grace added, smiling. ''Please don't tell me you still do that at thirty-three years old.''

''Hey, some habits die hard,'' Jenny said, shrugging. ''At least now I don't intentionally hide them—they just kind of end up there.''

Grace stared at her as though trying to decide if she was joking or telling the truth. Then she just shook her head and said, ''And what, little sister, do you do when you run out of socks and your underwear drawer is empty?''

''Buy more.''

She sighed. ''I don't know how you and I can be related. I seriously don't.''

''It's only a few dirty clothes under the bed.''

''Right,'' Grace said. ''I think I'll go ask Dr. Drake what it means when a grown woman hoards dirty clothes under her bed. Maybe it's some kind of aggressive behavior or something.''

''You will *not* tell Elliot Drake any such thing about my underwear, dirty or otherwise,'' Jenny said, pointing a finger.

A little smile escaped Grace's lips. ''Maybe *Elliot* Drake would like to hear about your underwear,'' she said.

''Stop it!''

''So, tell me what he's like.''

Uh-oh, here she goes. Grace was up to something. Jenny shrugged and picked at a hangnail. ''He's nice,'' she said, deliberately avoiding her sister's gaze.

''What's he look like?''

So they were playing twenty questions. Grace's favorite game. Only eighteen more to go. ''He's okay.''

''Okay? That doesn't tell me anything,'' she said.

''Aren't you supposed to be sick or something?'' Jenny said, shooting her a disgusted look. ''You're like a damn dog with a bone. You should be relaxing, not interrogating me like the Gestapo.''

She laughed. ''We *are* one-quarter German. And talking like this makes me forget about everything.'' Her voice trailed off. ''It makes me laugh again.''

''And I'm the butt of the joke,'' Jenny said. ''As usual.''

That made her smile again. ''Not, as usual,'' she said, looking surprised by the comment. ''It's just that you're not—'' she paused, searching for the right word.

''Normal?''

Grace shook her head. ''No. You're not . . . usual. That's it. You're different. Unique.''

''Weird?''

''Yes. In a wacky, loveable sort of way.''

''I'll take that as a compliment.'' Jenny pulled her legs underneath herself, sitting Indian style.

''Is he good-looking?'' she asked.

"Did I mention Joe's got a spot at the office for an investigative reporter? I think you're a natural."

"And I think you're avoiding the question," she said, raising an eyebrow to give Jenny that schoolteacher "I know you're hiding something" look.

"Okay," Jenny said, picking at the fringe on that stupid nubby pillow. "What was the question?"

Grace sighed. "Is he good-looking?"

Is he good-looking? Not, Is he GQ? Is he a hunk? Is he drop-dead gorgeous? Only Grace would phrase the question like that.

Jenny twirled a piece of fringe between her fingers. "I guess you could say he was good-looking in a Clark Kent sort of way."

"Oh."

"What?"

Grace was smiling, giving Jenny that little double nod that meant she'd gotten it all figured out. "Clark Kent, huh? Alias Superman?"

"I only said he was good-looking in a Clark Kent sort of *way,* not that I thought he was Superman." Jenny threw her a disgusted look.

"So, you won't be squeezing into any phone booths with him?"

"Grace!"

"What?"

"Can we change the subject? Please?"

"Fine. Fine by me."

Something was up; she'd given up too easily. She must be regrouping, analyzing her information, comparing Jenny's past history, and once she'd had a chance to think about it and reassess the situation, Grace would be back, loaded with more questions.

"So, how's your book?" Jenny asked, eyeing the book in Grace's lap.

"Depressing. If you want to have a good cry, just read Theodore Dreiser," she said, her voice fading out.

Jenny scrunched up her nose. "Theodore Dreiser? *An American Tragedy?* Why are you reading *that?*"

"It's a classic," she said, holding it up for Jenny to see.

"I'm not that ignorant," Jenny said. "Just because I'm part of the mass market fiction cult doesn't mean I don't know about Theodore Dreiser. It just means I don't read him. Why can't you read something else? Something modern-day?"

Grace looked at her as though she'd asked her to drink hemlock.

"Okay, then not modern-day. But why not try something a little lighter, say Mark Twain, for example?"

"Mark Twain?"

He seemed like a good choice. Humorous. Wise. And something Grace would approve of, no doubt: required reading in school, or at least it had been when Jenny was in school.

"I don't think so."

Jenny threw her hands in the air and said, "Well, fine then, if Mark Twain doesn't do it for you, then somebody else. But don't read that damn depressing stuff right now." Reaching over, she grabbed the book from Grace's lap and tucked it under her leg. "Not now, Grace. You don't have to be a psychologist to know that reading this kind of stuff when you've just been through what you have, is going to sink you fast."

Grace's shoulders slumped forward and she closed her eyes. "Maybe you're right."

Jenny nodded. "Damn straight I am," she said. "I may not be right often, but this time I am."

The phone rang just then, interrupting the rest of her speech. She was two seconds away from giving Grace a pep talk on the importance of positive thinking and relaxing, with breathing techniques and essential oils like lavender and chamomile.

Grace picked up the receiver and said, ''Hello?''
Pause.

''Oh, hi, Mom.'' She looked over and smiled. Jenny rolled her eyes.

''What?''

''What?''

''Oh, no!''

Chapter 14

"What?" Jenny whispered. "What'd she say?"

Grace waved her hand, held a finger to her lips. After five more "Oh, no's" and "What did the doctor say?" Jenny concluded that whatever was wrong with their mother was more aggravating than serious. But then again, it didn't take too much to set off Virginia Romano.

"Okay," Grace said. "I'll tell her. All right, Mom. Take care. I love you, too. 'Bye."

"What?" Jenny asked the second Grace pressed the "off" button. "What's wrong with her?"

"She's developed some kind of infection and the doctor said he doesn't want her traveling for at least three more weeks."

Jenny blew out a long breath. "Is she back in the hospital? On antibiotics?" She might not be able to spend fifteen minutes in the same room with the woman before one of them found an excuse to leave, but she was still her mother. Jenny had even survived the daily phone calls while Grace was in the hospital. Most of the time, she'd given her mother a quick report, answered ten minutes' worth of questions, listened to another five minutes of lectures, and then handed the phone off to one of the girls, saying they were dying to talk to her. It had been an effort, a supreme act of strength and discipline, but she had done it. Jenny had played the dutiful daughter.

Grace interrupted her thoughts. "No, she's not back in the hospital, and yes, she's on antibiotics. She's got to take them for fourteen days." She gave Jenny a look and added, "And not very happy about it."

"I'm sure that's a gross understatement," Jenny said, imagining her mother in all of her glorious displeasure.

"Very gross," Grace repeated. "She said she's damn tired of that damn doctor telling her what to do and as soon as she finishes that damn medicine, she's coming here, dammit."

"Damn straight," Jenny said, grinning.

"Damn straight," Grace added, her lips curving into a full-blown smile.

"Now, inhale, hold, exhale, *whoosh,* let the air flow through your body, through your fingers . . . your toes . . . that's it, open, open . . . expand your lungs, and *breathe.*"

Sydney let out a big *whoosh,* sucked in another breath of air, exhaled. "What's this supposed to make you do?"

"Relax," Jenny said. "It's supposed to make you relax and not be so angry or upset." This was the fourth time she'd been in Sydney's garden, her "Secret Garden," as she liked to call it. They were sitting yoga style on a blue-and-white comforter. "See those purple flowers over there, the ones in small clusters? That's lavender and it's a natural relaxer."

"What's that?" Sydney asked.

"Well, that means it's made up of things that help a person be calm just by smelling it. They make all kinds of things out of lavender—pillows, perfumes, lotions, candles . . ."

"Candy?"

"I don't know about candy."

"They should make lavender candy," Sydney said matter-of-factly.

"Oh? Why? Do you think it would taste good?"

Sydney shrugged. "I don't know, but kids could eat it and not get all hyper."

"Ahhhh," Jenny smiled, "good idea." She took another deep breath, held it.

"Is that the camera you use for your work?" Sydney asked, pointing to the Nikon on the edge of the comforter.

"Sure is," Jenny said. She scooped it up, zoomed in, and snapped Sydney midway between suspicion and intrigue.

"The one you use to take pictures of famous people?" She stared at Jenny, then scrambled to her favorite perch on top of a big rock surrounded by pink-and-garnet clusters of carnations. She was Queen of the Flowers and this was *her* rock, she informed Jenny the first time she tried to sit there. Her dad had picked it out just for her, put it on the edge of the flower garden, and painted her name on the side in pink and yellow.

"Some are famous," Jenny said, clicking off two more shots.

"Like who?" Sydney crossed her arms over her thin body.

"Well, I'm going to take photographs of the Pope in about a week," she said. "And I've done the Prime Minister of Canada, and the Governor of Massachusetts." Jenny flipped the angle, stepped closer, and zeroed in on her face. She wasn't a bad kid, just spoiled . . . and lonely.

"What about Britney Spears?"

"No, haven't done her."

"Back Street Boys?"

"No."

She scrunched up her nose.

"What?" Jenny asked, putting the camera down.

"You didn't do anybody good."

What? Okay, so maybe politics wasn't everybody's bag, especially a little kid's. But the Pope? The man millions of people flock to every year, wait for hours to see, just so he can hold up two fingers and bless them? *He* wasn't anybody good?

"Didn't you ever do anybody *famous?*"

Jenny clamped down on the two-wad ball of strawberry in her mouth. *Breathe lavender,* she told herself, *breathe lavender.* "I did do some singers," she said.

"Who?"

"Pavarotti." She frowned. "Enya." Sydney's blond brows pulled together like a rope, twisting. "Yanni."

"Never heard of 'em."

Jenny ignored her, asking, "What kind of people do *you* think are famous?"

"Britney Spears. Back Street Boys." She shrugged. "*NSYNC."

"I see."

They stared at each other. Sydney's lips thinned into a straight line. "My father doesn't like curly hair," she said, twirling her own pale blond, very straight hair around her finger.

Jenny ran a hand through her own tangled mop and said, "Really?"

"Yep. He likes straight, *blond* hair. And brown eyes, not—" she paused. "What color are your eyes?"

"Hazel."

"That's the color," she said. "He doesn't like *hazel* eyes."

"Did he tell you that he didn't *like* curly, black hair or hazel eyes?" Jenny asked.

Sydney cleared her throat and mumbled, "No." Then in a rush she said, "But he didn't have to."

"Oh?"

She fixed her gaze on a bunch of the pink carnations near her feet. "No. I knew what he meant."

"When did you discover this, Sydney? Did he say something?"

She shook her blond head. "Not really." She hesitated, then said, "Just that he thought you were really nice."

He said that? "And that bothered you?"

"He doesn't even know you. How can he say you're nice? You're not that nice. I think you're kinda mean ... and ugly."

The silence stretched long and uncomfortable over the grass, around the flower beds, creeping, creeping, until, finally, it circled Sydney and she looked up.

"Why are you doing this, Sydney?"

Her gaze flitted off behind Jenny and then back again. "Doing what?"

"Trying to make sure I don't like you. Trying to make sure I don't like your father."

"I am not."

"Yes, you are," Jenny said. "That's exactly what you're doing and I don't like it."

"You're wrong. You don't know anything about me." Her brown eyes narrowed. "You're mean and ugly, like a witch," she said. "I want you to leave."

"I don't want to play this game anymore, Sydney," Jenny said. "I thought we were friends." And then she dug deeper, to what might be the real problem. "I'm sorry your mother isn't here for you. Really sorry." Sydney buried her chin in her neck, refusing to meet Jenny's gaze. "But that doesn't give you a reason to treat people the way you do. You let me in *your* garden, but I can't touch anything unless I ask you. Not even a petal. And you order Mrs. Flatt around like she's your maid.'' She waited a few seconds to see if Sydney would say anything. The child held herself very still, a fine, pale curtain of hair shielding her face. ''I won't come in *your* garden anymore. From now on, I'll just stay with Mrs. Flatt. I think you're the one who's mean, Sydney, and that meanness makes *you* the witch. You, Sydney, you're the mean witch.''

Jenny's pulse beat hard and strong, pounding out sorrow for the child on the rock, as beautiful as the flowers surrounding her, but so alone, like an island, uncertain and unwilling to reach out for help. No one could help Sydney Drake. Not yet. Not until she, like so many others before her, learned that in life's most difficult challenges, the first step was always a solo one.

Jenny turned and made her way to the gate, camera slung on her shoulder, eyes straight ahead. Her heart felt like a bowling ball stuffed into her chest. Children should be happy. Children should not have worries. They should run in tall fields of grass, chasing each other, laughing, rolling, and howling, with the hard ground under their feet and the blue sky above. They should slurp chocolate ice cream and sip lemonade, bite into cotton candy and crunch caramel apples.

Children should be happy.

''Jenny?''

She swung around, waited. A little ''I'm sorry,'' that's all Sydney needed to say and they could start over. She'd even ask Eleanor if she could take her to Dairy Queen for an ice-cream cone—a very small one, since it was so close to dinnertime. Vanilla dipped in chocolate sauce.

''Yes?'' Jenny said, thinking about how upset Natalie would be if she found out Jenny had been to Dairy Queen without her.

"My dad *hates* long, curly, black hair and hazel eyes."

Jenny turned and walked out of Sydney's backyard wonderland. *Sometimes that's just what you have to do,* she told herself. *Walk away. Even when it's the very last thing in the world you want to do.*

Jenny wandered around Elliot's front yard for a while, taking in the ferns and begonias, and then went inside to find Eleanor.

The older woman smiled when Jenny came to the door. But then, Eleanor smiled all the time. "Hello, dear," she said. "Would you like a glass of lemonade?"

"Fresh squeezed with extra lemon?"

"Just like you like it," she said.

"Sold." Eleanor Flatt made the best lemonade this side of the Mississippi. Guaranteed. It was one of Jenny's favorite things about coming here. There were a few others too . . . one of them was tall and dark and . . .

"Here you go, dear," Eleanor said. "Just like you like it." She'd disappeared and reappeared while Jenny was still fighting with her thoughts, trying to ignore that pesky little voice that taunted her, telling her there might be something there after all.

"Thank you," Jenny said, accepting the tall glass, clinking with half-moon-shaped ice cubes and floating lemon wedges. She took a sip. *Zing.* Lemon attacked her taste buds head-on. "Mmmm. This is good."

"Glad you like it, dear," Eleanor said, moving over to her desk. She pulled out a chair, a navy tweed with oak trim on the legs, and plopped down. "I thought you were out back with Sydney."

Jenny took another healthy swallow. "I was."

"Is she still out there?"

"Yes."

"Oh. Well, maybe I'll go see if she'd like some lemonade,

too.'' She placed both hands on top of the desk and proceeded to hoist herself out of the chair.

''I think maybe she'd like to be alone right now,'' Jenny said. ''We had sort of a . . .'' She fished around, hunting for a name to tag onto whatever had just happened in the garden. Falling out? Argument? Nothing could quite describe it, so she settled on, ''Sort of a disagreement.''

''Oh?'' Eleanor's brow arched like a question mark.

Jenny nodded and gulped more lemonade. ''Sydney has yet to learn the fine art of diplomacy.''

''She will in due time,'' Eleanor said. ''She's only eight years old.''

She was trying to protect her. Of course, she was trying to protect her. Everybody probably tried to protect Sydney Drake from everything because her mother left when she was four, but nobody was trying to protect Sydney from her worst enemy—herself.

''I'm talking about getting along with other people, Eleanor,'' Jenny pushed on. ''Sydney says cruel things that hurt people.''

''She doesn't really mean them,'' the older woman said, placing her hands, palm side down, on the shiny desktop. She looked at Jenny with kind brown eyes. ''She's had a tough time. This is very hard on her.''

''Her mother left four years ago. How long is it going to be okay for her to treat people like five-day-old Chinese takeout? Like everyone exists to do her bidding?'' Jenny walked over to Eleanor's desk and lowered her voice. ''Don't think I haven't noticed the way she answers you back when her father isn't around. I've seen it and it's not right.''

''But she—''

Jenny cut her off. ''But nothing. She's a spoiled child who needs to be disciplined.''

Eleanor stared at Jenny, said nothing.

''Maybe if I had kids of my own, I wouldn't feel this

way. Maybe I'd be more forgiving." She raked a hand through her hair. "Maybe. But I know what it's like to be different, to do things for no other reason than to get attention. And get caught. And to want to get caught because of the attention you'll get. Even if it's bad." She'd spent the first half of her life doing things, anything, so her mother would notice her.

"You think Sydney wants more attention?"

"I think Sydney wants to be like everybody else. She wants to feel *normal*. Maybe even get yelled at once in a while. Does her dad ever tell her 'no'?"

"Of course he does," Eleanor burst out. "Surely." She paused. "Surely, he does—I think."

"Do you?" Jenny asked.

Eleanor cleared her throat and puffed out her over-endowed chest. "I discipline her."

"How?"

She thought a moment and then flashed Jenny a quick smile, obviously quite proud of what she was about to say. "Well, just the other day, she spilled her milk at breakfast."

"And you made her clean it up?" Jenny asked. Now they were getting somewhere.

Eleanor's smile slipped a little. "Why, heavens, no! I cleaned it up. But I made her apologize—yes, I did."

Jenny blew out a low breath. No wonder the poor kid was messed up. She could probably spit out watermelon seeds at the kitchen table and as long as there was a garbage can within five feet, Eleanor would label the activity acceptable.

"Eleanor, I think—"

"Jenny!" she cut her off. "You know what can fix this, don't you?" There was a bright, almost unnatural light in Eleanor Flatt's brown eyes.

"No." Jenny leaned in closer. "What?"

"A woman." She beamed.

"A woman?"

"Sydney needs a woman in her life."

"She has you, Eleanor."

Eleanor waved her hand in the air. "No, no, silly. I mean, a *woman.*"

Jenny stared at her. "And what are you under that dress? A man?"

She threw back her head and laughed. "I mean a woman as in a mother," she said, lowering her voice to a conspiratorial whisper.

"Ah."

"And I know just the person."

"You do?" Jenny asked, wondering if the lucky candidate knew she was being considered for sainthood.

She nodded so hard her gray bun flopped. "Oh, yes." The little extra flesh under her chin jiggled around, too. "And, she'd be perfect for Elliot."

Elliot. "Who?" Jenny tried to keep her voice even.

Eleanor Flatt smiled a wide, knowing smile that transported her back thirty-five years to pink chiffon and Saturday evening dances, where girls giggled into white rotary phones and fell in love before the third kiss. Jenny saw that young girl in those twinkling eyes, saw her looking at Jenny with wisdom and hope and recognition.

She lifted a finger and pointed to Jenny.

Me? Jenny opened her mouth to blurt out the obvious— at least it was obvious to her. *No!*

The door opened one-half second before the sound left her lips.

"Hello, Jenny."

Elliot.

Her mouth felt like sandpaper. She opened it and pushed a half-intelligible response out. "Hello." Jenny shot a side-long glance at Eleanor, who was sitting there, arms folded over her wide middle, smiling that smug little smile that said she'd figured everything out and soon Jenny would, too. Jenny shook her head but Eleanor's smile only got wider.

"Jenny?" It was Elliot. "Is something wrong?"

Her gaze flew up to meet his. "No," she said quickly, a little too quickly. "No." Inhale, hold. Exhale, *whoosh.* "I'm fine."

He looked at her once more and then turned to Eleanor. "I'd like to see Grace next Tuesday afternoon."

"Yes, sir," Eleanor said, flipping the appointment book on her desk. Jenny didn't miss the smile that hovered on her lips.

Grace came out of Elliot's office then, her eyes red, her nose puffy. Jenny walked over to her and squeezed her hand.

"Jenny," Elliot said, "can I see you for a minute in my office?"

"Sure." What had Sydney done, crawled through the window and finked on her already, she wondered. "I'll be right back," she said to Grace.

"I'll just wait outside," Grace said. "I feel like I need some fresh air." She tried to smile but her lips quivered and pulled into a straight line.

"Okay." *Poor Grace.*

Poor me. Now I have to face Elliot, tell him about Sydney and the incident in the garden. She cleared her throat, straightened her shoulders, and followed him into his office.

Elliot closed the door and turned to her. He didn't look angry. Maybe he wanted to talk to her about Grace. That was probably it. She blew out a little breath and rubbed the back of her neck.

"Do you like linguine with calamari?" he asked.

Huh? What did that have to do with Grace? Or Sydney? *Or anything?*

"Yes."

He smiled. "What about lasagna?"

"Uh-huh."

"Aglio olio?"

She nodded.

"Ravioli?"

What on earth was he doing? "Yes."

"Bruschetta?"

"Um-hmm."

"Manicotti?"

Enough. "Yes, yes, and yes!" she said, shaking her head. *"What are you doing?"*

Ignoring her question, he asked one more. "Veal Piccata?"

"No!"

He snapped his fingers. "I knew it. Why?"

So, Elliot was not only a shrink, he was a food critic, too. An Italian one, from the sounds of things. "I refuse to be involved with anything that's been locked away, hidden from the light, and killed before it can stretch and grow."

"I agree. That's why I went into this profession."

"So you could refuse to eat veal?" she asked, unable to keep a few specks of sarcasm from dusting her words.

He laughed and said, "No. So I can keep *people* from being locked up, usually in their own minds. Keep them from burying themselves in old habits and self-recrimination. Help them to stretch and grow in ways they never thought possible, physically, mentally, maybe even spiritually."

He had a way with words and a passion in his voice that made her want to curl up on his couch, lay her head on one of those beige, nubby pillows, and hear more. He had a cause and a reason for being. She wondered what it was like to have such confidence, such purpose, such direction. She'd bet *he* didn't flounder when he talked to *his* mother on the phone. And she'd bet he didn't need an extra dose of strawberry juice to face a very attractive, if not somewhat intimidating, member of the opposite sex.

"Jenny?"

"Huh?" He probably didn't sweat, either. Or leave that little bit of drool on his pillow like most normal people did every now and then, even though they'd never admit it.

"I know a great little Italian restaurant around here."

And he'd be one of those who rolled the toothpaste nice and neat from the bottom . . . What did he just say? "Excuse me?"

"I said I know a great little Italian restaurant around here." He paused and his lips turned up just a little. "And I'd like to take you there."

A date? Was this a date? She wanted to ask him if it was, but that would be so totally unchic of her. She'd look like a fool and then she'd be the one hiding from the light for the next century when he answered a surprised, *No, of course not. I just wanted someone to share a dish of pasta fagioli.*

"And I will swear off all veal dishes for the night if they offend you," he added.

Jenny let out a sick little sound that was meant to be a laugh but sounded more like a snort. It was just a nervous reaction. Very ladylike. He must be quite impressed. "Sure," she said. "Food is one of my great passions."

"Angelino's is one of mine," he said. "I always tell my mother, I've got to have some Italian blood running through me somewhere. Maybe some Italian girl and one of my ancestors had a little tryst a few hundred years ago." He smiled. "She gets furious when I say that. Her face turns all red and she shakes her head and tells me I'm English. One hundred percent."

"I love Italian food, too," Jenny said, standing there in the middle of Elliot's office, the scent of his Davidoff's Cool Water floating to her. "I also love Chinese, but I've never thought I might *be* Chinese."

He threw back his head and laughed. "I like your sense of humor."

"I was being serious."

"How about if I pick you up tomorrow night, say seven?"

Now was the time to tell him about what happened in his backyard. *I had an argument with your daughter. I told her I didn't like the way she treated people. And she told me you hated black hair and hazel eyes. Why, Elliot? What's she so afraid of to say that? Why?*

"If tomorrow doesn't work, we can make it another time," he said.

"No." *Tell him.* "Tomorrow's fine." *Tell him what happened in the garden . . . how she told you to get out . . . how you told her you didn't like the way she treated people . . .* "Seven."

"I'll see you then."

It wasn't until she was outside, heading down the steps and toward the navy minivan, that she realized she hadn't even asked him about Grace.

She'd wanted to hint around the idea of Heather Eastman, in a very casual way, to see if she could get a feel for what Grace did or didn't know. Not that Elliot would tell her, but if she asked the right questions, she might be able to read between the lines, figure it out. And hopefully, Grace would be blissfully ignorant of her husband's infidelity and the dream of a happy family, a circle of four, committed and faithful to one another, could live on. No one but Jenny would have to know it had been breached. Grace would grieve her husband in the way only someone who's suffered a great loss can, grieving not only the person but other, more intangible associated losses as well. There would be no father to bring in the Christmas tree this year or sing *Deck the Halls* in an off-key beat that always sent his daughters into giggles. Spring would arrive and Easter Sunday, but the man of the house wouldn't be escorting his "favorite girls" to Easter Mass. His wife would learn to sleep alone in the big four-poster bed, night after night, with nothing to warm her but a dual-control electric blanket, adjusted for one.

And as time passed, there would be bigger, more obvious holes in the family portrait. There would be no father to quiz the young men his daughters brought home, or load the car for college, or walk them down the aisle. His children's children would never call him Grandpa or Granddaddy or Grandpop. They'd call him nothing at all, except when pointing at pictures of him in old photo albums.

But his wife and children, and even his children's children, would think of him always and wish he could be there to share the joy of family. They'd gather him in their hearts and set up a memorial shrine, with a candle burning. And they would never let the flame of his memory burn out.

God knew what he was doing when he flat-lined Grant in ICU. In His infinite wisdom, He was preserving memories *and* saving lives. If Grant had lived and Grace had found out about her husband's infidelity, she would have been destroyed. The family would have been destroyed. How did that old quote from scripture go? *There but for the grace of God, go I? Amen,* she thought. *Amen.*

Chapter 15

"Try this one," Natalie said, holding up a red-and-black, tiger-striped knit top. "Elliot will think you're beautiful."

Jenny threw her a quick look and said, "Hardly." Personally, she thought the shirt had a certain coolness about it, kind of hip and funk all in one. But, she doubted Elliot would think there was anything cool about it.

"What about this, then?" Natalie pointed to a red jersey dress.

Red? No. She was searching for something more . . . more demure. Maybe sophisticated.

"If you wear this," Natalie said," and get s'ghetti sauce on it, you won't be able to tell."

Jenny ruffled the pile of curls on top of her head. "Thank you for such good advice, but I'm looking for something . . . different." Except different was not in her closet, at least not the kind she was searching for, and no matter how many times she rifled through the choices, it still just wasn't there. Her gaze swept over the pieces in the closet. Leather skirt, leather vest, leather pants. No. No. And no. Hot pink knit top, semi-see-through black silk pantsuit. No, and no. Low-cut, lime green halter dress. Big no. Second-skin red jersey dress. Absolutely no. Three long, flowing Indian skirts with jangle belts and matching tanks—purples and golds and midnight blacks, rusts and fuschias and lemon yellows. She flicked through the other choices and the most sedate outfit she could find was a tangerine-and-white sundress. From the front, it was presentable. Maybe it would do. As long as she stayed behind Elliot the whole night and didn't let him see the giant scoop of fabric missing out of the back.

Well, that was it—there was no choice left.

She couldn't go.

"Having a problem?"

Jenny turned around and groaned. Grace stood in the doorway, blue-and-white bandana wrapped around her head, a smile on her face.

"I can't go," Jenny said, shaking her head. "I have absolutely nothing to wear."

"Yes, you do, Aunt Jenny," Natalie said. "You got lots and lots of stuff."

"Well, yes, I do, but somehow, I just can't find the right thing."

"You've never had this problem before," Grace said.

Why was it that sisters loved to make those bold little statements that meant so much more than the actual words that came out of their mouths?

Maybe a simple pair of black pants . . . matching sweater. Great, except she and Elliot weren't going to a funeral.

"He's taking *you* to dinner, not your clothes," Grace said.

Jenny slammed a drawer shut and yanked another open. "I know that." Hmmm. White shirt. White slacks. Too virginal. "Damn," she said under her breath. She really *was* going to have to cancel. That was it. She straightened and turned around. "I can't go."

Grace rolled her eyes and turned to Natalie. "Honey, will you go get Mommy my slippers in the laundry room?"

"Okay. Be right back." She hopped off the bed and ran out of the room.

"All right, Jenny," Grace said, crossing her arms over her chest. "What's going on?"

"Nothing." Jenny pulled open the last drawer, even though she already knew what was in it: T-shirts, shorts, underwear. And a few pairs of socks. She opened it anyway and peered inside. Yep. T-shirts—red, blue, white, black, and yellow. Shorts—black, blue, green, and khaki. Underwear—black, black, and ... black. White socks. Nothing, all right.

"Jenny?"

Grace knew something was up—Jenny could hear it in her voice, in the slight dip and spill of the "n" when she said her name. She'd always done that, taken the middle of her name on a roller coaster ride, ever since that time when Jenny was eight years old and Grace had found her in the backyard burying her pet salamander. His name was Spot and he was fire-orange. Jenny had let him out of his bowl one afternoon and he'd escaped. She'd crawled on her knees, looking under every chair and table, crying until her eyes were almost swollen shut. A week later she found him, shriveled up in a corner of the kitchen by the heating vent. His fire-orange color had turned to coffee brown and his skin was hard with dark lines running through it. Jenny had picked him up and wrapped him in a paper towel. Then, she put him in a baggie, zipped it shut, and ran out back, to the far end of the property, where the weeping willows spread their arthritic, gnarled roots and they'd already buried two gerbils, a hermit crab, and three fish. It was there, in the black soil next to the white peony bush, that she started digging.

That's where Grace found her, shoveling away with her red-and-white spade, tears streaking dirt-stained cheeks. "Jenny," she'd called, so soft and sweet, rolling her name around like she was doing right now, making Jenny believe, making her want to believe that she could help, that everything would be all right.

"Jenny?"

Jenny sank to the floor and quietly closed the last drawer. "He's a nice guy, Gracie. A really nice guy. Like someone you would go out with." She pulled a hand through her hair and looked at her sister. "You know, I usually end up with the jerks. You know that." She gave a little laugh, shrugged her shoulders. "It happens . . . every time."

"It's only dinner, Jenny," Grace said, easing down beside her and crossing her legs. Their knees were touching. "He does seem like a very nice man. So, just try to relax and enjoy yourself."

"But that's just it, don't you see? *I can't relax.* I mean, really, forget the gum and the lavender. He'll be looking at me, watching me, studying me. And you know how I make those little noises when I kind of slurp my spaghetti? I'll have to order pizza or an antipasto." She shook her head and frowned. "Even though I love linguine and calamari, I won't order it. I can't." She ran a hand over her face, pulling at her cheeks and chin. "This is going to be miserable. *I'm* going to be miserable."

"No," Grace said. "You're going to be yourself."

"He'll never like that person."

Grace's brown eyes narrowed. "And is it important that Elliot like you, Jenny?"

It was a simple question, direct, fat-free, stripped to the bone. *Was it important that Elliot like her?* "I don't know." That was the truth. What was also the truth was that until she did decide if she wanted him to like her, she didn't want to blow it.

Grace laid a hand on Jenny's knee and smiled. "Just be yourself."

"I don't know why I'm acting so weird. I guess it's because he's so *not* my type. But, there's something about him, something I can't quite point out, that I find very—" she paused, tried to find the right word, then decided on "intriguing."

"So, what does a woman who finds a man *intriguing* wear on a date?" Grace asked.

"Actually, it probably shouldn't even be considered a date," Jenny said. "He just asked me if I liked Italian food and then he proceeded to name half of the menu at Angelino's. So," she lifted her shoulders, "he was probably just looking for a dinner companion and he figured I was Italian because of my last name and so he assumed I would like—"

"Jenny?" Grace cut her off.

"What?"

There was a firmness in her voice when she said, "It's a date."

"Oh."

"So get an outfit. One that *you* want to wear."

"You think so?" She was eight years old again, kneeling in the dirt, watching Grace push a handmade cross into the black soil of Spot's grave. It was made out of chopsticks, cut in half and held together with masking tape. *Do you think he'll go to Heaven?* she'd asked.

Grace had nodded. *Yes, I do.*

Really?

Really.

It was that way now, as Jenny waited yet again for her sister to nod and say, *Yes. Really.*

"I know so," Grace said, her blue-and-white-bandana-clad head moving up and down a fraction. "Really."

And then Jenny grabbed Grace's hand and let the warmth flow through to her. Even now, in her weakened state, she could still give Jenny strength. And Jenny wanted more than anything to be able to give it back to her.

"I've missed you so much," Jenny said, blinking hard.

"I've missed you, too," Grace said.

They were of the same blood, the same family, the same world, and yet, they were so different. And yet, they were sisters. And yet, they were best friends.

"I'll get it." Grace went to the door while Jenny fastened a second gold hoop in her left ear. Just a tiny one, to add a little California flair. She'd decided Grace was right. Tonight was just dinner. So what was the big deal? Underneath that scholarly exterior, Elliot Drake was just another guy.

"Hi, Elliot. Come in."

"Hi, Grace." His voice was warm and sure, like a flannel shirt on a winter night. Jenny felt her breath speed up, come in sharp, little rushes. Inhale, hold. Exhale, *whoosh,* she reminded herself. *Relax. Relax.* She sprayed her new cologne, Simply Lavender, on her wrists, her neck, behind her knees, on her wrists again. Then she capped the bottle and hurried out of the bedroom.

Elliot was standing in the foyer examining a photograph Jenny had taken last year of a butterfly resting on a daisy, the yellowness of its wings the same exact hue as the daisy's center. She'd been so excited about catching the colors and knew this would be a perfect gift for Grace, whose favorite color was yellow. She'd taken five or six shots, perfect, as the butterfly opened and closed its wings, spreading its beauty one second, hiding it the next. When she'd loaded her gear and headed for the car, she'd been so busy envisioning the type of frame she'd use, the blow-up, the matting, that she'd almost stepped on a yellow object by the left rear tire of her car. She'd leaned over, and there, pressed to the road, was a monarch butterfly, one wing crushed, one wing fluttering in the faint breeze.

Was it the same butterfly who moments before had spread its graceful beauty on a daisy? Jenny never knew, never wanted to know. She'd thrown her gear in the trunk and sped off but she hadn't been able to get the vision of the crushed butterfly out of her head. And after, when she'd given Grace the picture, a butterfly lighting on a daisy, that wasn't what she saw; her vision was crushed to the blacktop, one wing missing, one wing fluttering so faintly. That was life, she guessed—one minute, a gift; the next, gone.

"Beautiful picture," Elliot said, turning toward her. He was wearing an oatmeal polo shirt, almost the same color as the pillows in his office, blue Dockers, and brown loafers. *Elliot.* She smiled . . . and held her breath, just a second, as his eyes worked their way from her red-and-black leopard knit top, past her calf-length black skirt with the thigh split, which he noticed, to the black, strapless heels.

"Jenny," he said in a tone that made her feel drowsy and wired, all at the same time. "You look . . ." he paused.

Damn. Here it comes. Here it comes. And Grace said he was taking me out and not my clothes. Jenny shot her sister a look that told her what she thought of her advice. She should have worn the funeral attire, or maybe . . .

"You look wonderful."

"What?"

His lips curved into a slow smile. "You look wonderful, Jenny."

"Oh." *Oh.* "Thank you," she managed, certain her face was two shades darker than her top.

"I brought you something," he said, holding out a single

lavender rose wrapped in white ribbon with a tuft of baby's breath nestled in between.

"It's beautiful," she said, walking toward him.

"It reminded me of you." His fingers brushed over hers as he handed her the rose. "It's a Sterling rose. Very rare. Difficult to grow." They were close, very close. "It requires careful handling and unlimited patience. Most people won't waste their time on something as eccentric as the Sterling." His voice dipped. "But for those who do, the payoff is incredible."

Jenny swallowed, unable to find a single word in her expansive vocabulary to respond. A burst of feeling pounded against her rib cage, hard and strong, but it had no name. Elliot's words weren't laced with the usual carefully hidden sexual innuendoes of a first date. These were so much deeper, almost ethereal, saturating her brain, touching her soul.

He'd said the rose reminded him of her. *Very rare. Very difficult to grow. But the payoff is incredible.* That's what he'd said.

How? she wanted to ask him. *Tell me how it's incredible. Tell me more. Tell me everything.*

Instead, she barely fumbled through a simple, "Thank you." His smile deepened and Jenny felt something pulse deep inside. She looked away.

"Our reservations are for seven-thirty," he said. "Are you ready?"

"Uh . . . sure." She turned to Grace, took a quick sniff of the rose, and handed it over. "Would you mind?"

"Of course not," Grace said. "Have a great time."

Jenny didn't miss the way her sister's eyes shimmered when she looked at her. She gave Grace a quick hug and followed Elliot out the door.

She'd taken less than five steps when she stopped short and stared at the vehicle parked in the driveway. "Elliot?"

"Hmmm?"

"What is that?" Jenny pointed to the huge black-and-silver motorcycle parked in the driveway.

"It's a Harley-Davidson. Soft tail."

"I *know* it's a Harley-Davidson," she said. Of course she knew. She'd had a boyfriend a long time ago who owned one. *But Elliot?* What was *he* doing with one? He was a psychologist, for heaven's sake. He shouldn't be driving one. She pictured him behind the wheel of something reliable, secure, like a Buick, or maybe an Oldsmobile.

"Have you ever been on one?"

"Yes. Several times," she said, eyeing the black monster.

"I thought it would be a great night for a ride." He looked at her outfit and frowned. "I think you could ride like that, but if you're uncomfortable, you can change."

"Elliot?" She tried to keep her voice casual. "What are you doing with a motorcycle?"

He grinned. "Driving it whenever I can."

She shot a quick glance at the orange-and-white emblem on the side. He didn't look like the biker type; maybe if it were something a little tamer, say a BMW or a Honda, then it would all seem more plausible. *But a Harley?* "I just hadn't pictured you with something so," she paused, searching for a word that fit her confusion, "unconventional."

His lips twitched. "Sometimes I like unconventional, Jenny," he said.

"I guess," she said, frowning. Elliot Drake on a Harley? That was almost like seeing Mother Teresa in a miniskirt. The visual didn't work. At least not for her. They say there are always two sides to people: the one they let the world see and the one that's hiding underneath.

"Jenny, if it makes you that uncomfortable, I'll go home and get the car."

She looked at him. "What kind is it?" Buick or Olds? She'd bet the Buick.

"A Volvo station wagon."

Wrong, but right. Volvos reminded her of staid, comfortable individuals, men and women who wore oxford shirts with tiny stripes and scuffed loafers without socks. They had portfolios and brokers. And real estate. And interchangeable first and last names like Elliot Drake. Or Drake Elliot. Elliot was a Volvo man.

So, what in the heck was he doing driving a Harley?

"If you're uncomfortable with the bike," he said again, "we'll stop by my house and I'll get the wagon."

"I'm not uncomfortable with the bike," she said, avoiding his gaze.

"Okay, then what is it?"

"I'm uncomfortable with seeing *you* and the bike. The Harley," she corrected. "Together." There. She'd said it.

"Doesn't fit my image?"

Now they were getting somewhere. She'd been wondering when he'd start using psychology to figure this out. "No," she let out a shaky laugh. "It doesn't."

"Because guys who have Harleys are all long-hairs who wear black leather?"

"Pretty much."

"Lots of braided ponytails and bushy beards?"

"Right."

"And most have a road map of tattoos running up and down their beefy arms?"

"Most." Except for Ronnie, who'd been afraid of needles. She'd never told anybody, even after they broke up. It was better just to let everyone believe what he'd told them: he didn't want anything to mess up the natural lines of his biceps.

"They travel in groups with rough-looking blondes hugging their waists?"

Jenny laughed and looked at him. "Sometimes."

He was watching her and he wasn't smiling. "Their

mouths are dirtier than an outhouse after a camping week-end?''

She scrunched up her nose. ''How visual.'' She shook her head, flicked a wisp of hair off her shoulder. ''Not all are that way. Some are really nice. They're just into their bikes.'' Ronnie was like that. He'd loved being part of the group, loved the freedom of hopping on his bike with nothing but a pair of underwear and an extra T-shirt in his backpack and taking off down the highway, part of a caravan, like a winding black centipede inching along the open road. He'd loved the feel of the bike purring under him. Loved it so much . . . almost as much as he loved her. And Jenny, well, she'd *loved* his friends, but she'd only *liked* Ronnie . . .

''And you don't think someone like me could get into a bike like this?'' he asked, crossing his arms over his chest. His polo shirt pulled over his biceps and Jenny thought she saw a thin line of blue underneath his right sleeve. A tattoo? Of course not. *Of course not.*

What could she say? The truth? *No, I really don't think so. You seem more suited to something with doors and automatic windows. The deluxe edition package, maybe. Plush seats, climate control, CD changer.* Even she wasn't that bold, so she simply shrugged. ''I can picture you in a Volvo,'' she said, skirting the question.

A faint smile stole across his lips. ''Didn't your mother ever teach you about judging a book by its cover?''

Chapter 16

"My mother always says real Italians do not use a spoon to twirl their spaghetti," Jenny said, turning her fork sans spoon, three full rotations. A mountain of linguine clung to the fork, extra sauce dripping back onto her white plate.

Elliot paused and looked at the spoon in his left hand. "Then I guess it's a good thing I'm not Italian," he said and proceeded to wrap spaghetti around his fork with the assistance of a spoon.

"You are lucky," she said, smiling. "Your non-Italian orientation would exclude you from my mother's tongue. But, she would then spend the rest of the evening persuading you to put down your spoon and 'do it like an Italian.'"

That made him laugh. "What else does your mother say?"

Jenny finished chewing and thought about his question. Hmmm. It was a loaded cannon, aimed and ready to explode. On her, if she weren't careful. What to say about her mother? What *not* to say about her mother was the more appropriate question. Words alone could never describe her or their relationship. She tore off a chunk of bread, dipped it in the plate of olive oil and crushed black pepper and watched the bread turn pale gold. Straight to the arteries, no pit stops. Of course, olive oil was supposed to be healthy, but probably two to three tablespoonfuls, not two to three cupfuls. She flicked her wrist, shook a few droplets of oil off. "My mother says a lot of things," Jenny said, concentrating on the few specks of black pepper that clung to her bread. "She never stops saying a lot of things. There's always some lesson, built in, just like automatic sprinklers that come on at the same time every day whether you need them to or not."

Elliot reached over and touched the back of her hand. "It sounds like your mother isn't your favorite subject."

She shook her head, kept her eyes on the hunk of half-soaked bread. "No, she's not."

"Do you want to talk about it?" His voice was warm and soothing, like chamomile tea on a rainy night.

"No," she said. "No." She didn't want to talk about her mother. What was left to talk about? The story of the two of them was age-old with chapter after chapter of disjointed miscommunication, filled with bitter accusations and crushing disappointments. Worst of all, it just went on and on. Kind of like the last part of a prayer Jenny used to say as a kid. *As it was in the beginning, is now, and ever shall be, world without end. Amen.* That summed up the relationship she had with her mother. And there really was no *end* in sight.

"Okay," he said. "But if you ever do—"

She cut him off. "Did Grace tell you anything about me and my mother?" She wouldn't put it past her to try and weasel in a little bit of time for Jenny during her session with Elliot. Grace the do-gooder, always making sure everyone else was taken care of, busy mending those fences with her double-duty wire.

"No. She didn't say anything."

He seemed sincere, but then again, he was a psychologist, so he would know what "sincere" looked like, even if he weren't, wouldn't he? She tore into a piece of oil-saturated bread, dipped the crust in more olive oil, swirled it around, and thought of death by hardening of the arteries. At the moment, it was preferable to another altercation with Virginia Romano.

"Why don't we change the subject, Jenny."

She nodded, chewing. Changing the subject was a great idea. Only, she knew that Elliot would not forget these past few minutes. He was a psychologist. It was his job to analyze behavior. He'd probably catalog her reaction and responses about her mother and when he got back to his office, maybe he'd pull out his big, black medical book and flip through diagnoses until he found one that suited Jenny. Schizophrenic? Psychotic? Paranoid? Those were the only three psychology-related medical terms she knew, but she was sure he already had something in mind.

"I'd like to talk about Sydney," he said.

Jenny choked, coughed, spit up a tiny bit of black pepper. She grabbed her water glass and took a healthy swallow. Oh God, the subject material was going from bad to worse. "I can explain," she said. But she couldn't. She knew she couldn't. And she knew he wouldn't understand. Parents didn't take too kindly to other people scolding their children.

Elliot held up a hand. "Thank you," he said.

"Thank you?" It came out like a squeak.

He smiled and nodded. Jenny liked the way the red-stained glass lamp threw a faint cast on his hair, softening the black, accentuating the gray. She'd never dated a man with any gray on his head. Then again, who really knew? Many of the men she'd dated before would have pulled, plucked, and colored at the first sprout of gray, but not this man. He'd probably never even considered it.

What was she thinking? She wasn't *dating* Elliot Drake. He wasn't her *boyfriend*. She erased the "boy" part and left "friend." Better. They were bordering on friends, hovering at the fringes. That was enough for now.

"Yes, thank you, Jenny. She's been talking about you nonstop."

Jenny swallowed. Either he was quite adept at sarcasm or very misinformed. "Elliot," she said, jabbing at a piece of calamari. It was the one with legs. Her favorite. "I wasn't very . . ." she paused, started over. "We had a kind of . . . disagreement," she finished, her voice tapering down to little more than a whisper.

"I know."

"I said some not very nice things to her. And then I told Eleanor exactly what I thought of your daughter." She stared at the sauce on her plate, waiting. Fathers always protected their daughters. Always. How many times had her own battled her mother? Forty? Four hundred?

"I know."

He was talking but Jenny couldn't hear him. She was too busy forming the words in her mind, thinking about what she would tell him, how to make him understand. She liked Sydney, saw the little girl under the cruel words, even felt sorry for her, but she wasn't going to put up with her meanness.

She looked up and met his dark brown gaze. It was unsettling, really, those eyes that stared at her, into her, through her, as though they could see things no one else could, including Jenny. "I told her I didn't like the way she treated people. Especially Eleanor. She's just plain mean to her." Her voice dipped. "I told her I was sorry about her mother, but that didn't give her a right to act the way she did." That was it. She shut her mouth and stabbed another piece of calamari. She glanced back at him. What was he thinking? He sat watching her, like a hunter staring down the barrel of his shotgun, waiting for just the right moment to pull the trigger. "Sydney told me I was a mean witch," she blurted out, anxious to get it all out in the open, "and I told her that with the way she acted toward everyone, she was the one who was the mean witch." Jenny set her fork down. "I know I shouldn't have said it . . . I know it was wrong, she's just a child, but she *is* mean and everybody lets her get away with it because her mother walked out on her."

Elliot let out a long breath. "You're right."

She stared at him. "I'm right?"

He nodded. "I told you she hasn't stopped talking about you."

Jenny chewed on her lower lip. "What's she been saying?"

He rubbed his chin and said, "Let's see. First she said you were horrible and she never wanted to see you again. That lasted for about two minutes." He smiled. "And then, she fed me bits of trivia about you. Did I know you once rode a camel?" Elliot lifted a brow. *"And* an elephant? I've also heard all about the time you almost got locked in the zoo because you fell asleep in the monkey house."

She lifted her shoulders and shrugged. "I was tired." No one should travel through two time zones and then spend ten hours at a zoo.

"Or asphyxiated from the smell."

Jenny hazarded a smile. "What else did she tell you?" It was a tentative question. If she'd known Sydney was going to repeat everything she told her, she would have been more careful about what she said.

"She mentioned something about a horse throwing you to the ground." He coughed into his hand, tried to hide a smile. "Said you landed in a very . . . smelly place."

"It was smelly, all right," she muttered, recalling the time she went riding in white jeans and a white tank top. Just last year. It was her first experience with a horse and she'd been so impressed with her ability to stay seated that the minute she relaxed, the horse bucked her off, straight over his head, and into a pile of manure; so much for horses and white outfits.

"She seemed especially intrigued with the time you climbed a tree to save a cat."

Oh yes, that would be Mrs. Peters's tabby, Chloe. "I was fifteen, with more heart than brains at the time."

"I think she misses you," he said, lifting his wineglass.

"Yeah, like a boil on her backside."

"No. Like a real person." He paused. "A friend."

Jenny sucked in a deep breath. "What happened to her mother?"

He took a sip of wine and looked into his glass. She waited. He swirled the pink-gold liquid around the sides. When his eyes met Jenny's, they were guarded, careful. "She didn't want to be a mother anymore," he said, as though he was telling her he'd switched from whole milk to one percent. "She wanted to be," he paused, and then pushed it out, "an actress."

An actress? As in Hollywood? As in big screen? She had a million, no, five million questions for him. How did the woman go about telling him she was leaving? Was it heartfelt and painful, filled with tears and longing, or was it abrupt, a flick of her wrist as she walked out the door? Or were they having dinner, maybe sharing Chinese, little cardboard boxes lined up in front of them as they sat next to one another on the floor, knees touching, and in between forkfuls of pork lo mein, she said, "Oh, by the way, I'm heading to LA in the morning. It's been nice." Or was it a long, drawn-out, grievous affair, with Elliot pleading for her not to go, begging her to reconsider as she threw her clothing into a sleek black suitcase. First the silk underwear, pinks and cream with just a hint of lace. Then the hosiery—suntan, earth, taupe, black, and white, followed by five pairs of shoes—three pumps and two flats. All in varying shades of black and cream. When she got to the linen jackets and jersey tops, did he yank them back out and force her to face him? Did he demand answers? Or did he just let her leave, walk away, be done? And when the door clicked shut and she was on the other side, did he ache to pull her back, erase the words, the hurt, try to pretend it never happened?

Jenny blinked twice. An actress. "She sure gave up a hell of a lot."

"She never thought so," he said. "She made a few commercials, did some low-budget films, nothing spectacular. The last I heard she was living in Greece with an oil tycoon twice her age."

"I'm so sorry," she murmured.

He shook his head. "Don't be. Really. Claudia was never the maternal type. I knew that, yet even knowing that, I thought she'd change when the time came." He let out a harsh laugh. "I even thought I might be the one to help her change. Adapt to family life." His brown gaze met Jenny's, pulled her in. "Isn't that ridiculous, Jenny? Here I was, a psychologist, telling people every day that they can't change other people, that they can only be responsible for their own behavior, and then I went and ignored my own advice and actually thought I *could* change her." His mouth curved into a dry smile. "What the hell is wrong with that picture? It's kind of like the plumber who always has leaky faucets, or the accountant who never balances his checkbook. It's all okay as long as nobody finds out about it. You just keep spinning your wheels, trying harder, falling deeper into the hole, telling yourself you can do it . . . and believing you can. Then all hell breaks loose and you're left alone, with a flooded basement or ten bounced checks." He paused. "Or a child with no mother. It's a very humbling experience, actually—makes you much more human."

She nodded, wondering if Elliot's ex-wife—Claudia, he'd

called her—ever tried to contact him about Sydney. Did she think about her when she saw a little blond-haired girl with big brown eyes in a crowd? Or when she was flipping through the newspaper and saw an article about a disease that was crippling or killing children, did her heart beat just a little faster, her mouth go dry? Did she read each word twice, burn it in her memory? Did she even *think* about her daughter? Did she care?

"I've tried to compensate for Sydney not having a mother." He leaned back against the red leather booth and crossed his arms over his chest. "I think I've spoiled her." He looked at Jenny. "Okay, I *know* I've spoiled her."

"I think anyone in your position would do the same thing," she said.

"I know, but it isn't right. It's only going to make things harder for her later on." He gave her a rueful smile. "I do try. Some days, I actually think I'm making progress, that she's listening and absorbing what I'm trying to teach her. And then, there are other days . . ." He let his unfinished sentence dangle in the air.

"She just wants to feel normal," Jenny said in a soft voice, her thoughts rewinding twenty-plus years to a time when she felt very much like Sydney Drake. Oh, her mother might have been there, in the house, every day, cooking oatmeal with raisins in the morning, sprinkling brown sugar over the top and pouring milk so Grace and Jenny could make moats. And she'd washed Jenny's hair in the kitchen sink twice a week with Johnson's Baby Shampoo and then sprayed No More Tears on all the knots before she pulled a pink teasing comb through it. At least once a month, she'd get out a needle and thread to mend the hole in the knee of yet another leotard Jenny had managed to rip.

Jenny saw these visions in her head, memories of her mother, doing, always doing for her, but never *being*. Not the way she was with Grace. And that was all Jenny had ever really wanted from her mother. Just to *be* with *her,* not always Grace.

So, yes, she understood Sydney's pain. Even though the child tried to hide behind cruel words and stony faces, Jenny could see her pain. She knew it. *She'd lived it;* the pain of loss, of wanting and not having, of never being enough. That's how it had been with her mother then. That's how it still was now. They could be in the same room, talking, touching, and still they were worlds apart.

Jenny looked up to find Elliot studying her, probably trying to figure out what was going on in her head. She wanted to tell him that he really didn't want to know; it was too psychotic, too Freudian, probably, but instead, she smiled and took a sip of zinfandel.

He smiled back. "Sydney said Ruby Red misses you."

Jenny opened her mouth and the words came out whisper-soft, like a warm breeze on a summer's night. "Tell her I miss her, too."

It was 1:10 A.M. when Elliot brought Jenny home. He walked her to the door, took her hands in his, and leaned forward, brushing his lips against hers, once, twice, making her body thrum like his Harley, and then he pulled away. She wanted to yank him back, press her lips, her body, against his, tell him not to stop just yet, but instead she stood there, watching him turn away, get on his Harley, wave good-bye.

Elliot Drake filled her senses as she let herself in the house, slipped off her sandals, and padded across the foyer. He was right; she shouldn't judge a book by its cover. There was so much more to the man than horn-rimmed glasses and diplomas on the wall ... so much more ... and she was beginning to realize that she wanted to find out so much more ...

She stifled a yawn, slung her sandals in her left hand, and tiptoed upstairs. That's when she heard the noise—a low, keening sound, coming from the far end of the hall. Grace's room.

Grace! Jenny ran the rest of the way up the steps, down the hall, a million dreadful possibilities racing through her head. She'd hurt herself, fallen down, blacked out. Or maybe she'd experienced some kind of delayed problem from the accident.

"Grace!" Jenny let out a fierce whisper as she opened Grace's door. It was pitch black. She stood in the doorway, listening. Nothing. She flicked on the light.

"No!"

Grace was huddled in the far corner of the room, head bent, an orange bandana lying several feet away, hugging her knees to her chest. Crumpled pieces of paper lay at her feet. "Grace? What's wrong?" Jenny started toward her, wondering what could have happened in the few hours she'd been gone to put her in such a state.

"No!" she sobbed again. "Turn out the light!" She jerked her head up and met Jenny's gaze. The woman staring back at her looked nothing like Grace. This woman's eyes were red and almost swollen shut, her nose puffy, her lips pulled into a straight line. But it was the torment etched across her face that shocked Jenny most.

"Turn it off. Please." Her voice was flat, her words empty.

Jenny leaned over, switched off the light. "Grace?" she said, inching her way forward in the dark. "What happened? Is it the girls?" Fear ripped through her. "Are they all right?"

"Fine," she said. "They're fine. Laura has them."

"Did something happen after I left?"

"Bastard," she whispered. "Goddamn bastard."

Grace never swore. "Who, Gracie?" Jenny asked in the most gentle, reassuring voice she could muster, considering her heart was about to beat out of her chest. Had she taken the pain pills Dr. Shaffer sent home with her? If so, how many? Grace got tipsy on half a glass of wine. Maybe she was having some kind of reaction to the stuff.

"Bastard," she said again, but this time her voice quivered.

Jenny worked her way toward her sister, feeling along the edge of the bed. When she heard her sniff, she knew she was close. "I'm going to sit with you, Gracie," she said, easing herself to the floor in the darkness. She swatted away a few crumpled pieces of paper. One of them got stuck under her foot. She reached for it, felt its glossy edge. It was a photograph. Grace had been mutilating pictures of something. Or someone.

"Just put your hand out so I know where you are," Jenny said. She moved her own hand in the air, sweeping it back and forth until she came into contact with Grace's fingers. "There." She grasped Grace's hand, like a mother soothing her child. "It's okay, Gracie. It's okay."

The tears came then, great sobs that wracked Grace's body as she clung to Jenny. "It's okay," Jenny murmured, stroking her back. "It's okay." How many times had Grace comforted her, held her just like this and whispered these same words? But Jenny's grief was usually related to some wrong committed against her, perceived or otherwise, some misdeed or misunderstanding that revolved around her bruised feelings. But never, not once in all of their years together, had Grace ever come to Jenny for comfort . Until today. Right now.

Something was wrong, very wrong. The key to Grace's pain might well lie on the floor, on the glossy, ripped pages of the balled-up photographs. Jenny had to see what they were, what image or images could make a person like Grace lash out with such malicious intent and cause such destruction. Reaching out, Jenny felt around for one of the pieces of photograph and pulled it into her hand.

After several more minutes, Grace's sobs dwindled to an occasional hiccoughy sigh. "Grace," Jenny murmured, "I'd like to turn the light on and talk to you now."

Grace sniffed again and eased out of Jenny's embrace. "I'm okay now," she said. "I'm fine. Just a little . . . overwhelmed, I guess."

"Let me turn on the light," Jenny said, scrambling to her feet. "I'll get the one on your nightstand." *Whose picture have you annihilated, Gracie?*

"I think I'd rather just be alone," she said. "I'm fine now. Really."

No way. "I'm not leaving you now," Jenny said, flicking on the small bedside lamp with the rose-colored shade. "Not until I find out what's going on. If you'd found me like this, you'd be making me spill my guts."

Grace shook her head, pressed her fingers against the bridge of her nose. "It's not the same. This is . . . this is . . ." her voice trailed off.

"What?" Jenny asked, making her way back over to Grace. Her gaze caught a splash of black-and-white on the edge of a torn photo. She knelt down and picked it up, slowly smoothed it out. It was a half-picture of Grace on her wedding day, looking beautiful and very much in love. She was smiling at someone, presumably Grant, but nothing more than a hand remained in the picture. The rest had been torn away, severed, ripped in half.

Jenny picked up another photo. It, too, had been brutalized, husband and wife badly mangled. A third did have the couple holding hands but Grant's head was missing. Jenny looked at her sister, whose head was buried once again in her knees.

"Gracie? What's going on?" She put a hand on her sister's arm. "Tell me."

"Why?" she moaned. "Why did he have to . . . ?"

Why did he have to die? Jenny wanted to tell her that she was better off with the slime-bucket dead, rotting in hell, where he deserved to be, but Grace was grieving and that wouldn't solve anything. She'd loved him, loved him still. He was the father to her children. Jenny sucked in a breath and said, "I know how much you loved him. And I'm sorry." *Sorry that you had the misfortune to care about somebody who used you.*

Grace's shoulders started to shake with new tears. Jenny sat there, helpless, watching her sister shrink away and curl up like a flower that's seen its last bloom. Jenny had to do something, say something. "Oh, Gracie, *please* talk to me."

Maybe it was the pathetic sound in Jenny's voice or her desperate plea that got Grace's attention. It didn't really matter. All she cared about was that Grace had heard her and had started to inch her head up, not even trying to stop the tears that rolled down her cheeks. Her brown gaze met Jenny's and once again, there was pain and torment there. "I . . . did . . . love him," she said.

Jenny nodded, tried to smile. "I know," she said, pushing back the bowling ball in her throat to get the words out.

"And now," she gave a deflated sigh and leaned against the wall, closing her eyes, "I hate him."

Chapter 17

Jenny blinked. "What did you say?" she asked, leaning forward a little.

Grace's eyes fluttered open and she stared at Jenny. Her voice was flat, hard. "I said I hate him."

She said she hated him. No, Grace loved him. She'd always loved him. Always. Ever since they were freshmen in college. Jenny was the one who hated him.

"Grace?"

Grace let out a little laugh that died a second after it left her lips. "I loved him with my whole heart," she said. "With every part of me. I would have done anything for him." Her voice dipped, scraping the depths of her agony. "And now, I can't stand to hear his name."

"What are you talking about?" Jenny asked, settling down next to her. Tiny prickles of dread inched up her spine. She had this horrible feeling . . .

"He had a girlfriend," Grace said, tossing the statement out as though she was telling her he wore a size 12 shoe.

Casual. Matter-of-fact. "She was a brunette." Her shoulders lifted in a little shrug. "Long, black, curly hair, kind of like yours. I always did think he liked long hair better." Another half-laugh slipped through her lips. "I wonder what he'd think if he saw my hair now."

She knew. She knew about Heather Eastman.

Grace reached up and patted her spiky head. "It doesn't matter. He'd lie to me anyway. Just tell me something so I would believe he really cared." She swiped a hand over her eyes. "At least I don't have to worry about that anymore."

"How . . . long did you know?" Jenny asked, still dazed by her confession.

"Which time?"

Jenny thought she was going to be sick. Her whole world started spinning, swirling out of control. She tasted the aftermath of her food working its way up her throat. *Oh, my God.* "There was more than one?" She pressed her fingertips to her temples and started massaging in little circles.

"Oh, yes," she said. "There was another one, three years and four months ago. Her name was Lisette, but I never actually saw her."

How could this be happening? How could Jenny be sitting in the dark, in the corner of her sister's bedroom, listening to Grace confessing her husband's infidelities? Jenny swallowed twice, trying to work up enough saliva to speak and push her half-digested food back where it belonged. By the third attempt, she managed to croak out a few words. "Why didn't you tell me?" That's what she really wanted to know. Why didn't her own sister tell her that her world was crashing in around her? Why did she let everyone continue to believe that everything was fine? Wonderful? That she had a perfect marriage?

A perfect husband?

A perfect life?

Why?

Grace balled her left hand in a fist and held it over her knee. "How was I going to tell you, Jenny?" she asked, her voice rising with each word. "What should I have said? My husband's sleeping with another woman, please pass the ketchup?" She blew out a long, heavy breath. "Natalie was two years old when I found out about the first one. Danielle was only five. I thought about leaving him then, I really did, but I just couldn't. Not yet." She closed her eyes and when she spoke again, her words were soft and hypnotic, as though she were reading a story from a book. "I used to tell myself I stayed with Grant because the girls would be devastated if we split up." Her lips curved into a faint half-smile. "But that's not the whole truth. Not really."

She paused, went on, *"I wanted the dream,"* she breathed, "white house, picket fence, children, and a man who couldn't live without me." A low moan escaped her lips. "I wanted it so bad that I was willing to do just about anything to get it. We never talked about the affair after that first night when I found out. It was something we agreed on. Start fresh, don't bring up old hurts. New beginnings. I read every book I could get my hands on about putting the spark back in your marriage. *Love and Marriage Can Equal Great Sex. How to Pleasure Your Mate. Keep the Love Alive.* You name it, I read it. I even planned little romantic meals, wore red lipstick. Grant seemed to want to try, too. He came home with flowers and cards and a diamond-and-ruby bracelet. And they were beautiful and I was touched."

A single tear fell down her pale cheek. "But I could *never* erase the image of the letter she wrote him, every graphic detail of their last sexual encounter, what they did, what she was going to do to him the next time they were together. It was branded in my brain, like Lady MacBeth and that damnable spot of blood. Weeks could pass when I didn't think about it and life would be almost like it was before and then something would happen that would bring it all back, like one of those zoom lenses on your cameras. It could be anything. Maybe, Grant was running late or the woman in front of me at the checkout counter was young and attractive and I'd think, *Is that what she looked like? Is that her?* Or the new bank teller's name was Lisa, reminding me of Lisette. One little, insignificant event would start off a whole chain reaction that plummeted me into days of depression.''

Another tear fell and then another, sliding down the path from cheek to chest. "And not once," she said, her voice cracking, "did we discuss it. Not once.'' She pressed her fingers on either side of her nose.

"I wish you would have talked to me," Jenny said. "Just tried. It wasn't right for you to keep it all inside.'' She laid a hand on Grace's knee. "No one should have to live like that.''

Grace shrugged. "I couldn't talk to anyone. That would have meant admitting we had a problem. I ... I just couldn't.''

"I know," Jenny said, but she didn't know. Not really. Actually, not at all. Everyone was used to Jenny with her multitude of problems. It was natural, even normal, to see her dangling from some crisis line or other, albeit usually minor but blown up larger than one of Jenny's 16x24 glossies. Even Gerald and Stefan had taken to questioning her about her latest turmoil, whether it be something as aggravating as lost luggage in Bangkok or a little more significant, like a blind date who turned out to be a cross-dresser. It was always something, and it was always happening to Jenny. Grace said it was because she plowed forward, feet first, jumping into every situation without testing the water and worse yet, most times, not taking time to make sure there was even any water to jump into.

Well, Grace was probably right; Jenny did tend to be a bit impulsive. And that impulsiveness did sometimes create "situations" that needed to be resolved. That's when she called her sister or visited Stefan and Gerald—to hash out a plan, devise a bailout program.

But Grace, falling apart, messed up?

"About six months ago, I started to relax a little," Grace said. "I wasn't so paranoid if he walked in the door fifteen minutes late or if I called his cell phone while he was on an errand and that sterile prerecorded message came on, telling me the phone was either off or out of calling distance." She sighed. "I actually started to *believe* him when he said he loved me. I really did. But then one night I woke up around two in the morning and he wasn't in bed." Her voice dropped to a whisper, as though someone were blocking the air in her windpipe. "I jumped up and my heart started racing, and I knew. Jenny, I *knew*. But then I thought I was crazy, because I found him in the study working on a brief. I felt stupid, like *I* was cheating him, cheating both of us of another chance, so I told myself I was going to stop checking up on him, start trusting him. That's why I planned a surprise for our anniversary—lunch and a hotel room. God," she swiped at her cheeks, "what a fool I was."

"Grace—"

"No, let me get it all out, because I don't know if I can do this again. I tried, Jenny, I did. Laura talked me into going to Victoria's Secret and buying a piece of lingerie," she half-choked on a laugh, "so there I was, standing in the middle of Chantel's and then I see them. First, I see Grant and it doesn't register right away, but then I see her, and *then I know.*" Pause. "And she was beautiful, really beautiful."

"Don't do this, Grace, don't torment yourself."

She looked at Jenny, her eyes bloodshot and swollen. "And she looked so familiar, like I should know her from somewhere . . . like I've seen her before . . ."

"Grace—"

". . . and I couldn't take my eyes off of her . . . and then it hit me."

An image of Heather Eastman standing on Grace's front porch, stuffed into a blue jersey dress, flashed through Jenny's head. She sucked in a deep breath, and waited.

"She looked familiar because . . ." Grace met her gaze, her bottom lip quivered, "because she looked like . . . like . . ." her voice dipped to a pained whisper, "you."

"Me? *Me?*" She couldn't have heard that right.

Grace nodded, "She looked like you, Jenny, same hair, almost same-color eyes, tall . . . gorgeous . . . I saw her."

So did I, Jenny wanted to say. *But me?* Well . . . maybe . . . *maybe* . . .

"I always knew he thought you were beautiful," she paused, swiping her cheeks. "I remember the first time he came home with me from college. Remember? He couldn't stop telling me how stunning you were, how . . . exotic . . . even though you were still in high school."

I don't want to hear this, I don't want to hear this.

". . . and later, when you were always flitting off to Europe or some other adventure for your photo shoots, he used to comment on your Bohemian lifestyle, your 'wild side,' as he called it. He acted like he didn't like it, as though he thought it was inappropriate, but deep down, I think he did. Sometimes, he'd say, 'You should be more like Jenny. You don't see her cowering in the corner, afraid of her own shadow, do you? She hops planes to Athens, or London, and you,' he'd say, 'you won't even take an overnight trip in a car.' "

"Oh, Grace, I'm sorry, I'm so sorry."

"Maybe he was right," she said. "Maybe I was just too afraid to live my own life, afraid to make a mistake. Maybe that's why he found somebody else."

"No, how could you even think that?" Jenny stroked her

sister's hand. "You are so strong, Grace, so confident, in charge—"

"I'm afraid," she interrupted. "That's why I try to control everything, keep it all manageable." She let out a small laugh. "I tried to keep my marriage manageable, too, after," she paused, stumbling over the next words, "after the first girlfriend. But it was all a lie, Jenny, just a lie and sooner or later it had to explode. I should've seen that, should've been stronger, but," her voice cracked, "I really did love him."

"I just wanted to get away. From him. From the memory of her kissing his hand, him touching her hair. From everything. But he kept talking. He just wouldn't stop. And the more he went on, the faster I drove." She dragged her hands over her face as though she were trying to reshape it, change herself into someone else. Anyone else.

"When he told me he loved me, I went nuts. I started screaming." Her eyes were squeezed shut and Jenny knew she was reliving that moment all over again. "He grabbed for the wheel and jerked it . . . hard. That's the last thing I remember before I woke up in the hospital.

"This was not supposed to happen." Grace's right hand opened and closed in a slow fist. "I did everything I was supposed to do. Everything." Her shoulders slumped along the wall. "I don't deserve this, Jenny. I don't deserve this."

"I know," Jenny said. Guilt hung over her, pushing her down, trying to steal the air from her lungs. Grace was right. She didn't deserve this. Jenny was the one who'd defied convention, tested boundaries, flipped off rules.

"Gracie—" She felt so helpless, so pained to watch her sister in her private torment. "I'm so sorry. I wish to God it hadn't happened to you."

Grace's lower lip started to tremble. "Why, Jenny? Why couldn't he just have loved me enough not to do this?"

"I don't know, Gracie. I just don't know." Jenny reached

out and drew Grace into her arms and for the second time that night, consoled her as her heart ripped open once again.

"Don't leave me, Jenny." Her shoulders shook. "Not now ... not yet. Please ... please ... Please don't leave me."

"Hello?"

"Elliot? Hi. This is Jenny. I'm sorry to call you so late, but I really need to talk to you ... it's about Grace." She took a deep breath, pushed the words out. "Something's happened. She needs to see you again—tomorrow, if possible."

"What's going on?" he asked. His voice touched her like a fleece blanket on a winter afternoon, wrapped tight and tucked in at the toes.

"Oh, just about everything, right now." She tried to lighten the tenseness in her voice with a quick laugh, but it came out like a squeak. Sometimes humor was best left at the door, especially when there were important issues to discuss. Like how was Grace going to get through her life, hour after hour, day after day, without thinking about her dead husband's betrayal? And what about all the well-wishers? How was she going to look them in the eye, shake their hands, accept their most sincere condolences for the loss of her husband, when what she really wanted to do was scream that he was nothing but a lying bastard and she was glad he was dead? How was she going to do *that* and still stay sane?

"Talk to me, Jenny." She liked the way he said her name, dragging the "n" an extra half-second so it kind of rolled into a lazy familiarity.

She'd promised herself she would protect her sister. She would not betray her, would tell no one about the true state of her marriage or her husband's philandering ways.

Pretend—that's what she would do, pretend they were the happiest, most devoted couple in the neighborhood. No, the city, or maybe the world. She would offer a faint smile and nod sadly when people said it was unions like theirs that inspired love songs and greeting cards.

She would pretend until Grace was strong enough to accept the truth, and then, Jenny would stand by her side, help her face her new life.

Something started clawing at the lies, trying to dig out of the black hole deep down in Jenny's gut, like a rabid beast seeking to escape. Was it the truth tunneling its way to the surface, demanding to be heard? Maybe. She couldn't tell. Not yet.

Truth. Lies. All rolled into one, like the insides of an eggroll; it was hard to pick the tiny pieces of shrimp out of the cabbage, no matter what utensil a person used. After a while, you just gave up and stuffed it all in your mouth because you couldn't tell where one stopped and the other started. Sometimes, that's how little difference there was between a truth and a lie. Sometimes. And sometimes, it was much greater, like the difference between a Java Jolt and a Colombian Decaf. But, Jenny thought, there was no such thing as black and white, split down the middle like a Dairy Queen twist-cone. Half chocolate. Half vanilla. No such thing at all. After the first lick, when the chocolate swirled over the vanilla, it was all the same.

But if she closed her eyes and scrunched down on the floor next to her bed, the feel of thick carpet between her toes and spaces between her words, she could see the truth. It was there, flashing before her in vivid shades of blue and green and yellow. *I will not betray my sister.* She used to believe that meant burying Grant's crime with him and never speaking of it to anyone. Ever. But Grace's knowing changed everything. Her knowing was killing her; Jenny had been witness to it, like an open wound, draining life, one memory at a time. Grace needed help and Jenny was the only one who knew just how much; she was the only one who could make sure her sister got that help so she had a chance of pulling out of the black hole of her life.

"Talk to me, Jenny," Elliot said again.

"It's really bad, Elliot. There are . . ." she hesitated, "things that happened." God, why did this have to be so difficult? Why couldn't that jerk have just kept his pants zipped? Then she wouldn't need to have this conversation. Jenny fished around in her shirt pocket and pulled out a piece of Bubble Yum. Sanity dipped in strawberry. She peeled off the wrapper and popped it in her mouth, savoring the first burst of tangy flavor exploding on her tongue. Relief.

She sighed and started again. "Grace and Grant didn't have the ideal marriage we all thought they did," she said, trying to think of a way to say what she had to say without really coming out and saying it. It was hard referring to sexual things with Elliot Drake. Probably because there was something in the way he'd looked at her tonight, with that intense stare probing, exploring her perimeters, that was almost sexual. Not that it was, but almost. Or it could be. At least from her perspective, but who knew what a man who plumbed people's brains every day would think? Maybe he'd have no perspective, everything would be grossly analytical, and she would be just one more glob of gyrus and cortex or whatever other goop made up the brain.

But Jenny's take on the situation was that talking about sex in a direct or indirect manner, between married or other parties, with Elliot Drake was going to make her turn the color of her very pink T-shirt. At least, two phones and several miles separated them. For that, she was thankful. She cleared her throat and took the plunge. "They had some problems in their marriage. No one knew, but it was bad."

"What kind of problems?"

"The kind that kills a marriage." She chewed hard. "Rips

it apart, sucks out the inside and leaves the shell. That's all Grace had left, just the shell. But she held on because she didn't know what else to do and now I think even that's getting ready to crack.''

"Maybe she did the best she could at the time."

"Yeah," Jenny said, pinching the bridge of her nose. "Maybe she did."

"How can I help?"

"She needs somebody to tell her it wasn't her fault."

"It wasn't."

"Not the accident," she said. "The other. The thing that tore them apart."

"That wasn't her fault, either," he said.

She cleared her throat. "Well, I know. But I think in some way she feels that she fell short—blissful expectations and all that kind of thing. Who would have known twelve years ago that they'd end up like this?"

"There is something to be said for avoiding fortune-tellers and tarot cards."

A little laugh fell out of Jenny's mouth. "And crystal balls," she added.

"Definitely crystal balls," he repeated. His voice was warm and comforting and very masculine. She wanted to wrap herself in his words and listen to him talk as she drifted off to sleep. She could do that, she realized. Drift off to sleep with his soothing tone lulling her through layers of slumber.

"Can you bring her in tomorrow afternoon?"

Jenny lay down on the floor, stretched out, her head resting on the crook of her elbow, a chunk of hair falling over her face, blocking out the rest of the world, blocking out everything but the voice on the other line. "Sure," she said. "What time?"

"Why don't you bring her in around four?"

"Okay. Fine."

Silence.

"Jenny?"

"Yes?"

"Are you all right?" His voice dipped even lower, making her insides do weird little flips.

"Sure," she said. She *was* fine, really.

"If you need to talk, I'm here."

That got her attention. Fast. She jerked up, quicker than a dog who'd just tasted the current in one of those invisible fences. She'd let herself get a little too close to the man, and bam, he'd zapped her. "I'm *fine.*"

"Well, if you ever want to talk—"

A very long pause filled the line.

Then Elliot was speaking. "I was talking about on a personal level," he said in a quiet voice. "As a friend."

She clutched the phone, hard. "You want to be my friend?"

"I'd like to."

"Why?" She brushed the hair out of her eyes and pushed herself up into a sitting position.

He laughed and her insides felt like forty miniature marshmallows melting in a pan of butter for Rice Krispie treats. "Why *what?* Why would I want to be your friend?"

"Right," she said. "Why would you want to be my friend?"

He laughed again and the last of the marshmallows swirled into the others in one white, gooey confection. "Because I've never met anyone quite like you, Jenny Romano."

A little smile snuck onto her lips. "Just friends?" Her mouth went dry. She pictured him sitting in that red leather booth at Angelino's, his long fingers wrapped around his wineglass . . .

There was a part of her that, for some crazy reason, wanted him to say, *Oh, no, Jenny, I want to be much more than friends with you. So much more.* And then there was the kiss, a mere brush of mouths, yet hinting of a deeper longing . . .

But there was another side, the dark, scared side, working faster than ten masons throwing up mortar and brick, that wanted him to say, *Oh, no, Jenny, you could never need anyone. You're so self-assured, so self-sufficient, so self-contained, that I want nothing more than to be your friend.*

This man said neither. He sidestepped the question altogether with, "All great relationships start with friendship."

Okay. Well, there it was, out in the open. They were going to be friends and . . . maybe something else. Or maybe not. Part of her was relieved with his answer—the other part, disappointed.

"Jenny?"

"Okay," she said. "So, we'll be friends." She ran a hand through her hair, her nerves jumping under her skin. At 2:10 A.M. she was suddenly very wide awake. "And you're not going to try and analyze me or play shrink?"

"You give me too much credit, Jenny," he said, and she could almost see him smiling that little half-smile thing he did when he was amused. "Even with all of my education and experience, I doubt I'd know where to begin with you. I don't think anyone's ever figured you out."

Jenny smiled, a very smug smile. "Right you are, Dr. Watson. Right you are."

They both laughed and then he said, "So, I'll see you tomorrow."

"Okay," she said. "Tomorrow."

And then there was a click on the other end of the line and the dial tone humming in her ear. She pressed the "off" button and cradled the phone between her hands. *Something* had happened just now, something between the spaces and words of that conversation. She could feel it, low and hard, thrumming through her body, radiating from her arms and legs, calling her to awareness, seeking her out. She couldn't identify it or analyze it, nor did she want to. But it was there. And now, everything was different.

Chapter 18

"When the hell are you coming back here where you belong, Romano?"

"Joe." Jenny sucked in a deep breath. *Relax, relax.* She glanced at Grace, who was sleeping in the recliner. "I was just getting ready to call you."

"How about that? *You* were supposed to call me two days ago."

"I know, I know." She lowered her voice as she made her way into the kitchen, out of earshot. "I'm sorry—something came up."

He blew out a long breath. "So? I'm waiting."

"Well," she looked out the kitchen window, settled her gaze on a lilac bush. "It's Grace." How to tell him her sister was falling apart, one memory at a time, because of an unfaithful husband? "She's having a really tough time adjusting to her husband's death."

That part was true, but what was even truer was the fact that Grace couldn't adjust to the death of her dream, her fairy tale. *That* was the death that tore her apart, made her stare straight ahead, listless.

"What are you saying, Romano?"

Jenny took a deep breath. She *needed* this assignment; it would gain her much-needed credibility after the debacle with her last job, and it would earn her the respect she deserved. Grace would never want her to turn down this opportunity. She'd tell Jenny she'd only begged her to stay the other night because she was beside herself, that she'd be fine, really. Grace would tell her this even if it was a lie.

That was just Grace, always thinking of everyone but herself, so unlike Jenny, who always thought of herself before everyone else.

Jenny said, "Is there any way we can postpone the trip a few more weeks?" Maybe, maybe in a month Grace would be doing better, more like the old Grace.

"Jesus, I can't wait that long. You know this business—postponing deadlines is like committing hara-kiri. I need you on that plane, next week."

"I can't leave her, Joe." The words fell out of her mouth, a promise to her sister.

"You can't leave her," Joe repeated, his voice filled with disbelief.

"I'm sorry, Joe. I really am. I have to stay here and take care of Grace. She needs me now."

"*I* need you, Romano. You're the best damn photographer I have and I need you for this shoot."

"I'm sorry, I can't." She wasn't leaving Grace for three weeks.

He swore under his breath. "Ah, Jesus." Joe paused. "When are you coming back? You know this business, it's run on deadlines. I start missing them and we're out of business."

"I know." She rubbed the back of her neck. She *did* know; she also knew that she might have just blown the biggest opportunity of her career, but she *wasn't* leaving Grace.

"So, when are you coming back here where you belong, Romano?"

"I don't know Joe." And it was true, she didn't know. "I owe my sister."

There was a long pause at the other end of the line and then Joe said, "Can you get away at all? A day or two, tops? I've got a shoot in D.C. If I send Gravitz to Italy, I need somebody to handle it."

"D.C.?"

"Yeah, big white building, you know the place?"

She ignored his sarcasm. "When?" The extra money would help and maybe Laura could manage things for two days . . .

"Next week. Tuesday, Wednesday. It's not anywhere near the scope of Italy, but it's a paycheck."

"Yeah, I could use one of those." But Grace . . . would she be okay, would she think Jenny was deserting her?

Joe's rough voice interrupted her anxieties. "We're doing a story on five senators and their families."

"Oh." Laura could keep the girls during the day while Grace rested . . .

". . . feature stories on the families. One has a kid in rehab. Another has a daughter being treated for bulimia. And, another has a grandchild who's been diagnosed with ADHD."

"What?"

"You know, Attention Deficit," he said. "When the kid can't sit still."

She rubbed the back of her neck. "And these people have all agreed to these stories?"

There was a long pause. "Sort of."

"Meaning?"

"They'll tell *their* stories and we'll get *our* stories."

No, they hadn't agreed, not really. Probably didn't even know that Joe was only featuring the politicians to get to the meatier subjects: substance abuse, eating disorders, attention deficits. Real issues that mattered a hell of a lot more than balancing the budget or overseas spending. Everybody knew somebody who drank too much, took too many pills, ate too little or too much, or couldn't settle little Johnny down long enough to have him finish his homework. Everybody knew somebody . . .

He cleared his throat. "It might get a little tricky. People tend to guard their skeletons, especially politicians."

"Joe—"

"But the public needs to know these kinds of problems don't discriminate."

"Joe," she said, a little firmer, "who—"

He cut her off again. "Anything else is bullshit, dammit. Just a Band-Aid. But a senator's daughter who pukes up her guts every time she eats, now that's real. And that kind of exposure can help every closet puker across the country. It's a damn national crisis we're dealing with and you can make—"

"Joe!"

"What!?"

"Who's going to talk them into the piece?"

"I'm sending Reynolds. She's young but she can do the job."

"Okay, fine."

"You sure you want to do this?"

"I'll do it," she said, wondering how she was going to tell Grace.

"Be there next Tuesday. Greta will call you with your itinerary. And Jenny," he said, "I'm counting on you. Don't let me down."

The phone clicked in her ear. End of conversation. Possibly, end of her life, as she knew it. *Don't let me down.* Joe's words spun around in her head, faster and faster, until she thought she'd throw up. She sucked in a breath, willing herself to concentrate on nothing but the exchange of air in and out. *Breathe . . . breathe.*

She had to tell Grace. Now. Jenny set the phone down on the kitchen table and made her way back to the living room where Grace was sitting, eyes closed, lips pulled down into a half-grimace.

"Grace?" she said in a soft voice.

Grace's eyes fluttered open. "Oh, gosh, I think I must have dozed off." She let out a big yawn. "What did your boss have to say?"

So, she had been listening, at least to the beginning. Jenny picked up a pillow, pulled a piece of fringe between her fingers, and forced herself to meet her sister's gaze. "He said he wants me to go to D.C. next Tuesday."

"What about Italy?"

Jenny shook her head. "I'm not going. My Italian's rusty anyway, and the showers were horrible the last time I went. You know, rusty water, leaky pipes." She paused, scrunching up her nose, "Poor sewage system."

Grace just stared at her, said nothing.

"It's only for a few days," Jenny rushed on, trying to make it sound like she was taking a trip to the grocery store instead of several hundred miles away. "I'll make sure Laura can cover for me. I'll get the house stocked before I go— Wonder wheat bread, Jiffy peanut butter, two percent milk, Charmin toilet paper—"

"Jenny," Grace tried to cut her off.

"Munchem's, the ranch kind, Kraft Singles, red grapes, and Yoplait yogurt. Any of the reds—raspberry, cherry, strawberry. No strawberry-banana." She sounded like a mouse on speed. "Oh, and Lever soap." She grabbed a pad and pencil from the coffee table and started jotting down the list.

"Jenny, stop."

"Just a minute," she said, adding one dozen large eggs to the list. Was there another margarine in the freezer? Brummel and Brown, right?

"Now!"

Her head shot up. "What?"

"What are you doing?"

"I'm making a grocery list so I can have everything ready before I leave."

"I'm not an invalid, you know."

Jenny nodded, "I know."

Grace leaned over and snatched the pad from her hand. "So, stop treating me like one. Go to D.C. It's okay. I'll be fine."

Grace was right. *She was fine.* Laura called Jenny the first night and told her that she'd taken Grace shopping at the mall—not too long, a few hours—just to look and see if she could find a nice summer outfit, a skirt and top maybe, with a matching scarf for her head. Grace had found four! And then there'd been dinner, and a game of Aggravation with the girls after that, and by nine o'clock, Grace had yawned and said if she didn't get home she'd fall asleep at the table.

The second day had gone much the same as the first, with Laura keeping Grace busy and moving so she wouldn't have too much time to think. Laura just thought Grace's overall quietness was the aftermath of grief over losing Grant. If she only knew . . .

It was Jenny who couldn't stop thinking about Grace, worrying that she might have a relapse and curl up in the corner of her bedroom and hide or, worse yet, curl up in a corner of herself, deep inside, and *never* come out again. But Elliot assured Jenny that she was doing everything she could, they all were, and now, much of what happened was up to Grace.

Elliot. She missed him. Odd, that a person she'd known such a short time could occupy such a large section of her thoughts. He was planning to pick her up at the airport tomorrow afternoon. She'd told him no, she'd driven the minivan and would get herself home, but he said he'd be there waiting for her, by baggage claim. And she hadn't argued—had actually been . . . pleased.

Jenny decided there were three things she really liked about Elliot. Actually, there were about thirty things, but three stuck out above the rest. First, she liked his smile. It was a lazy curving up at the corners, the kind that invited a person to relax and join in. No pressure, nothing forced, just the steady, languorous movement of skin and muscle rolling over and into one another. When he smiled at her like that, her insides turned all gooey, like melted caramel. Oh, yes, she liked that smile.

The second thing she really liked about him was his hands. They didn't fiddle. Unlike Jenny's, that were always in motion, twirling a piece of hair, picking at a hangnail, pulling on pillow fringe, scratching the spot at the base of her neck. Elliot did none of those things. His fingers were strong, capable, devoid of rings, with a faint tracing of hair just below the knuckle. She liked to watch his hands, liked the way he raised them in one fluid motion, graceful and with purpose, not scattered and ill-directed like hers.

She marveled at the way he carried on whole conversations with his hands crossed over his stomach or resting on the arms of his leather chair. How did he do that? she wondered. How? Jenny couldn't say one word, two syllables, without using her hands, or at least her fingers. She swung them in the air, slashed them across, arced them out wide. When she was younger, everyone told her it was the Italian in her, but she didn't think that was the reason because

Grace came from the same mother and father and she was as calm as Elliot.

And then, there was his voice. She thought that was at the top of her list, his voice. It drew her in, soothed her, encouraged her in deep, gentle tones. But it wasn't just the way he said things, it was *what* he said. And what he said to her. The other night, she'd just stuck a second piece of Bubble Yum in her mouth—strawberry, of course—and he'd asked her why she did that. She'd shrugged and tried to pretend it was because she loved the taste, which was true, but not the real reason. He just kept staring at her and she just kept going on and on about how the burst of flavor in her mouth was so exhilarating and did he want to try some? He shook his head and told Jenny just to relax, not be so nervous around him. She'd stopped chewing and held his gaze, feeling like he'd just stripped her bare and could see all of her flaws, from the two-inch scar where she'd had her appendix out, to the annoying, red, blotchy spots at the base of her scalp that required special prescription shampoo to stop the itch. But he went deeper still, past the flesh, into her brain, around her heart, into places she did not want him to see. And yet he did.

She'd been the first to look away. He didn't say anything, no questions, no probes. Just a light touch on the back of her hand that shifted to a gentle stroking, and then he'd lifted her chin with his other hand, his thumb and forefinger holding it steady. She'd met his gaze, saw the longing, the need, in the depths of those brown eyes and knew he saw the same in her own. Her eyes had drifted shut as she waited for the pressure of his lips, remembering the first time he'd kissed her, when he'd taken her home from Angelino's, and wanting to feel that kiss again, wanting *more* than just a kiss. It was inevitable; she'd known it in some elemental way, from the first. His lips brushed hers, once, twice, his tongue tracing her lips, gently probing, seeking. Jenny had moaned when she felt his tongue touch hers, had wound her arms around his neck and pressed herself against the hardness of his body. She'd been hot, cold, shivering, wanting, *needing,* and then he'd pulled away, leaving her dazed, confused, and greatly disappointed. He'd touched her mouth with his fingers, and said, *First, we have to be friends. And that means we have to open up and learn to trust one another.*

She'd swallowed and said nothing.

Open up? Trust?

She'd wondered what that had to do with this *need* pulsing through her body. Jenny only trusted three people: Grace, Gerald, and Stefan. And with that trust came honesty—sometimes, a bit more than they might have cared to hear. Like the time Gerald asked her if she thought his hair was getting thin in the back. Stefan had suggested he see someone about Rogaine treatments because he could see traces of Gerald's scalp. That comment sparked an enormous fight between the two and Gerald demanded that Jenny act as mediator. She did; she told him that when she looked a certain way, she could see gaps, big ones, not just traces of pinkish-white scalp. He'd clamped his mouth shut, stalked next door, and stayed away for three days.

Could she do it? Could she open up and trust Elliot? The only time she'd ever trusted a man in a relationship had been Reed in college and he'd dumped her—said he was looking for someone more "corporate," *more like Grace.*

But Elliot seemed different. Maybe. No, he really did seem different. But it was just too soon to tell. She was touched, in a way, that he wanted to be friends before the relationship could grow into whatever it was going to grow into. Most other men, even the honest ones, would be saying it with their mouths and reaching for her breasts with their hands.

So what if they did get open, share secrets, maybe even fears? Then what? She was leaving in the next month or so anyway, wasn't she? Well, wasn't she? What was the point of getting involved, especially with someone like Elliot, if she weren't going to be around?

Or was that maybe a stall tactic on his part, she wondered. Maybe he wasn't really interested in her in *that* way at all, and he was just being nice, biding his time because he knew she was leaving. *Was that it?*

Oh, God, she was so confused. And there was only one person who could set her straight, be honest, tell her the truth, but she'd cut her tongue out before she asked him. Wait—that's what she'd do, wait. And breathe . . . inhale, hold. Exhale, *whoosh.*

The plane was beginning its descent. Soon, she'd be following the rest of the passengers down the tarmac to the gate . . . and Elliot. He'd be there, waiting for her. Her heart did a weird little extra thump. *Soon.*

She closed her eyes and leaned back. The trip had been a success, despite the initial reservations of the parties involved. But Stephanie Reynolds had gotten the okay for the stories she'd wanted and Jenny had gotten her pictures. It hadn't really even been that difficult. Stephanie had just been honest about what she was trying to accomplish, she hadn't tried to manipulate the truth and bury it under layers of fancy words that didn't bear the slightest resemblance to their real objective, and that had done it.

Jake, the seventeen-year-old in rehab for habitual heroin use, was a sad, pathetic testimony to a young boy whose well-meaning parents never taught him the word *no.* Like so many other baby boomers, the senator and his wife were determined to give their son everything their own middle class upbringing had lacked. Cars, trips to Europe, endless spending sprees. Only, they gave too much, too soon, too often, and Jake ended up with a needle and a spoon and a heroin habit that landed him in an alley, beat-up, naked, and half-dead.

Allison, the bulimic fifteen-year-old, was a sweet, shy girl with big blue eyes and a body that looked like skin pulled over bones. At ten, she'd been a healthy, rosy- cheeked child with dimpled knees and an extra layer of winter protection around her belly. At twelve, the excess was gone and her parents noticed her increasing obsession with the bathroom. By fourteen, her cheeks were hollow, her skin sallow, and she hadn't had a period in months. Allison's parents were shocked the first time the word *bulimia* was mentioned in connection with their daughter. How could a bright, beautiful, popular child who didn't have an extra ounce of fat on her body fall victim to such a degrading disease? They refused to listen to doctors for another year until, at age fifteen, she was rushed to the emergency room spitting up blood.

And then there was Clay, the nine-year-old, redheaded little roughhouse who was diagnosed with ADHD. The senator and his wife had raised five brilliant children who went on to receive graduate and postgraduate degrees from places like Princeton, Harvard, and Rutgers. There had never been an individual on either side of the family who hadn't excelled in academics. *Never.* So, little Clay got labeled uncooperative, undisciplined, and unwilling to buckle down and do what was expected of him when he squirmed in his seat and flicked pencils on the floor. Not until the school psychologist suggested that Clay's behavior might well go beyond stubborn willfulness did the family even consider the term ADHD.

Three separate families, one pain. It tore at hopes, crushed dreams, and ripped expectations back to the most elemental level—survival. These families would need to help their children adapt to a different world—not the one they thought would welcome each of them into its fold, but another, far more essential universe that knew and understood. And cared. Jake, Allison, and Clay's parents and grandparents might feel disappointment, anger, maybe even some shades of resentment over dreams and hopes lying scattered in barren soil. But they would have to push past the selfishness, tunnel through the grief to emerge on the other side, committed to helping these children adjust and overcome their limitations.

Jenny believed they would.

A vision of Natalie crying in the night, clinging to her sister, shot through her head. And Danielle, whose grief had channeled itself through anger directed at Jenny for being the one to tell her she was fatherless. They were only children, trying so hard to adjust to an adult world with adult situations. And then there was Sydney, another victim of an adult's carelessness. Thinking of Sydney made Jenny think of Sydney's father, and just how much she was looking forward to seeing him. She glanced at her watch, took a deep breath. Soon . . . very soon.

Chapter 19

She saw him when she was still a good fifty feet from baggage claim. He was standing off to the side, arms folded, newspaper tucked under one arm, wearing tan Dockers and a navy blue polo shirt. Jenny's heart skipped as she closed the distance and he saw her, his expression serious, searching. And then he smiled.

Jenny moved toward Elliot, pulled by a force stronger than herself, willing her body to his. When she reached his side, she felt suddenly shy, self-conscious, feelings that were as foreign to her as peppermint gum.

"Has it really been only two days?" he said, his voice low, gentle.

She laughed, a nervous hiccoughy sound, as she checked the calendar on her watch. "Yup. It's only been two days."

"I missed you, Jenny."

Oh, God, I missed you, too. She nodded, said, "Me, too."

He took her bag, set it down beside them, took a step forward. "Come here, Jenny."

She took two steps toward him, her gaze never leaving his. This is what she'd been waiting for. *This,* she thought as he wrapped his arms around her, pulled her against him. Their lips met, melded, tongue to tongue, searching, exploring, honoring. She pressed her body against his, close, closer. His hand slid down her back, kneaded the top of her hip.

"Dr. Drake? Is that you?"

Elliot broke the kiss and stared at the sixty-something woman with the pink-rouged cheeks and sweatshirt that said, "Seniors Do It Better." "Mrs. Abblebee." He struggled to regain his composure. "What . . . what are you doing here? I thought you were going to visit your daughter in Arizona."

"I did," she said, "but I came back a bit early." She smiled at him, winked at Jenny. "You know how it is when you miss your man," she said.

Elliot turned a dull shade of red. Jenny felt her own face heat up.

"Who's your lady?" Mrs. Abblebee said, turning to get a better look at Jenny.

"This is my friend, Jenny Romano."

"Your *friend,* Dr. Drake?" She laughed, a tinkling sound filled with years of knowing. "You meant *girl* friend, didn't you? You're a pretty one," she said to Jenny. "Lucky, too. We were all after him, but nobody could seem to land him." She smiled then, a broad smile that showed a mouthful of bridgework. "You take care of him, you hear?" She tsk-tsked. "The girls are going to be heartbroken, Dr. Drake, just heartbroken when they find out you've got a girlfriend."

"Mrs. Abblebee—"

"Ida," she corrected him. "How many times did I tell you to call me Ida?"

"As many as I've told you to call me Elliot," he said, sounding more like his old self.

"Well, in my day, it was a sign of respect to call a doctor a doctor—none of this first name this and that." She waved

a hand in the air. "So, to me, you'll always be Dr. Drake."
Ida Abblebee leaned toward Jenny. "Now, you take care of
this young man, 'cause if you don't, we've got a whole line
of eager females who will."

Jenny nodded, wondering if "the line" was all white-
haired senior citizens.

"Good-bye, Ida," Elliot said.

"Good-bye, *Dr.* Drake." She waved. "Good-bye Dr.
Drake's girlfriend."

Elliot grabbed Jenny's bag and clutched her hand. Then
he turned and said under his breath, "Let's get out of here."
They worked their way to baggage claim, moving fast. They
didn't speak again until they were in his car. "I dropped
the van off at Grace's last night." He gestured at the cream
upholstery of the Volvo. "I didn't think the Harley would
be too practical with your luggage."

"No. Good choice." It was all she could manage. *Elliot's
girlfriend?* Is that what she was? Well, he hadn't denied it,
but he *had* introduced her as his friend. So, what *was* she?
More importantly, *what did she want to be?*

"Jenny," Elliot reached over, took her hand, ". . . I'm
sorry. I didn't mean to embarrass you back there."

"It's okay." What did he mean, the part about Mrs.
Abblebee . . . or their kiss? And who was embarrassed, him
or her? She wanted to know and yet she was *not* going to
ask him.

"No, it was poor judgment on my part. I'm sorry."

"Elliot," she turned to him, unable to keep her mouth
shut. "What was poor judgment?" She felt the heat rising
in her face. "Telling Mrs. Abblebee I was your girlfriend
or the other . . . the kiss?"

He hesitated a second, cleared his throat. "Well, actually—"

She yanked her hand away. "Forget it, I don't want to
know."

"Jenny—"

"I said forget it, really. I don't want to know." She crossed her arms over her chest, staring straight ahead. It felt like college all over again, *all over again,* Reed taking her home to meet his parents and the next thing, *bam*, she got tossed out like day-old Chinese food, soggy carton and all. And now, Elliot was going to try and pacify her, use some psychology on her; he'd be an expert on that, and then, just when she finally let her guard down and opened up to him, he'd inch away, tell her she didn't fit into his "professional" persona. He'd do that, she knew it, so she'd do it first, *before* they got any more involved, *before* they slept together, *before* she fell in love with him.

"Jenny, what are you doing?"

She kept her vision on the car parked in front of them, a black Lexus, shiny, with a sunroof. *Stupid, stupid, stupid*— why did she have to be so stupid when it came to men?

Jenny saw Elliot out of the corner of her eye. He was leaning against his door, arms folded over his chest, watching her.

"Can we please leave?" she asked.

"No, not until we talk."

"I'm not in the mood to talk right now."

"I missed you, Jenny."

She said nothing.

"And all I could think about was touching you, being with you."

Her insides started to heat up, curl into a tight ball, low in her belly.

"God, when I kissed you, I forgot where we were, what we were doing, what I wanted to do . . ." his voice trailed off, ". . . and then Mrs. Abblebee popped up out of nowhere and reminded me that we were in a very public place and I was well on my way to doing some very private things to you."

Like what? she wanted to ask. *Tell me, every detail.* Instead, she said, "Then you weren't embarrassed that it was me you were with or that you'd been kissing me?"

"What are you talking about? Hell, no, it had nothing to do with you—it had to do with me and protecting you, protecting our privacy."

"Well," her heart started fluttering like a balloon blowing in the wind, "it's not like we did anything *that* personal."

"You wouldn't be saying that if you knew what had been running through my mind." His voice was dry, matter-of-fact.

She turned to him then, her breathing coming in short, choppy puffs. "I . . . I just didn't like the way it made me feel, like I wasn't good enough to be seen with you in public."

"My God, Jenny, there's nothing further from the truth." He leaned forward, stroked her cheek. "I'm proud to be with you." His voice dipped. "It wasn't about you at all." His fingers trailed down to her neck, hovered along the opening of her cotton blouse.

She wanted him to touch her, wanted him to . . .

Elliot snatched his hand back. "Christ," he swore under his breath.

"What? What is it?"

He shook his head and raked a hand through his hair. "Do you remember when I told you we needed to be friends, establish trust and honesty before the relationship could go any further?"

"I remember."

"Well, I lied." He met her gaze, his brown eyes almost black. "We've got the friends part down, but the rest, the trust and honesty, we've got a long way to go. We're still feeling each other out, figuratively speaking, and yet, that's all I want to do, literally."

She stared at him but said nothing.

"You're driving me crazy, Jenny. When I'm around you I can't think straight—all I want to do is touch you, get close," his voice dipped, "as close as I can get."

A low thrumming ran through her body. "And that's a problem?"

"Hell, yes, it is. I'm not like that—I've never been like that. I respect women, respect their choices. I'm not the kind of guy who meets a woman at eight and tries to get in her bed at eleven. I like to take my time, understand the situation, analyze it, ponder the possibilities, know what I'm doing and where I'm going."

"So, where are you going with me, Elliot?"

"I don't have a clue."

"That's not always bad, you know ... especially if the woman wants to go there with you."

He smiled at her, a long, slow smile that made her tingle all over. "Truth, Jenny? Truth? Okay. I haven't been able to think of anything but touching you." He trailed his finger along the inside of her shirt, traced the outline of her breast. Her nipple peaked into a tight bud, left her aching, wanting. "Honesty? I couldn't think of anything but touching you." He spread his fingers, cupped her breast. She moaned and leaned forward, trying to get closer. "When I'm around you, I can't think straight ... frankly, I can't think much at all."

"Oh, Elliot ..."

He slid his hand between her legs, pressed his fingers against her, then found her mouth with his. She was drowning, drowning in her own need ... He filled her mouth with his tongue, deep, deeper, she pulled him in, sucking, stroking. She moved her hand up his thigh, cupped his groin, felt the hardness pulsing beneath her fingers.

"Jenny," he broke the kiss, his breathing ragged. "I ... we've got to stop. Let's ... let's go somewhere ... anywhere."

She ran her hands along his thighs, brushed her lips against his ear. "We are somewhere . . . Her fingers moved closer to his groin. "We're here."

He groaned, let out a ragged breath, and caught her hand. "Jenny. Stop . . . just stop . . . go sit . . . over there . . ." Elliot sucked in a deep breath, gripped the steering wheel, and stared straight ahead.

"Elliot?"

"Don't talk, Jenny. Okay? Don't move . . . just give me a minute. Okay?"

"Okay." She leaned against the passenger door and crossed her arms over her chest. "It's hot in here, isn't it?" She undid the top button of her blouse, watching him. His eyes were closed, and he looked like he was meditating, lost in another world. Elliot had just admitted how much he wanted her; the knowledge made her giddy with excitement and, at the same time, powerful. "Whew!" She flicked another open and then another until her white cotton blouse fell away to reveal the thin scrap of silk covering her small breasts. Jenny lifted her right leg, crossed it over her left, hitching her skirt up several inches to reveal a long expanse of skin. There.

She wanted to teach Elliot Drake that sometimes it was okay to lose your self-control; sometimes, it was downright necessary.

"Elliot?" Her voice was low, seductive.

"Hmm?" His eyes were still closed.

"Look at me, Elliot."

He opened his eyes, turned toward her. "Jesus, Jenny!" He leaned over, pulled her shirt closed. "What are you doing?" He tried to smooth her skirt back into place.

"Just showing you the *truth* behind what you've been imagining these past several weeks."

"Cover up, Jenny. Someone might see us." He looked around. The lot on level 6 was deserted.

"They might," she said, shrugging out of her shirt, "and then again," she slid her bra strap down, "they might not."

"What are you doing?" He looked like a desperate man, his eyes burning into her breasts, her stomach, her thighs. *"What are you doing?"*

"Teaching you, Dr. Drake, that sometimes even you need to lose your self-control." She lifted her leg higher, exposing more flesh.

That did it. Elliot fished his keys out of his pocket, turned the ignition, and threw the car in reverse. The Volvo roared out of its parking place and tore through the lot.

Well, so much for teaching Elliot about losing his self-control. The man was made of steel and she'd just made a complete fool of herself. Jenny pulled her shirt together, edged back into her seat, and stared at the arrows in front of her. But instead of going down, they were moving up. What was he doing? Elliot pulled the car out onto the top level, which was deserted except for a white Honda Accord and a green Toyota Camry parked at the opposite end of the lot. He backed the Volvo into the far corner, threw it in Park, and turned off the ignition.

His breathing was heavy, uneven, and when he looked at her his eyes were bright, almost glazed. "So, you want me to lose my self-control. Is that it, Jenny?" His words were low, deliberate.

"I . . . yes."

"Okay." He flipped his trunk open, got out and retrieved a blue-and-green windshield sun screen. "Just remember one thing. You asked for it," he said, positioning the sun saver on the windshield. Their eyes met, held. "I'm very, very close to losing the last ounce of self-control in my body." Elliot opened the back door, climbed in. "Come here, Jenny. Let me show you what happens when I lose my self-control."

Her body was hot, burning. She scrambled out of the front

seat and climbed into the back. He sounded so normal, so in control, and she would have thought he was, except for the twitching on the right side of his jaw. He turned to her, pulled her onto his lap. She straddled him, steadied her hands on his shoulders, moaned when he massaged her buttocks. She was falling apart, one moan at a time. When he suckled a nipple through the sheer fabric of her bra, she let out a cry.

"Oh, God, Jenny," he groaned. "Oh, God." He unfastened her bra, slid it down her shoulders to expose her breasts. His hands palmed them, his lips and tongue moving over each nipple. "I want you." He buried his fingers inside her panties, stroked her swollen flesh. "And that's the God's honest *truth.*"

"Make love to me, Elliot." It was a whisper, a plea. "Make love to me."

The next seconds were a whirl of sound and sensation: a zipper sliding down, a low groan, hard flesh against her fingers, a foil packet, the feel of latex, tongues tasting, licking, pleasuring, and then, when she thought she'd explode with the next flick of his finger, he lifted her by the hips and impaled her.

The joining was furious, desperate, with Jenny moving over him, up and down, her whole body tingling, begging for release. Elliot grabbed her buttocks and guided her, his hips jerking up to meet hers. Their mouths met, their tongues mated, harder, deeper, reaching, touching, body to body, heart to heart, soul to soul, until their worlds fell apart, shattered one stroke at a time, hurling them both over the edge and into a free fall of oblivion.

They dozed for minutes or longer, Jenny didn't know. The sun was high in the sky when she opened her eyes, the world outside of the Volvo a foggy existence, nebulous, unclear. She was still on top of Elliot; he was still inside of her.

He was the first to speak. "You know, there's a bottle of wine chilling in the fridge at home and a blanket on the lawn in the garden." He ran his hand along her arm and she shivered. "I'd planned on a picnic, just the two of us— a kind of welcome home, just for you."

She sighed, snuggled against his chest. "I can't imagine anything better than the welcome home you just gave me," she murmured.

He kissed the top of her head, pulled her to him. "Except, perhaps, more of the same."

They were lying on a green-and-white striped comforter in the backyard, their clothes scattered where they'd thrown them a short while ago. Elliot had stripped Jenny naked, kissed her everywhere: the hollow at the base of her neck, behind her ears, the bend of her elbows, the underside of her breasts, the soft swell of her belly, the inside of her thighs, the back of her knees, her toes . . . And she had flung off his clothes, and done the same. When she found the tattoo on his right arm, a Harley-Davidson emblem, she laughed and kissed it, too.

Their lovemaking this time was more languid, rolling over and into one another, a joining that moved like a dance as they shifted and stroked, sighed and pleasured, one to another, all the time, reaching, reaching, until the final crescendo that left them exhausted yet filled with peace.

Elliot plucked a grape off the platter Eleanor had fixed and eased it between Jenny's lips, his fingers lingering there.

"Remind me never to tell you to lose your self-control again," she said, smiling at him.

"I perform on command, madame."

"And you do it so well."

He leaned over, kissed her. "So do you."

She could stay just like this, basking in the afterglow of

their lovemaking, the sun warm on their backs, the heady aroma of the flower garden filling their senses. Perfect. It felt perfect.

"Jenny, look," Elliot said in a low voice, pointing to a cluster of lavender. "The butterfly, see it?"

"It's beautiful," she whispered. It was indeed beautiful, black with vibrant blue-and-green markings, one that she'd never seen before. She watched as it flitted from lavender to iris to lupine, its wings opening and closing like a fan in a flutter of grace and iridescent brilliance.

"It's a pipevine swallowtail," Elliot said, "I've only seen it in the garden a few times."

"I wish I had my camera." It would be a spectacular shot.

"You, naked, with your camera?" He let out a low laugh. "That *would* be a spectacular shot."

She rolled her eyes. "I meant the butterfly, not me."

"Oh, the butterfly—well, it'd be a good shot, too, but not as great as the one I'm picturing."

She gave him a small smile but her eyes were on the butterfly, trying to figure out a way to capture him on film. Damn, if she could only get to her camera. "I think I'll throw some clothes on and get my camera," she said, as the butterfly dipped to a low-lying rosebush.

"Don't bother. He'll be gone by then."

"I'll hurry," she said, sitting up and reaching for her shirt.

"I've tried it, Jenny. Trust me, he'll be gone—just enjoy him now, while he's still here."

"But—"

As if on cue, the pipevine swallowtail flew to a group of pink lupine, hovered, then lifted, higher, higher, and fluttered away, over the fence.

Jenny sank back onto the blanket, her gaze fixed on the

spot where she last saw the butterfly. "Do you think he'll come back?"

"Maybe someday."

"Did you ever try to catch him?" She could see the picture of the butterfly in her mind, one hundred times more vibrant than the monarch photo she'd given Grace.

"Catch him? He'd die. You can't catch something like that, Jenny." His voice was low, serious, filled with a quiet sadness. "You can't catch a creature like that any more than you can catch a person. You can only create an environment that they might want to live in. That's it. The rest is up to them."

Jenny looked at him, knew by the expression on his face that he was talking about much more than a butterfly. "It's your ex-wife, right? That's who you're thinking about, isn't it?"

He shrugged. "Not really. I'm talking about life and people in general."

"Oh, the old 'If you love something, set it free' thing?"

Elliot smiled at her. "Yeah, something like that."

"I never caught anything long enough to set it free," she said on a half-laugh that sputtered out into silence.

He was watching her, his dark eyes intense. "Why haven't you ever married, Jenny?"

That came out of nowhere. She opened her mouth to throw out a flip answer, tell him she couldn't find a guy with the right highlights in his hair or some equally ridiculous answer, but the words wouldn't come out. *Truth and honesty,* he'd said.

"I almost got married once, in college." She looked away, her eyes on a cluster of lavender. "His name was Reed Maxwell and he was in his second year of law school. I used to sit in the library and write, 'Mrs. Jennifer Maxwell' all over my notebook, in cursive, block, print, curlicues, you name it. I thought he loved me, and I think maybe he really did, but then he took me home one weekend to meet his parents and when we came back, he dumped me—told me he didn't think I'd make a 'good corporate wife,' said I was too Bohemian, too outspoken. And then," her voice fell to a whisper, edged in pain, "then, he asked me why I couldn't be more like my sister, more like Grace."

"He was a fool."

She went on as though she hadn't heard him. "And I think that's what I resented the most—not the fact that he didn't approve of the three-inch hoops I wore or the suede satchel I carried everywhere. It was the comparison to *Grace*, the fact that he made a point of bringing it out in the open, making a statement. 'Why can't you be more like your sister?' I'd spent my whole life hearing my mother say that, wondering it myself, and then to hear it from the man who claimed to love me? For a long time after that, I resented him, and for a while I even resented Grace. I used to do outrageous things just to get a reaction from people, even if it wasn't what I really wanted to do. It was just something I felt I had to do, a way to hold onto my own identity. But sometimes I used to wish I *was* more like Grace. Then I would've married Reed—not that it would've worked, because obviously, it wouldn't—but it would've been my choice and it would've been so much *easier* to be like her."

"And how is she, Jenny?"

"Accepted."

"And you're not?"

She shrugged. "Not always."

"I accept you, Jenny."

She looked at him and there were tears in her eyes.

He leaned toward her, brushed her lips with his mouth. "Never change, Jenny," he whispered. "Never change."

Chapter 20

Elliot lifted an orange dahlia from the plastic flat beside him, plopped it in the hole next to the marigolds. He tamped the ground around the flower in place, whistling as he turned back to the flat.

"Well, well, aren't we in a chipper mood this morning."

He shielded his eyes with his forearm. "Hello, Eleanor."

"And I can tell you, the last one, the biochemist, she never made you whistle like that. No indeed." She waddled toward him, her gray bun flopping with each step. She was wearing a bright green skirt and a white, short-sleeved blouse with stockings and green sandals. He was wondering how someone as round as Eleanor had such tiny feet. Jenny's were long and slim, her toes, delicate . . .

"So, how is our Jenny?"

She'd taken to calling Jenny "our Jenny" to try and give him an extra push in Jenny's direction—not that he needed it, not after yesterday. His pulse started pounding in his ears. God, was he ever going to be able to think of anything but yesterday? Jenny lying naked underneath him, Jenny straddling him, Jenny throwing her head back in ecstasy, Jenny . . .

"Elliot?" Eleanor raised her voice. "How is our Jenny?"

"Fine," he mumbled, turning back to the dahlias. And her touch, soft and gentle . . .

"And?"

. . . and her tongue, oh, God, her tongue . . .

"Elliot Drake, are you listening to me?"

He shook his head, trying to push Jenny and her throaty laugh out of his mind. "I'm listening, Eleanor."

"So, tell me, what did you two do?" She moved so she could see his face. "Did you go to dinner? Talk for three hours?" Her voice dipped. "Stare into each other's eyes? Kiss? Did you kiss her, Elliot, make her all flushed and flustered?"

Flushed and flustered? Now *there* was a question. He cleared his throat and said, "Yes, Eleanor, yes to all of the above."

Jenny had just laid the last bag of groceries on the kitchen table when the doorbell rang.

"I'll get it," Grace said, pushing her chair back.

"You will not. Just sit right there. It's probably some salesperson anyway, and you don't need to deal with that." She hurried out of the kitchen and through the living room, preparing her "Thank you but we're not interested" speech.

Jenny opened the door, and stared. A tall, very handsome man was standing there, holding a huge bouquet of white roses. He had a deep, golden tan and high cheekbones with a straight nose that reminded her of a Greek god. His eyes were silver, shiny like a new coin, and his hair, the color of warm caramel, brushed his shoulders, with golden highlights and a cowlick in the front. He was wearing a black T-shirt with a camel-colored sport jacket, black pants, and black Italian loafers.

"Hi. Is Grace here?" His voice was smooth and velvety, like a fine bottle of chardonnay.

"Uh ... sure. Come in." Who was this man? Correction—who was this *gorgeous* man and why was he holding a mountain of roses?

"Guy!" Grace was walking toward the man, eyes bright, a smile spreading over her lips. "Oh my God, Guy! I didn't know you were back."

The man named Guy was at her side in three long steps, his face filled with concern, his silver eyes on Grace. "I didn't know, Grace," he said, and there was pain in his voice. "I didn't know ..." His words trailed off. He set the flowers down on the end table and pulled Grace into his arms, hugging her. "I'm so sorry."

Grace sniffed, swiped at her eyes. "Thank you. How could you have known, Guy? You were halfway around the world—who would've told you?"

"But I should have been here, the way you were here for me."

Grace smiled and there were tears in her eyes. "I wasn't alone. Jenny was here." She turned to Jenny, who felt as though she was in a play where someone forgot to give her a script and she didn't know who any of the characters were. "Jenny, I'd like you to meet Guy Delacroix. Guy's the art teacher at Keystone Elementary, or was—he took a sabbatical to paint in France. He and I have known each other for years." She extended her hand. "And Guy, this is my sister, Jenny."

He smiled at her. "Ah, the infamous Jenny."

Jenny smiled back. "Infamous? I don't know if I like the sound of that."

He stepped forward and took her hand in his. "I've heard only good things from Grace."

"Of course, I showed him pictures of your condo," Grace said.

"I especially liked the herb garden." He nodded and she saw the glint of a gold hoop in his left ear. "Your designer is quite creative."

"Yes, Stefan does pride himself on his creativity." *Who was this man, really?* Why was he here? Jenny hadn't missed the way he looked at Grace as she walked toward him . . . like a long-lost . . . what? Soulmate . . . friend . . . *more than friend?*

"Come in, Guy. Sit down and tell me all about France."

"First, I want to hear about you, Grace." He touched her shoulder, his voice dipped. "I want to hear how you're doing."

"Well, I think my hair suffered the most," she said with a laugh, patting the pink-flowered bandana on her head. "It's a close second to ground cover."

Guy didn't laugh. "You had beautiful hair."

"It'll grow back." She motioned toward the couch, sat down beside him. "I'm so happy to see you, Guy." She smiled at him. "And thank you so much for the beautiful roses." She glanced at the bouquet behind her, reached out, and fingered a petal. "Now, I want to hear all about France."

"But you—"

"I really don't want to talk about it." Her voice shook, leveled out. "I've lived it every day for weeks. I . . . I just want to let it go, okay?"

He took her hand, smiled. "Sure, Grace. That's fine with me."

Jenny slipped away into the kitchen but neither of them noticed.

For the next two hours, Jenny put away groceries, made hamburger patties for dinner, and stared out the window, reliving every minute detail of yesterday afternoon with

Elliot, down to the whisker burns on her right breast, and wondered about the man in the living room.

She tried to catch snippets of conversation, but aside from an occasional laugh or an, *Oh, really,* Jenny couldn't tell what they were saying and it was driving her crazy. Finally, at four o'clock, Guy Delacroix left.

Grace was just closing the front door when Jenny flew into the living room, flopped down on the couch, and said, "Okay, what gives?"

"Excuse me?"

"You know, the guy. Guy? Who is he?"

"I told you," Grace said, dropping into her recliner. There was color in her cheeks, and her eyes were bright, happy. "Guy is a friend from school."

"Right."

"Grace, for heaven's sake." She shook her head. "His wife and I shared a kindergarten class. I had mornings and she had afternoons. Guy and I became friends when Pam was diagnosed with leukemia." She paused. "She only lived five months."

"I saw the way he was looking at you," Jenny said, crossing her arms over her chest.

"What way? He looks at everybody that way."

"I doubt it."

"We're *friends,*" Grace said. "That's all."

"I'll bet he'd like it to be more."

"Jenny, how can you even talk like this? Grant hasn't been dead—"

"Grant? What's this got to do with Grant? He had a girlfriend, remember?"

"He was still my husband." Grace sucked in a deep breath. "I still loved him."

"I know. I'm just asking about this Guy person."

"This is so silly—he's not even my type."

"Oh? From what I could tell, a man who looks like that would be just about any woman's type."

"He's younger than me."

"Oh?" She raised a brow. "How much younger?"

"He's thirty-two," she said, playing with the fringe on a beige pillow.

"So what's four years?"

"He's not my type."

So. Had she thought about it? *Possibly considered it?* "How do you know that?"

She looked at Jenny. "His hair touches his shoulders."

Jenny laughed. "Oh, my God, Grace. His hair *touches* his shoulders? He should be jailed."

"Oh, be quiet."

"Is his hair length the major reason that you've decided he's not your type?"

"No." She said the word with such authority, such finality.

Jenny waited.

"He," she paused, looked away, "has an earring."

"That's right, I noticed. Which ear was it?" Jenny asked. "Oh, forget that. You can't go by that anymore."

"He's not gay."

"Good. He's not gay, he's thirty-two, gorgeous—let's not forget that—with hair touching his shoulders. And he has an earring. Anything else?"

"No. He's just a really nice guy. That's all. A *friend,* Jenny," she said, "a friend."

"I'll carry the watermelon," Jenny said, hefting it onto the kitchen table with a thunk. "You get the macaroni salad."

"Fine."

Grace had her back to Jenny, staring out the window, shoulders ramrod straight. Jenny glanced at her watch. Laura had expected them at her house fifteen minutes ago. Grace hadn't wanted to go to the block party, had tried every excuse to beg off: she needed more time, everyone would be looking at her, asking too many questions, drawing too many conclusions, her hair was too short, her smile too wobbly, her pain too new.

And she was probably right. But Jenny had persisted, pushing past her initial resistance and convincing her to make an appearance, take a stand, shoulders back, head high, as a woman, alone, yes, but proud and alive. A survivor. She could do it. And Jenny would be right by her side, fighting the inquisitors, warding off the too-curious, spurning the naysayers.

"Are you ready, Grace?"

"Just give me a minute."

Something in her voice caught Jenny's attention. Grace was staring out the window, but her right hand was clutching a wooden spoon, her knuckles white and straining.

"Grace?"

"What?" She tore her gaze from the window and plunged the wooden spoon into the macaroni salad, turning it with quick, forceful strokes. Or perhaps *pounding* would have been a better word. Ten more rotations and they'd be eating mush salad instead of macaroni salad.

Jenny grabbed the end of the spoon. "Stop," she said. "What's wrong?"

"Nothing," Grace said, with about as much conviction as a thirteen-year-old saying he'd rather eat his mother's meatloaf than a Big Mac.

"Come on, Gracie. It's me, remember?" Jenny let out a little laugh. "I'm supposed to be helping you, coming to your aid in time of need and all that, so do me a favor and tell me what's wrong."

Grace turned to her then, a little half-movement, but it was enough to see the agony carved out on her face. "Oh,

Jenny,'' she said, her voice raw with pain, ''I don't know if I can go through with this.''

Jenny touched her sister's shoulder and squeezed. ''Sooner or later, you have to, Gracie. I'll help you.''

''But all those people,'' she breathed. ''Laura said most of the neighborhood would be coming.''

''What better time to show everybody you're alive and well?''

''Look at me,'' she said, swinging around to face Jenny. ''Look at me! I'm pitiful. No, I'm more than pitiful. I'm pathetic.''

Jenny looked at her sister, tears shimmering in eyes the color of molasses, and thought she was beautiful. But then she'd always thought that, ever since they were kids. Not in the classic lines and shapes that people write about and magazine covers try to enhance as angular, hip fashion, but a soul-deep, connected, luminescent type of beauty, the kind that touches you when she smiles and makes you say, ''Ah, yes!''

''I think you look beautiful,'' Jenny said. And she did. Not quite the same as before, because her hair was clipped and covered with a burgundy bandana. But there was something else, something deeper than the mere visual that changed her appearance. Maybe it was vulnerability, hovering just below the surface, spreading through her into her smile, her eyes, her fingers. Spreading everywhere.

''Haven't you noticed the way I tremble sometimes?'' Grace asked, a tear spilling down her cheek. ''For no reason?'' She held out both hands, palms down. ''I think of the accident, of what happened, and it starts.'' Her eyes grew wider. ''And even when I force myself *not* to think of it, I still feel my body shaking.''

Maybe Jenny had seen it once or twice, a fine shiver running over her that she'd attributed to cold or maybe a split-second recall of the accident; either way, it was fleeting and Grace never mentioned it. Neither did Jenny.

"I wake up in the middle of the night and I'm soaking wet," she said. "Elliot tells me it's anxiety." She laughed, a brittle sound filled with despair and betrayal. "Anxiety, Jenny. Think of that."

"I'm sure it's normal, Gracie," Jenny said. "You've been through a lot."

"Normal?" She swiped at a stray tear. "Normal? Nothing will ever be *normal* again." She shook her head and sniffed. "Not for me."

Jenny rested her hands on her sister's shoulders, met her gaze. "Then you'll do the best you can," she said, giving her a gentle squeeze. "You *will* get through this."

"I'm so tired." Grace closed her eyes. "So tired of pretending. I just don't think I can face everyone today. They'll all be telling me how sorry they are, what a wonderful couple Grant and I made, how tragic and pointless it all is." She drew in a deep breath, held it a second, blew it out. "And I'll have to just stand there and nod and smile, when all I really want to say is what a cheating, lying bastard he was and how I'm better off without him." Her eyes flew open, and she met Jenny's gaze. "I'm glad he's dead, Jenny," she whispered. "Isn't that horrible to say about the girls' father?"

Jenny shook her head. "No, not considering the circumstances." Or the fact that if he weren't already dead, Jenny would have killed him herself—after she'd castrated him, of course.

"I feel guilty," she said, swiping at her eyes. "I should put it all behind me, go on. Maybe even try to forgive him. I know that's what I should do. I know it's the healthy thing to do. Mentally, physically, emotionally." Her lower lip started to quiver. "But God, you have no idea how I hate him."

No, Jenny didn't know. If it was her, she'd still be plotting revenge, even though he was six feet under.

"Hate is so insidious. I know that. And yet, I can't seem to help myself."

"I know."

"But Elliot says that there will come a time when I have to choose between feeding the hate or living my life."

Jenny chewed on her lower lip, thought of Elliot. "I think he may be right," she said.

Grace nodded and her eyes welled up again. "But not now. Not yet." Her gaze shifted to the refrigerator. Jenny's followed. There were three magnetic picture frames trimmed in white daisies, lined up on the white door just below the Frigidaire logo. Inside the cut-out vinyl frames were three smiling faces: Grace, Danielle, and Natalie. There had been a fourth frame, next to Grace's. Jenny had noticed it the day she arrived, the day Grant died. Now, it was gone, all traces of its existence erased, a sad testimony to love, marriage and the age-old institution known as family.

Twenty minutes later, Grace blew her nose, splashed water on her face, and picked up the glass bowl of macaroni salad covered with green plastic wrap. Ten minutes after that she followed Jenny, Danielle, and Natalie down the street to Laura and Hank's backyard, the central food drop-off and grilling location. They'd just deposited the macaroni salad and watermelon on one of the long red-white-and-blue-paper-covered picnic tables when Jenny heard a familiar voice.

"Grace!"

Samantha Steward's voice reached them a full five seconds before Jenny saw her. Even the sound of Clint Black on the outdoor speakers didn't diminish her distinctive shrill.

"Grace!" she called again.

Jenny looked to the left, and saw her big, gold hoops dangling as she made her way toward Grace like a hawk swooping down on its prey. "You look wonderful!" She leaned over and kissed the air near Grace's cheek.

"Thank you," Grace said, running a hand over the back of her head. Once, twice, three times.

"I mean it," Samantha said, her white smile gleaming between bright red lips. "Even with the new 'do,' " she gestured to Grace's scarf-covered head, "you look just great."

Grace nodded, her lips turning up into a faint smile.

Samantha turned. "Jenny, nice to see you again. Been planting any more flowers?" It was a simple question, innocent enough, perhaps, but coming from those red lips, it was too much. Samantha brushed back a lock of hair, black and shiny, like the glossy finish on a photograph. Jenny imagined she thought of her entire world as gloss, while everyone else was only matte.

Jenny pasted a half-smile on her face and said, "Not yet, but I will be." She cocked her head to one side and tapped a finger on her chin. "I've talked Grace into something a little more . . . daring. More artistic." *There, put that in your silk Armanis.* "I'm thinking of poppies," she said. "Lots of them, kind of a Georgia O'Keeffe landscape."

"Poppies?"

Grace nudged Jenny's ankle with the toe of her sandal. "Jenny still thinks she's in California," she said with a short laugh. "Bigger, bolder, better—that's her motto." She turned to Jenny and her eyes narrowed a fraction, just enough for Jenny to know she thought she should have shut up ten sentences ago.

Well, someone needed to put this woman in her place. Jenny knew she could do it, and why not? It wasn't like she was going to ostracize her from her bridge club or anything. She had nothing to lose and the rest of the women on this street had everything to gain. Like individuality, for starters. She glanced at Samantha Steward's painted red nails. She'd probably been the type in high school who said yes to the blonde with the tight pink sweater and no to the brunette with the double chin and cat's-eye glasses. Jenny could just picture it all now, in minute detail—the hopeful face of that pathetic young girl with glasses and a few extra pounds, desperate to belong, to fuse, to join, willing to do homework favors, write extra papers, carry books. Anything. Anything at all, to be a part of a bigger whole . . . to be accepted. Jenny had seen it in high school and she saw it now, fifteen years later.

A smile stole across Jenny's lips. "Oh, Gracie, Samantha's got style," she said, pointing to the woman's matching sweater and shorts. White linen with a thin stripe of blue. Ralph Lauren? Or maybe, Liz? "I bet she knows what I'm talking about." Jenny leaned over and whispered in Samantha's ear. "It's all about art. Bold. Vibrant. Painting a canvas that stretches the senses." Jenny laid a hand on the woman's shoulder, a conspiratorial pretense, and said, *"You* know what I mean."

Samantha Steward cleared her throat twice and murmured a polite, "Of course."

"Poppies," Jenny said in a low voice. She gave her a quick nod and held her arms wide. "Stretching across America." She winked at her, enjoying the look of total bewilderment on Samantha Steward's perfectly sculpted features. "Think of it. From Grace, to you," Jenny swung her arms wider in the air, "to the postman in Des Moines, to the retired schoolteacher in Scottsdale, to the dance instructor in Reno, to . . . me."

Samantha Steward nodded her dark head and worked a closed-mouth half-smile on her red lips.

"If it was me, I'd set the trend, get out of the box, make a statement." Jenny hiked her chin up a notch and gave her a smug smile. "You know everyone will follow your example, Samantha. You're a leader."

The woman's smile spread and she actually had the good grace to blush. "Poppies," she repeated.

Jenny nodded a silent yes and said, "Poppies."

She watched as the other woman patted and smoothed her perfect hair. "Oh, my, I almost forgot," Samantha Steward said, glancing at the gold watch on her left hand. "It's my turn to serve." Her blue gaze swept over Grace and Jenny. "If you'll excuse me?"

"Certainly," Jenny said, but the woman was already moving away from them—on rather quick feet, it seemed.

"Bitch," Jenny said under her breath.

"Jenny, I swear, if you ever pull something like that again, I'll never forgive you." Grace's voice was low, hard, very serious.

Jenny turned and looked at her. "She's a manipulator, a user, and I don't like her. I figured all that out five minutes after our very first conversation. What I want to know is why you give her the time of day?"

"You can't just be rude to everyone you don't like."

Jenny raised a brow. "Rude? Was I rude?"

"You were playing with her, trying to make her look like a fool."

"No, I wasn't. I was trying to teach her a lesson in humility. I want to see her dig up all those flowers in her yard and plant a sea of poppies." Jenny smiled, picturing the woman with garden gloves and matching trowel—royal blue or sunshine yellow, maybe—crawling around with sweat trickling down her neck, the sun beating on her perfect, shiny head, and the whole neighborhood staring after her.

"Why?" Grace asked. "What does it matter to you? Why can't you just ignore her?" There was a quiet, controlled anger in her voice that surprised Jenny.

"Because I don't like what she's saying beneath the words

coming out of her mouth. It's like she really thinks she's better than everybody else.''

''Samantha's just . . .'' Grace paused and took a deep breath, ''just Samantha. Most of us just ignore her comments.''

''I think you should all tell her to take her red lips and kiss off.''

''It's not that easy, Jenny. You can't just say that to everybody who annoys you.'' She shook her head and frowned. ''But right now, it's awfully tempting.''

Jenny stared at her. ''Are you talking about me?''

Grace didn't answer.

''What? What did I do? I was only trying to stick up for you.''

Grace shook her head again and turned away, heading toward a group of people to the left of them.

What? Jenny watched her disappear from view. *What?*

Chapter 21

Jenny watched Grace for the next twenty minutes, engaged in a serious conversation with two men, scholarly-looking types with close-cropped beards and white polo shirts, and a woman who looked like the men minus the beard.

So, fine, Grace was going to ignore her. Fine.

Jenny sipped a Molson Light and looked around. There were clusters of men and women, a kaleidoscope of color and motion—eating, drinking, talking, laughing, usually all four in succession. Children covered every inch of green space, chomping hotdogs, spitting out watermelon seeds, hot, sweaty bodies, hair sticking straight up or out, braids undone, pigtails crooked, bangs smashed down. When the ground proved no more conquest, they took to the air, some hoisting their tanned little bodies to the top of the jungle gym with a sturdy, yellow rope, bony legs pushing off wooden supports for strength. Others chose the easier way to their "heavenly retreat" by using one of two side ladders or crawling up the attached sliding board.

Grace and Jenny had a swing set when they were kids. It was metal, red and white, with two swings, a mini sliding board, and a glider. Jenny used to pump that glider, pump it hard, until the white poles jumped out of the grass and wobbled back and forth in short, choppy skips, threatening to tip them over. She loved making the swing set "walk." Faster, harder, higher—she'd laugh and shriek in equal amounts of delight and fear as only a child can.

Grace, unfortunately, had never shared her enthusiasm. She'd clutched the bar of the glider, knuckles white, eyes wide, mouth open, knees clamped together. When Jenny's legs gave out and the poles stopped jumping, the glider would just kind of slide to a stop. And then, that's when Grace came to life, yelling at Jenny, telling her what a dangerous thing she'd done and how they both could've been hurt and maybe even broken their arm like Tommy Latser did at school. After a while she refused to go on the swing unless Jenny promised not to make it "walk." And no matter how Jenny tried to tell her that the whole fun of it was making it do things it didn't usually do, wasn't *supposed* to do, and how it turned her insides jiggly-jumpy and stole her breath with one giant jump, it didn't matter. Grace didn't care. She said she didn't need to feel that way, didn't *want* to lose her breath or her brains. She said there were rules for playing on a swing set and Jenny should learn them. Rules were important, she'd said. There were rules for everything and six years old was old enough for Jenny to start understanding some of them.

Well, Jenny hadn't done a very good job of following rules back then and it looked like she was still struggling with the concept, at least where it pertained to unspoken expectations from a neighborhood busybody.

A blur of hot pink in sandals and matching scrunchie tore through her absentminded nostalgia. Jenny swung toward the image, saw the blur chasing another fast-moving object, a boy, dressed in khaki shorts and a blue shirt. They sped along the outskirts of the crowd, heading in the direction of the front yard. Two seconds later, they were gone, swallowed up by a flowering hydrangea and an oversized boxwood. The pink swirl was Natalie, the khaki-blue, she didn't know.

Kids, they had all the fun. Jenny took another pull on her Molson, started to turn away, but stopped. Where was the rest of the Freeze Tag brigade? Wasn't there supposed to be more . . . four, six, seven? She spotted Danielle hoisting herself up on a big rope. She obviously wasn't part of the game. There were a lot of other little bodies, dressed in summer yellows, greens, and reds, climbing, sliding, swinging, jumping, and digging. But running, flat out, arms extended, legs flying?

No. Jenny glanced at the spot where she'd last seen Natalie. Men and women gathered in small clusters, sticking together like giant popcorn balls, exchanging gooey bits of information, sweet and sickening at the same time, with an aftermath of tidbits that stuck in their brain long after the last kernel was flossed away.

Where was Natalie?

She made her way to the side of the house, past the conversation about Jessica's swimming classes and Michael's thumb-sucking, and the "he-he" panting in the last stage of labor, and the beautiful cerulean blue of the EPT. Morning sickness, night sickness, *linea negra,* hemorrhoids. She moved faster, excusing herself with a slight shrug of her shoulders and an innocent smile. A man with a half-buttoned Hawaiian shirt and ten strands of slicked-back brown hair blocked Jenny's exit from the suburban fantasia that occupied the Montgomerys's backyard. He was holding a Miller in his right hand and waving a cigar in his left, complaining about the "shitty" return he got on his investments last year. *Too heavy in the European market,* he said. *Too much foreign stuff.* The woman, a thirty-something, bottle redhead with pancake makeup that didn't hide the pockmarks dotting her cheeks, nodded and sipped from her plastic glass. She had that glassy-eyed stare that said she had no idea what he was talking about and no desire to find out.

Jenny worked her way around the man, with effort, and broke out into the open, on the other side, where a world existed apart from pacifiers and IRAs. She passed a few stragglers—mother, father, and two children, carrying covered dishes and diaper bags. The little boy, a towhead with a buzz cut, dragged a plastic bat behind him, scraping the lime green tip along the sidewalk. His sister, at least she assumed it was his sister because she had the same white-blond hair, bounced a red ball several paces behind the rest of the family. When they passed Jenny, they smiled, exchanging a stranger's niceties.

Where was Natalie? Jenny reached the front of the house, walked over to the porch, called her name.

"Natalie?"

Nothing. She was nowhere in sight. Neither was the speed demon she'd been chasing. "Natalie?" Strains of the Doobie Brothers whirled around her. *"Natalie?"* She spoke louder this time, with more urgency. Nothing. Had she left the yard, gone to the boy's house? Jenny sucked in a deep breath, clenched her jaw, unclenched her jaw. Should she tell Laura, ask her if she knew where Natalie might be? Or should she . . . What? What should she do?

"Natalie!" She should try to find her first. No sense in alarming the rest of the neighborhood because her five-year-old niece had decided to chase a boy and had disappeared. She could have circled around to the backyard by now. What did Jenny know, anyway? She was probably the only childless person in that group. What did someone who'd never been a parent really know about the intricacies of the family obedience system? Maybe kids were allowed to roam around during neighborhood parties, go to each other's

houses, use their bathrooms, try out their colored antibacterial soaps. Maybe, Jenny was being paranoid, envisioning child-snatchers hiding behind sugary smiles and the thick oak trees crowding out the tree lawns, just waiting for some unsuspecting five-year-old to come racing by so he could scoop her up. Maybe she'd seen too many horror movies. Maybe her imagination was too wild, too twisted.

"Natalie!" She also could have slipped into Laura's house and was at this very minute sticking her finger into a big bowl of Cool Whip. Jenny bounded up the porch steps. Or, she might be stuffing her face with Lay's, dipping half the chip into a bowl of French onion dip. Jenny opened the door and slipped inside, breathing in the aroma of fresh-baked biscuits and hoping she'd find Natalie munching one at the kitchen table, crumbs stuck to both sides of her mouth. But when she reached the kitchen, she found nothing but ten bags of Lay's on the almond Formica countertop and two trays of biscuits cooling on square wire racks.

"Natalie?" *Damn, where was she?*

A growl, low and feral, came from nearby.

"Natalie?"

Another rumble, like a warring animal . . . coming from under the kitchen table. Jenny bent over, lifted the gold plastic tablecloth decorated with red apples along the edges, and peeked underneath.

"Natalie!"

She was huddled up, knees tucked under her chin, bare arms wrapped around bruised shins, staring at Jenny from a blanket of wild hair. "She's not a monster." It came out more hiss than word.

Jenny knelt down on the floor, scooted toward her under the table, placed a hand on her knee. "Who, honey? Who's not a monster?"

"And she does not look like a buzzard. Jerry Lenning looks like a buzzard!"

Oh. So, Natalie hadn't been playing Freeze Tag. She'd been after that little bolt of lightning, Jerry Lenning, but why? And what would she have done if she'd caught him? Punch him in the nose? The shins? The gut? *Had* she caught him? It was hard to picture Natalie doing any of those things until Jenny looked at her, crouched low, thin-lipped, white knuckled, and breathing hard. Then, she could see her niece pummeling the poor kid, splitting his lip open, maybe even giving him a black eye.

But who had Jerry Lenning called a monster and a buzzard? Who had she been trying to protect? A sickening sensation gurgled in the pit of her stomach, worked into a boil, spilled like toxic froth, burning a hole right through the lining, right through sense and decency and countless blind efforts to protect the girls. The painful, searing truth was that they could not be protected, not from a young boy's cruel words or an adult's raised brow.

Children could be cruel, adults could be cruel, *life* could be cruel.

God. So this is what it felt like to be a parent.

Jenny pushed back a chunk of hair from Natalie's cheek. "Tell me what happened, honey."

Natalie's bottom lip quivered, straightened, quivered again. "He said Mommy looked like a buzzard."

Jenny moved closer and hoisted her onto her lap. "That wasn't a very nice thing for him to say." Natalie buried her head against Jenny's chest, arms clinging around her aunt's middle, knees bent to her chin. They clung to each other under the Montgomery table with its apple-coated plastic covering, a safe haven, shielding them from the outside world and all of its injustices. For the briefest of seconds, Jenny almost felt as if she *could* protect her.

"He's mean and I hate him!" Natalie's words came out muffled against Jenny's shirt.

Jenny stroked her back, pulled her closer. "I know you

want to hate him, because he said something that hurt you. But don't, Natalie. Don't hate him. It will only make you feel bad." She planted a soft kiss on top of her niece's head.

"I already feel bad." She sniffed. "And mad."

"But you'll feel worse."

Another sniff. "Mommy's not a buzzard," she said. "She's not." Her voice trembled, faded. "She's not. She's not." The same words, over and over, more tenacious than a prizefighter battling the final round, bloody but not broken, until at last, the words stopped, her breathing quieted, and she slept.

Sleep had always been one of Jenny's greatest pleasures. There was something about the way twilight wrapped itself around her half-conscious being, pulled her under, transported her away to another place, another time, *another life*. She'd always prided herself in possessing the innate ability to close her eyes and drift off, no matter the situation or surroundings. Cars, trains, buses, planes, hotels, villas, condos, elevators. Yes, elevators, if there were more than fifteen floors and she'd passed the third stage of exhaustion. But usually, she just closed her eyes and floated into that other world, the one with no deadlines, no expectations, no ulterior motives. And every smile was a real smile and words were commitments that didn't require legal documentation to enforce or interpret.

And life was good, without the hassles or deceptions.

But not last night—last night, sleep wouldn't come. Not with a temple massage, not with thirty pages of Thoreau's *Walden,* not with side one of *Mozart for Meditation,* or side two, either. The lavender-and-chamomile body lotion didn't work, nor did the serenity candle burning on her nightstand. She knew the reason, knew it before she looked at the clock for the sixth time. A deeper, darker vision had control last night, running through her mind, unsettling her brain, disrupting conscious thought, and nothing would erase it. Nothing would take away the sight of Natalie crouched under Laura's kitchen table, fierce warrior come to do battle for her mother. And when the fight had drained from her small body, she'd curled up and fallen into an exhausted sleep, her fingers clutching Jenny's shirt. That was the dark vision that imprinted itself on Jenny's memory, wiping out any hope for a peaceful night of ordinary slumber.

At 4:15 A.M., Jenny got up, threw on her UCLA sweatshirt, and followed the tiny ray from the night-light down the hall into the kitchen. The light was still on over the stove, a habit Grace carried from their childhood. Some things never changed, whether they knew it or not ... whether they admitted it or not. Jenny could still remember their mother closing up the house at night, turning off every light except the one over the stove. That stayed on for their father, whose job as a second-shift foreman at Webber's Tool & Die kept him out until midnight. The light was his beacon, his guide to safe harbor, his path home.

Jenny headed for the Mr. Coffee and flicked the "on" button. For the next hour and a half, she sat in the dark, Indian style on a kitchen chair with no pad, sipping a steaming Colombian Blend.

So, this was what it felt like to be a parent. No wonder there were so many childless couples. Sleepless nights and Natalie's quivering, 'She's not.' *Worry. Worry. Worry.* Jenny sighed and closed her eyes.

"Shhh. She's sleeping."

"You sure?"

"Of course I'm sure."

"How can you tell?"

Pause.

"For one thing, her eyes are closed and they're not all scrunched up like yours are when you're pretending."

"Oh."

"And see the way she's breathing? It's all even and she's not holding her breath."

"Oh."

"So be quiet and don't wake her up."

"Okay." Pause. "Danielle?"

"What?" Sigh.

"Are we just gonna sit and wait for Aunt Jenny to wake up?"

"Yes."

"Then are we gonna show her what we did?"

Another sigh. "As soon as she opens her eyes she'll know."

"Oh. Okay." Long pause. "Danielle?"

"What?"

"Do you think she'll be mad?"

Very long pause.

"I don't know."

"Oh."

Silence.

Jenny had been awake since the second whisper. Sleep had come to her sometime in the predawn hours, luring her under, away from thoughts of Natalie and buzzards. Her arms ached from their position as a makeshift pillow, her neck felt like it had a permanent crook in it, and both of her legs were stiffer than cardboard. But she didn't care, didn't even want to think about the whopper headache she'd carry around from too little sleep.

Right now, all she wanted to do was open her eyes and find out what Danielle and Natalie were talking about. What little secret were they keeping and why would Jenny know about it as soon as she opened her eyes? And why did they both think she might be mad once she found out?

"She twitched her nose," Natalie whispered.

"Shhh."

"She did. Watch."

A flutter of warm air brushed over Jenny's face. Closer, closer. *Natalie*. Jenny could tell her smell anywhere, an odd mix of graham crackers and Johnson's Baby Shampoo. She couldn't stand it any longer. She inched open her right eye.

"What the—!" Jenny jerked her head up, mouth open, eyes staring.

"Hi, Aunt Jenny," Natalie said, her voice timid, unsure.

Danielle edged closer to her sister, her small mouth pulled into a straight line. She said nothing.

Jenny unfolded her legs and stood up slowly, shifting her gaze between both girls, unable to believe the two urchins in front of her were the same children she'd seen less than twelve hours ago. Oh, their faces looked the same, maybe a little flushed from sleep, and they were wearing their usual sleep attire—oversized UCLA T-shirts she'd sent them last Easter. But that's where the similarities ended. Jenny hazarded a quick glance at the top of their heads. *Good God!* Natalie's black curls were sliced and mangled to within two inches of her scalp, tufts sticking out around her head like a mini-Afro. She had no bangs, only pieces of curly fuzz framing her forehead.

Danielle's hair was chopped to just above her chin— long, short, shorter, long, short, shorter—in some crazy, convoluted pattern. That beautiful sable hair, so like her mother's, gone! Her bangs were gouged out a good two inches above her eyebrows.

"What happened?" Jenny dug past shock and disbelief, pulling the words from the bottom of her gut.

Danielle shrugged. "We cut our hair."

That was the understatement of the year. *Cut* was much too mild a term. Massacred, mutilated, butchered, buzzed, chopped, killed, destroyed, annihilated . . . those were more adequate descriptions of what these two had done with a pair of scissors and an idea.

"Why?" *But Jenny already knew why.* Of course she knew why, even before she asked the question. Her brain bounced back to yesterday, with Natalie clinging to her under the Montgomerys's kitchen table, fiercely insisting her mother was *not* a buzzard.

"I wanted to be like Mommy," Natalie said. "And her hair's short."

Jenny nodded. "Yes, it is," she said, trying not to stare at the quarter-sized spot of white on the left side of Natalie's forehead, where she'd done a little extra rambunctious trimming. Right to the scalp.

Danielle cleared her throat and took a step forward. "She was cutting her hair in the bedroom with Mom's sewing scissors. Big chunks," she said pointing to her sister's right side. "When I found her, half her hair was chopped off. I tried to fix it, but I had to keep going shorter and shorter." Her eyes grew larger, her voice softer. "I tried to fix it, but I couldn't."

They were the most words Danielle had spoken to her since the night Jenny told her that her father was dead.

"So she cut hers to look like mine," Natalie chirped in.

Jenny couldn't speak, couldn't find the words, and when she did, she had to fight past the bowling ball in her throat to get them out. She knelt down and ran tentative fingers through the fringes and tufts on their heads. "I think you're both very brave," she said, blinking hard. Her voice went from gentle to raspy. "Very, very brave."

"Then you're not mad?" This from Natalie.

Jenny shook her head, felt the weight of her own hair scattering around her shoulders, stretching her scalp. She swallowed twice, the feel of saliva pooling in her mouth. "No," she said. "I'm not mad."

Natalie let out a big sigh, an enormous sound in such a

small body. It was relief mixed with a weariness that should be prohibited in one so young. But it was there, nonetheless, in the whoosh of breath swirling about her, the slump of shoulders leaning forward, pushing her down. "She doesn't look like a buzzard," she whispered, meeting Jenny's gaze.

"No, she doesn't," Jenny whispered.

"Now we all look alike."

"Yes, you do," Jenny said, running her fingers along the side of Natalie's face. "And you are both so beautiful. Do you know that, girls?" she asked, opening her arms to them. Natalie rushed forward, flinging herself at Jenny. Danielle looked at her aunt's outstretched arms, took a step closer, lower lip trembling, eyes bright. Their gazes met, locked. *Come to me, Danielle. Come to me.* She took another step, and then another, and Jenny pulled her close, pressing her small body against her own. The tears came, pouring over them, in a ritual of forgiveness and renewal.

This was love, Jenny realized. This doing, this *being,* this was it. She rubbed her cheek against their shorn heads, over the soft and stubby parts, breathing in the faint scent of Johnson's Baby Shampoo, letting it roll over her senses, capture her, coax her, fill her with the strength she needed to stand beside her nieces, equal in task and commitment.

They held each other a long time, Danielle and Natalie giving and Jenny taking. When she pulled away, ever so gently, she looked into their faces, saw the courage and innocence, maybe a hint of trepidation, but only a hint— nothing like the boulder Jenny had pushing against her back. By some intuitive nature, without prodding or persuasion, they seemed to know their roles, know what they could do to help their mother get well.

If they could be so brave, so selfless, so loving, so could she. Jenny fingered a chunk of hair that had fallen onto her shoulder. *So can I,* she told herself. *So can I.*

* * *

Three hours later, Jenny pulled the minivan into the garage, right between the snow blower and the Crazy Coupe. She shut off the ignition and hit the garage door button.

Jenny, Danielle, and Natalie sat in silence and semidarkness, with only a sliver of illumination from the small octagonal window on the side entry door. The minivan's air conditioning pinged three times and was done.

"Should we show her now?" Natalie whispered from the backseat.

Jenny turned and smiled, running a hand through her hair. "Might as well."

"With or without hats?" Danielle asked, pulling the flopping denim hat with the red rose Jenny had bought her at Kmart over her head. Natalie stuffed a matching one on her head, too.

"Whichever way you like," Jenny said. "I think you look great either way."

"Are you gonna wear yours?" Natalie asked, peeking over the front seat at Jenny's hat. It was denim, too, a little more fitted, with a bright orange flower that looked like a cross between a rose and a poppy.

Jenny ran a hand through her hair again, stopping just below her neck. "No, I don't think so."

"Okay. I won't wear mine, either." She yanked hers off and set it beside her.

"Me, neither." Danielle removed hers, placed it in her lap. "At least not yet."

Okay. Okay. Jenny took a deep breath, inhaled, held, exhaled, *whoosh.* "Let's go find your mom." What would Grace say? How would she handle this latest twist in her life? Two daughters trying to ease her pain by chopping at their hair with sewing scissors? At least, they looked a little better, more uniform in a pixyish kind of way, thanks to the help of Amy at Styles Like Us. Jenny touched her neck again, felt the skin, scratched it.

What will Grace say when she sees me?

"Okay, kiddos," Jenny said, unfastening her seat belt. "Let's go."

The girls flicked open their seat belts and bound out of the car. Jenny grabbed the Kmart bag filled with an assortment of glitter clips, citrus-colored headbands, red, blue, green, and pink scarves, and fashion barrettes with daisies, butterflies, and turtles—just about every imaginable accessory for the "cropped-minded" girl.

Jenny sucked in another breath and followed Danielle. Natalie was already ten steps in front of them, rounding the kitchen corner, heading for the living room.

"Mommy! Mommy!"

Grace's shriek hit them with the force of a dump truck pinning their bodies under a two-ton load of dirt. Jenny froze in place, listening.

"Natalie! What happened!?" There was disbelief in her voice, shock.

"I got my hair cut. Just like you," Natalie said. There was a long pause. "Don't you like it?" she asked. It was a child's offering, innocent, heartfelt, yet suddenly unsure.

Pause. "It's not that I don't like it," Grace answered in that warm way that reminded Jenny of when they were kids and Jenny had done something stupid. Again. Grace knew just what to say and how to say it, to make Jenny feel better, make everything seem all right. "It's just different."

"Like yours," Natalie said.

"Like mine." Grace's voice faded out.

Danielle and Jenny turned the corner, took two steps down the small hall, and stood at the edge of the living room. Grace was facing them, head bent, leaning over Natalie, one arm wrapped tight around her, the other stroking her head.

"Aunt Jenny said you would like it," Natalie mumbled into her mother's shirt.

Grace's hand stilled. "She did?" There was a sharpness in her words, buried beneath casual inquiry, but Jenny heard it. Did she think Jenny was responsible for Natalie's new look? Obviously, yes.

"Uh-huh."

One little half-formed word that wasn't even really a word to crucify Jenny, make her look like an irresponsible idiot. *Does Grace really think I'd do that?*

"I see."

"But only because me and Danielle tried to cut it ourselves and we got it all crooked."

"What?" Grace jerked back, stared at her. Then her gaze shifted, and she saw Jenny and Danielle. Her mouth went slack, inched open, but she said nothing.

Jenny touched the back of her neck again, felt bare skin. Again. "Hi, Grace."

"Jenny, what happened to your hair?"

Jenny shrugged and forced a laugh. "Short seems to be in."

Grace rushed over to Danielle, ran both hands through her daughter's short locks, and whispered, "Danielle? Why?"

"We wanted to be like you, Mom," she said, eyes wide, lips unsmiling. "We didn't want you to be alone."

"Yeah," Natalie chirped. "And Jerry Lenning better not open his big mouth, either."

"But your hair," Grace said, her voice cracking.

"Aunt Jenny said it'll be a lot easier to wash," Danielle said.

"And she bought us tons of stuff for our hair," Natalie added. "Where's all that stuff, Aunt Jenny?"

Jenny held out the Kmart shopping bag. "Here you go."

"C'mon, Danielle." Natalie grabbed the bag and ran toward the steps.

"Let's spread it out on our beds and we'll pick," Danielle said, racing after her.

They flew up the stairs, chattering and laughing as only the young can do following a disaster. They didn't dwell on their misfortune or bemoan a state of unfairness or dissatisfaction. No, they counted their losses, wiped their noses, and moved on.

Jenny wished grown-ups could do the same thing.

"Jenny?" Grace's voice was tentative, confused.

"When I woke up this morning, they'd already done the deed," Jenny said. "It was much worse, if you can believe that." She let out a little laugh and shook her head. "Much worse. Natalie had butchered half of her head and then Danielle tried to fix it."

"But why?" Grace ran a hand over her face. "Why would they do such a thing?"

"They told you," Jenny said. "They wanted to look like you. They're protecting you, can't you see that?"

Grace blinked hard, turned away. Jenny watched her as she walked to the recliner, sank into it, and closed her eyes.

"Grace? Are you okay?" Jenny sat down on the couch and picked up a pillow, playing with the fringe.

"When is it going to stop, Jenny?" she whispered. "When is the pain going to be done?" Tears streamed down her cheeks, but she didn't bother to wipe them away. "Every day, I think it will be better, that I'll forget and move on with my life. But then, something happens that reminds me of—" she stopped, sucked in a breath, and said, "everything. Then it all comes rushing back at me and I *can't* stop it. It just keeps coming, all the lies, the deceit. The hate."

It all came back to Grant. Again. He was still controlling her and he was six feet under and stiffer than a board. "You have to try and let it go, Gracie."

"I can't." It came out like a moan, low, keening.

Jenny leaned forward and took her sister's hand in her

own. Grace's fingers were cold. "You have to try. Just try. If you don't, it'll destroy you."

"I hate him." Her eyes flew open and she stared at Jenny, her gaze hard and glassy. "I hate him."

"I know." How could she make Grace listen to her, make her understand that she had to at least try to *start* letting go? "Sooner or later, you have to let that hate go. You don't ever have to like him again, or forget what he did, but you have to let it go."

She shook her head. "No. No. I can't."

Jenny bit the inside of her cheek. This was not the right time to talk about forgiveness or letting go or any other feel-good kind of thing. Maybe it was too soon. Maybe it was the way Jenny had gone about it, too straightforward. Maybe she should have sugar-coated it a little more. *Maybe . . . maybe.* She just didn't know anymore.

They sat in silence after that, Jenny leaning forward, stroking Grace's fingers, and Grace resting her head against the back of the recliner, taking slow, even breaths. Her tears had pretty much dried up, leaving the faintest trails on her cheeks.

God, but Jenny felt old, sitting there . . . so much older than her thirty-three years. It was the worry that did it, she guessed. It pulled a person's face down, gave them wrinkles and a permanent frown. Worry. No wonder so many parents walked around looking so miserable. It was the worry, distorting faces, gouging out creases between eyebrows, yanking lips down, clenching and unclenching jaws, stripping away peace, dumping the life from them.

It was the worry.

Now Jenny knew what it felt like to know that worry. She reached up and felt the skin between her own eyebrows. No furrows yet. But soon, if things didn't improve with Grace, they'd be deeper than a spring planting bed.

Her hand ran to the back of her neck, a deliberate habit

in the last few hours. It was only hair, she told herself. And if it would help Grace get back on track, feel more like her old self, then it was worth it. Heck, she'd shave off all of it if it helped her sister deal with that jerk husband of hers. Correction. *Dead jerk husband.*

Jenny pressed the spot between her eyebrows again, tried to flatten it out. Worry. It was enough to make a normal person insane.

Jenny stuffed three wads of Bubble Yum in her mouth, then she sprayed Simply Lavender body splash on her neck, wrists, forearms, and legs. That should do it, but just in case, she lifted her shirt and sprayed twice more.

Her mother was here, less than a hundred feet away in Grace's living room. She'd heard her open the door, yell, *Yoohoo, girls, I'm here. Is anybody home?*

Oh, God. Oh, God.

Jenny forced herself to leave her bedroom, then pushed her feet, one in front of the other, until she made it down the hall to the steps, first one, two, three, six, seven . . .

"Jenny! What in heaven's name did you do to your hair?!"

. . . she hadn't even made it to the landing. "Hi, Mom." Her chest tightened, squeezed, tightened again. It was starting already and her mother's suitcase was still in the car. *Chew, chew,* she told herself. Jenny leaned over, gave her mother a kiss on the cheek and a quick hug.

"It's so short."

"I know."

She shook her head. "You had beautiful hair. I don't know why you got it in your head to go and cut it all off."

Jenny shrugged. Had that been a compliment?

"Grandma! Grandma!"

The girls came tearing down the stairs, freshly bathed and

dressed in matching yellow-and-white sundresses scattered with daisies. Wide yellow headbands with a daisy on the side covered a large section of their heads. Grace had insisted on getting them ready by herself. She wouldn't even let Jenny help wash their hair—not that it would require great effort, but still.

Hours before Virginia Romano walked in the door, Jenny could feel her presence slowly creeping in, taking over, permeating the house, the walls, the inhabitants. Grace was already trying to take command again, be the dutiful daughter, the one in charge, the organizer, calculator, fixer-upper . . . the one who diminishes her own needs for everyone else.

And once again, Jenny was being pushed to the background, a casual piece of landscape, interesting to look at but ineffectual. Useless. She chewed harder.

"What happened to your hair?!?"

Déjà vu.

"We cut it, Grandma." Natalie pulled back from her grandmother's comfortable middle and gave her a toothy smile. "Jenny cut hers, too."

Virginia Romano pierced her daughter with her dark eyes—deep, brown, Italian eyes, the kind that bore into a person, and never shone, not even when they were exploding with joy. Opaque eyes, Jenny called them. They fit her mother. She was an opaque kind of person, at least to Jenny she was; there was no getting behind the words or the behavior to figure out the person.

"Are you responsible for this?" she asked Jenny, stroking the top of the girls' heads.

"*We* cut it, Grandma," Danielle said in a quiet voice, as though she sensed the accusations beneath her grandmother's words. "Jenny only fixed it for us." She looked at Jenny. "And then, she got hers cut, too."

"The lady didn't want to cut hers," Natalie said, looking at her aunt. "But Aunt Jenny made her."

Virginia Romano's dark gaze flitted over her daughter but she said nothing.

"Well, don't go doing anything so foolish again. Do you hear me?"

She was looking at Danielle and Natalie, but Jenny felt the words just the same, knew they were intended for her more than the girls. How long had Grace said she was staying? Two weeks? Three? Jenny chewed harder.

"Hi, Mom."

Grace.

Everyone turned and looked at her, the woman who'd brought them all together. Sister, mother, daughter. Grace was all things to all of them. She looked beautiful walking down the steps, like she was floating, with that sad little smile on her face, her hair pulled back into a pale pink headband. Her hair was growing—every day it looked better and Jenny made sure she told her so.

"Oh, honey," Virginia Romano said, holding her arms wide. Danielle and Natalie scattered apart, drifting over to Jenny.

"Mom," Grace murmured, falling into her arms, the pain and weariness of a beaten soldier pulsing in that one little word.

"It's okay, now. I'm here. It's okay."

Jenny watched the reunion, a play of depth and feeling, like a dance in slow motion, one soothing the other, touching, offering comfort and hope.

She turned away when the tears came. It was more than she needed to see. She swiped a hand over both eyes and went to check on the lasagna.

* * *

"This meal is delicious," Virginia Romano said, helping herself to a second piece of lasagna. "Just like mine." She smiled and a map of tiny wrinkles spread out from the corners of her eyes. "But, I guess it should be, since it's my recipe." She slid an end piece onto her plate, cut a small section, and plopped it into her mouth. "Mmmmm. Delicious."

"Thank you," Grace said. "Jenny helped."

Her mother arched a brow in Jenny's direction. "Did you really?" She took another bite. "It's very good."

"Thank you," Jenny mumbled into her napkin.

"Any reason for this sudden domestication?" she asked.

"No."

"Not cooking for any man—"

"No." She was not going there.

"What about Elliot?" Natalie asked.

"Elliot?" There was that tone, a soft lilt that disguised blatant prying as casual curiosity.

Jenny shook her head. "He's a friend," she said. Oh, God, hadn't she practically gone ballistic on Elliot when he'd introduced *her* that way to Mrs. Abblebee at the airport? Well, her mother was different. Virginia Romano was a national broadcast and critique service, all wrapped into one.

Grace intervened and, once again, made sense out of a senseless situation. "Elliot is the psychologist the girls and I have been seeing," she said, taking a sip of water.

"Oh."

Jenny could tell that was not going to appease their mother. Not her. Nothing short of a divine revelation would make her quit without more information.

"So, what does Jenny have to do with him?" She was looking at Grace, fork paused inches from her mouth, and Jenny felt as though she were watching a play, where the main character isn't present. Except that Jenny was, very much so.

"I met him first when I took the girls," Jenny said. "Later, I encouraged Grace to see him." There. That was the truth.

Virginia Romano looked at Jenny, eyes narrowing to fine, dark slits, just like she used to do when Jenny was a teenager and her mother had asked her if she'd been riding in Tommy Angelo's Chevy. Jenny met her gaze, exactly as she had back then—no blinking, no frowning, and no flaring nostrils. The last was always a giveaway.

Then her mother straightened in her chair and said, "I'd like to meet this Elliot."

Jenny blew a little air out of her nostrils, just a tiny bit, so she wouldn't see the relief. She was through with the thirty questions for now, but her mother wouldn't forget about Elliot. Oh, no, she'd be listening and watching for clues as to the nature of Jenny's relationship with him—if for nothing else than to voice an opinion.

"Fine," Grace said. "I'm sure he'd like to meet you."

"Can I be done?" Natalie asked, putting her fork down and looking at her mother.

"It's 'May I be done,' " Virginia corrected. " 'May I be done, *please?'* "

"May I be done, *please?*" Natalie repeated, smiling at her grandmother.

"Wipe your mouth, and then you may be excused," Grace said, in what could only be called a valiant effort to maintain control over her own children.

"Me, too?" Danielle asked.

"What do you say, young lady?" Virginia Romano, *Miss Manners.*

"May I be excused, please?"

She nodded.

"Go ahead, and take your dishes to the sink," Grace said.

Ah, it was amazing that in the minuscule span of three hours, Virginia Romano had invaded the Clarke household, dug around in one daughter's fragile relationship with her sister's psychologist, usurped the other daughter's control over her children, and all of this before dessert.

No one spoke again until the screen door banged against the frame a second time. Natalie ran, yelling after her sister to wait up for her. When their voices faded out, Virginia turned to Grace and said, "I'd like to go to the cemetery tomorrow."

Jenny had always heard of people turning white or gray, usually from fear or dread, but she'd never actually seen it. Until those words came out of her mother's mouth. That's when Jenny turned to Grace and saw her switch from a normal skin tone to ash gray faster than the double click on a camera. Zap. Done. Jenny thought Grace was going to be sick; she opened her mouth to speak but nothing came out.

"She hasn't been to the cemetery yet," Jenny blurted out.

Virginia looked from Grace, to Jenny, to Grace again. "Why not?"

Grace's nostrils flared, just a little, but Jenny saw them. Grace's hands were in lap and Jenny would just bet she was shredding her napkin into a hundred pieces. "I just haven't made it yet," she said in a quiet voice.

And you won't, either, Jenny thought. *Not if I can help it.*

"Well, now that I'm here, I'll take you there."

Grace met Jenny's gaze. Her skin shifted from gray to pasty white.

"I think she needs to rest and get better," Jenny said, turning to her mother. "She's hardly been out at all, except to go see Elliot and a few times to the grocery store." She forced a smile to push her point. "We've been to the mall once. That's it."

"All the more reason to get her out and about." Virginia shook her head, a salt-and-pepper color, more pepper than salt.

"She hasn't been up to it, Mom," Jenny said, a little more forceful this time. "The doctor only let her start driving this week and she doesn't even feel much like doing that."

"It's her duty to her husband—she knows that."

"Duty?" Jenny balled her hand into a fist under the table. *Duty?* To that cheating jerk? If she only knew.

"A wife has a duty to her husband, whether he's dead or alive," she said, as though Jenny hadn't spoken. "When your father died, I brought fresh flowers to the cemetery every week. They didn't let you plant anything in the ground back then, so I brought my own vase, filled with flowers . . . sometimes carnations, or daisies." She stared at her glass. "A few times, I brought him roses. Red was his favorite. Even in the winter, I made sure something was there . . . Holly, mostly." Her voice faded and Jenny imagined she was remembering that square granite headstone that read: *Joseph A. Romano, 1926-1987, Devoted Husband/Beloved Father.*

"She hasn't felt well enough to go," Jenny repeated, watching all the color sift from Grace's face.

"We'll go tomorrow."

Jenny rubbed the back of her neck. God, but she could be persistent. "Things are different now, Mom. People don't necessarily honor the dead in cemeteries anymore." She shrugged. "There are a lot of different ways to pay respect." Jenny had been to her father's grave once, the day of the funeral. But she thought of him every day.

"That's a sacrilege," Virginia Romano said, shaking her head. "Everything today is about convenience. People don't want to go out of their way to do anything anymore."

"It's not that," Jenny said, but her mother cut her off before she could say anything else.

"Yes, it is, Jenny. It is exactly *that.*" She looked at her, dark eyes burning. "If it doesn't fit their schedule or falls during prime time television, they don't want to be bothered.

It's considered an inconvenience.'' She let out a sigh. ''No wonder we have all the crime we do today. Everybody's just out for themselves.''

All Jenny had said was that Grace hadn't felt well enough to go to the cemetery . . . and now this . . .

''I'll go tomorrow,'' Grace said, her quiet words plowing through the tension that hung over them, heavier than wet snow.

''You don't have to go if you're not up to it,'' Jenny said, willing Grace to meet her gaze. Why was she buckling under their mother's bully tactics? Couldn't she tell that Jenny was trying to help her, throw her a lifeline, give her a plausible out? Why wasn't she taking it, holding on with all her might, standing strong?

Why? *How* could she even consider going to Grant's grave when they both knew even the thought of him tore her apart?

Jenny didn't understand. She really didn't.

''Jenny, she said she'd go.'' There was a sharpness in her mother's voice that said the discussion was over. She'd won. ''We should all go. It's the least we can do for that poor man.'' She sniffed. ''He was like a son to me.'' Another sniff, then she cleared her throat. ''Such a tragedy. Such a horrible tragedy.''

Jenny wanted to throw her glass against the wall, jolt Grace out of her stupor, and watch the glass shatter in a hundred pieces, water dripping down the pale green wall.

Then she wanted to yell until her lungs hurt: *Did you know he was screwing some long-legged brunette? Did you know he was with her the day he died? Did you know she wasn't the first?*

Did you know she looked like me?

Did you know?

Did you?

And did you know Grace knew?

But she didn't, she didn't do any of those things. She just sat there, staring at her fork. Four tines, tiny scratches, faint scrollwork at the base. Her gaze narrowed on a speck of red wedged between the last two tines on the left. Sauce, no doubt. She could barely hear her mother's eulogy for her dead son-in-law—a low droning that went on and on about everything from the time he installed a new garbage disposal for her to the way he made blueberry pancakes every Saturday morning. There was too much in between, too many "wonderful" recounts of "such a wonderful man." Jenny wanted to ask her if she thought shoveling snow in sub-zero weather was fair trade for overlooking a husband's screwing around? But she didn't. She just sat there, staring at her fork, clenching and unclenching her right hand, and waiting for Grace to say something.

But she didn't.

When her mother paused, Jenny jumped up, gathered her plate, fork, and glass, and mumbled something about having to be somewhere. She moved fast, rinsed off her dish, and stuck it in the dishwasher. Then, she started on the kids' dishes, faster yet, like the Energizer Bunny after two jolts of Colombian Supreme. She had to get out, get out, get out!

Chapter 22

"Jenny, are you okay?"

Elliot.

She fell into his arms, pressed her body close to his, pulling his strength into her. "I'm just a little . . . stressed," she said. "My mother came this afternoon."

"Oh."

"Yeah." She pulled back a little, tried to smile.

He tipped her chin up, brushed his lips over hers. "You look different," he said, his gaze moving from her floppy jeans hat with the big orange poppy-rose to her red tank and jeans shorts, to her sandals, and then back up to her hat. "Did you do something different or have I forgotten what you look like?"

"It's only been twenty-three hours," she said, her voice soft.

"Can't be," he said, running his fingers down her bare arms. "It feels like twenty-three days."

"No, it's not. I've been counting." His hands were so gentle, so soothing, and yet, so . . . exhilarating.

"Oh," he said, his voice dropping an octave. "So, you've missed me." He led her further into the foyer, which was covered with large, leafy plants, burnt-orange walls, and black-and-white pictures of Sydney.

Jenny opened her mouth to make some flippant remark about not missing anybody, but when she looked into those brown eyes, they pulled her in, sucked her under, and all she could do was close her mouth and nod.

Her honesty seemed to surprise him. He probably expected her to banter, maybe even try to deny what was happening between them, and when she didn't, another line of defense fell. "I missed you, too," he said, his voice low, husky.

He leaned toward her and Jenny's eyes fluttered shut, anticipating, wanting, needing. When their mouths met, opened, shared, she pressed herself closer, trying to absorb the feeling. Elliot gripped her face between his hands, his tongue probing, filling Jenny's mouth. His hands moved to her hair, pushed the hat away.

"What the hell—" He pulled away, staring at her head. "What did you do!?"

Jenny twisted her fingers together, then let out a noise that was more squeak than laugh. "Oh, yeah. I guess I forgot to mention I got a haircut."

"I loved your hair."

She bit her lower lip. "It's still my hair," she said, running a hand through it, touching her neck. "Just not as much of it."

"Why?"

"I had to," she whispered, wanting all of a sudden to cry. It was only hair. Just stupid hair. Why did everybody have to make such a big deal about it? She swallowed, then settled her gaze on the dark, springy hairs peeking out of Elliot's red polo shirt, right at the second button. "Natalie and Danielle cut their hair,'' she said, trying to keep her voice even. "Really short, chopped right off. When they told me they'd done it to look like their mother, I couldn't get over how brave they'd been, how truly incredible, for such little girls. So, I joined in their cause and got mine cut, too.'' Jenny lifted her eyes to his and tried to smile. "But, I also told them, no more scissors or sharp utensils. Period."

He didn't say anything for a few seconds. Then he lifted his hand and ran it through her short curls, like a soft caress. "I think you're the brave one, Jenny Romano," he said, pulling her into his arms.

And then the tears came.

Elliot led her to the living room, to an old navy couch with soft, oblong pillows trimmed in beige piping, worn at the edges. He sat down and settled her on his lap, his arms wrapped around her, protecting, offering comfort while she poured out the whole story about Grace, and the cemetery, and her refusal to stand up to their mother. At some point, the crying stopped, and Jenny rested her head on his shoulder, letting exhaustion take over as she drifted in and out of quiet slumber.

Ruby Red was curled up at Elliot's feet, an occasional whimper sneaking out of her as she passed from half-sleeping to half-dreaming. The television was on, a *Perry Mason* rerun droning in the background. Jenny wondered what it would be like to always have everything figured out, like old Perry did, to be able to fight past the doubt—in a wheelchair, no less—to champion justice. How did he do that when she couldn't even get a five- and eight-year-old to agree on the same flavor of ice cream?

"Feel better?" Elliot brushed his fingers over her bare arm, a slow, even rhythm that both lulled her and gave her goose bumps.

What was it about this man that could soothe her one second and excite her the next, and, sometimes, do both at the same time? She shifted a little, nuzzling into his shoulder. She was too tired to think about it now, too tired to do anything but feel.

"Hmmm," she murmured.

He laughed, low in his throat. "I'll take that for a yes."

"Yes," she whispered. "Thank you."

He brushed his chin over the top of her head. "For what? You did all the talking."

"With your help. You made me see that Grace has to make her own decisions, right or wrong, and I have to stop butting in."

"That's my girl," he said, kissing the top of her head.

"Unless she's so off base that I just can't keep my mouth shut," Jenny said. "Then, it's my *duty* to say something."

"No, it isn't," he corrected. "Unless she asks you for help."

"Wait a minute," she said, lifting her head off Elliot's shoulder so she could look him square in the eye. "Are you saying that if she's totally screwing up, and I mean big-time, I should just let her *go*? Let her sink herself and not do a thing to try and help her?"

"It's got to be her decision or she'll resent you."

She rolled her eyes. "So? She'll get over it."

"It's got to be her decision, Jenny," he said again, as though she hadn't heard him the first time. "She has to realize what's at stake and what she wants to do about it, if anything."

"That's crazy. I can't just sit there and smile while she messes up her whole life. It's not in my nature." She was wide awake now. She jumped off the couch and started pacing. "If it were really bad, I'd *have* to say something, try to make her see."

Elliot shook his head. "Jenny—"

Before he could finish, the front door opened and Sydney called out, "Daddy, I'm home!"

Ruby Red jumped up in full alert, letting out a string of barks as she went in search of her owner. Jenny swung around, her gaze darting to the narrow hallway leading from the entranceway. Sydney. She'd only seen her twice since the day she'd kicked Jenny out of her garden and made the bold statement that her father hated women with long, curly, black hair and hazel eyes. Well, at least one of those adjectives no longer fit. The two other times they had seen each other had been fleeting—once to pick up Grace and once to drop off Danielle and Natalie.

Jenny stood near the couch, bracing herself. Any second, Sydney would round the corner and see her . . .

"In here, Syd," Elliot said, holding out his left hand and motioning Jenny toward him.

Jenny shook her head, just one quick jerk. No. She planted her feet, waiting. Some things needed to be faced alone and a confrontation with Sydney Drake was one of them. Would she try to kick Jenny out of her house? Create a huge scene? Cry and throw a fit so Jenny would leave?

"You should see what Aunt Eleanor bought me." She was chattering away, coming closer with each word. Ruby Red rounded the corner first. "It's this big, stuffed raccoon—"

She saw Jenny then and her words fell away, like a handful of pebbles scattering off a cliff. Going, going, gone. Jenny and Sydney stared at each other, both locked in position, waiting. How could it be that an eight-year-old could make Jenny's palms sweat and her breath jam up in her throat?

Jenny didn't need to think about it for longer than a half-second before the answer stretched itself between them, an elastic rubber band of will and tenacity, pulling woman and child apart and thrusting them together with equal force. The answer under layer after layer of supposition was simple and had little to do with the fact that Sydney was Elliot's daughter. It wasn't about him at all. It was about Sydney.

She reminded Jenny of herself when she was that age: unac-
cepted, rebellious, different . . . determined not to let anyone
else get close enough to hurt her. Not like her mother had.

Yes, Sydney was just like she had been.

"Hello, Sydney," Jenny said, keeping her voice casual.

Sydney said nothing, only stared back at Jenny out of
wide, brown eyes.

*At least she hasn't started screaming or tried to boot me
out yet.* "I like your stuffed animal," Jenny said, nodding
to the masked bandit she held in her arms.

Silence. Perry Mason gave his closing argument in the
background.

"What's his name?"

Nothing.

She'd prepared herself for this, but the rejection still hurt.
Jenny turned to Elliot and forced a smile. "I think I'd better
go."

"You cut your hair." Sydney's words rode on a sucked-
in gasp of air, one big whoosh, and then she was finished.

Jenny met her gaze, wide-eyed and open-mouthed, just
short of gaping. "Yeah, well," she said, running a hand
through her short pile of curls, "it's much easier to wash
this way."

Sydney hugged her spot, fingers clutching the raccoon.
"Your hair," she murmured.

Jenny shrugged, faked a smile. "Pretty short, huh?" She
didn't think it looked *that* bad. It was short, not hideous,
but Sydney was looking at her as though she were Medusa's
twin.

"It was beautiful." A flat, empty statement, rolling off
Sydney's lips. Her hands dropped to her sides, the raccoon
dangling from her right hand, his bushy tail sweeping the
floor. Ruby Red sniffed its tail, trotted back to Jenny's side,
sniffed her hand, and plopped down at her feet.

Sydney didn't seem to notice. She hadn't taken her eyes off of Jenny's hair.

Was she referring to my hair? My long hair? The hair she said her father hated? Did she think *that* was beautiful?

"You cut it because . . ." she faltered, started again, "because . . ." She couldn't seem to get past the "because" part. Her voice grew higher, wobbled, cracked. "You cut it because of me." The tears came then, spilling over and down her pale cheeks.

Jenny rushed to her, forgetting that Sydney had kicked her out of the garden, uttered cruel, hurtful things, and warned her away from her father, from herself. Jenny pulled her into her arms, resting her chin on Sydney's silky head. "It's not your fault, Sydney. It's okay."

She sobbed into Jenny's shirt, great tears of loneliness and misery. "I'm . . . sorry. I'm . . . sorry." Jenny heard the muffled apology and tightened her arms around the child.

"I know," she murmured, over and over, a soft lullaby of forgiveness and hope floating around them.

Sydney's arms snaked around Jenny's waist and she hugged her. "Ruby Red really, really missed you, Jenny."

Jenny swallowed hard. "I missed her, too, Sydney. Very, very much."

Jenny and Sydney were in the garden, cutting lavender.

"Just rub a little bit of the purple between your fingers," Jenny instructed her, "and sniff."

"It smells good."

"Take a deep breath." She inhaled, held it. "Then let it out. See, doesn't that make you feel all relaxed?"

Sydney made a face. "It tickles my nose."

Jenny swatted a piece of lavender at her chin and laughed. "It's *supposed* to make you relax. You should see how much stuff I have that's made with lavender—candles, body lotions, body sprays, linen fresheners, soap, potpourri.'' She inhaled again. ''But nothing's better than the plant itself. This is the best.''

''Jenny?''

''Huh?''

''You can take as much as you want, any time, even if I'm not here.''

Jenny looked at the little girl and saw the earnestness in her eyes. ''Thank you, Sydney. Thank you very much.''

''Are you gonna leave?''

''What?''

''You know,'' she picked off a lavender bud, rubbed it between her small fingers. ''Leave. Go back to California.''

''Well . . . eventually.''

''Can't you just stay here?'' There was a pleading note in her voice.

''I . . . I have a job back there.''

''Can't you get a job here?''

''Well . . .'' Joe had been pleased with her D.C. piece, had told her there'd be more East Coast work if she was interested. Why had he offered that? Had he sensed something she hadn't, that maybe she didn't *want* to leave, that maybe she wanted to stay in Ohio?

''So?''

This was crazy. ''So, I have a home, a condo.''

''You could get a home here, in Ohio . . . maybe even with Daddy and me.''

Jenny coughed, half-choked. A home . . . with Sydney . . . and Elliot . . . She brushed the thought away—now she knew she was losing her mind. ''And I have friends, lots of them, who would really miss me if I weren't there.'' Okay, so Stefan and Gerald were her only real friends, but they *would* miss her.

''I'm your friend,'' Sydney said in a small voice, ''and if you weren't here, I'd really miss you.''

"I'd miss you, too, Sydney." And she *would* miss her very much . . . and Elliot.

"Just say maybe—can you just say maybe?"

Jenny opened her mouth to say "no," she was sorry but she couldn't even consider it, the whole idea was ridiculous, she belonged in LA with a job that jetted her all over the world, but the word wouldn't come; it lodged in her throat and wouldn't budge. When she did finally speak, the words that came out surprised her. "I don't know, Sydney. I just don't know."

Sydney smiled.

"Why are you smiling?"

"Because tomorrow you'll say 'yes.' " Her smile got wider, showing off her dimples.

"Why do you think that?" Why would she think that when Jenny was more confused than any of them and she was the one making the decision?

"Because, when Daddy says 'I don't know,' I just wait and ask him the next day." She nodded her head, gave Jenny a knowing look. "And then he says 'yes.' "

Jenny shook her head, wondering who the real psychologist in the family was, Sydney or her father. Out of the corner of her eye, she saw a butterfly land on the clump of lavender where she'd been taking cuttings. It was a monarch, its yellow wings fluttering amidst the purple.

"Look," Sydney whispered, "let's catch it." She swooped out her hands, trying to cup the butterfly between them, but he was too quick and flew out of reach before she could grab him. "I almost got him," she said, her gaze following the butterfly in the air. "Come back here," she called. "Come back here, butterfly."

"Sydney, do you know if you catch him, he'll die?"

"I don't want him to die—I just want to keep him."

Jenny shook her head. "You can't. Where would you keep him? In your house?"

"I'd want to train him, keep him outside, in the garden," she said, her eyes following the butterfly as he landed on a lilac bush.

"And even if he would stay in the garden, even if you could put him in a fenced-in garden, do you know what could happen when you tried to catch him?"

Sydney met Jenny's gaze, shook her head.

"If you tried to catch him, some of the color could rub off of his wings, and that's what helps him fly. And then do you know what happens?" Jenny knew because she'd done it herself once—caught a monarch, touched his wing, got yellow powder on her fingers . . . and watched him die.

"No, what?"

"When his color rubs off, he can't fly anymore, and then he dies."

. . . and then he dies.

Maybe Jenny and Grace weren't so different from the butterfly . . . maybe they both needed to just be who they were, stop trying to wish themselves into something else, *someone else* . . . or *their* color would get rubbed off . . . by unmet expectations, friends, family . . . even themselves. Maybe, just maybe, it was time to learn to accept who they were . . . time to learn to protect their color.

Chapter 23

Jenny put the last dish away and closed the dishwasher. She had just picked up the latest copy of *People* and was headed for the backyard when she heard the car doors slam.

They were back.

Grace had gone to the cemetery, after all. She hadn't had the strength or the guts to stand up to her mother and say, *You can pay your respects to the bastard. You don't know what I know. You go. If I do, I'll spit on his grave.*

How could Grace play the game, and play it so well, when she hated him so much? *How could she do it?* Was pretending she'd had a loving, faithful husband and a wonderful marriage more important than being real? And at what point did fact and fiction blur into a zillion indistinguishable particles of a fragmented self? At what point was there no "self" left?

Part of Jenny wanted to ask her all of these questions, wanted to shout them out, demand answers. And yet, another part, softer, more forgiving, did not want to know.

"Tomorrow, we'll bring him some daisies," Jenny heard her mother say as they came in through the side door. "I'll cut a bunch from the Shastas out back."

Grace said nothing.

"Jenny, there you are. Grace, what time did we leave? Nine A.M.? And you were still sound asleep. We've already been to the cemetery, the post office, *and* the grocery store."

"Hi, Mom." Jenny leaned against the kitchen sink, glanced at Grace, who was wiping her nose with a tissue.

"I'd like to say living in California did this to you, but you were like this before you ever left."

Did what to me?

Virginia Romano shook her head and set her tan purse on the kitchen table. "I could never get you to budge in the morning. It was always a hassle. Your father was the only one who could get you moving."

"I've been up since nine-fifteen."

Her mother's brow shot up. "Then you should've gotten up a half-hour earlier and gone to the cemetery with us."

Jenny shot Grace a quick look. She looked away. Her eyes were all puffy and her nose was red.

"I told you, Mom," Jenny said, "I don't go in much for cemeteries."

Her mother let out a disgusted sigh. "It's not about the cemetery, Jenny. It's about respect. Simple, honest respect." Jenny watched her as she made her way over to the coffeepot and pulled a mug down from the cupboard. It was blue with "We Love Daddy" scrawled in white and spattered with tiny white handprints along the bottom. Figured. "That man deserves it. He cherished your sister." She poured a drop of cream in the mug and stirred. "You should be so lucky to find a man like that."

Jenny looked at Grace, watched her fidget with her bandana, pulling it first to the right, then to the left, and finally back to the right again. Her head was bent, her gaze cast downward.

Jenny crossed her arms over her chest, cleared her throat, and said, "Grant was one of a kind."

"He was a saint," her mother said, pulling out a chair to sit down. She set her mug on the table and made the sign of the cross. "I sent in a Mass card for him. The Brothers of St. Francis will celebrate a Mass in his name every month for the next year."

"Good." *He'll need it.*

She took a sip of coffee and looked at Grace. "I think we will bring those Shasta daisies to the cemetery tomorrow. They'll be a nice touch. Light, airy, delicate." Her black-and-gray head slowly moved up and down. "It'll be a perfect contrast to the roses we brought today. Don't you think so, Grace?"

"Yes," Grace said, her mouth barely moving.

"Good. And then there are begonias and pansies." She tapped an index finger to her chin. "Maybe even petunias."

She carried on for another full minute, naming flowers and color combinations, oblivious to everything but her own words. There were carnations and mums in just about every shade imaginable, though she thought pale pinks might be best. And a few sprays of lavender tucked in with baby's breath would complement the purple violas she'd seen at the greenhouse this morning, though they'd most likely wither in this infernal heat. On and on it went.

How could she not notice Grace's glassy stare, fixed and dull, focused on the edge of the plastic tablecloth? Or the faint white line around her lips, drawn tight and unsmiling? And what about the way Grace kept picking and pulling at her clothes with her right index finger and thumb? Didn't she see that, her own mother?

Silence swirled around them, a thick, opaque fog, threatening to submerge them in darkness, snuff the life from their bodies, suck their souls dry. Didn't she *feel* it?

And what about Grace? Worst of all, *what about Grace?* She *knew.* Grace knew. How could she let herself be dragged under, suffocated, plunged into an existence that had no meaning?

How could she? *How could she betray herself?*

Jenny stuck her trowel deep into the dark brown soil and scooped out a four-inch pile of dirt. Okay. Well, she'd see if Elliot was right about his little manure tip, or if it was just a bunch of bull*shit.* Funny. At least she still had a sense of humor, though she hadn't used it much in the past two hours, not since she'd interrupted her mother's litany on flowers for Grant's gravesite. Jenny had faked a coughing fit, got up, and downed a glass of water. Then she'd nodded that she was okay, and beelined out the back door.

Relief. Blessed relief, that's what she'd felt when her foot hit the bottom step and her mother's voice faded away. Jenny had gone around the side of the house to the garage and pulled out garden gloves, a trowel, a four-pronged digger, and a fifteen-pound bag of manure that she'd bought at Kmart yesterday. She needed to dig around in the soil, bury her hands in the black earth, even if they were covered in lime green garden gloves. It didn't matter what she planted; it could be dandelions or three-inch squares of grass, for all she cared. She just needed to plant.

She decided to separate those damned Shasta daisies that her mother was planning to take to the cemetery tomorrow. Why not? She karate-chopped a third of the plant with five solid whacks, and then proceeded to dig it up. It would look good, five plants down, past a black-eyed Susan and three variegated hostas, in the vacated spot of a shriveled-up viola.

She plunged the trowel into a fresh section of soil. This *shit* better work.

"Jenny?"

Grace.

She stiffened, her trowel filled with dirt and a fat, juicy earthworm.

"What?" Jenny stared at the worm, watched him try to burrow back to the safety of the soil. She did not turn around.

"I had to go. You know that, don't you?"

Jenny lifted her shoulders. *Keep your mouth shut*—that's what Elliot had said, but in a much more diplomatic manner.

"You do know that, don't you?" There was persistence and a bit of something else laced in those words. Desperation, maybe?

Her choices have to be her own. "You did what you thought you had to do," Jenny said.

"Yes. Yes, I did." She took a few steps to the right so she could see Jenny's face. "If I don't go with her to that damned cemetery, she'll know something's wrong." Her right index finger and thumb started picking at her T-shirt. "She'll start asking me questions, digging around." The fingers picked faster. She hesitated. "I can't risk that."

Jenny dropped the trowel, letting the worm tunnel back home. "What do you want me to say, Grace?" She leaned back on her heels. *Don't say anything. Keep your mouth shut. Keep your mouth shut.*

Grace's voice grew high, almost shrill. "I want you to stop looking at me like you think I betrayed you. Like you think I should have refused to go."

Jenny shot a glance toward the house. "Are you ever going to tell her?" she asked, lowering her voice.

"No!" she said, in a fervent whisper. "Absolutely not!"

Jenny gnawed on her lower lip. *Shut up. Don't open your big mouth.* Don't. Don't. "It's only going to get worse." The words flew out of nowhere. "Pretty soon you'll be saying the rosary for him.'' They just kept coming. ''And wait until she starts having his picture laminated on everything, like she did when Dad died.'' She couldn't stop now. ''You won't be able to go to the bathroom without seeing his face right above the toilet holder.''

''I can't tell her.'' Her voice wobbled, cracked. ''I can't.''

To hell with keeping her mouth shut. ''Yes, Gracie,'' Jenny said, ''you can.'' She flung off her glove, reached up, and squeezed her sister's left hand.

''You have to.''

Grace stared at Jenny, eyes bright and shining, lower lip trembling. ''You don't understand,'' she said, pulling her hand out of Jenny's grasp. ''You never understood.'' She sniffed and took a step backward. ''You have no idea what it's like to have everybody watching you, *expecting* you to always do the right thing.'' She swiped her hands over her eyes. ''No mistakes. No room for error. *How could you possibly know?* You always did whatever you wanted.''

The truth slipped through Jenny's lips. ''I wish someone would have expected something from me.''

''Hah! No, you don't, believe me.'' Grace's voice dipped, rose, dipped again in a roller coaster of emotion. ''I never did anything without worrying if it was the *right* thing, the noble thing to do.'' She let out a laugh that came out more like a choking gasp. ''And where did it get me? I'm visiting a dead, philandering husband's grave. And bringing him flowers, to boot.''

Jenny clenched her lower jaw, released it. ''So, stop it now. Stop the cycle. Before it destroys you and you don't know who you are.''

Tears rolled down Grace's cheeks, but she didn't try to stop them this time. ''Who am I, Jenny? Huh? *Who am I?*''

Before Jenny could answer, she dove in. ''I'll tell you who I am. I'm a thirty-six-year-old widow with a shaved head and a bunch of broken dreams who still can't say no to her mother.'' She covered her face with her hands. ''Pathetic, isn't it?''

''Oh, Gracie.'' Jenny stood up, reached for her. She had to try to stop the pain, absorb some of it into herself—she had to do *something*.

''No.'' Grace lifted her hands and stepped back, just out of Jenny's reach. ''No.''

''Let me help you.'' Jenny felt the sting of her own tears spilling over, pouring out grief and remorse.

''No,'' she whispered. ''Don't you see, Jenny? Don't you really see?'' she asked, choking on her words. ''I can be so strong for everybody else, forgive them their mistakes and shortcomings. But not for myself. I know I should go in there right now and tell her about Grant. Tell her everything. But I won't because I'm a coward. I want her to go on believing he was perfect, my life was perfect, everything was perfect.''

''You'd rather fake it all than tell her the truth and be done with it?''

She met Jenny's gaze, her eyes red and swollen. ''I've been faking it since the day I found out about his first affair.'' She sniffed. ''I'm actually quite good at it.''

''But,'' Jenny hesitated, ''it's all a lie, Grace. You're just living a lie.''

She smiled then, a pathetic, half-tilt of the lips. ''But it's the perfect lie. And it's all I have left.''

In seven days, Jenny was going back to LA. Joe had called and told her he needed her in Seattle to shoot a priest-turned-techie spread. He said it was big stuff and it was her last chance. She'd told him she'd be there.

She'd also called Stefan and Gerald, told them she was coming back and was dying for a bowl of Gerald's bouillabaisse.

"You don't sound very excited," Stefan said, the night she called him. "Actually, you sound a little . . . down."

"Why wouldn't I be excited to be coming back to the best neighbors in LA, not to mention best friends, best decorator, and best chef? Huh? You just have Gerald start cooking and I'll be there." Her words might have been upbeat, but her tone sounded flat, even to her own ears.

"Jenny?"

"Yes?"

"What is it?" Stefan prided himself on picking up telepathic waves—"getting vibes from people," as he called it.

"There's just a lot going on here." That much was the truth. "Grace is having a tough time," she paused, adding, "and my mother is still here."

"Ahh . . ." then, "Have you been using the lavender and chamomile oil?"

"Yes, but actually, I know someone who *grows* lavender and chamomile, so I've been picking it fresh and practically burying my face in the smell."

"Something else is bothering you. I can tell. Is it that brute Joe Feltzer, bullying you back before you're ready?"

"No." Should she tell him about Elliot, tell him that she was leaving in seven days and he hadn't even once asked her to stay? Or to write, or visit, or whatever it was that romantically involved people who lived thousands of miles away did?

When she'd told him about Joe's phone call, they'd been lying on a comforter in Elliot's backyard, the scent of the garden drifting over them, the moon and stars covering them from above. He'd been stroking her arm, slow, gentle, driving her wild with desire. And when the words were out, there'd been a half-second hesitation as his fingers paused, and then he began stroking again, telling her it sounded like a good opportunity and he was confident she'd do a good job. She'd waited, actually hoped he would take off his horn-rimmed glasses and pinch the bridge of his nose like he did when he was thinking, and then look at her with those soulful brown eyes and ask her to stay. But he didn't. He hadn't even said he'd write.

Grace was another story. When Jenny had told her she was leaving in seven days, the Arctic freeze between them seemed to melt a few degrees. But not much. They hadn't really talked since the day she'd come to Jenny in the back-yard and told her that her life was a lie and she knew it and there wasn't a damn thing she was going to do about it.

Their mother must have sensed the tension between them, because she was actually civil to Jenny. Hard to believe, even shocking, but true.

Three days before Jenny was scheduled to leave, she and Grace were folding clothes on the kitchen table. Jenny was in charge of socks and underwear, Grace shirts and shorts. They both did the towels. Their mother was ironing Natalie's cotton sundress with the big daisies on the border.

"Mommy! Mommy! Mommy!" Natalie came tearing into the kitchen, with Danielle at her heels. Their faces were pink with excitement, their breathing coming in quick, shallow gulps. "Guess what we found under your bed!" She held out her small hand, balled into a fist.

Grace smiled, a faint, tolerant smile that only another mother can understand. "What did you find under my bed?" she ventured, cocking her head to one side.

"Guess?" This came from Danielle, who seemed equally enthralled by the mystery.

"Hmmm," Grace said, picking up one of Danielle's powder blue tank tops. "Dust bunnies?"

The girls shook their heads and said, "Nope."

"A monster?"

"No!" Their giggles filled the room and made Jenny smile, probably only the fourth in as many days. But how was a person supposed to smile when her sister was on the outs with her? When the man she was crazy about was letting her go two thousand miles away without a word to try and keep her? When her mother was taking every opportunity to laud her dead son-in-law's attributes in the hope that one day Jenny, too, might find such a wonderful man?

It was enough to make a person crazy. Really crazy.

"Look, Mommy! Look!" Natalie squealed as she turned her hand, palm up, and uncurled her fingers.

Three objects sparkled in the middle of her tiny palm. Two rings, sprinkled with diamonds. Grace's wedding rings. And a bracelet, gold, covered with rubies and diamonds.

"Where on earth did you find those?" Their grandmother moved in for a closer inspection.

"Under the bed, Grandma," Natalie said.

"Oh, baloney. Did you take these from your mother's jewelry box?"

"No," they said in unison.

"You girls both know that God doesn't want you to fib."

"No, Grandma. Honest," Danielle said. "They were under the bed. We were crawling under there with our flashlights and saw them."

"Yep." Natalie's short curls bounced as she nodded. "That's right. And we knew Mommy would be happy we found them for her."

"This makes no sense. How could they have gotten under the bed? Grace?" Virginia Romano looked at her daughter and frowned. "These are your wedding rings. And the bracelet looks quite valuable. You told me you couldn't wear the rings because you lost too much weight. But you didn't tell me you lost them. And how could you lose the bracelet? Under a bed, no less. I don't understand."

No, she wouldn't, but Jenny thought *she* did. The night Grace confessed Grant's infidelity she was crouched down on the floor in the corner of her bedroom. Jenny didn't remember if there was anything in her hand, but there could have been. And if she'd thrown them in a fit of rage, they might well have landed under the bed. There was certainly rage that night, enough to explain discarded wedding rings and a diamond-and-ruby-studded bracelet.

"Grace?" It was their mother again, persistent as ever. She was not going to let this go.

Jenny leaned forward and snatched the jewelry from Natalie's outstretched hand. "Thanks, kiddo. Your mom was looking for these." She fluffed the top of her niece's head and Natalie giggled.

"Welcome." The little girl turned to her mother and her smile faded. "You should be more careful with this kind of stuff, Mom."

Grace looked at her youngest daughter and merely nodded. She hadn't moved since Natalie opened her hand to reveal the jewelry. Her face was pasty white, her eyes fixed and glassy.

How was she going to explain this one? *I was cleaning under the bed and they fell off? I dropped them and they got kicked under there? I lost so much weight they just slipped off in my sleep and rolled under the bed?* It all sounded untrue. Like the big lie that it was.

"Why don't you kids go bring this pie plate back to Mrs. M," Jenny said. She didn't want them around when Grace started on another lie.

"Okay," Danielle said. "Can we stay there and play a little, Mom?"

"Sure." One word, faint, distant, forced.

"Okay. 'Bye." They each gave Grace a quick hug around the middle, then Danielle snatched the aluminum plate from Jenny's hand and bounded out the back door, screen door slamming.

"All right. What's going on?"

"Nothing, Mom," Jenny said. "Grace just misplaced some jewelry."

"Just misplaced some *jewelry?*" Her brow shot up. "They were wedding rings. You don't just *misplace* those."

Jenny shrugged. "Well, she did."

Their mother's nostrils flared and she turned to Grace. "What's going on?"

"I—" Grace started, stopped. "I took them off one night," she rubbed her forehead with both hands, "and put them on the bedside stand. They must have fallen and rolled or gotten kicked under the bed."

"When?" Virginia Romano knew how to interrogate.

"I don't know." Grace shrugged. "A week ago. Maybe two."

Their mother let out a grunt that sounded half-snort. "You lost your rings *and* a bracelet and you don't even remember when?"

"No." Grace inched the word from her lips.

"Why did you take them off?" She held up her left hand and displayed the plain, gold band. "I never take this off. Never. Not even when I'm cleaning."

"They were too big. I was afraid I'd lose them." Grace was a terrible liar.

"So you put them on the nightstand instead of in a jewelry case? Because you didn't want to lose them?" There was a shrillness to Virginia Romano's voice, an accusation almost, as though she knew Grace was lying to her.

But there was too much at risk for honesty to shatter Grace's image or the dreams she'd built in the pre-tide sand, even if she had to guard them with a bucket and her last vestiges of self-respect.

"That's right," she said, her gaze darting to Jenny's right hand.

Jenny clenched her fist around the jewelry, felt the stones

digging into the soft flesh of her palm. *I won't betray you,
Grace.*

"This whole situation is totally ridiculous." Virginia
Romano shook her head and let out a loud breath like she
always did when she was too disgusted to put her annoyance
into words. The magnified exchange of air usually did the
trick. Her daughters heard it, recognizing it for what it was:
anger and annoyance. And then Grace would try to appease
her.

But not this time. Grace was silent. She'd picked up a
white sock and was pulling at a long string on the stitching,
head bent, intent on her mission.

"Jenny, give your sister those rings and that bracelet. The
least she can do is put them on." She clucked her tongue
on the roof of her mouth. "I swear, is this what happens
when you come to stay with your sister? *She* starts to do
crazy things? Behave as irresponsibly as you?"

Jenny bit down on her lower lip, hard enough to taste
blood. *Do not say anything. Keep your mouth shut.*

"Go on, Jenny," she repeated. "Give them to Grace."

Jenny hazarded a quick glance at her sister. Grace's face
had changed from white to gray with her mother's first
command. The stones dug deeper into Jenny's palm.

Now what, Gracie?

"Come on, Jenny. She needs to get them back on. You
know it's very bad luck to take your wedding ring off for
longer than an hour at a time."

Where did she hear these things? Jenny wondered.
Between her sayings and superstitions, she could publish a
book. Correction. *Books.* Volumes one, two, *and* three.

Grace was pulling on another string, this one along the
edge of the sock. *Grace? What am I supposed to do? Help
me out here. Say something.* Grace yanked hard and the
string broke.

Jenny held up her hand, trained her gaze on Grace's face,

and watched her sister study the two-inch piece of string in her hand; then she slowly unbent her fingers.

"Now," their mother said, snatching the rings and bracelet from Jenny's hand. "I want both of you girls to stop this foolishness. Right now. Here, Grace, put these on." She held out her hand, waiting for Grace to take the jewelry.

Jenny balled her hands into fists, felt the sharp edge of nail digging into flesh. Tighter. Tighter. Pain. And still she waited. What now? *What now?*

Chapter 24

Grace took a step back, clutching the sock in her hand.

"What's the matter with you?" Virginia Romano was not a stupid woman. "You're acting like you don't want to put these on." She paused. "Oh, I see." Her dark gaze shot over at Jenny, then swung back to Grace. "I see what's going on here. Your sister's trying to fill your head, isn't she? Talk you into dating and acting like a single woman. Well, don't even think about it. It's much too soon."

Grace lifted her hand, extended it, and came within inches of touching the wedding band. Then she let out a cry and jerked her hand away. "No," she said, shaking her head, the pain pulsing in her words. "I can't." Her voice was raw, whisper-soft. "I can't."

"Grace?" Alarm shot out of that one little word.

"He cheated on me, Mom," she said in a ragged breath. *"He cheated on me."*

"Oh, my God." Their mother leaned back against the

table, working a hand over her face. *"Grant?"* She shook her head. "Grant was having an . . . *affair?"*

Grace's dark eyes brimmed with tears. "The day he died, I found him at a restaurant with his girlfriend. That's why he was in the van with me." She swiped a hand over her eyes. "Trying to tell me another lie. And it wasn't his first," she finished on a weary sigh.

"Oh, Gracie, why didn't you tell me?"

"How, Mom? How could I tell you that the marriage you thought was so perfect, to the man you adored, was all a lie?"

"You should have tried. I would have helped you."

"I couldn't. Not then." She let out a hoarse laugh. "I refused to believe it myself, so how could I tell anyone else?"

"Oh, my God—oh, my God."

"That's what I say every night when I get into an empty bed." Grace sniffed. "That's why the jewelry was under the bed. I threw it there. I never wanted to see it again."

Virginia Romano looked like the life had been punched out of her; her eyes were glazed over, mouth slack, breathing labored. She clasped the edges of the table, half leaning, half sitting. "You knew?" she said, looking at Jenny. "You knew about this?"

Jenny nodded. There was hurt in her mother's voice, and a hint of accusation.

"She wanted me to tell you," Grace said. "But I insisted on keeping it all a big secret. I told myself it was better for you, easier if you thought I was a grieving widow." She coughed, cleared her throat. "I didn't want you to know that truth. But when Natalie opened her hand and I saw the rings and that bracelet, I knew I couldn't go through with it."

"I wish I had known."

"I know, but I didn't think you'd want to. Not really.

You were so proud of me, the girls, Grant. I didn't want you to start criticizing me.''

"Why would I do that?" She seemed genuinely surprised that Grace would say such a thing. "I would never do that.''

"Sometimes you do, Mom," she said, shooting a quick look at Jenny.

"Well, only if they deserve it." It was her turn to give Jenny the once-over.

Grace shook her head. "That's not true. You don't like it if somebody has a different opinion from yours. You make it very difficult for them.''

"That's because some people are too impulsive, too outspoken, too . . . unstructured.''

Why didn't her mother just come out and hook her name on the front of those words. *Jenny is too impulsive. Jenny is too outspoken. Jenny is too unstructured.*

"Some people are honest, Mom," Grace said. "Some people tell you when they don't want to make pies from scratch. Others will go through the motions, never uttering a word, and hating every minute of it.''

"It's important to know how to make a good crust.''

Grace's lips turned up into a sad smile. "That's not the point. I was too busy thinking about what *you* wanted to consider what I might want. I should have done that, I really should have.'' She looked at Jenny then, her brown eyes brimming with tears. "I just needed someone to give me a little push.''

Jenny swallowed, felt the sting of tears in her own eyes.

"I wish I would have known how you felt, Grace.''

Good old Mom. She just never quit.

Grace shrugged. "Well, I guess now you know.'' She ran her hands over her face. "I think I'll go lie down for a while. I'm exhausted.''

"Fine. Go lie down.'' She nodded her head.

"I love you, Mom," Grace said, taking a step forward to give her a hug.

"I love you, too, Grace."

Jenny clamped down on her bottom teeth, willing herself not to cry. *So, she doesn't show this kind of emotion toward me. So what? So what?*

Grace pulled away and turned toward Jenny, arms outstretched. Jenny stepped into them, and they clung to each other, absorbing one another's pain. "I love you, Jenny. Thank you," she whispered.

"I love you, too, Gracie."

Grace sniffed and let out a shaky laugh, releasing her hold. "You'd have to, to put up with me these last few months."

"Yeah, you've been a real pain. I guess we'll be even in about thirty years."

That made her smile.

"Go, get some rest," Jenny said.

She nodded, looked at Jenny, then at her mother, and walked out of the kitchen.

"Well," Virginia Romano said, pulling out a chair and sinking into it with a thump.

Jenny picked at a piece of skin on her thumb. "Yeah."

"I really wish she'd told me. I could have helped her."

Jenny pulled the skin straight up, felt sharp pain, let go. "She said you really helped her."

Jenny shrugged, feeling suddenly self-conscious. "I did what any sister would do."

"That's true. You did," she agreed. "And that's what surprises me most."

Jenny's head shot up. "Did you think I wouldn't? That I'd bail out?"

She didn't say anything for a few seconds, just stared at Jenny with those dark eyes that revealed nothing. "I wondered."

Of course she did, Jenny thought. *She wondered how long I'd make it. And how screwed up everything would be by the time she got here.*

Her mother's gaze dropped to the tablecloth. "But, you know," she said, drawing a pattern on the plastic covering with her fingernail, "I don't really think you needed me here. You could've done this by yourself."

What? "Was that a compliment?" Jenny wasn't trying to be sarcastic—she really didn't know.

Her mother hesitated. "Yes. Yes, it was."

"Thank you," Jenny managed, feeling awkward and elated at the same time.

"You're welcome." She shifted in her chair.

Jenny wondered if her mother felt awkward and elated, too. Probably just awkward.

"You know, Jenny," she started, working her gaze up to meet her daughter's, one inch at a time, "things haven't always been easy between us."

Jenny forced herself not to laugh out loud. *Right,* she wanted to say. *And the Pacific Ocean is a creek.*

"It's just that," she paused, licked her lips, "you were always so *different.* I never understood you. Not like Grace. She was easy, predictable. You were like a storm, crashing in, veering right, then left, invariably hitting dead center, flattening everything in your wake." She stared off into space. "Your father said to leave you alone. You were the baby." Her voice dropped. "His pride and joy. I couldn't, though. Not at first. I tried so hard to protect you ... the time you tried to ride your sister's bicycle and wrecked into the tree. Fell right on your left arm, broke it just below the elbow."

"I was the first kid on the street to get a cast."

"True. And then, when you were in seventh grade, you tie-dyed a shirt and a skirt for the school dance. I told you not to wear it, but you did anyway. I knew the kids would laugh at you.'' Her eyes grew misty. ''But you insisted on going in that ridiculous big shirt and long skirt. And they did laugh.''

''Not all of them,'' Jenny said, remembering the snickers and hoots as she walked into the gymnasium. She'd been going through her Janis Joplin–Beatles era, and tie-dye seemed like the thing to do.

''Enough that the principal called me because he was concerned.'' She shook her head. ''I stayed up all night, worrying about you, wondering how you were ever going to mesh into society with all of your crazy ideas. Your father said to let it be. You'd do just fine.'' She looked at Jenny. Hard. Like she was really looking at her, into her, maybe for the first time. Or maybe it was the other way around. Maybe it was the first time Jenny was really looking at *her*. ''So, I let it go. And the next time something happened, I let that go, too, until after a while, I let everything go.''

''I never thought you cared,'' Jenny said, sounding six years old again.

''Never cared? I cared too much. So much that it was driving me crazy.''

''But you tried to control me.''

''I did. I thought if I controlled you, then I could understand you. And then I could protect you.'' A tear slipped down her cheek. ''But it all backfired. We ended up enemies, on the opposite side of a war no one could win.''

''So, you chose Grace.'' Jenny couldn't keep the hurt from her voice.

''I didn't *choose* Grace over you,'' she said, swiping at her eyes. ''I always loved you both. Grace was just so much easier to be around. She didn't fight for the sake of fighting. She was much easier to *like*.''

Tears sprang to Jenny's eyes. She swallowed, hard, and pushed the words out. ''I just wanted you to care about me, Mom. To look at me the way you looked at Grace.'' She swiped a hand across her cheek. "But you never did. So, after a while, I created things to get your attention, the worse the better. And then, by the time I became an adult, I didn't care anymore." Her voice dipped. "I *told* myself I didn't care anymore."

Her mother was crying now, big, fat, honest tears rolling down her face.

"I'm not Grace. I can't be. I'm me," Jenny said, jabbing an index finger at her heart. "Me. Jenny Romano. Yes, I love flying cross-country on a moment's notice. Yes, I have an herb garden painted on my kitchen wall. Yes, I sometimes eat cake for breakfast. And yes, I still do, on occasion, leave my underwear under the bed." She reached out, and covered her mother's hand with her own. "But that's me, Mom. That's what makes me, *me*. Please don't try to change that."

Her mother placed her other hand on top of Jenny's. "I can only promise to try."

Jenny smiled. "That's a start."

"I do love you, Jenny."

"I love you, too, Mom."

Her mother's lips worked into a slow smile. She leaned closer, looked Jenny square in the eye, and said, "Now about the underwear under the bed . . ."

"Don't forget, you promised Mom you'd visit her for Christmas."

"I know. I will, Grace." And she would. Jenny and her mother were in the tenuous stages of rebuilding their relationship after a twenty-some-odd-year hiatus. It was the least Jenny could do. And for once, she didn't feel like she *had* to do it. She wanted to do it.

"I'm a little surprised she didn't stay here longer, at least wait until you left."

Jenny wasn't surprised. Not at all. They'd said a lot of

things to each other, years of words, built up, packed tight, layered with the veneer of misunderstanding, peeling and yellowed, needing to be scraped clean.

Her mother needed time. Jenny needed time.

"It's okay," Jenny said, realizing that it really was.

"Has Elliot said anything about the two of you still seeing each other once you leave?"

Crash. Back to the acid-eating dragon gnawing on her stomach lining. "No."

"You've still got two days." She covered Jenny's hand with her own. "He might."

"Come on, Grace," Jenny said, meeting her gaze. "I'm not six anymore. We both know if he wanted this relationship to go any further, he would've said something by now. He's had plenty of opportunities and it isn't as if I haven't broached the subject, several times. He just keeps skirting around it, changing the subject."

"Maybe he's afraid, you know, after his wife ran off and all." Her soft brown eyes misted.

"Yeah, well, maybe we're all afraid." *And maybe I'm dying inside, damn him.*

"Give him time."

"Forty-eight hours, that's it, and then I'm gone."

The house was quiet. Too quiet. Jenny wandered around, trying to decide if she should exercise her improving culinary skills and bake chocolate chip cookies, take a walk and enjoy the sunset, or, and this kicked her salivary glands into fourth gear, dig into the new gallon of Heavenly Hash in the freezer. It took about 2.2 seconds to opt for the Heavenly Hash. Three scoops and a cherry on top later, she plopped down on the couch, spoon in one hand, remote control in the other.

Ain't life grand? she thought, plunking a big spoonful of

Heavenly Hash into her mouth. She flicked through the first six stations. Baseball, golf, and more baseball. *Click*. A man and a woman kissing. *Click*. A man, a woman, and a baby. *Click*. A man in a black tuxedo and a woman in a wedding dress. *Click*. *Click*. Off.

Why hadn't she and Elliot talked about her leaving, or, better yet, talked about her staying? He was the one who was the psychologist—wasn't he supposed to know when a person needed to talk, get something cleared up? Well, wasn't he? Wasn't there even the tiniest piece of him that wanted her to stay? How could he just let her walk away, as though they had shared nothing more than a caffe latte or a stroll in the park, as though they hadn't come together, body, heart, soul?

She loved him.

God, yes, she loved him. Didn't he love her, even a little bit? The pain of rejection hit her square in the gut, right on top of the half-pint of Heavenly Hash she'd just devoured. Why was it when she finally found a man she could love, he didn't love her back? *Maybe she wasn't professional enough, traditional enough ... maybe she just wasn't enough?*

She'd told Elliot in a roundabout way that after this next assignment, she was considering taking Joe up on his offer to cover all of the East Coast assignments. It wouldn't be as glamorous as shooting on the Thames, or leaning out of a second-story window in Venice to capture an old man peddling cherry tarts and fresh-baked bread, but it would be solid. Real. And close to the people she cared about. Close to Grace, Danielle, Natalie, Sydney ... Elliot.

She dumped another spoonful of Heavenly Hash into her mouth.

Grace didn't need her here anymore. There was a shine in her eyes, a kind of glow about her that spoke of self-confidence and second chances. Jenny had seen it when

Grace opened the door this afternoon and let Guy Delacroix in. He'd come to pick her and the girls up for pizza and a matinee. And Jenny had also seen the way he watched her. If Grace thought he only wanted to chum around with her as a teacher pal, she was in for a big shock. A pleasant one, though, or at least it would be once she got past the age thing and the longish hair. Oh, and the tiny gold hoop in his left ear.

She shoved the last bit of Heavenly Hash into her mouth.

So, why the hell couldn't Elliot Drake love her the way she loved him? *Why?* Had it been nothing but sex with him, had she been nothing more than a diversion with long, black hair? Hadn't he felt the deep soul-promise when they were together, body to body, heart to heart, soul to soul?

Dammit, hadn't he?

Jenny plunked the empty bowl on the table, tossed the spoon inside. Well, if he hadn't, he'd have to tell her himself. She jumped off the couch and grabbed her keys. In two more days, she'd never have to see him again, but tonight, tonight she'd have her answers.

Chapter 25

Jenny slammed the van door and ran up the sidewalk to Elliot's house, oblivious to the ferns and pots of begonias on the front porch that usually gave her so much pleasure. All she wanted to do was find Elliot and confront him, *now*.

She rang the doorbell to his office, waited. Nothing. Then she tried his other doorbell, the one for his home. Again, nothing. *Damn.* Where was he? He usually worked Thursday afternoons, so where were his patients and where was he?

Jenny blew out a long breath, tried to think. Maybe she should just go back to Grace's, wait until she'd calmed down and could be more civilized about the whole thing, then call him, be polite, perhaps even a bit removed. Maybe say something clever like, *I've really enjoyed these last several weeks but it seems reality calls . . . or, It's been great fun, thanks for the memories . . . and even, If you're ever in LA, call me . . .*

Maybe that's exactly what she should do—go back to Grace's, have a glass or two of chardonnay, and then call

Elliot and just say good-bye and not bother with the whys
and the why nots—what did they matter? He'd chosen not
to continue the relationship, if not by his actions then by
the absence of them. Why torture herself by seeing him
again? It would only prolong the inevitable: she was going
back to Los Angeles and he was staying here in Ohio, and
there was more than the 2200-plus miles separating them—
there was a different belief in what they'd shared. She'd
changed, somewhere between that first meeting when she'd
sat in his office and he'd looked at her over his horn-rimmed
glasses, and now, when she couldn't think of him without
remembering how he pinched the bridge of his nose when
he was thinking, or the way he jingled his car keys when
they were walking, or the color of his eyes—deep, Hershey
chocolate—or the feel of his body pressed against hers . . .

Jenny had thought there was promise with Elliot, deep
soul-promise. It had called to her in the velvet midnight of
his voice, in the gentle honoring of his touch, rolling over
her senses, devouring her heart, her mind, her soul. She had
thought he felt it, too.

But she'd been wrong; if he'd felt anything for her, he
would have tried to keep her. He would never have let her
just walk away. *Damn him.*

Anger pulsed through ever inch of her body. *Damn him.
No.*

She wasn't letting him off the hook that easy. She'd wait
for him to come home, confront him, make him tell her he
wanted her to go. *Where was he?* She raked a hand through
her hair, and decided to wait in the garden; at least she could
enjoy its beauty and maybe, maybe find a little peace there.

She walked to the backyard and opened the gate. It was
midafternoon and the sun was still high in a cloudless sky,
a perfect summer day. She'd always remember this garden,
the first time she saw it, the brilliant colors and shapes of

lowers and shrubs, and rocking back and forth on the swing with Sydney . . .

She stopped, stared.

Elliot was sitting on the wooden swing, head back, eyes closed, a bunch of lavender pressed against his chest. Pieces of his short hair were sticking up and his face looked pale beneath his tan. Jenny's chest tightened.

He doesn't want me. He's letting me go. He let me believe he cared about me.

"Goddamn you, Elliot Drake, how dare you do this to me?"

Elliot's eyes flew open. "Jenny?" He looked surprised, maybe even confused.

He started to get up but she took a step and said, "Stay right there, Elliot. You're going to talk. You know I'm leaving in two days, don't you?"

His expression looked pained. "I know," was all he said.

"I thought we had something." Jenny slashed her hand in the air. "Maybe not serious enough to make a lifetime commitment, not yet at least, but I thought we might have actually been on our way." She sucked in a deep breath, pointed a finger at him. "So tell me how I could've been so wrong about us? Huh? Didn't you feel anything, Elliot? Was it just a way to pass time? Was it just about sex?"

He stared at her, shook his head. "No, Jenny, it wasn't just about sex."

"Then you cared about me?"

He nodded. "I did . . . and I do." His voice was quiet, drawn.

"And you were just going to let me walk away, go back to California and not try to stop me, keep me here, or," she clenched her fists on her hips, "at the very least let me know that you wanted to continue seeing me? You were just going to say good-bye?" The words were shrill, angry.

Elliot pinched the bridge of his nose.

There, he was doing it, just the way he always did when he was thinking. *Well, try to think your way out of this one, Elliot.*

"Tell me," she demanded. "Were you?"

"Jenny, I couldn't ask you to stay. It wouldn't have been fair."

"Says who?"

He shrugged. "It just wouldn't have been. How could I ask you to stay when you have a whole other life back in California?"

"Maybe I don't want that life anymore? Huh? Did you ever think about that?"

He didn't answer right away. When he did, his voice was flat, unemotional. "You might think that now, but you'd miss it—"

"You think you know everything, don't you? You've got it all figured out. Why, then, didn't you at least tell me you wanted to see me again, keep in touch, call me, for God's sake? Why, Elliot?"

"I thought it would be easier this way . . . and once you got back home you wouldn't feel obligated to," he hesitated, ". . . for anything that happened between us."

"Oh, my God. *Oh, my God.*" She clenched her hands, unclenched her hands. "I could just hit you over the head with all those damn degrees of yours. How can you be so smart and yet be so *stupid?* I've been dying, Elliot, do you hear me, *dying,* thinking you didn't want me, didn't want what we shared. Ugh! You . . . you . . ."

"I couldn't keep you here, Jenny. I had to let you go, set you free."

And then it hit her, what he'd once told her about the butterfly and setting it free if you loved it and how if it came back it belonged to you and if it didn't . . .

Now she understood, now it all made sense. He was letting

her go because he thought it was what she needed, what she really wanted. But he was wrong.

She took a step toward him, and then another, until she was standing next to him. "Elliot," she said, in a soft voice, "would you please ask me to stay?"

"I can't, Jenny." There was real pain in his voice. "It's not fair to you."

"Ask me. Please?" Her words were whisper-soft.

He sat there, clutching the cluster of lavender to his chest.

"Please?" she said again.

"Will you stay?" His voice was thick, tortured.

Jenny reached out, touched his cheek. "Yes, Elliot. Yes, I'll stay." A smile spread over her lips, deepened. "Do you know why? Because I love you and I want to be with you, and Sydney. I love both of you."

"Oh, God, Jenny—"

"And I'm not going to run away, Elliot. I'm not your ex-wife." She ran her fingers over his lips. "I'm the butterfly who came back."

He set the bunch of lavender beside him, pulled her onto his lap. "I love you, Jenny." His voice was raw, tortured. "I love you with every part of me." He reached up, cupped her face with his hands. "That's why I had to set you free." His lips spread into a slow smile as he said, "But I will thank God, every day of my life, that you came back to me. Every day," he whispered, as his mouth covered hers.

A pipevine swallowtail flitted near the bunch of lavender lying on the bench beside them. It dipped, once, twice . . . and landed.

Epilogue

Five months later....

"Grace, you're only going to be gone for four days, not four months." Jenny lay hunched down at the head of the bed, one leg crossed over the other, watching her sister unload two drawers and stuff their contents into a paisley suitcase.

"I just don't know what I'm going to need," she said, refolding a pink turtleneck.

Jenny let out a long sigh, exaggerated enough to catch Grace's attention. "Listen, you're going skiing with Guy for four days, right? All you need is a toothbrush and that little black nightgown you've got tucked away in your bottom drawer."

"Jenny!"

"Okay," she said, laughing, "forget the nightgown. It'll just get in his way."

Grace glared at her. "Guy invited me to go skiing. That's
t."

Jenny nodded. "And aren't you staying in the same
oom?"

Her sister rolled her eyes. "That's because the lodge only
ad one room available."

"Right."

She ignored Jenny. "And there are two beds."

"Good," Jenny said, smiling. "That way you can use
ooth."

Grace flung the turtleneck in the suitcase and turned
around. "I swear, sometimes I don't know how we can be
sisters. I really don't." She yanked open another drawer and
started pulling out underwear. Pink. Yellow. White.

Ugh. Grace, Grace, Grace. Jenny leaned over and snatched
a Victoria's Secret bag from the floor. "Here," she said,
holding out the bag to her sister. "I got you a little something
for your trip."

Grace turned and eyed the bag, then Jenny, and then the
bag again as though they were both explosives, mere seconds
from detonation. "Take it," Jenny said, plopping it into her
suitcase.

"I don't need any of those things," she said, her eyes
narrowing on the pale-pink-and-white-striped bag.

"What things? You don't even know what's in there."

"I can guess."

"Come on, Gracie, you know I'm only teasing you."
Jenny sat up and leaned forward. "I think it's great that you
and Guy are still seeing each other and that you're such
great *friends.*" She dropped her voice, met her gaze. "But
I think he'd like more and I think maybe you would, too,
but you're afraid. I'm just trying to lighten up the situation
a little, make you . . . consider it."

Grace sat down on the bed, rubbed her face, combed her
fingers through her hair. It was much longer now, thick

and shiny, with wispy bangs and a back that touched her shoulders. "I have been thinking about it," she murmured. "A lot."

"Good."

"But, Jenny, I'm so scared."

"I know."

"I've never been with anyone but Grant."

"I know."

"I feel like a dinosaur caught in the twenty-first century." Jenny smiled.

Grace looked at her, eyes brimming. "I just don't want to get hurt again."

There it was. Beneath all of the doubt and insecurity, and talk about dinosaurs, that was the real reason.

"Believe me, I know."

She smiled a little. "I know you know."

And Jenny did. She'd gone on a real tightrope for Elliot, without so much as a net, and had been scared to death, was still scared some days. But most days, she loved her choice as much as she loved the man and his daughter.

Grace swiped at her cheeks, sniffed, and reached for the Victoria's Secret bag, pushing aside the pink-hearted tissue. "Oh. Oh, Jenny." She looked up, grinned. "Thank you," she whispered. "They're beautiful."

"You're welcome."

She lifted the tissue paper and four pairs of underwear spilled out: silk lace, French cut. Magenta. Turquoise. Black. Red.

"You should wear those," Jenny said, "even if you're the only one who sees them."

Grace picked up the magenta pair, traced the lacy side panels. "I doubt I'll look like the models in the magazine," she said, letting out a little laugh.

"You'll look beautiful." Jenny grinned. "And if Guy ever gets to see you in them, I'm sure he'll agree."

She smiled then. "Maybe."

"He's crazy about you, Gracie. Give him a chance."

She didn't say anything for a long time, just sat there, fingering the silk and lace. Finally, she murmured one little word. "Maybe."

That's all Jenny had to hear. She leaned in closer and grabbed the edge of the suitcase. "Well, don't forget about protection. There's stuff out there that can kill you today, not just make you pregnant. And if it doesn't kill you, it can still stay with you forever, like chlamydia, warts, and a whole host of other STDs."

"Jenny!"

She shrugged, determined to have her say. "You've been living in the Dark Ages all this time, Grace. You need to know this stuff and be aware. Not that Guy hasn't probably been walking around with something in his pocket all of these months, hoping it'll be his lucky day, but you can't be too sure."

"I got tested a month ago."

"Huh?"

She looked at Jenny, held her gaze. "I had a husband who was sleeping around. Remember? Well, I got tested for all of those things. As far as they can tell, I'm okay."

"Oh."

"So, I know the risks." She shook her head. "I've always known them. I just didn't think they applied to me if I had a husband. Guess I was wrong."

"All men aren't like Grant."

"I know that. I really do. Guy is so different. He really cares about . . . me, and what I think. I'm just being careful."

"I don't blame you," Jenny said. "Not one bit."

She laughed. "Look at this role reversal. I used to be the one worrying about you and your relationships. Now, it's the other way around."

Jenny laughed. "Does this mean that I'm finally growing up?"

"And it's only taken thirty-three years." Grace's smile faded. "Elliot is good for you, Jenny."

"Elliot is more than good for me, Gracie. He's fantastic."

"I can tell. Anybody who could make you quit that horrible bubble gum habit of yours is a winner in my book."

"I haven't had a piece in over three months, and the weird thing is, I don't really miss it."

"That's what love will do to you."

"I guess."

And she loved him. Oh yes, she loved him.

"Any plans on making your arrangement permanent?"

Jenny shrugged. "We talk about it. It's just too soon to say. Maybe in a year or so, who knows? Right now, I'm thinking about getting the condo in shape. I talked to Gerald and Stefan the other day, and they've agreed to come for a visit this spring and paint my walls."

"The infamous herb garden again?"

"No," Jenny said. "This time, I want walls of lavender, and Shasta daisies, and poppies, every inch covered with color . . . and a black lab in the background . . . and butterflies, monarchs and pipevine swallowtails . . ."

"Sounds like Sydney's garden."

Jenny's lips curved into a slow smile. "It *is* Sydney's garden," she said in a soft voice.

Grace covered Jenny's hand with her own. "She's a very lucky little girl."

"I think we're both lucky."

"I think you're right."

"There's something else I want to tell you, Gracie." Jenny met her gaze, held it. "When Gerald and Stefan come, I want them to paint your bedroom ceiling with a zillion stars. Tiny, glow-in-the-dark ones. That way, when you flick

the switch off and get into bed, you'll always beat the light."
She squeezed her sister's hand. "Always."

A single tear trailed down Grace's cheek. "Yes," she said, with strength in her voice, "I will, won't I, Jenny? Finally, after all these years, I'll beat it." Her eyes sparkled with determination. "I'll win."

"You've already won, Gracie," Jenny said. "You've already won."

And from the deep swelling in their hearts, filled with hope and possibilities and tomorrow's dreams, to the moonbeams shooting through the window, they both knew it to be true.

About the Author

As a child, I can still remember crowding around our black-and-white television with my brothers and sister, anxiously awaiting the annual showing of *The Wizard of Oz*. I was petrified of the flying monkeys and the wicked witch's scary face, and *that* voice, but I was perplexed by the narrator at the beginning when he told viewers the first half of the movie would "look" different from the second. Ours never did—not until our black-and-white television died and our parents bought a color set. (After much deliberation, I must add!) *Then, I understood.* And that's what writing has done for me—put the color in my life. I have always been grateful for my family—my husband, my children, stepchildren, mother, brothers, sister—and all of God's gifts, even the heartache along the way that has made me stronger. But writing is the gift I give myself, in full-blown color, and it is the gift I wish to share with you . . .

I would love to hear from you, whether it's about my books or just to tell me what "colors" your life! My e-mail address is **mary@marycampisi.com** and my Web site address is **www.marycampisi.com**. Snail mail should be directed to Zebra Books.

By the way, I live in Ohio with my husband, my three children, and two stepchildren, (yes, that equals five!) and our resident queen, a seven-year-old black lab named Molly.